DYING PHOENIX

LORETTA PROCTOR

Cover design by Bradley Wind.

Matador
9 Priory Business Park
Kibworth Beauchamp
Leicestershire LE8 0RX, UK
Tel: (+44) 116 279 2299
Fax: (+44) 116 279 2277
Email: books@troubador.co.uk
Web: www.troubador.co.uk/matador

ISBN 978-1783062-874

British Library Cataloguing in Publication Data.
A catalogue record for this book is available from the British Library.

Typeset in Aldine401 BT Roman by Troubador Publishing Ltd
Printed and bound in the UK by TJ International, Padstow, Cornwall

Matador is an imprint of Troubador Publishing Ltd

To John and Lawrence

Also by this author

The Crimson Bed
Middle Watch
The Long Shadow

Author's Note

Dying Phoenix is a sequel to my first Greek novel, The Long Shadow, in which we follow the story of Dorothy Clarke, a Red Cross nurse who goes to Salonika in the First World War and falls in love with a Greek Officer. Her son, Andrew, born and brought up in England, leaves England when a young man in a quest to find his Greek roots. In his turn, he falls in love with a refugee, a girl from Smyrna called Anna Manoglou.

This story, Dying Phoenix, opens in 1966, the year I returned to Greece as an adult with my husband, John. I hadn't been there since I was a very small child, taken by my Greek mother to see my grandmother in Athens. The following year, in April of 1967, a group of Colonels took over the country and kept it under an oppressive military rule for seven years. By chance, my mother and I were obliged to return again to Greece in May 1967 on family business. I was too young at that time to notice anything very different in the political climate. Beaches, blue skies and tavernas were far more enticing. My mother's cousin, George Iliadis, worked for *Mesimvrini*, one of the papers run by Eleni Vlachou and the character of Aris Praxiteles is to some extent based on him. In one way or another some of the attitudes, stories and sayings from my Greek family have crept into the narrative with names shuffled about but the main characters are all my own invention and any real persons mentioned are famous – or infamous– ones. My knowledge of the dry cleaning business is thanks to my cousins in Thessaloniki; three brothers who ran dry cleaning shops there.

Many thanks are due to numerous others who helped by telling me their unique experiences during the time of the Junta.

Some found it a good time while others with more liberal and left wing leanings did not. I have tried to represent both sides of the argument. On the whole, however, most people will agree that behind the smiling face of the Junta lay terror, torture and an abominable flaunting of human rights.

Thanks go to Gregory Mosiadis, a great and patient guide, who took me around in his taxi and helped when I was researching in Thessaloniki. He introduced me to his friends, Lexi Triandafillidou and Efthimis Triandafillides, from whom I gained valuable insight into running a Greek garage and repair shop. In the UK, Ray Sellars and his sons also provided information on the running of a repair workshop in the sixties. Greg also introduced me to Aris Manarazian, an old Thessalonian of eighty with an amazing memory. The International Trade Fair of Thessaloniki gave me a marvellous book with references to the history of the Fair and how it began.

In Athens my thanks go to Alex and Ella Lekka, parents of Annia Lekka Blazoudaki, a wonderful author friend. Also to Anne and Dimitris Trigatzis who introduced me to Antonis Papandonakis and his wife, Annette, over a delicious dinner. Antonis kept us engrossed with his boyhood memories of the Junta and the late sixties. Meanwhile, a chance encounter on the aeroplane with Thanos Kokotopoulos gave a very right wing view of it all as told to him by his father. All these marvellous stories gave me flavour and insight into the minds of ordinary working people at the time. I gathered left, right, middle and detached views everywhere. It has been an interesting insight into the Greek mind; no – the human mind. These atrocities are not simply a Greek problem. They have been perpetrated everywhere by every nation and extreme national party. And I suspect always will be.

Thanks as always to my dear daughter, Thalia, and my husband, John, for encouragement and valuable help. Also to my good friends and writer colleagues, Mary Cade, Rebecca Lochlann, Anna Rossi and Gordon Thomas who read the first draft and gave me some brilliant feedback. And a special thanks to Bradley Wind who designed the beautiful, striking cover.

Greek Glossary

Aliti	(insult) a bum, a tramp
Andartes	partisans /resistance fighters
Anthropi mou	my man
Avgolemono	a thin lemony soup into which an egg is stirred
Bougatsa	a filo pastry made with cheese or custard filling
Cafeneion	café
Despinis	Miss
Dolmades	vine leaves wrapped around rice or minced meat
Doula	female servant
Embros	hello (on telephone)
Epitaphios	a cloth icon used during Holy week
Filotimo	pride/ honour
Filoxenia	hospitality
Glyko	sweet. Often a spoonful of jam in a dish offered with a coffee and glass of cold water to a guest
Haloumi	a hard goat's cheese
Kaimenos/Kaimeni	poor thing (m/f)
Kali orexi	good appetite (as in wishing Bon Apetit)
Kalispera	good day

Kalosorizate	welcome
Karotsaki	horse-drawn carriage
Koulouria	ring of bread coated with sesame seeds
Koumbaros	best man or godfather
Komboloi	a string of beads used mainly by men as a calming tool for nervous, restless hands. Better than cigarettes!
Koproskilo	Insult: translates to dogshit
Kyrios	Mr
Kyria	Mrs
Makaronia	oven-baked macaroni
Malaka	wanker
Me sihoreite	sorry
Mitera	mother
Moira	Fate
Mou	my. Often affectionately added to someone's name, e.g. 'Maria mou'
Moussaka	a baked dish with aubergines, potatoes and mince
Ohi	no
Paidi	child
Palikari	a brave fellow, a real man
Panayia	the Holy Virgin Mary
Pantocrator	the creator – large portrait of Jesus on the dome of the church

Papoutsakia	a delicious dish made with scooped-out aubergines filled with mince and baked in the oven. The name means 'little slippers' because they look like the little shoes worn by women in the old days
Papse	shut up, be quiet
Pastitsio	baked macaroni and meat dish
Raki	a drink, raw spirits rather like vodka to be drunk in tiny glasses
Retsina	resinated wine
Romanzo	romance. A popular Greek magazine in the 1960s
Saloni	sitting room, salon
Souvlakia	diced pieces of meat on skewers, usually grilled
Soppa	shush
Stifado	beef stew
Taverna/Psarotaverna	eating place/one specialising in fish
Tavli	backgammon
Tiropites	cheese pies made with filo pastry
Xeni	foreigner
Yia sou	goodbye (singular) also 'cheers'
Yia sas	Goodbye (plural)
Yia yia	grandmother
Yiatros	doctor
Zaharoplasteio	confectioner's shop

PART ONE: THE GREEK WOUND

Wherever I travel, Greece wounds me
Curtains of mountains, archipelagos, naked granite
They call the one ship that sails *Ag Onia 937*

'In the manner of GS', George Seferis

Chapter 1

Thessaloniki, Greece: September 1966
Early Evening

Max Hammett loved the lingering twilight time in Greece. Just now he was in a reflective mood with no desire other than to join the idling promenaders. Tired after a long day, but mentally alert, he wanted to savour the situation.

I'm here in Thessaloniki at this very moment. It's not a dream. I'm here in Greece, where I love to be, feeling the breeze on my face and arms, smelling the briny sea, hearing the music and chatter, seeing the sun setting over the horizon, the full moon rising over the hills.

It was good to think this way, be totally aware, touch a moment as if it was something to hold briefly in his hands. Water trickling through his fingers, tangible but not graspable, and all the more delightful for being transient … yet the moment of euphoria faded quickly. He ought to be happy but there was too much missing and his heart ached with unspeakable sadness.

The hour was hardly late; things were just beginning to get underway. September was the tourist season for Thessalonians and the city hummed with distant sounds of music from tavernas near the seafront. Cafés were packed with people enjoying an ice cream, drinking Fix beer or sipping the mud that passed for Greek coffee. In the parks and along the promenade, people strolled with aimless pleasure in the cool fresh night air or sat on the red painted benches, gazing out romantically over the darkening sea.

Crossing the main road, he sauntered along one of the side streets. A woman with a dusky mass of waves passed by. A sensual fragrance walked along with her, a mingled scent of talcum and some oriental perfume, an essence that breathed from her skin and haunted the trembling trace of a breeze. He almost ran after the woman – but for all the wrong reasons. It was because the perfume reminded him of Nina. More than all the other senses, scents brought situations and sharpened memories to mind that he desperately wanted to forget. Putting these thoughts out of his head, he turned his attention once more to the scene around him.

From a little open-air theatre came faint bursts of music and clapping. On the other side of the street bars teemed with life, their bright lights splattering across the pavement till they melted away into the gloom of pine trees. The narrow side street he was walking in opened out onto the broad, tree-lined avenue of Tsimiski, the Oxford Street of Thessaloniki. Crowds flowed along the pavements on each side, a stream of enthusiastic, chattering people who peered in brightly lit windows full of fashionable clothes, furs and jewellery. Few could afford these delights but they loved to look and hope. After looking at the best and most expensive goods, they would shrug philosophically and then turn off the avenue and make for the cheap and cheerful products of the Modiano market.

At the far end of this long avenue was a park where, poised squat and round, was the *Lefko Pirgo*, the White Tower of Salonika, that ancient remnant of Venetian occupation surrounded once by white walls, long taken down. It stood lit up against the deep blue-black of the night sky. Beyond it the promenade, Leoforos Nikis, twisted like a broad white snake about the harbour. In the far distance, ship lights glittered and danced, shimmering over the waves, while the lighthouse at the end of the bay beamed its message to fishing boats far out at sea. Hands in his pockets, Max stood for a long time at the edge of the promenade. He stared down into the tideless waters of the Mediterranean, half-mesmerised by the gentle lap and swell against the stone jetty.

'Eh, I knew I'd find you here!'

His reverie was broken by a cheery voice and his back slapped so hard he almost pitched forward into the sea.

'Oh, for God's sake, Dimitri, can't a fellow have a bit of peace!'

His grin belied the irritability of his tone. Dimitri stood, hands on hips, surveying him with amusement, shaking his head at him.

'What the devil are you talking about; you don't come to Greece for *peace*, my boy. You've been wandering around long enough. I feel ready for action. That shower did me good. You should have come back with me and had one too.'

'What, that communal shower on the roof? Open for the world to see you? No thanks.'

Dimitri looked offended. 'What are you talking about? No one can see you all the way up there. It's the coolest place when it's hot like this.'

'Last time I showered up there, a little girl poked her head round the terrace door and stared at me. She was probably shocked out of her wits.'

Dimitri chuckled. 'That'll be Toula's daughter, Efterpe. She's a nosy brat and likes seeing naked men. Nothing would shock that kid.'

Max shrugged. 'That's not the point. Doesn't Yiota grumble about it?'

'*She* won't use it, it's true. She washes at the sink and prefers *me* to use the shower. She says I'm always covered in oil. I work with machines, don't I? What's she expect, the silly woman? How else will I feed the family if I don't get my hands dirty? Ech, she's always grumbling about something. She can't wait to move away and keeps nagging me about it. But what can a man do? I have to stay where the work is. I'm not a millionaire, am I? I can't afford to live in smart places. Can just about afford the rent as it is.'

Max said nothing, but reflected that Dimitri's flat in Vassilis Georgiou was not exactly the smartest accommodation for a growing family. It was two floors up from the busy street and opposite the Paradiso open air cinema. In the summer the flat was unbearably hot, the only air coming in from a tiny balcony perched over the traffic fumes. The constant noise from the cinema formed a background of yells, music, and incomprehensible speech till the early hours of the morning.

'Anyway,' Dimitri continued cheerfully, 'never mind all that. Come on, time to hit a bar, have some fun. Have you eaten yet?'

'Not a thing,' Max confessed.

'You haven't eaten since that disgusting hot dog at lunchtime? How's a man supposed to survive on that? Yiota keeps saying you have to come over for a meal. She wanted you to come over tonight but I said we'd hit the bars. How about it, eh? A nightclub, maybe.'

'Tomorrow, Dimitri, old man. I'm really whacked tonight.'

'Whacked?'

'Tired, shattered, exhausted. Don't forget I stepped straight off the plane this morning and been busy with machinery and paperwork ever since.' Max looked troubled for a moment. 'D'you think we'll sort it out in time? The Trade Fair starts officially in two days, the Prime Minister is probably rehearsing his opening speech right now, and one of the tractors is still at the docks awaiting clearance. And I'm worried about that. Last time they hauled one up so carelessly the wing mirror smashed to pieces.'

Dimitri peered at him. 'Okay, you sound like you've had it. But food at least, some *retsina*. Come on, you can't get food at the Galaxio. It's a flea pit. Which is another thing. Yiota says come and stay at our place. Why go to that lousy hotel?'

They began to walk along the promenade towards the harbour, Dimitri gesticulating in his usual excitable manner, bright eyes glittering like two black diamonds. His face wore a constant expression of repressed merriment, as though life was continual fun and it was only with difficulty he refrained from laughing aloud all the time. There was a bounciness in his walk, a vibrancy, a virile strength in his small firm body. Max smiled down at his wiry, dark-haired companion.

'Okay, glass of *retsina* and a pork chop,' he agreed, 'but then

I'm off to bed. I can start the serious drinking when the Exhibition is over. I'll be delighted to come and sample some of Yiota's delicious cooking; tell her so.'

'And you'll come and stay with us?'

They entered one of the dimly lit cafés and sat at a table with a blue and white checked cloth on it. A radio played music in the background, some wailing tale of loss, Greek-style, as if the very being of the singer was twisted in an agony of love and pain. After they had ordered their food, a bottle of retsina, and swallowed a tiny glass or two of *raki*, Dimitri repeated his question.

'Come on back with me to our place, what d'you say, Max? Don't be all English and proud, I shall be insulted, Yiota will be insulted, the kids will be insulted.'

'Oh, for heaven's sake!' laughed Max. 'Thank you, Dimitri, old friend – but I need tonight on my own to recover. You have to admit, your apartment is small and ... well ... I'm not used to kids.' He was apologetic but firm.

'They make a lot of noise,' admitted Dimitri. 'I'm not much better, I know.'

'No, you're not. You sing all the time, you and Yiota shout and yell non-stop. I mean, what do the neighbours say about it?'

'They're just as bad,' his friend said despondently. 'That bastard downstairs has the radio on day and night. He drives me crazy!'

'There you go, that's my point. And there's that damned cinema. If I have to listen to Laurence Harvey in *The Running Man* for an entire week – which I did last time I stayed with you and Yiota – I'll go over and murder the projectionist. Seriously, I need my beauty sleep. And anyway, Basil Petrakos is coming back from some business he had in Athens on Wednesday. I'm invited over there for a meal on Thursday. You know he's my old buddy from university days. I can't say no to him. I missed seeing him and his wife during the Trade Fair last year because they went to the States to see some long-lost relations.'

Dimitri spread his hands out and shrugged his shoulders. 'But, of course, your old friend, Basil. And he has a big apartment in a posh part of the city, plenty of bedrooms, so it's all nice and quiet.'

'Don't be offended now. You've offered, Basil's offered … but I find it easier to stay in a hotel while I'm working. I need to get away from it all – you know me. And you know I love to come over to see you and Yiota. No one cooks *stiphado* better than she does. Thing is, I haven't seen Basil for a couple of years. It'll be good to catch up, meet Athina and the kids again.'

'His wife *is* a beauty,' said Dimitri, putting his thumb and forefinger together and flinging a kiss in the direction of some imaginary person.

'He always did have an eye for the best-looking girls.'

'He never struck me as a woman-chaser.'

'No, not Basil. A true gentleman.'

'Boring,' chuckled Dimitri, 'boring, eh? Not like you, Max, you like the girls a lot. And girls here like tall, fair Englishmen like you. Eh, listen, I know a place along the old Monastir Rd where you can have a girl, nice and private. I'll take you some time.'

Max shook his head. 'I'm here on business, no time for that sort of thing just now. Plus, I'm a reformed man. Doesn't Yiota ever guess what a rogue you are, Dimitri? You've got two kids, for goodness sake.'

Dimitri shrugged again, threw open his hands.'I have to practice, you know, or the bloody thing will fall off. Yiota's almost turned celibate since she had Georgie. I mean, a man has to keep going.'

Max laughed. 'Well, let's hope it doesn't fall off!' He raised a glass to that. '*Yia sou*!'

'*Yia*!' responded his friend and the two men clinked their glasses and fell to eating their pork chop and chips with a ravenous appetite.

After their meal, they brought out cigarettes and smoked peacefully over tiny cups of thick, sweet Greek coffee. There were times when even the 'mud' seemed good. Max felt the tiredness ebbing away and stared out into the street beyond, watching married couples walking by, children running and chattering by their side. He felt again that wave of sadness as he watched them. A woman stooped to pick up a little girl who then clung to her neck, raining kisses on her mother's cheek, and Max sighed despite himself. Dimitri was watching him and said after a while, 'You miss her, don't you?'

Max snapped back his gaze, picked up the coffee cup and pretended to drink the already unwholesome dregs in the bottom to avoid making a reply.

'You miss her,' said Dimitri, almost to himself. 'Admit it.'

Max raised his head and looked his friend in the eye. 'No. I don't miss her at all. I don't miss her. It just didn't work, Dimitri.'

Soho, London, England : September 1966.
Early evening

'wherever I travel Greece wounds me.' George Seferis

Nikos Galanis watched her covertly as she sat opposite him in the fashionable London bar. Her long, slender fingers moved up and down the stem of the wine glass as if caressing it, but her thoughts were elsewhere. Nina Hammett was a beautiful woman, there was no denying it. Her dark hair was sleeked back into a loose bun at the nape of her neck. On anyone else it would look unfashionable and severe; on her it looked elegant and poised. It was something to do with her eyes as well, he thought, looking into them now: unfathomable, enigmatic pools of brown, deepening almost to black.

When she spoke, her voice was low but clear. Her Greek was impeccable, without a regional accent. An educated woman and an intelligent one.

'I have always admired Lambrakis,' she said, 'and I always will. I met him just before he was murdered. He was a friend of my great aunt, Christoula. Auntie lived in Kavalla but she had a flat in Thessaloniki as well where she used to hold little soirées.

I met him at one of these in 1962. I followed his athletic career even as a child. All those gold medals he got at the Balkan Games! What an achievement.'

It was three years now since that left-wing politician, Doctor Grigoris Lambrakis, was mown down by a vehicle and clubbed to death during broad daylight in the streets of Thessaloniki. For heaven's sake, the man was dead and gone and still she thought of him! Nikos wished a woman would speak of him with such admiration. How little he had accomplished compared to the brave and splendid things which that martyr Lambrakis had done in his short life. Perhaps it was now time to make his own mark on the world. He glanced over at Nina, who was staring at the table as if lost in thought.

Nina sipped her wine and went on with her musings. 'But what I admired most of all, Niko, was the fact that he was a resistance fighter like my mother. Did you know she was an *andarte* in the war? My mother, Anna?'

'I had heard,' he replied, his voice respectful.

'Yes, she was a brave woman and she was hung by the Nazis. The damned Nazis, Niko. She was tortured and hung but she gave nothing away.'

They both fell silent for a while as Nina drank the rest of her wine, her eyes smouldering with hurtful memories. He went to refill her glass but she put her hand over it and smiled at him, tilting her chin in Greek fashion, to indicate a 'no'.

'I personally admire Sartzetakis for taking an unbiased, detached view of the matter and bringing Lambrakis's assassins to justice,' Nikos said. He kept his voice smooth. Nina smiled back at him and he knew his comment had hit the right note.

'Mmm, me too. A good man, a truly good man. He's a bit of a right-wing character but he put his political feelings aside and stood for justice. It was brave of him. I heard the rumour that a lot of difficulties were thrown in his way to prevent the truth coming out.'

Nikos nodded, his face sombre. 'Yes, yes. It's not easy to get justice done in Greece these days. I wonder if the murderers will really pay the price. They don't seem to have dealt with them yet. One despairs.' Nikos sighed as he said this but his face remained impassioned. He was watching Nina with narrowed eyes as if weighing her up with care.

'Which is worse? The Americans, the British? They make a pawn of Greece. If Frederica hadn't come to England, Lambrakis might still be alive.' Nina looked sorrowful. 'All he wanted was to help that poor woman, Betty Ambatielos, whose husband was still in prison. He – as always – wanted to fight for justice and peace and came to talk to Queen Frederica herself. But would the cow speak to him? Not her. The coward, the despot, the traitoress! Instead she arranges his assassination.'

Nikos looked around and lowered his voice, 'Shh … not so loud, Nina. Even here there may be Greeks who will hear you. This is traitorous stuff.'

Nina glared at him. 'You think I care who hears me? I'm not imagining it either. I know many things; I still have friends who were in the army, old friends of my grandfather's. I know what's going on over there.'

'Do you? Do you really know what's going on? My dear, you may be safe here. But you will be making it unsafe for yourself when you visit Greece if people hear all this talk. I'm just saying have a care.'

Nina subsided a little and gave a shrug. 'It's hard, Niko. I hate to see how Greece escaped the wretched Turks only to become a pawn for Britain and America. Nothing is sacred, democracy is lost. Plato would love it. He always liked an oligarchy. Nevertheless, his vision *was* one of reason and order. We have little left of that.'

'There's a splendid way to restore order.'

'What way – revolution?'

'No, no. That's too bloody. There are ways, there are always ways.'

Nina frowned, but he refused to say any more.

'I sometimes wish there was something I could do for my country,' she burst out, her voice passionate with feeling. 'I'm a Greek but I feel I do nothing, just keep comfortable. Especially when I'm back at Downlands with my father. I feel like a child wondering what to do to prove myself.'

Nikos couldn't help a smile. 'You are indeed a Greek, Nina. Your grandmother's English blood certainly doesn't show. Yet you married an Englishman. Why didn't you come back to Greece and marry one of your own?'

Someone like me, he thought. He glanced at himself in the huge mirror on the wall beside them. He had been handsome enough in his youth but at forty-one his hair was thinning on top, wrinkles were furrowing his eyes, a paunch was beginning to overlap his trousers. These days he had begun to wear a corset but it did little to hide the rising tide of blubber. He pulled himself up a little straighter and hoped she hadn't noticed.

'Oh, but I love English men. I love England. Dad always said he felt as if he belonged to both countries and yet belonged to neither, a citizen of the world. I understand what he means. Yet, I know my mother's Greek warrior blood stirs in me, Niko. I know it does and I want to live up to her fierce, brave memory.'

Nikos Galanis looked at her with some admiration. To make a woman like this love him! He brought out a packet of cigarettes and offered her one. She took it from him and he lit it, holding her hand a little longer than he should, slightly rubbing her fingers with his own. She took her hand away quickly and stared at him for a moment but made no comment, just exhaled a long stream of smoke.

'I went to the funeral, you know.'

'Lambrakis' funeral?'

'Yes. My husband didn't want me to attend. He thought it was too dangerous, but there were thousands of people there. Max doesn't understand that this is the way Greeks express themselves – at funerals. They show what they truly feel in those moments. What danger was there when hundreds followed the coffin? And it was right to mourn so great a man. A doctor, an athlete, a peacemaker, a great man.'

She fell silent and her eyes focused on the past. He wondered what it was that made her sound so unhappy. Something was troubling her deep inside.

'You and Max ...?' Nikos didn't finish his sentence, just shrugged questioningly.

Nina smiled, but her eyes were sad. 'We've separated, Nikos. It had to be. We were quarrelling too much.'

'Are you seeking a divorce?'

She hesitated and her eyes softened a little – then just as suddenly became hard again and she pulled herself up straight as if confronting some inner enemy. 'I'm not sure. I don't want it. I hate the idea of divorce. But it's hopeless. In the end there was no trust. I know he loves me ... loved me, anyway. He had a stupid affair, promised it would never happen again ... but how can I believe that? Once is enough for me. It's disloyal, it's wicked.'

Nikos couldn't help a little smile at this. 'Now if he was a Greek, I think you'd accept it like all Greek wives do.'

'That's stupid!' she fired at him. 'I'm not one of these women who thinks a man can do as he pleases while a woman doing the same is labelled a whore. But I suppose I did think as an Englishman he'd be honourable. So it was all the more disappointing.'

'Does that leave the field clear?' asked Nikos, with another of his little smiles.

Nina regarded him thoughtfully. He felt a sudden sense of panic at her steady gaze that seemed to move through the layers of conceit, pride and falseness that was his nature, through to the very heart of him. The dark, sensual, cruel heart of him.

She smiled and looked down at her hands, twisting her golden marriage band around her finger.

'I'm not ready for men, Nikos. Not just yet. I want to *do* something, not spend time on my back.'

He laughed and motioned to the wine bottle again and this time she let him pour in some more and they made a toast.

'To Greece, may she be forever free!'

Chapter 2

Thessaloniki: Preparing for the Trade Fair

Exhausted by the hectic activities of the day, Max slept well. The Galaxio hotel was a plain three-storey building in one of the narrow side-streets off Egnatia. They had given him one of the 'best' rooms, so called because it boasted a little sink and a tiny shower cubicle. The shower was a half-cold douche fixed to a tap almost halfway down the wall, but it was adequate. In order to wash his hair he had to stoop his tall frame so he decided it would be simpler to get a local barber to deal with it when required. For some reason there was no private toilet installed in the room but a communal one located down the hallway. But at least there was a proper toilet bowl in there, not one of the squatting kind to be found in many houses and tavernas. Despite these minor setbacks, the room was clean with a decent bed and an array of mosquitoes on the ceiling which he swatted with a rolled up newspaper before turning in at night.

The hotel was situated away from the main road but the location was still noisy with people shouting till late in the night and the hammering and clanging of incessant building works. To his chagrin he realised there was an open air cinema opposite his room so he hadn't escaped that affliction, after all. You couldn't seem to get away from a cinema in Thessaloniki. Thankfully, a cheery Greek musical was showing each night which was somehow less irritating than *The Running Man.*

Now a long day lay ahead and Max had a good many matters to attend to before the official opening of the

Thessaloniki International Fair. After a shower, shave and light breakfast, he planned to take a taxi to the docks and see if the missing tractor had arrived safely from England, then hire a driver at the docks to bring it to the Exhibition Park. Thankfully the designated open air stands were ready and in order.

Although there was a British Pavilion that year, sponsored by some Greeks who represented various British businesses, his own employers had hired a private stand which was situated near the outskirts of the park. The International Trade Fair was becoming so popular that space was beginning to be a problem and there was talk of acquiring more ground. It had come a long way since its origins in 1925 on the Field of Mars, a far smaller area near the 3rd Army corps buildings.

The ground occupied by the present Fair had once been the old Muslim cemetery in the days when the Ottoman Turks ruled Macedonia. It was a huge area but every year, as the exhibitors grew more and more numerous, new ground was constantly acquired. This year, Max's firm had to make do with what they got as they had entered their vehicles rather late. However, the position of the stand didn't affect sales. Dimitri saw to that.

On the whole, because each pavilion oversaw their own security, there was seldom any real trouble. The tractors seemed safe enough, hardly an easy item to drive off in the middle of the night past the security guards. But last year, Max had a furious row with the TIF organisers who, in his opinion, needed a better system of patrolling the grounds. A great deal of swearing, arm waving and aggravation made it an unpleasant experience. The stumbling block was due to an inexplicable act of vandalism in which two of his prize tractors had their thick rubber tyres punctured by a chisel driven into them – which must have taken some force – wing mirrors smashed and vital parts removed from the engines.

'Such a thing has never happened before,' one organiser stated angrily. He made it sound as if the fault was carelessness on Max's part. The damage occurred despite the supposed night patrol of security men around the grounds. He had sworn he would never bring his machinery back again.

However, he enjoyed coming to Greece and loved Thessaloniki. He had his friends there and wanted to come back again. Despite the fact that even his boss seemed to imply he should have taken more care, Ford had asked him to return this year with the tractors and other vehicles from Basildon to take their place at the Fair and declare how wonderful were all things made in England – even if they were an American firm! He promised his employers that he would sleep on the stand if necessary and as for the TIF, they were determined not to allow any more incidents to occur again. It was bad for business. He was assured that all possible precautions were being taken this time.

Once all the paperwork was sorted out, he intended to take a bus back to Karabournaki for a pleasant reunion with Basil Petrakos at that gentleman's commodious apartment near the sea. It was over two years since he had seen his old friend. Basil was once as close to him as a brother during those far off days when they were both students at London University. Basil had undertaken business studies; Max had a bent for practical things and was so adept at taking apart cars and putting them back together again that he got a sponsorship from Ford at Dagenham and went in for engineering. The two men struck up a friendship despite, or perhaps because, they were so very different in nature. However, about two years into his studies, Basil's father, Ignatio, died suddenly from a heart attack and the young man was obliged to cut short his stay. He returned to Thessaloniki to help carry on his father's dry- cleaning business, marry a charming and beautiful girl called Athina, and to take care of a large family of which he was now the head.

Tall, dark, heavy and grave, Basil was serious about all he did, the antithesis of Max who, though equally tall, was light-haired, had greenish-blue eyes and appeared wittily amused by life. He regarded it as a passing show of which he was a curious observer. 'All the world's a stage and all the men and women merely players' might well be written for him alone. However, it was this lightness that helped Max accept and even enjoy the company of Basil Petrakos. Others often found the latter a great deal too sombre and heavy but Max liked the intensity; a counterpoint to his own nature. It pierced his shell occasionally and made him for a moment feel as his friend did, carried away by a sincere emotion. There were even times when Max wished he could cast aside his cynicism and experience life as profoundly. He found it hard to believe in anything much. But he also realised this was a lack in his nature that did not make life better. It made it easier, but not better.

Max seldom spoke a good deal about his early life. He preferred to forget it. Which was why he had taken to calling himself Max when he left school. His full name was Edward Maximillian, the more romantic name added on the insistence of his mother who had once read a story about some Austrian emperor. As for his father, he called his son Eddie, and the boy always hated this dreary rendering of the name of so many great English Kings. His father insisted on Eddie, partly out of spite.

'Trust your mother to think up a poncey name,' he sneered. 'Eddie's good enough for an East End kid.'

Well, it wasn't good enough for Max.

It was after Basil returned to Greece that Max met Nina Cassimatis at a friend's party. She was accompanied by another man at the time but they appeared to be friends rather than lovers. Max was also with a friend – but to his mind, Shirley Mason was nothing serious. No woman was anything serious as far as that went. Marriage was certainly not on his mind at that time. He'd decided that he was not the man for a home, a wife to cook and fetch slippers, children rushing noisily about. Plus, he suspected that he was never likely to be a faithful partner and women always wanted you to love them only. When it was so easy to love them all.

He spotted Nina at once, saw her across a crowded room just like the song said and their eyes met. He tried to hold her gaze; it was one of his sexual techniques. But her eyes slid away. She looked elsewhere and seemed rather bored.

He poured out a glass of shandy for Shirley and introduced

her swiftly to Alan Shelley, one of his old friends. After a few polite moments of shared conversation, he turned to his girlfriend. 'Excuse me a moment, Shirley, my dear,' he said patting her on the arm gently and with a leave-taking expression that she easily interpreted when she saw him take off across the room towards the dark and exotic-looking Nina. She shrugged and turned back to Alan. In her sensible opinion, a bird in the hand was worth a dozen in the bush and it was Alan who was now gazing at her with admiring interest. Max could do what he liked, she didn't give a damn.

Nina had just put down an empty glass, which provided Max with a cue. The fellow with her turned away for a moment and engaged in conversation with someone else. Max took Nina by the arm and steered her swiftly and deftly away towards the bar.

'You need a drink,' he stated, 'and I'm the man to get it for you. I can provide all you need, dear lady, trust me. If you need a troubadour, that's me. A man to sit at your feet and play a lute … or a guitar … or anything that may amuse you.' His green-blue eyes gazed at her with admiration, his smile utterly engaging. Nina looked surprised for a moment then smiled and gave a little shrug. 'Okay. I'll have a gin and tonic. There's no need to sit at my feet though.'

'But I would like to,' he said earnestly. 'Beauty is to be worshipped.'

'What nonsense you talk!' she said. Her sternness turned him on. He enjoyed the challenge.

He found her the drink, refusing to let go of her arm, then led her to an empty seat in a far off corner and sat at her feet as promised.

'Not such nonsense, my fair maid,' he said, raising his glass, 'because you *are* beautiful. So, here's to beauty. I might even dream up a poem in true troubadour style. Something like …

A maiden fair was she,
With eyes like stars at night,
I looked into that face
And then my soul took flight … what do you think of that?'

'I think you've drunk too much.'

'I'm as sober as a judge. And they have to be sober or they're in trouble. I feel as if I've known you for a thousand years, maybe in another life, if you believe in such a thing. And just at this moment, I'm inclined to believe it. But still, we need to observe the formalities. Let me introduce myself. I'm Max Hammett. And your name?'

'Nina Cassimatis.'

'A soft, sweet name. Just right for you.'

She looked at him, seated on the floor at her feet, cross-legged, balancing a drink in one hand and trying to fish a packet of cigarettes out of his pocket with the other. He looked up and gave her a merry grin. Her face was serious and she didn't smile back. She just regarded him thoughtfully. He offered her a cigarette.

'You know,' he mused as he lit them up, 'you remind me of my good friend, Basil. You've the same sort of serious, unsmiling look. But I like it because it means you're a thinker. And … though you may not believe it, Nina, I'm a thinker too.'

'You certainly don't give me that impression.' Her voice was sarcastic.

'Ah well, you only see the mask; the mask of smiles and laughter. You must look beneath. See the real face.'

She blew out smoke and kept her eyes on him, scanning his face as if to challenge his allegations. 'I see nothing but a charmer, a teaser. You must prove it.'

'Okay. What would you like to discuss? Nietzche, Schopenhauer, Freud?'

'They're all too gloomy, only interested in madness. Kazantzakis would be more inspiring.'

'Aha. I have, as it happens, read all his works. *Travels in Greece* is one of my favourites, *Christ Recrucified* is a tad heavy for me. *Zorba* is always going to be his best. His style is a bit over the top, a bit too dramatic for my taste – but most of the time I concede that he writes like a poet.'

Nina looked surprised. 'Yes, he is a philosopher and a poet,' she agreed. 'As a child I used to quote passages from his books. I've forgotten how to do that now.'

She spoke perfect English and behaved like an

Englishwoman, yet she was dark-eyed, her hair a lustrous black, her figure shapely in a close-fitting black dress that was simple and expensive but elegant. She wore a necklace of graded pearls about her neck, one large lustrous one in the centre resting in the hollow of her collar bones. Little pearl earrings were fixed in her ears. There was an aura and glamour of something mysterious and foreign about her. She was exquisite and he made up his mind to seduce her. Thoroughly seduce her so that she would beg for more. The mere thought of it made something lurch inside his solar plexus.

'I know everyone must ask you,' he smiled. 'I just wondered if you were Greek?'

'People often think I'm Italian,' she replied.

He shook his head. 'No, you haven't the softness of an Italian. There's a kind of strength in your face, that jawline, that chin and high forehead. A flash in your eye. You have to be Greek. My great friend, Basil, introduced me to a load of Greeks over here. I've got the feel of them. Plus you like Kazantzakis. What Italian would talk about him rather than Dante Alighieri? So that's a giveaway!'

Nina stared at him with surprise. 'Well, you're the first person who's guessed correctly. Britons seldom manage to distinguish one foreigner from another; they tend to have a few role models and Greeks don't often figure amongst them. You're right. I'm three-quarters Greek, actually. My paternal grandmother was English. She met my grandpa in the First World War when she was nursing over in Salonika. He was a Greek officer.'

'That sounds romantic.'

'It was. They were madly in love.'

'So they got married.'

She hesitated for a moment. 'They were formally engaged. Then Gran got pregnant with my dad and was sent home. Later, she was told that Costas … that was my grandpa … had died in the war.'

Max was intrigued. 'And had he?'

'Oh, I don't talk about these things,' she said and drew her eyes away. A sense of something closing, an inner door shutting him out. 'They're family things.'

He wanted to know more. He resented her reticence when people generally opened up with ease to his approachable, candid manner. The desire to penetrate her literally and metaphorically possessed him so strongly that he was almost surprised by it. Often, if a girl proved difficult in some way, which they seldom did, he would simply move on. It was never worth the bother of prising open a hard, unyielding shell however sweet the promise of the nut lying inside.

'Why not?' Max shook his head at her, his eyes humorous and questioning. 'It's a story to you and me. All the amazing things our grand parents and parents did in those wars are just romantic stories for us younger ones. Our memories of the war are a few air raids … unless we lived in London or on the South Coast. I was an East End kid and they sent me away at first. Life was quiet enough in a Shropshire village. But I never returned to my old home. It was blitzed to the ground. My mother was out at the time, luckily. Dad, of course, was off fighting in the Med. They ended up in a council house. Dad had a few tales to tell but he was never really the same after the war. He drank a lot more, seemed hard, cruel even – and didn't seem to care about anything much. Ended up dying of kidney failure. Mum reckoned it was the war made him change, said he was a kinder man before. I'm not so sure. He was a bully.' He paused for a moment, surprised at himself for telling this stranger so much. 'I wonder if we'll have such stories to tell our own grandchildren.'

'My memories are not of air raids,' Nina said. Her eyes had a fire in them that intrigued Max. She seemed to burn from within and something incandescent appeared in the deep brown irises. It glowed about her like a halo. He looked at her with fascination. If he had believed in such things as saints, he'd swear she had a nimbus of light about her head.

'No, not air raids,' she replied in answer to his raised eyebrow. 'I was born in Salonika just before the German occupation and I was still there when the war ended and lucky not to be taken away by the communists in Greece. My grandpa Costas told me so. But sometimes …' she broke off and smiled a wicked little smile that charmed Max, ' … sometimes I wish they had taken me with them and I could have become a fighter for freedom like my mother. She was a heroine.'

Max shook his head, bemused by her words – which at that time were meaningless to him – and bemused by the amazing quality of intensity that pulled him towards her as if he was a moth to her flame. When she spoke, she moved her graceful, elegant hands expressively. Her nails were oval-shaped and polished a delicate pearly pink like the inside of a shell. He watched these fluid hands, fascinated by their movement.

'So Costas wasn't dead after all?'

'No, but it's a long story.'

'I'd like to hear it some day. You make me feel my life has been very suburban and boring, Nina.'

'Better a boring life,' she answered. 'Isn't it the Chinese who say "let me *not* live in interesting times"?'

Max frowned at her. 'That's a world-weary statement for such a young girl. Only I'm allowed to make comments full of *ennui.*'

She laughed. 'But I'm not unhappy.'

'I'm glad,' he replied with sudden warmth, taking her hand and clasping it for a moment between his own as if to draw her towards him in some way, to make a physical contact that allowed his desire to pour towards her. She allowed him to do so, looking down at him with narrowed eyes, then suddenly broke into a delightful warm, open smile.

'You're a kind person, Max. I see it in your eyes. You're very kind.'

'How kind would you like me to be?' he grinned. She made no reply to this and he regretted it as a fatuous question. This was not the sort of girl to take a direct approach with. She was subtle, mysterious. He needed to take greater care. Instead she now took his hand, held it palm upwards and looked at it thoughtfully as if seeing a wealth of information in it.

'You have an interesting palm,' she said after a few moments, tracing lines and whorls with a long slim finger. Her touch made desire and longing spring up inside him. It almost shook him with its force. He stared at her, amazed. What power this young girl had! Seductive power without trying to be seductive. Sexuality without needing to make it obvious. She was unique. Unique to him, at least. He had never known a woman like her before. 'Maybe your life won't always be as boring as you think,' she added, looking at him with a smile.

'I suspected you were a little witch! A palm reader and probably read tea leaves as well. But you haven't answered my question.'

'Your question? There is no answer to that question – Max.' Her eyes were serious still and he could tell she was not to be easily drawn into the circle of his charm.

'I'll keep asking until you think of a suitable answer,' he smiled.

She shrugged. 'You're assuming we're going to meet again.'

He took both her hands in his again and this time she clasped his back, entwining their fingers together. They stared into each other's eyes for what seemed a very long time. He wanted pull her forward and kiss those full lips but something held him back and she made no move towards him either. Yet he knew, somehow he knew, that this girl was his destiny and he was hers. Whether she had seen this in his palm or not he had no idea.

'Oh, there's no doubt about that, Nina,' he said. 'We'll meet again.'

And for once his life he felt very serious indeed. A year later they were married.

Chapter 3

Gloucestershire, England: September 1966

Nina looked out upon the utter darkness beyond as the train rattled through the Gloucestershire countryside. She always regretted leaving London behind but it would be nice to have a little break and see Dad and Helen. Her feelings about Downlands were always mixed. She loved the huge old house and sometimes vaguely speculated what she would do to improve it if it ever belonged to her. Her father often told her it was to be his wife's home as long as she lived, but on Helen's decease it would be hers. That was natural enough as Helen had no children – largely, Nina felt sure, because her stepmother had no desire for any. Helen was a cold woman. So different to her warm, impulsive father. What had attracted him to this woman, she wondered? True, Helen lived up to her classical name with a slender, fair, heart-stopping loveliness. There was always something fragile and delicate about her – the porcelain skin, china-blue eyes, statuesque figure. One could only think of Helen in terms of adjectives like these for she was as remote and inaccessible and as precious as the best china locked away in the hall cupboard and seldom used.

It had to be said she was a good wife. She did everything beautifully, placidly and without demur. She was a gracious hostess, well-read, intelligent and interesting to converse with. And if she was unhappy at Downlands – and sometimes Nina felt quite sure she longed for other things – she never really betrayed it or seemed to want anything to be altered on her behalf.

Towards Nina, she had always been kind, calm, cool. Never close, never acting like a mother. But then no one could take her mother Anna's place. No one. And Nina wondered, in her heart of hearts, if perhaps her father felt the same and that Helen was a complete contrast on purpose. And wondered too if Helen also suspected this and bore it with calm resignation.

The train drew into the station. Nina gathered together her small bags and leant out of the window. She saw her father, Andrew Cassimatis, waiting on the platform and felt a wave of love and affection. He was so young looking, not yet fifty, still slim and handsome, his thick black hair slightly greying at the temples which made him all the more attractive. He looked so Greek, so much more a Greek than an Englishman, and yet he never seemed that comfortable with his Hellenic nature. He always felt happier playing the English country squire. Nina felt regretful about this.

'Pa-*pa*!' She flung open the door and descended from the carriage. Her father caught her up in his arms as if she was still a young girl and kissed her on the cheek.

'My lovely girl… . so glad you're home.'

Nina had never really felt Downlands was her home but would never have told Andrew so. She knew how much he loved the place. Almost as if it was a part of his own body, an extension of his being.

'Is Grandma Dot here?'

'She's coming over tomorrow and looks forward immensely to seeing you. Here, give me those bags … the car's waiting at the front. We'd better move it or the station master will be after us, but I didn't want you to walk about in all this mud so I came as close as I could. It's been raining cats and dogs lately. The trees look wonderful this time of year. You'll see them tomorrow. We'll go for a walk round the woods and gardens.'

'Lovely.'

They made their way to the old, patient, somewhat battered Ford estate car parked outside the railway station. Nina felt at times that this car had belonged to Andrew for years and years; all her life! In fact, she knew full well that Max had helped

Andrew buy it cheap at an auction about six years ago. It looked as if it had passed over miles of muddy fields and lanes since then.

'You've still got this old jalopy!' she exclaimed.

'Of course, Would never get one better. When I like a thing, I like it.'

Nina smiled. 'That *is* you, Dad.'

They bowled along for a few moments in silence then Andrew half turned and said, 'Oh, it's so good to see you, Nina. *So* good. I've told Helen to keep you something hot. I knew you'd be hungry.'

'You're so thoughtful, Dad.'

'Anything for my baby.'

Nina laughed. 'Some baby! … An ageing baby.'

'What nonsense. You're just twenty-nine and look lovelier than ever. I have to say, you look a lot happier since you left that good-for-nothing husband of yours.'

'He wasn't good-for-nothing, Dad. He was good for a lot of things. Too good at one thing, though.'

'Yes – fornicating! He was a bastard, Nina, admit it.'

'Dad, you're just being possessive. You always hated Max.'

Andrew laughed. 'Hate's a strong word. Of course I didn't *hate* him. But I have to admit I didn't trust him a lot. Too easy, too charming. Made me suspicious … but it's just the stuff that women go for, of course. I bet you thought you'd rule him with ease.'

'I did rule him most of the time.'

'Hmm … but he was too sneaky even for you, wasn't he?'

Nina sighed and looked away into the darkness as the car sped along the narrow lane that took them to Downlands. 'Don't let's talk of it, Dad. It's over. He's in Greece now at the Trade Fair and I've started my new job in London.'

She thought in her heart how ironic it was that Max had learned to love Greece through her and was able to go there on business while she had not visited her own country for a year now. Just at present she was too busy with a new job working for her father's cousin's newspaper. It was proving hard work but it was fun too and she was feeling a fresh joy in life because of it.

'Will you make me some *keftedes* tomorrow?' Andrew asked hopefully.

Nina laughed. 'Oh, Dad, you ask that every time I come home! It's time I taught Helen how to make them.'

'She *has* tried. But no one can do them quite like you, with fresh mint and that delicate hint of spice, just perfect, so soft and tender. Not that I'd ever tell Helen that. She does her best, you know.'

'You're really making me feel hungry now. What's Helen made tonight?'

'Shepherd's pie.'

'Oh goody! She does that very well. Get me home quick!'

Nina sat in the comfortable, old-fashioned drawing room and relaxed her limbs before the roaring fire. The place always had a comfortable, cluttered look about it with magazines on occasional tables and huge mahogany bookshelves, filled with faded red, blue and brown leather-bound books, ranging the yellowing buff walls. Any spaces left in between were filled with gold framed pictures of eighteenth-century landscapes, floppy Basset hounds and manic-looking chestnut-coloured horses. Pieces of china covered every available shelf; familiar little dogs, horses, cats and flouncy china ladies that were never moved from their spot except to receive a dusting once a week.

As a child, Nina had imagined them all talking to one another at night when the human beings had gone to bed, like the ornaments in a Hans Andersen tale. The ladies would ride the horses, the dogs would bark at their heels and the cats would sit on a doorstep washing their paws and making wise comments. She smiled, remembering these fantasies and the pleasure they once gave her. In the centre of the room, winged chairs cluttered the space, together with a sagging old sofa that had been around for donkey's years. She'd snuggled up with her father on that as a child.

In a way she could see why Andrew felt happy here. There

was this sense of continuance for him, a security in the familiar objects passed down through the generations who had lived in this house. She knew he loved being here, loved the quintessential Englishness of it all. Yet he had told her that as a young boy he had looked very foreign, and estranged from his relations. Dorothy, his mother, was always kind and loving but in a dream of her own – pining, as he later discovered, for his father, a Greek officer, and her lost love. It had been a strange childhood and Nina knew he had stories about that time which he refused to share even with her. She sensed her grandmother did too and that these shared events created a secret bond between mother and son which at times excluded everyone else.

However, she held no resentment over this. Everyone had their secrets. And Andrew never failed in his love for her. Whenever he spoke of her mother, Anna, it was with respect and love, his warm, feeling brown eyes stirred by past emotions.

'She was the love of my life, Nina,' he would tell her when they were alone. 'You were born from the deepest love.'

'So, how are you enjoying the new job, my dear?'

Nina's grandmother, Dorothy Cassimatis, sat opposite her at the breakfast table and spread thick marmalade onto a thin piece of buttered toast. She smiled at her granddaughter as she asked this, a warm and loving smile, then popped a piece of toast into her mouth and looked appreciative.

'Helen makes delicious marmalade,' she murmured blissfully.

Nina smiled back. She loved her Grandma Dot: so undemanding, modern in outlook and, though in her late sixties, still a handsome woman. It was easy to imagine her as a nursing sister in the First World War. There was always an air of command and efficiency about her, a dignity in all she said and did. It amused Nina to know that this sedate-looking county lady had been a bit of a tearaway in her youth. Now she lived in London with her younger son, Fred, and his large family but visited Downlands often. She loved it as much as Andrew, had so many happy childhood memories from before the First War. The pair seemed inextricably tied to the place.

'I love it, Gran,' she replied, 'but dear old Cousin Reggie is unashamedly making me his favourite and everyone will hate me as the boss's pet.'

'No one could possibly hate you, what nonsense! You only have to smile at them and they'll adore you. People have always adored you, Nina. Yes, they have. No use blushing. And you've always been Reggie's pet. Have you done much reporting yet? It all sounds very exciting.'

'I'm assigned various roles but my main task is to help interpret French, Greek and Italian bulletins or help in interviews where an interpreter is needed. And I have interviewed a few really interesting people lately. I want to earn my place, Gran, not be promoted because I'm a relation of one of the bosses.'

'That's understandable and commendable. And just like you, my dear.'

'We must be true to ourselves,' shrugged Nina. 'I'm actually rather proud of an article I wrote on the Greek situation.'

'There's another Greek situation?' sighed Dorothy as she poured herself and Nina a cup of tea from the pot.

Nina laughed. 'Oh, indeed, always a Greek situation. King Constantine is so naive, I don't honestly think he knows what to do with his people. Greeks have never loved their foreign Kings.'

'His Danish wife – what's her name? … Anne-Marie … she's a pretty little thing,' mused Dorothy. 'People like *her,* I believe. And despite what they say now, I thought the old one, Queen Frederica, did a lot of good after the war. Helped organise centres to aid the poverty stricken women in the villages? I remember reading how she travelled a road that had been mined. It blew up the day after and her escape was deemed a sign from God that she was saintly.'

'Oh, that's the way the superstitious villagers would see it – I call it luck. But, yes, she did a lot of good things in those days,' Nina admitted. 'Then she started to get involved in politics and that's when she became interfering and unpopular. She tried to influence people. Even threaten them to do things her way. Now people really hate her. I'd love to get an interview with

King Constantine though,' she added, a mischievous smile on her face, 'wouldn't that be a scoop?'

'Wouldn't you be one of his detractors, though? Hmm, I rather think so, poor chap. I rather like the look of the lad. He's a handsome man, isn't he? He reminds me of your Grandpa Costas in his youth. Though my Costas was a lot tougher and more manly looking. They do say the King is a bit of a playboy, thinks of nothing but sailing and playing tennis with that friend of his, Michael … something.'

'He's young, I suppose,' Nina shrugged. 'No, I'm not his detractor. To be honest, I feel a bit sorry for him. But a playboy? … not unfaithful, I imagine … but who knows with men?' A shadow passed over her face and Dorothy, seeing it, knew her granddaughter was thinking of her husband Max,.

Silence fell between them. Dorothy wondered whether to broach the subject. Nina was not an open person; hard at times to fathom what was going on inside her heart.

'Do you still hear from Max?'

Nina sighed and lowered her eyes. She picked up her teacup and drank a little before replying.

'I do. He writes to me quite often. I know he wants me back again but I can't go back, Gran.'

'Because you're enjoying your freedom?'

'No, nothing to do with that. Max never stopped me from doing anything I wanted to do. It's … it's something he will never understand. Max is brilliant at superficial relationships with people. He's got hundreds of acquaintances. But I begin to think that he finds it hard to commit to a real deep relationship with anyone. On the surface he's all charm and bonhomie but his heart is shut somewhere deep inside.'

'I got that feeling too,' Dorothy remarked.

'Did you? Oh Gran, you understand people better than I do. I thought he'd change – don't we always? It's the music hall joke. He did love me, I know that. I think in his way he still does. But life is a play to him; he doesn't *engage* in it, somehow. And *you* know I'm not like that. When I truly love something or someone it's with all my passion, all my heart and soul. When I decided to finish with Max, it plunged me into such terrible anguish. I thought I was teetering on the brink of madness. He just said nothing, nothing, just looked at me quite calmly and turned and walked away from my life. He said I wouldn't listen to him, so what was the point. I can't go through all that again. He didn't understand how much it hurt, how cruel he was. I wanted him to shout, sob, beg my forgiveness. He feels if he says "sorry, my dear" it will all be fine again and the merry play can go on.'

Dorothy looked at her granddaughter with compassion. It was like hearing herself speak as a young woman. She had also been full of passion. Her love of her nursing work, her love for Costas Cassimatis, had taken her over and she had never been able to let go of that passion in all those years. And she knew that Andrew was made from the same mould. He had loved Anna Manoglou deeply and though he had said little, her terrible death at Nazi hands haunted him still. His joy at finding that Anna had left him a beautiful daughter, so like her mother in looks and temperament, had mitigated the pain. But it was still there. She knew it was.

'Oh, Nina, darling,' she sighed, 'you must move on. There'll be another man somewhere for you. Maybe you'd be better with a Greek. Someone who also has passion in him. But we all go for opposites, for some reason.'

Look at your father, she felt like saying. Helen was so entirely the opposite to Andrew's first love, Anna. Dorothy felt that this woman he had chosen to be his wife and a stepmother to Nina was more like his maternal grandmother, old Mary Clarke, in temperament – and Dorothy's relationship with her own mother had always been very difficult, very fraught.

'You know, at times, Nina, you do remind me of my beloved Costas. He was always aflame with some cause or another – and the flame died down in him towards the end. He was ill, feeble and burnt out. Don't get burnt out following causes, dear child. Find a good man, enjoy a happy life, enjoy your work. It would be lovely if you could have some children to fill this house with some laughter and joy again.'

'It would be wonderful, yes, I know,' replied Nina but her smile was sad, her dark eyes held grief in them. 'But …'

'But you still love Max, I suppose.'

'Sometimes I hate him! *Hate* him, Gran. Hate him for the pain he gave me. He was so tender, so loving, so gentle as a husband and I truly thought he was my best friend and soul-mate. He insists he still is. But I see now we never really knew one another at all. I'm going to throw myself into my work and forget him. I'm *not* interested in men.'

'Methinks thou protesteth too much?'

'Oh, Gran, you're just an incurable romantic. I'm not. Not any more. I've become a cynic. Yes, truly…don't smile! I'm going to try and do something useful, something to help my fellow men and be of some worth, as my mother was. I don't care to be a housewife, just have kids and look after a huge house like this. I want to…to do something. I don't know what exactly but I know there's a need for reforms in Greece. I want to go back there and see if I can help with something like the Lambrakis Youth Movement. Lambrakis was a man I much admire. I wish I could meet a man like *him* now…'

'So what's this Lambrakis Youth Movement, then? Not like that frightful Youth Organisation of Metaxas, I hope?'

'Oh God, no! Quite the opposite. These are young intelligent people with dynamic views. They set up libraries and theatres in villages and try to educate and help people. There are scholarships, they gather together popular songs . It's not just political, you know. They do a lot of social work too; plant trees, restore churches, give blood and many, many other things. They are the new youth of Greece. They'll *help* to restore democracy. I mean, Metaxis was a dictator, a fascist! His Youth movement was little better than that of the Nazis.'

'I think you're being a little bit harsh, my dear.'

Nina made a face. 'Gran, there's no excuse for dictatorship. Greece is supposed to be the cradle of democracy.'

Dorothy also made a face and pursed her lips,'Hmm … and Britain invented railways but that doesn't mean they run on time here half as well as they do in Germany.'

Nina looked exasperated. 'Oh, Gran, if you're going to be flippant…'

'I'm not being at all flippant,' Dorothy protested. 'I'm simply saying that because an ideal was brought to birth in one place in the past, it doesn't mean to say that the present generation understand or uphold it. Greece forgot to be a democracy during all those centuries of Turkish occupation. But they never lost their spirit or allowed themselves to die out as a race. They just need a few more centuries to re-adjust again. And let's be truthful, my dear, do any of us uphold our youthful ideals any more? The world has turned cynical and disillusioned with religion, politics and all else.'

'I uphold *my* ideals,' cried Nina, her eyes alight with that strange, slightly manic fire, that sometimes possessed her. 'I believe that Greece *is* capable of greatness again. The leaders and visionaries are there, people like Papandreou and his son, like Theodorakis and Lambrakis and many, many others who want to help Greece to change and enter Europe as a strong nation.'

Helen walked into the kitchen at this interesting point in the discussion and Nina stopped talking with reluctance for she knew that Helen was not interested in Greece or Greek ways at all and evinced no desire even to visit the country. She preferred Spain, Majorca or France and that was where she and Andrew spent their holidays. If Andrew wanted to visit Greece, which he seldom did nowadays, she declined to go with him and said, 'Take Nina instead. You'll want to visit relations and talk Greek all the time, and it's so frightfully boring for me. I've seen the Acropolis and Delphi and that will do. It's very pretty but I don't understand the people very much. They always sound angry and seem to be quarrelling a lot of the time.'

So it would annoy her to hear Nina 'spouting politics' as she always put it. The young woman felt sad about this. Even her father was no longer interested in Greece. He was far more concerned with the devaluation of the pound and the horrors of having a Socialist government in power. In this, as in many things, she and her father were not in agreement. But nothing ever marred their deep love for one another.

Chapter 4

Thessaloniki: Dinner at the Petrakos apartment

The table, covered in a large delicately embroidered white cloth, was almost sinking with the weight of plates and delicious dishes full of aromatic morsels. Basil poured out the wine and the adults all clinked their glasses together in salutation to the banquet and to health and happiness. Their two children, Yiannaki and Nitsa, copied them with little tumblers full of watered-down wine.

'You think you will be more successful this year?' asked Basil after they had all indulged in some silent moments of appreciation of the abundance of *mezes* before them. Max scooped up some more *melitsane* pate with a small piece of pitta bread and considered the matter.

'If Manos Katsarakis gives me any more grief, then I won't be,' he declared. 'He's a problem, that fellow. I'm convinced he was behind all the damage to my machinery last year. They never got to the bottom of that destruction but I'm certain it was him and his bully boys. He's a nasty piece of work who resents our success at the Trade Fair. I think he was trying to get some deal with a Yugoslavian company to supply farm machinery but they ended up coming to us. We did so well, even better than the Americans that year. I used to send Dimitri round the farming community in advance of the Trade Fair telling them to come over and see the British stand. They were most impressed and the tractors and other farm machinery were selling like hot cakes. And they certainly need them when you looked at the antiquated stuff they are still using in so many parts of Greece. Oxen, even – I mean, they're still using *oxen*!'

'Dimitri is a certainly a good salesman,' observed Athina.

'He must be one of the best salesmen there is. He could sell a fridge to an eskimo, as they say.'

'He's a good man. We always get our cars repaired by him. There's nothing he doesn't know about mechanics,' added Basil.

'I agree; he's a godsend. Thank you for introducing him to me.'

'What makes you think Katsarakis was behind last year's damage?'

'Well, I haven't an ounce of proof. But he was heard making threats against me.'

'He *is* a trouble maker,' said Basil thoughtfully. 'One of those lefties who infest our cities and live to stir things up. I wouldn't be surprised if he's behind half these riots we've been having lately. He probably hates the Americans like so many of them do.'

'So I suppose that means he hates the British too?'

'Ech, he's the sort who dislikes all foreigners. And Manos Katsarakis deems even the miserable refugees from Istanbul and Smyrna "foreigners" just because they have a Turkish accent.'

'He's a Cretan, I imagine?'

'He is. But not one to be proud of.'

Max sighed. 'Politics aside, the bastard never forgave me for the fact that his wife took a fancy to me. I didn't encourage her, I swear it.'

Athina gave a little laugh at this.

'I didn't, Athina, on my life!' Max lowered his voice and glanced over at the children, who were still occupied with their food. 'He was beating the poor girl, slapping her around. I took her part, that was all. I told him I'd punch him in the face if I saw him hitting a young girl like that again. I was already "eating wood" – as you lot say – from Nina who seemed to think every woman I looked at was after me and that I was after her.'

Max was relieved that they were talking in English at present as he had no wish to discuss this subject in front of the young children. Yiannaki, a highly intelligent ten year old lad, had spoken to him in quite decent English earlier on and was apparently learning German too – but he felt sure the child would not understand the conversation fully.

Athina and Basil both looked at one another and smiled again.

Max shrugged. 'Give a dog a bad name,' he muttered.

'Of course the girl fell in love with you if you act the knight in shining armour,' said Athina, throwing him an amused look. 'This is half your problem, Max. You can't help but go to the rescue of those you see in distress. It's always going to get you into trouble.'

Basil nodded and looked serious. 'Athina's right. Let the likes of Manos Katsarakis and his woman sort themselves out. Anyway, she may well enjoy being knocked about. Some women do, strange as it seems.'

'Oh, yes?' countered his wife. 'Well, I'm not one of them. You'd better not try. I have a big frying pan in the kitchen.'

'You wouldn't hit Papa with the frying pan?' said Yiannaki in horror. He spoke in Greek but it was evident that he was following this conversation too closely for Max's comfort and appeared to have a greater grasp of English than he'd realised. He sometimes wished Greek children could be in bed at an early hour and not left to join in with adult conversations so much.

'Wouldn't I?' nodded Athina. Her fierce words were so incongruous with the soft prettiness of her face and her gentle blue eyes that they all laughed except Nitsa who was beginning to nod off on her chair, her little chin sinking slowly towards her plate.

Athina disappeared after a while to fetch in the next course of sea bream served with mayonnaise. This was followed by a course of grilled partridge with salad and pureed potatoes. After everyone was replete with good food, the dining chairs were pushed back a little and the adults enjoyed a cigarette with their coffee. Max reflected that he would never have eaten as well as this at the top restaurants. He sighed with pleasure.

Yiannaki had decided to come and sit beside Max at the table and shyly looked up at the older man who smiled down at him and offered him a slice of peach on the end of his knife. Yiannaki declined. He sat and polished his glasses on his napkin for a while then, speaking in Greek, asked, 'Is it true that in England they have red buses with stairs that go up to the top?'

'It certainly is true. And we have trains that go underground like your Athens metro, but they go for miles, right out across the city. And stairs that go down to the underground trains called escalators that move so that you can stand on them and go up and down without having to walk. How about that?'

'I want to go on those.'

'Maybe some day your father will bring you to London.'

Yiannaki's eyes lit up and he stammered with pleasure, 'I would like to go with you; I would like to see England and London. I want to see Trafalgar Square, Buckingham Palace and Madame Tussaud's. Papa says they are the places to see.'

Nitsa had been nodding off on her father's lap but she sat up indignantly now and said, 'I want to go too.'

Her father popped a grape in her mouth and said cajolingly, 'When you're a bigger girl, then we'll see.'

The child turned her head and spat the grape out then pursed her lips. 'No, now! I'll go back with *Kyrie* Max. I want him to take me home with him and go on the top of the bus and on the moving stairs. I want to!'

'You can't go home with *Kyrie* Max, don't be so silly,' said her mother. 'This is a change of heart! What would he want with a bad-tempered little girl like you?'

'He doesn't want Yiannaki either,' muttered Nitsa, her lips trembling ominously.

'I'll take you both some day,' Max promised.

'Me too,' said Athina, 'why should they have all the fun?'

'Not too sure about *fun* in London,' said Max.

'But, of course – isn't it the swinging city? Isn't it the height of fashion, Carnaby St and the Beatles, shops, money, nightclubs?'

'Good God, must I disillusion you?'

A slight frown crossed Max's face. He thought of London, home in Earl's Court, the Basildon office, the grey day he had left behind him. The dreary streets, the occasional bomb damage that still lingered around the city, reminders of those grim battles in the skies. A flash or two of light ... brightly lit Piccadilly, the art galleries, the Mall with its long imposing tree-lined walk down to the Palace, the cheerful pigeon-infested madness of Trafalgar Square. Then his favourite places: Fleet Street late at night when newspapermen scuttled in and out of cafés and offices like rabbits in a complex warren. And St Paul's springing into being amongst dim street lamps as the spotlights were switched on and that comfortable, sacred edifice of the daytime became a strange ghostly monument of dark hollows and lonely white light. Dear, dirty, noisy, graceful, fascinating London!

He knew that Athina's vision of London was Oxford and Regent Street, elegant shops and parks, swinging, ringing life in the West End. Not the London he cared about. He had been brought up within the sound of Bow bells and felt himself to be an East Ender at heart though he had moved a long way from those humble beginnings.

Athina seemed to sense his thoughts. 'All cities have their beauty and their ugliness,' she said. 'I understand, Max.'

'I want to go,' reiterated Nitsa.

'You'll be bored,' Max laughed. 'England is cold and wet and we live a long way from the sea. You'll soon be tired of moving stairs and buses.'

But Nitsa was cross and fretful now. Not even the most solemn promise could convince her that one day she would be allowed to go to England with Max. She began to cry and, slithering from her father's lap, ran off to the sitting room where her howls could be heard ascending to the skies.

'Put the child to bed,' said Basil with a wave of his hand at his wife.

'She's drunk too much wine, *vre* Lakis,' scolded Athina, 'you shouldn't let her drink so much, it makes her ill.'

'She's hardly had a mouthful,' replied her husband. 'She's just being naughty. Put the boy to bed as well.'

'Let me stay a little more, Papa,' begged Yiannaki.

'Bed!'

Nitsa's howls gradually faded away and Yiannaki quietly removed himself to the far end of the room where he might stay unobserved a little longer. A peaceful silence fell as the two friends smoked their cigarettes. It was dark now and the room was lit by the gentle light of a green-shaded lamp that stood in a corner. Cool night air wafted in through the veranda windows. Basil rose to close the French doors and shutters as it was turning a little chilly. The sound of distant traffic was now very faint. The room smelled of cut peaches and the sweetness of grapes.

Athina returned and invited them all to come and relax in the *saloni*. She made some more coffee and poured it out, smiling and looking serene and gentle as she always did, a woman who exuded a sense of calm and relaxation. She looked very beautiful in the soft lamplight as she bent toward her husband and brushed some crumbs from his lapel with solicitous tenderness before sitting down to sip her coffee. Max paused to light another cigarette and took in the scene. He studied her long slim arms, the natural fairness of her hair, the whiteness of her skin, the little gold cross on a chain about her neck that disappeared into the demure bodice of an orange patterned cotton dress. There was a time when he had felt very attracted to Athina and envied his friend this devoted, caring wife. He adored Nina but life with her wasn't always as easygoing and loving as Basil's marriage appeared to be. Nina was always so independent, restless, and fiery. But neither would he have wanted a clinging woman, or one who didn't have courage and character as she did. He sighed. Loving was a complex business. He desperately wanted Nina back but how was he to persuade her to return?

A cosy sleepiness pervaded the atmosphere. Yiannaki had fallen asleep resting on his mother's arm which encircled him in a warm, motherly embrace. Max felt the happiness of this charming family atmosphere so different to his own early life. He let his mind wander back to his own childhood and all its harshness and sadness, thought of his mother scraping pennies from a jar to afford the fare into town. Sometimes she would leave him in the library where he spent happy moments reading books in the reference room while she went shopping. His father, however swore at him if he caught him reading too much at home.

'Bloody idiot! You'll end up a pale ponce like that, not a real man,' he would shout, snatching away the book and tossing it aside. 'Get off your bloody backside and go out and play football with the lads in the street.'

And so Max went to play football and his father sometimes stood at the door and watched the boys as they careered around the streets shouting and yelling. As Max was quite a good scorer, his father was actually proud of this accomplishment for once.

'That's more like it,' he'd say approvingly. 'That mother of yours will turn you into a milksop with all her nonsense. *We* were educated by life,' he added, nodding his short cropped head and pulling his moustache fiercely, 'that's the only education worth having. The rest is just make-believe and the opinion of fools who sit at desks and don't experience a thing. It's all trash – novels, newspaper stuff, no one can believe any of it. I've no time for it. Football, that's worthy. Horses – they're real.'

But, reflected Max, the money his father gambled on the pools and on the horses might have been equally real, the money he spent on gallons of drink in the local pub would also have been real. Instead it disappeared into the grasping hands of the bookies or was pissed down the toilet and the family suffered from poverty and debt.

Chapter 5

Thessaloniki: Trouble at the Trade Fair

'*Ade re aliti,* come and have a bite to eat, I'm starving.'

Max, who was busy checking over the machinery, looked up as Dimitri, full of his usual vigour and energy, came bustling up. Max's face and neck were scarlet in the heat of a midday sun which poured relentless rays upon the white cement of the open air stand. There was a canopy at the back of the stand and a small lock-up office where they kept documents and papers. In front of this little office stood the gleaming tractors and combine harvesters looking solid, grim and purposeful. Max looked on them with a certain British pride.

'Dimitri, you never think of anything but food and sex,' complained Max. 'I've got a mound of forms to fill in and dozens of calls to make later. My boss rang from Basildon earlier but I missed him because you wanted a coffee. Then I couldn't get hold of him after that. It's a rotten line. So it's all very well, but there's work to do.'

'Nah, work's boring,' said his cheery colleague. 'Food and sex, you say ... but of course, they're the only things that keep the world turning. You have to agree with that. Come on, it's getting late in the afternoon – we'll only be half an hour.'

'I'm not leaving the machinery for half an hour. It may be insured but I'm responsible for any damage and you remember what happened last year.'

'Ach, that was bad,' admitted Dimitri, 'but I still reckon it was some kids. I caught a couple of them trying to get over the railings this morning. Standing on each others shoulders, what next!'

'Kids aren't after tractors and farm machinery,' said Max, a grim expression on his face. 'They're after money or food or a place to do what you like doing. Getting their cocks into some girl – or up each other's backsides.'

Dimitri laughed then looked serious again. 'So you really think it was that *koproskilo*, that Cretan dogshit, Katsarakis?'

'I do. It needed strength to do that kind of damage. Strength and angry intention.'

'Well, you would mess with his woman. He's a regular fanatic. She's lucky he didn't kill her. You know those Cretans have a big thing about honour.'

'Look, I didn't make love to the girl, Dimitri. I was chatting with her and next minute she threw herself at me, holding on tight as if she'd never let me go. And, yeah ... just at that moment her boyfriend came along. It was a put-on show to make him jealous and he knew it, I'm sure of that. Heavens, I was trying to fend the girl off. Thing is, he started slapping her about and I couldn't let him do that. I suppose he thought then that I really did fancy his bitch. And as he still isn't sure what went on, he's had it in for me.'

'He beat her up, so she didn't get away with it, you know, whatever her game was. She had a couple of black eyes for days.'

'Well, I don't give a hang what he did to her now. That wrecked machinery got me into a good deal of trouble back home, nearly got me the bloody sack and they're still wrangling over the insurance claim. So I'm making sure I don't talk to a solitary female on the site and don't leave my precious machines unattended.'

'Eh, no problem. Look, here comes Antoni and his mate. They'll keep an eye on things while we take a break.'

And sure enough up strolled Antonis Tatsis, one of the security men who patrolled the grounds and a great friend of Dimitri. Everybody was a great friend of Dimitri, who seemed to know practically everyone in sight. Streams of visitors who had nothing at all to do with governments, farming or anything else came up during the day and cluttered up the stand, generally getting in the way. It took a good deal of persuasion at times to move them.

Max sighed but gave in. His own stomach was rumbling now. He locked up the little office and chatted briefly with Antonis, who agreed to leave one of his men there while they went to have a break. The two men strolled away down the broad avenue in the centre of the exhibition grounds that led to what Dimitri euphemistically called the 'restaurant'. It was in fact a self-service counter in a small building with a terrace that commanded a high level view of the grounds. A dirty, smelly place, crowded with people of all nationalities who jabbered and chattered like a thousand multi-lingual sparrows. Inside the building it was hot and stuffy but far worse out on the terrace where the sun blazed and burned, a stifling infernal blanket of heat. The only cheerful sight was the forest of brightly coloured flags flying over the grounds.

Every seat was taken and people spilled over onto the walls or on the ground which was littered with paper and the remnants of food. The crowd was happy, noisy, gesticulating furiously while consuming their coffees, stale sandwiches, hot dogs and odd-looking meatballs, the smell of which was enough to turn one green. Sweat poured out of armpits and from foreheads to mingle with the stink of rotting food and indifferent cooking. Children ran about heedlessly, scattering crumbs and toys and screaming with temper whenever they fell over which they frequently did. The hubbub and the heat were immense.

Dimitri managed to find them a small space on a low wall that encircled the terrace and they sat there struggling to eat a hot dog, dry as a bone and as tasteless. None of this perturbed Dimitri who hummed cheerfully, his fingers turning over the amber beads of his *komboloi* with a steady click-clack.

'*Afto pou arheisi oreo teleoni me ponos…*' he sang softly.

'How true,' Max agreed,' "that which begins beautifully ends with pain".'

The heat sapped his blood, an invisible vampire that was slowly reducing him to a limp heap of flesh and trickling water.

He turned to his beer, tongue hanging out in longing. It was flat, warm and disappointing. The sausage in the stale bread was positively nauseous and he threw it away with an expression of disgust that made Dimitri burst out laughing.

'Not the best of Greek cuisine, eh?'

'I'll buy some stuff outside the grounds tomorrow,' said Max.'I'm not putting up with this every day.'

'There's a nice revolving restaurant on the new tower.'

They both looked over to the slender OTE Tower built that year, now providing the first black and white TV broadcasts to Greece.

'I can't afford that every day on my salary,' said Max, 'hot dogs it'll have to be.'

'There's that fuckster, Katsarakis,' muttered Dimitri through a mouthful of sausage.

Max turned his head slightly and met the hard stare of a man who was approaching the café. Katsarakis was a tall, beefy fellow with a permanently sour and distrustful expression on his square florid face. His thick wiry hair was brushed away from a balding pate, his mouth full of gold teeth gleamed a dull yellow when he stretched his thick lips in what resembled a smile … or perhaps a leer or a sneer. Hard to tell. There was nothing friendly about it, anyway.

Max returned the stare, his own eyes hardening and angry. He would so love to give this fellow a good pasting but he knew full well he would come off the worst for it. Katsarakis was not a man to be trifled with.

As the Cretan passed by the two men sitting on the low wall, he kicked over Max's beer and sauntered on, hands in his pockets.

'*Malaka*! That wanker is just full of shit,' said Dimitri feelingly. 'What was the point of that?'

'The point is, he'll do anything to irritate me,' said Max with a shrug. 'He'd love it if I was never allowed to return to the Fair.'

'He hangs out with a very strange crowd, that guy,' said Dimitri, frowning.

'What sort of crowd – gangsters?'

'He hasn't got that much brain. He's just a bully boy for the Lefties. Now there's no way I'm right wing or anything as far fetched as that. Me, I'll always be for George Papandreou, a good man, a democrat.' He lowered his voice and murmured, 'And I hate that little shit, King Constantine. He's a regular mummy's boy. He chucked out Papandreou just because he wouldn't do as he was told and stood up for democracy. You know that? Just sent him packing like a naughty boy. And still hasn't called for elections. Just put in his stooge, Novas. And I bet you what you like the Americans are behind it. They're behind everything that goes on here. We all know it, but what can we do? They have us by the balls. Pouring money in and making us dependent on their milk when it's time we got weaned. You mark my words, there'll be trouble because of this. There's sure to be a revolution or something. And the mob that idiot Katsarakis is probably working for may well be mixed up in it. If they get rid of that brat, Constantine, then I'll support them myself.'

'Better to steer clear of politics, Dimitri. That's a dangerous game in any country. And even more over here. I tell you, I had enough of all that with Nina. She loves her causes and her wretched political schemes more than she ever loved me.'

Dimitri looked at his friend and shrugged. 'Women are all a pain. But I have to say,' he added,'Nina is a Greek, Max. You married her, knowing what she'd be like. She's going to care about the country she was born in even if she did get brought up in England. It doesn't matter, she'll always be a Greek at heart. Look at George Papandreou's son, Andreas. He had it all in the States: money, position, respect, the lot – yet he came home and became a Greek again, gave up his US citizenship and all to fight for a free Greece.'

'It wouldn't surprise me if Nina gave up her British citizenship some day for a free Greece,' Max said bitterly.

'You do still care about her, you know,' said Dimitri with a sad smile. 'You should get together again, you two. You love each other, you fools. That's not to be given up lightly.'

'She won't have me back.'

'Have you tried?'

'Yes … no – and I won't.'

'Bah! That's pride speaking. Take her in your arms and fuck her hard next time you see her. That'll do the trick. Are you a man or aren't you? Women are all the same when it boils down to it.'

Max couldn't help a laugh. 'Oh, Dimitri, old friend. You make it sound so easy. But my opinion is that women like Nina are very complicated beings. I will never get the hang of how to deal with women. Come on, let's get another beer, foul as it is.'

At night, the Exhibition Ground took on a new magic that it could never possess in the harsh light of day. Now it was a glittering, gleaming carnival of light and shadows, colours and sounds. Music played in bursts of gaiety, the smell of sausages and fried onions assaulted the nostrils and actually seemed appetizing. The hum and chatter and surge of life made the place take on the aspect of a merry fairground.

It was a warm night, rather close and promising thundery weather but occasionally a warm breeze would spring up from the sea and waft about one's face, mingling many strange things together in a pot-pourri of scents. Dimitri had set off home earlier and promised to be back later on with his entire family. Max had set a couple of Dimitri's men on the stands to keep an eye on things and answer any queries from would-be purchasers. He sat in his office and busied himself with some paperwork and drank disgusting half-cold coffee.

Later on he went for a stroll about the grounds, visiting various exhibitions and pavilions and watching the people surging in under the new ultra modern arches that marked the entrance. He always enjoyed watching people, noting their expressions and foibles, listening to amusing snatches of conversation. They were much the same everywhere, he reflected, be it a fairground in Greece, Austria or England.

Dimitri eventually rolled up with Yiota, the two children and an aged mother in tow. They all started to jabber at Max at once. He held up his hands in surrender.

'One at a time, one a time!' Then he hugged Yiota, kissed her on both cheeks and swung the young ones aloft to squeals of laughter.

Yiota was a small, plump woman in her late twenties with short curly brown hair that framed a full-moon face. Her skin was pink, clear and glowing with health, and she had large deep brown eyes, heavy-lidded so that she always appeared to regard one through half-closed eyes. She tilted and moved her head in a manner that was feminine and attractive and when she spoke, her voice was girlish with a pleasing lilt to it. Though not a pretty woman, she had a lively charm and warmth.

The old *yiayia,* on the other hand, was a wrinkled creature like a brown dried fig; her eyes glazed over with ill-health, her mouth was thin and turned down at the corners as if in a constant state of disapproval. She fixed her rheumy eyes on Max as if trying to read his every fault. His open-necked shirt and rolled-up sleeves seemed to displease her greatly. Max knew the old lady considered him a sloppy Englishman but he also knew how to get round her and bowed and kissed her hand like a courtly gentleman.

She drew her shoulders up at this, giving him a thin and reedy smile of welcome, '*Kalosorizate*. Welcome, *Kyrie* Max.'

'I hope you're well, *Kyria* Dora,' he responded.

'Well enough,' she sighed.

'You look most elegant tonight,' added the arch charmer, Max. The old lady fluttered a little and gave another tight smile. 'But you need to take care walking about in those high heels,' he added, 'the ground's very uneven.'

'I keep telling her she's getting too old to wear heels,' said Yiota, exasperated. 'She's sure to fall over, she always does, the stubborn old woman.'

'*Papse, vre*!' the old lady exclaimed. 'Just shut up, daughter in law! I'm not that old yet! And I will never wear those nasty flat shoes you keep buying me. I've always been an elegant woman all my life. I'm not stopping now. *You* can look like something the cat's brought in if you like. That's your problem.'

Little Georgie took Max's hand and tugging him, said, 'Let's go and see the boxing!'

'Take him, Max. I'll hang on here, you have a break,' said Dimitri.

Yiota, *Kyria* Dora and little Savva decided to go to some other stalls. Savva already had eyes that reflected a million lights as he gazed around at all the marvellous things on display and began to demand whatever took his fancy.

'*Soppa, vre paidi mou*!' scolded her mother, 'just be quiet, child!' But her youngest son ignored her and began to shout and yell out his demands.

Max decided the boxing with Georgie was the better option and allowed the youngster to cart him away. They approached the newly built Alexandreio Melathron, the Palais de Sports, which was now the largest hall in Greece and looked most imposing. It was a large closed-in building that was like a theatre or arena, like the amphitheatres of old. Seating themselves on the tiers, they looked around in happy anticipation. The next contest was announced and the two opponents ranged themselves on opposite sides of the makeshift ring.

'Can you fight like this?' asked Georgie, his eyes alight.

'Yes, I can box. I was taught at school.'

'I'm going to learn all the rules,' said the child, 'I want to learn to box. I like it.'

'It's not my favourite sport,' Max replied, 'but it's useful to learn a bit of self-defence.'

He looked around him as he spoke and saw the hated Katsarakis with his wretched wife, Zoë, seated some way off. Max felt a pang of compassion for the girl. She appeared cowed and miserable and glanced over at him with a sad expression on her face. He looked swiftly away again as Katsarakis turned his beefy head in his direction. There was no way he wanted any more trouble with that nasty brute.

They wended their way back after the boxing bouts were over and Georgie exclaimed in delight over all the goods on offer. Max bought him sausages and sweetmeats and they stopped to look at the stand advertising the televisions.

‘I wish we had one of those,’ said Georgie, his eyes riveted by the black and white pictures that flickered over the screen.

‘Clever, isn’t it?’ said Max. ‘Comes via Yugoslavia, I believe. And then the new OTE Tower sends signals all over Greece.’

‘I want to be on television when I’m big. I’m going to be famous,’ the boy announced. ‘I don’t mind how. But I’ll be famous – and rich,’ he added. ‘I want to buy my mamma a bigger flat. She keeps saying we need a bigger flat.’

‘Good luck, then.’

They got back to the stand and found Dimitri deep in discussion over the merits of some recent models, the Super Major and the Super Dextra tractors, with a wealthy landowner of Macedonian tobacco fields and a farmer from the rich agricultural lands of Thessaly.

‘Nothing wrong with the Fordson Major I bought years back, it’s still a beautiful machine,’ said the farmer. ‘And cheap to run on diesel. But I need another machine now.’

‘You must have bought the Major after the war,’ said Max, surprised.

‘I did. I bought it in ’51 when I was in England and had it shipped over. I believe in modernisation and just loved that tractor. An American friend of mine lent me the money and he’s never regretted it. I’ve paid him back twice over. What would we do without the Americans, I ask you, eh? I couldn’t have afforded it otherwise. The locals were still using the old plough but seeing what my tractor could do soon woke them up. Though there are still many who feel I cheat or that it’s the Devil’s work and all the rest of it. Bloody peasants are stupid everywhere.’

‘This is the most up to date now, the Ford 5000 mid-size range,’ said Dimitri with pride, patting the shiny blue and white tractor on the stand. ‘You won’t beat this for value. Look at the thing: four cylinder, diesel, a cabin with weather protection. It’s at the top of the tree.’

‘Not that you need that much weather protection in Thessaly,’ smiled Max.

‘What are you on about? You’d be surprised how wet the

spring can be,' the farmer replied, looking over the engine as he spoke.

After some discussion the farmer agreed to order one of the newer models to add to his expanding farm. The Macedonian landowner said he would give it consideration. It was getting late, and the old *yiayia* had taken the protesting children back home with her. Dimitri fancied going with Yiota to the Wine Festival where they could sample food and wine then dance on the rough platform erected in the centre of the tables. Max, however, now wearied by the noise and smells, decided to stay and finish off some paperwork in his little office by the stand. Few people came that way, having drifted to the more entertaining venues of the Fair.

Max finished filling in his last piece of paperwork, stretched his tired arms over his head and decided to call it a day. He put his papers in a briefcase and glanced at his watch. It was almost ten o'clock. He wondered whether to join Dimitri and his family at the Wine Festival but decided against it. His head and back ached, he yearned for a shower and some time alone in his room at his hotel where he could read a book, smoke a few cigarettes and turn in for the night. The sounds of the festival were now a hum in the distance and he had a strange sense of unreality, of being in a dream. Too much of that awful coffee and indigestible food. He needed a walk to clear his head and unlock his body.

There was a soft sound at the door of the office, a timid knock. As he turned towards the sound, he smelt a familiar cheap perfume that made him turn even quicker to confront the small, slim blonde girl who had slipped inside. She shut the door swiftly behind her. Her face was a mask of terror, her cheek and lip cut open at the side and bleeding profusely.

'Zoë, what the hell...!'

She ran over and flung her arms about him. He tore her arms from his neck savagely and swore when he saw blood on his shirt.

'Get the hell out of here! What are you playing at now, damn you? Just stop these blasted games of yours.' He tried to propel the girl towards the door but she clung to him with desperation.

'*Kyrie* Max, help me. That man's a madman, he'll kill me. Save me, for God's sake, save me!'

'Look, you chose that bastard, Zoë. It's not my problem, get it? Go to the police or something. Go and see Antonis Tatsis. He's out there somewhere.'

'You don't understand,' the girl said. Her eyes were open wide and she swivelled her head about as if trying to hear sounds of pursuit. Her fear was so real that Max paused a moment. What the devil was going on here? He had an uneasy feeling that he was being set up again.

'You and that husband of yours are always trying to get me in trouble. I don't want to know about your problems. Get out of here now and ask a brother, father, someone to take care of you. There's nothing I can do.'

'I don't have anyone,' she sobbed.

He gave her a handkerchief and she dipped it into the glass of water on his desk and began to make an attempt to staunch the blood from her lip, flinching in pain. 'Listen, he took me from the orphanage. I'm all his, nowhere to go, no one to care. My parents were killed in the war, they died of starvation in the street. You showed me that you cared before so I ran here hoping you'd help me. English men don't beat their wives. You could take me away with you. Please, please take me away with you!'

'Are you joking? I can't take you anywhere, you stupid girl. And Englishmen beat their wives just as hard as Greeks, don't kid yourself.'

His mind flashed back to childhood scenes when his father would take off his leather belt and whip his mother with it. Her screams still echoed in his mind and heart.

'But not you,' Zoë pleaded.

She tried to re-adjust her blood-stained blouse. The sleeve had been torn in some struggle. Max looked at his bloodied shirt and swore to himself again. He had no idea what to do. It looked as if they had been in a tussle together, as if he had been the attacker. Was that the idea? Would a vengeful Katsarakis now burst in claiming he, Max, had slapped his wife about? Yet the girl seemed genuinely afraid and his heart, ever ready to rescue a woman in pain, was stirred. He thought again of his mother cowering in a corner, shielding her head with her arms while his father, his brutal work finished, would fling the belt aside and collapse in a drunken heap on the sofa. He remembered running to her side and dabbing her cheek as he now dabbed at this young woman's lip.

Leave the bitch alone, d'you hear … leave her alone, you little brat. How do I know you're even mine, eh? Howsa man know …she was whoring around while I was fighting a bloody war…

No, he could never let a woman suffer at the hands of a brute. And a liar. His mother had never 'whored around.'

The girl began to sob now, deep racking sobs. She clutched at the hand Max was using to attempt to clean the congealing blood on her face.

'You're a good man, a *palikari,*' she whispered, 'I knew you were good. Take me somewhere safe, *Kyrie* Max. I can't stay any more with him. He goes mad when I speak or even look at another man. He's worse than ever nowadays. He says he'll kill me next time and he will, I know he will – or I'll kill him. I'll take a knife to him, I swear on Christ I will!'

'We can't stay here,' said Max. He switched off the light and prayed no one had noticed or heard anything. Luckily the Ford stand was near the outskirts of the park, away from all the fairground shows and activities. The door was shut and he had just a simple anglepoise lamp on his desk. He put his head out of the door; all seemed quiet enough. A few people were strolling along the path and the guard had his back turned to the office, sitting chatting to someone at the other end of the stand. Somehow, Zoë had slipped past him while he was thus absorbed. So much for *his* vigilance. The air was humid and heavy with the feel of a thunderstorm.

'Put on my jacket to hide some of this mess you're in and get out into those trees over there where you won't be seen. Slip out in ten minutes and meet me outside the front gates along

Angelaki – but keep out of the way. For God's sake try not to be noticed. I'll get a taxi when I get out myself.'

'You *will* come for me?'

'Yes, I'll come, though I haven't a clue what to do with you, Zoë, except take you to a police station.'

The girl looked frantic at this. 'No, *Kyrie* Max, you mustn't, they'll just hand me back to him. Don't do that. He has friends, they're all bought, all in these things together. He's one of the bastards who was involved in that Lambrakis thing.'

Max was shocked. 'I though he was a leftie.'

'Bah! He's nothing, just out for himself. He pretends, he spies, he's mixed up in all sorts of things.'

Max sighed deeply. 'Okay, well, off you go, quick … while no one's looking.'

She slid out into the night and ran silent and swift as a little fox into the trees and bushes, now dark looming shapes that lined the sides of the railings.

Max shut the wooden door, locked it with care and walked along the path, making sure he kept in the shadows. The guard looked over at him and called a cheerful greeting,

'You going to the Wine Festival?'

'Later,' said Max, mustering a smile. 'Maybe a shower first.'

He prayed that the bloodstained shirt wasn't visible and held his briefcase against his chest to hide it.

'Good idea, it's a shit of a night, too hot,' grumbled the guard. '*Yiasou*. see you tomorrow then.'

'*Yia*. See you.'

The firework display was just starting and the night flared up with shooting stars, echoing with bangs, explosions and cheers that came from the distant arena where the crowd had gathered. The noise made Max jumpy; it was like gunfire and his nerves were frazzled enough without the lurking feeling that the brutish Katsarakis may be searching for Zoë and that his animal-like instinct would surely lead him in Max's direction.

He walked along in the direction of the gates and debated whether to get a taxi. That bastard might well bribe the taxi men to tell him if they'd seen anyone with Zoë. Better to walk perhaps, keep to the shadows and take the girl … where? To his hotel? Hardly. That would raise far too many eyebrows in such a small, gossipy place. To Basil's place? How would he explain her to Basil and Athina? And the children would want to know what was going on. What the hell was he to do with her?

He walked over to the trees where she had gone to hide. At first there was no sign of her and he swore to himself but also felt fleetingly relieved. Then he saw a movement in the shadows of the walls and he found her curled up beside an acacia bush, her head down in her hands. Again, he saw that terrifying flashback to his younger days and it made him feel sick to the pit of his stomach. Raising the girl gently, he put a comforting arm about her. She was shivering, despite the heat. He was sure now that her terror was real and knew he had to do something to help her. But what?

Chapter 6

Ladbroke Grove, London, England

Nikos Galanis leant back in the swivel chair, the last patient gone. He could hear his nurse, Toula Papadopoulos, bustling around in the reception area as she drew down blinds and prepared to go home. His surgery was on the middle floor of a double-fronted Victorian house in a street off Ladbroke Grove. It was a pleasant, quiet street lined with plane trees that shaded the road in a mantle of green in the summer. However, today was cloudy and dreary and most of the leaves on the trees had long shivered their way into the gutters to be cleared up by a stupid-looking lanky fellow with a broom and a barrow.

He hated England. It was a cheerless, grey country where it never stopped raining and where the people were polite, distant, cold and unreachable. Thankfully his clients were mainly all Kensington Greeks and Embassy staff or from various Cypriot outposts such as Finsbury Park and Camden Town. Not that he liked the Cypriots either. They had abandoned their own country from fear of the Turks or else from greed and cupidity. They were making good money by tempting lacklustre Britons with food or else they ran sweatshops making clothes that fell apart in five minutes. In his opinion they were all ignorant peasants. Some were now affluent peasants, however, having fled to this land to woo the bored and jaded British palate with meatballs, lamb kebabs and rich sweet honey-cakes, most of which were adapted over the centuries from Turkish cuisine. In the end it was foreign food, not bombs, that conquered the xenophobic

British; hardly surprising when one considered the bland tastelessness of their own cuisine.

They took the easy route. It was far harder to fight against oppression and invasion as his grandparents had done against the Turks. His parents had fought against the Nazis, but Nikos always had a secret admiration for Hitler which he would never have dared voice in his home. His father would have beaten him and thrown him out. True, the Nazis had been invaders, starved the population, but they had the right idea. A pure race. Keep all the races pure and not mingle them up into the filthy tasteless human soup that was fast becoming the norm. At least the Germans were European and Christian. He was so angry with the Russians. The Russians had always been their allies, their brothers before God. How could they have abandoned their beautiful Orthodox faith and turned to Communism?

He was always happier when a client was a Greek from Kensington. These were mainly diplomatic wives and daughters with various minor problems which they puffed up to amazing hypochondriac proportions, or else pregnant women who wanted private treatment with a fellow countryman in attendance. They grumbled about climbing the stairs to his surgery but it was good for them, rich, idle and pampered women, equally stupid in many ways but at least they spoke beautiful Greek, were well-read and held proper views about life. Not this immoral, irreligious attitude so prevalent here in England and creeping slowly but surely into Greece, poisoning the very foundations of his beloved country bit by bit.

Democracy! This was what you got with democracy. You got a mish-mash of ideas, no proper rules and boundaries to life. Anything was allowed and nothing was done. It meant life was no longer orderly and secure but chaotic and frightening in its formlessness. He wanted order and form. It was vital to existence. A body without a skeleton and skin to give it structure would be just a shapeless mess. And Greece was becoming just this shapeless mess. England already was. He wanted to howl with anguish over it.

But what could he do?

He smiled. Oh, there was plenty he could do. Plenty was being done already and his heart swelled with pride to think he might have a place in the future of a stronger, wiser Greece. He had friends in the Greek army and he knew there were rumours flying of a brilliant coup. Not the coup that foolish young King was planning with his generals. It was much braver and more heroic than that.

Again Nikos smiled to himself and drew down the blinds over the windows before leaving his surgery.

The Old Brompton Road, London

Nina lived in a small ground floor flat off the Old Brompton Road, the home she had once shared with Max. It was a three-roomed apartment in a street of once-elegant old houses, now mainly let off in single rooms to a variety of Australian students and hippy couples. Earl's Court had, for some reason become the Mecca of Australians in London, but they were a friendly, cheerful bunch and she got on well with those she encountered. It was hardly a salubrious area and she knew her father often wondered why she and Max chose to live here when they were married. But then, his idea of Heaven was his beloved Downlands, Elgar, the countryside and being an English country gentleman. Even Cousin Reggie had offered to help them, telling them they should try and find a better place in the suburbs.

'It's not that far to travel on the Tube, is it?' he said. 'So much pleasanter in Putney or Barnes, you know.'

'But not so interesting,' Nina had told him. 'I don't want the uniformity of suburbia and smart houses all in neat rows with neat front gardens. There may be mess and litter and sad homeless people around but it's alive, it's busy, it's full of unusual characters. I like that.'

She loved these rooms they rented with their high white ceilings, decorated with trailing rows of plaster acanthus leaves and uncertain fruit. She liked the feeling of history this place gave her; in fact, she'd always liked the area, especially the beautiful old cemetery across the road. Brompton was said to be the finest of the seven great cemeteries built on the outskirts of London in the Victorian era. She was reluctant at first to enter the cemetery. The mere thought of all those dead people horrified her, quick and living and full of passionate energy as she was; horrified to think one day she would no longer exist but lie in such a place. Strangely enough, it was Max who persuaded her, the last person she would have expected to like such a place. 'You'll love it in there,' he said,'it's not morbid at all, it's serene and peaceful. In fact, it's full of life.'

'How can it be full of life?' she queried. Curiosity won her in the end and she went in with him and indeed, it *was* full of life. Squirrels, foxes, birds, butterflies, beetles inhabited the wilder areas while people walked about the paths between the well-tended graves or sat in the shade of the sycamores. She was enchanted by the place.

She and Max often took long walks there when they were first married. How happy they were then, so in love. It always made her think of Max when she walked in the cemetery and since they had parted she had ceased to go in there. However, tonight she felt a need to stretch her legs after a long day working at the newspaper office.

Her article finished and handed over to the editor, she hurried home. The day was cloudy but dry for once; a longing for some green space after staring at a typewriter all day called her forth. Changing into jeans and plimsolls, she ran down the front steps, greeted an incoming tenant who lived in the rooms above her own, crossed the road and passed joyfully beneath the huge Victorian archway that marked the north entrance to the cemetery as if entering the gates of Paradise. Ahead of her stretched a long wide avenue lined with lime trees, which in the early summer were scented honey-sweet but had now turned golden yellow and were shedding their leaves abundantly upon the pathways. At the far end of the avenue loomed the beautiful white chapel with its rotunda, said to be based on St Peter's in Rome. On either side, stretching in all directions, were the elaborate and exotic headstones, carvings and mausoleums raised by the Victorians to house their mortal remains. In these decaying stone and marble palaces, the inhabitants were reduced to the utter simplicity of bones and names. The ancients had thought of the skeleton as the greatest symbol of purity, stripped of the fantasy of flesh, desire, ego. Flesh was corrupt; it defined one as male or female, young or old, beautiful or ugly. But bones were simple, straightforward, bringing all to equality.

Names however, were another thing. Old families, local names, foreign names, famous names were recorded here. As always, Nina paused by the memorial to Emmeline Pankhurst, a lady she much admired. Many, many heroes lay there, men who had won the Victoria Cross or otherwise distinguished themselves in battle. She admired them also, these men who had fought as soldiers and died for the sake of their country. She could understand that. Her father and her grandfather had been soldiers; her mother a partisan, a soldier in her own right.

Max's attitude when she expressed such thoughts always annoyed her. He was flippant, dismissive. He reminded her at such times of Reggie, her father's cousin and her employer. He too had voiced similar thoughts to her when she was young, scathing about war and battle. Reggie had been a conscientious objector in the Second War whereas she believed in fighting to maintain democracy and freedom. If there was a war now, she felt sure Max would also refuse to fight in it.

'Heroes?' Max laughed. 'Men who have to kill whether they like it or not. Or get shot themselves? *Dulce et decorum est* isn't for me. I've no wish to sweetly die for my country or get shot if I don't. Can't see the bravery in that.'

'But these men and women fought to keep out invaders, to keep us free, Max. What, you'd be a conchie like Cousin Reggie? Would you? You'd *want* to be taken over by another country, your freedoms curtailed, become slaves, prisoners ... worse if you were a Jew! Never, never would I give in to tyranny. I'd fight till my last breath. I'm *glad* they are honoured. But I still wonder at all this elaborate Victorian worship of dead bones. The Greeks are wise. They gather the bones after so long and put them all in an ossuary. It saves space.'

'I don't really think about the graves,' he replied with a smile, 'I just look on this place as a beautiful park, a serene place to be in after a hot, heavy day.'

'How can you not think of the graves when they're all around us? Here Death has swallowed people. People who lived and breathed and had stories to tell. I often wonder what their stories might be – look at all these foreign names – Polish men and women and so many others. And the heroes, and the artists and writers and so many amazing people. You were right; it's not a morbid place. I find it good to be reminded of how short life is, Max. It's a reminder to get on with life and do something useful with it.'

'You look after me, that's useful,' he joked and put his arm about her, tried to kiss her. But she shook him off, annoyed at his flippant response, his lack of understanding.

Remembering all this made her pause a little. Despite everything, her heart swelled with yearning. She missed him so much. She missed his jokes, his teasing ways, his fun and lightness, the way he always made her laugh. Maybe she *was* a little too serious. She sighed. But Max needed to learn to be *more* serious just as she needed to lighten up, as he would put it. *Lighten up, Nina!* She almost heard his voice and turned for a foolish moment thinking he was there. Instead she saw a slim dark-haired young man walking a little way behind her. He smiled and raised his hat in greeting. She looked away and carried on with her walk. As the young man passed her by, he raised his hat again and said, '*Kalispera*, *Kyria* Hammett.'

She nodded and gave him a half smile, wondering who he was. A Greek who obviously knew her but she had no idea who he could be. A son of a friend, perhaps?

Shrugging, she carried on with her walk till she came to the semi-circular colonnades, underneath which were the catacombs. Spaced at regular intervals were broad flights of stone steps that led down to wrought-iron doors which guarded the dead laid in these underground tombs. The young man who greeted her earlier had walked down one of these and was peering in through the grilles of the locked doors. She smiled a little. She had once done the very same thing, then run back to Max and urged him to come and take a look. 'It's like the catacombs of Rome,' she had said, 'rows and rows of shelves with coffins on them. Like the Christian catacombs, isn't it, Max?'

But he had just laughed and said, 'There's no way they're putting me in there. Rather be out in the open under God's sky.'

Yet, she felt that the thought of those hidden tombs had affected him, touched a nerve somewhere. It was strange the way he'd reacted – the only time she felt he was unable to be flippant, make a joke about it all. It really bothered him and they never walked down those steps again to look at the rows and rows of coffins laid in there.

The walk revived her spirits and she returned home slowly as dusk was falling. Outside in the street, the trees swayed in the evening breeze, shedding drifts of leaves with every movement, while the lamps, now alight, made haloes of pale incandescence appear in the damp misty air. There was always a slightly Dickensian atmosphere about London at this time of night.

She had a bath with a lot of foamy suds scented with the sweetness of lily of the valley, her favourite floral perfume. Drying herself with a huge fluffy white towel, she dressed with care in a simple slim-fitting midnight-blue dress, pearls at her ears and throat. She always wore pearls, it was her trademark. Pearls were elegant, feminine and sophisticated. Her grandmother had given her these pearls for her twenty-first birthday. They were quintessentially English. They represented the English portion of her nature.

Nina had agreed to meet Nikos Galanis that evening. He had rung her earlier that day and told her he had something important to ask her. She had known him for many years; his grandfather, Petros Galanis, was a close friend of her grandfather Costas. The two men had fought side by side against the

Bulgarians back in 1917 while Nikos's father, Andreas, had fought again in the Second World War. Then, after all that, the poor man had come home to be accidentally killed in the terrible Civil War in Greece between the communist faction and extreme right wing sympathisers which broke out immediately after Greece was liberated from the Nazis. He had become caught in crossfire, shot through the heart by a sniper's bullet. She knew that it had affected Nikos badly, the loss of his father. He always said it was a communist bullet that killed Andreas Galanis and silently nurtured an abiding hate for all that the communists represented. It wasn't based on any fact, just an idea. It could just as easily have been a British bullet or one of the right wing supporters who had slain Andreas.

Nina understood that Nikos was an unhappy man. She felt pity for him. He too was wounded in some way, scarred in his own heart by the bullet that had killed his father and made his beloved mother a widow. Yet, she felt a certain, irrational dislike for the man. He was always bland, elegant, polite and passably good-looking in his early youth. Though only forty or so years old, his face had already become puffy and jowly and his attitude was middle-aged. He never seemed to have enjoyed his youth and spoke of his student years with bitterness.

He had always admired her, she knew that, and it felt good to be admired again, to feel feminine and attractive once more. She hadn't felt like that for such a long time. Nikos was erudite, clever, interesting to converse with. But there was something ... she couldn't put her finger on what it was that irritated her. Perhaps she felt he was never quite honest. He always agreed with what she said, what anyone said. That alone was suspicious in a Greek man. Had he learnt to do this here in England in order to conform with his new post? ... No, he'd always been the same.

He arrived in his smart white MG at the exact time agreed. Nina was ready and waiting. She knew he hated anyone to be late. Opening the door of the car, he gently helped her in, taking her arm and guiding her as if she was some fragile doll.

They drove in the direction of Camden Town and talked

about the weather, the trials of finding a parking place in London these days and other such banal matters. It took a little circling round but at last they managed to find a slot in which to park.

'It's a bit of a walk, I'm afraid.'

Nina shrugged. 'I don't mind a walk.'

'How do you ladies manage it in those high heels?' smiled Nikos, glancing down at her shapely legs.

'Practice, Nikos. We practice from childhood with our mother's shoes. In my case with my grandmother's. She had a black pair and a grey pair for best and a white pair for the summer. Never that high in the heel. Mostly she was always sensible and wore low heels or flat shoes. She used to be a nurse and said she always felt uncomfortable in high heels. But I've always loved them.'

'You have the legs for them.'

He ushered her into the restaurant ahead of him and clicked his fingers at the young waiter who was hovering near the door, speaking to the man in Greek.

'I reserved a table at the back.'

'But of course, *Kyrie* Galanis. Come this way.'

They were led to a table tucked into a discreet corner where the lighting was subdued. Nina looked at Nikos wondering whether this was a prelude to seduction. If so, it wasn't going to work. All the same, it was nice to flirt a little. She would enjoy that. It felt a long time since she had flirted with a man, a long time since a man had said he loved her. Yet it was only a year, in truth. A year ago that she had flung her husband out of their flat in a fit of rage and jealousy. What had that been about? It seemed so stupid, looking back. However, she refused to regret it. Finding he had been having sex with that little peroxide blonde who worked in his office was too much. Surely she was worth a hundred times more than *that* woman.

They sat down and the waiter brought the menus over, fussed with napkins and poured iced water from a jug into the two waiting glasses. As they sipped at their aperitifs and sampled the meze of olives, feta and hummus, the restaurant owner bustled over to them and bowed to Nikos.

'*Kalosorizate, Kyrie* Galanis, so good to see you. Come and see what we have prepared today. And your lovely lady too. Choose your dish.'

They went into the kitchen and the chef opened several pots and pans and enumerated his various dishes. Nina chose her favourite, *papoutsakia*, baked halves of aubergine stuffed with mincemeat so that they looked like little black slippers, hence the name. Nikos ordered lamb *souvlakia* and chips.

The bouzouki music was merrily blaring out popular Greek songs. Nikos glanced up, irritated.

'Turn that music down, I can't hear myself think,' he ordered the waiter.

'At once, *Kyrie* Galanis. At once.'

Nina played idly with some pitta bread and a little hummus. She wondered if all this masculine stuff was meant to impress but knew it was just the way Greek men liked to act. Particularly a man like Nikos. He was vain at the bottom of it. On the whole, she felt that she could never have married a Greek. Women friends in Greece had often told her that an Englishman was a better husband, more manageable. She sighed. Max *was* a wonderful man in so many ways, kind, tender, warm and caring. Why had things gone so wrong between them? Was it her fault? Had she not satisfied him enough sexually so that he'd felt the need to take up another woman?

Max had accused her of spending all her energy getting involved in politics.

'I'm never sure what you're up to,' he once told her. 'You aren't getting mixed up with the Commies, are you, Nina? That's a dangerous road to tread here in Britain, let alone in Greece. If you must get into left-wing politics, why not join the Labour Party over here or something.'

'English politics are of no interest to me,' she replied. 'They're too tame.'

'Too tame? What the hell does that mean?'

'Max, I'm a Greek. We like danger, we like battles, we like to fight for our homeland. It's in our blood and bones. The English seldom have the energy to fight. They're apathetic most of the time. That's why you never have revolutions over here but cling to the old, mellow ways of life. You're all too lazy and too used to your comforts.'

'There's plenty to fight for here. There is still poverty and injustice.'

'In the Victorian era, in the thirties, yes. But now you've got a Welfare State. Everyone can have free teeth and glasses and medicine. People out of work can live quite comfortably compared to their unhappy forefathers who were thrown into workhouses. That's a wonderful thing in so many ways – who, after all, wants dire poverty and starvation? But strangely it isn't always for the best. Not for any of us. Too much ease destroys something that wants to fight, to rebel in our human nature. Comfort means there's no incentive for men to work or fight any more. My father always said it was destroying the backbone of this country and if we Greeks ever get too comfortable, it will destroy us too.'

'Do you begrudge ordinary people these comforts after all we've been through, Nina? After all this country has done to defend itself and defend Europe, liberate your beloved Greece?'

'And then interfere immediately afterwards against what they saw as a communist threat,' she retorted angrily. 'The British and Americans are always interfering, always think they know what is best for other countries. But you northern nations have a different nature. We Greeks are of the south; we are passionate, freedom-loving individualists. We would never turn over to Communism, don't they realise this? Democratic Republicans, yes. That's different. '

'Well, the British are a quieter nation, a calmer nation,' Max replied. 'We don't "do" revolutions, I agree, and thus we are stable and on the whole accepting. We have had our riots, our Civil War, our decapitated king, but on the whole, we don't have an aggressive spirit as much as a defensive spirit. We'll do anything to defend our shores and our way of life. And we have done. We've given the best of our nation.'

'Yes,' agreed Nina,'the best, the most beautiful. And Britain is left with the dregs now. It will never be the same nation again.'

Max had thrown up his hands in surrender.'You like to have the last word, don't you? Oh, Nina. Forget all this stuff. Come and kiss me instead. Darling, what can we do about anything? Life goes on, things change – but, as the French say, in the end nothing changes. It goes round and round in crazy circles.. I can't see how we can prevent anything in the long run. Don't you Greeks call it *Moira*? Fate?'

He'd tried to take her in his arms, make her forget her political passions in the passion of lovemaking. Once that would have quietened her restless soul, brought her back to earth. But this time she had turned sharply away, still full of her ideas and anger over what she perceived as the injustices, the lethargy of others when so much needed to be done.

Perhaps it was true. Her libido had been driven elsewhere and sex, while enjoyable, was never her first thought in life. There was so much else to occupy the heart and soul. She wasn't sure she wanted children whereas Max liked kids and, though he'd never said so, she knew he longed to start a family. She was a bit of an Amazon, really. Maybe marriage wasn't for her at all. Andrew had said her mother, was like that. Nina had inherited Anna's warrior spirit, love of freedom and individuality.

'Come, come, Nina, your mind is elsewhere. Isn't the food good? Do you want to change the dish?'

Blinking a little, Nina brought her thoughts back to the present and smiled at Nikos, who was regarding her with puzzlement and a slight touch of annoyance. He wasn't used to being ignored, even for a few minutes. Nina was usually so full of conversation and cheerfulness.

'I'm sorry, Niko *mou*.' She patted his arm. 'Yes, my mind was elsewhere. It's so rude of me. A walk down memory lane.'

'They didn't look very pleasing memories.'

'They weren't.'

They chatted in more general terms and finished their

meal. Nikos proffered and lit a cigarette for Nina then one for himself and sat back.

'So what is the important thing you had to tell me, Niko?' she asked.

He regarded her silently for a moment or so. 'Are you planning to return to Greece?' he asked.

She nodded. 'Yes, I'm going there after Christmas. I always spend Christmas at Downlands with Papa. He'd be very upset if I didn't.'

'Interesting that my father knew your grandfather, isn't it?'

'One of those things,' Nina shrugged. 'How are your mother and brothers?'

'They're all well. Mother's getting on, a real old *yiayia* now. Dresses in black and looks twice her age. She moved in with my brother Spiros and his family when they went to Faleiron a year ago, leaving the house for me when I return home. She said Athens was getting too noisy. Now she misses all her old gossiping cronies.'

Nina laughed heartily at this. 'Oof, they always want peace and quiet when they get older. My father's just the same. No longer interested in travel. He even talks of retiring from his practice soon and he's still a young man. He wants to manage Downlands and the farm, go fishing all day and write his memoirs. Or so he says. He'd be bored in five minutes.'

'What is it your father does?'

'He's a doctor, a local GP.'

'Well, I understand his feelings, then. That's what happens as you get older. You don't want trouble any more. That's why you have to act while you're young and enthusiastic about life, still believe you can change things. I'm thinking of returning to Athens, Nina. I'm seriously thinking of it. I'm fed up with London, the English, the weather, the practice. Totally fed up with it.'

'This is a sudden decision.'

'Not at all, I've been considering it for some time. I have a feeling things are changing in Greece. I want to be involved. I think I could advance myself a lot better over there than I ever will here. Our country needs us.'

She looked at him thoughtfully. 'What sort of changes?'

He ground out his cigarette in an ashtray. 'I can't say a lot. Things are afoot, Nina. I mean to leave after Christmas. Will you come with me?'

'To Athens?'

'Of course. Will you come?'

She looked at him for a long while, till he shifted his gaze. 'I may go to Thessaloniki,' she said, 'maybe stay at our house in Mistres.'

'Don't go to Thessaloniki, Nina, come with me. I'm asking you to … to be my companion. I have my parents' house in the suburbs. I have money invested in olives and a family vineyard and they're doing well. Things will be wonderful.'

'Live with you, d'you mean? Are you joking? The gossip will kill you. You're far too straight-laced, Niko. What's come over you to make a proposition like this?' She seemed amused.

'But obviously not live with me as a *mistress*! I want to marry you, Nina, when your divorce comes through. I love you,' his voice sank to a whisper. 'I want you. Desperately. Will you agree?'

She sat up and looked at him again with those clear, all-seeing eyes that made him flinch inside. 'Niko, I'm not divorced yet and haven't even begun proceedings. Max and I are simply separated. I'm still married to him. Nothing as final as divorce has been discussed between us. Not yet, anyway. He'll maybe join me at Downlands after he returns from the Trade Fair. Then we'll talk things through.'

'But you don't love him any more, surely? You said yourself …'

'Women say such things,' she replied, 'but the fact is, I do still love him. I … like you a great deal, Niko. But I don't love you and certainly don't intend to run away to Greece and be your "companion", as you put it.'

He dropped his eyes and a faint angry flush came over his cheeks. She put a hand on his and said, 'I'm sorry, Niko. Truly I'm sorry. I really didn't expect this, you know.'

He looked up quickly. 'But you'll think about it? Okay, I did spring it on you, I know. Clumsy of me. But I thought you realised how much I admire you, Nina. How much I love you.'

'No, I didn't realise,' she admitted. 'The truth is I'm a bit shocked. We've been friends some time and yes, it was good to see you over here when you first arrived. It felt like a part of Greece had come close to me. I'm fond of you, Niko, but you're almost as old as my father!'

'As old as your father! I'm nowhere *near* as old as your father.' He looked disgusted.

'He's only forty-eight, you know. He met my mother when he was twenty years old, just before the war broke out. It was so romantic.'

'Many women prefer older men!' Nikos snapped. He was angry, but she couldn't do much about that.

After a long silence, he looked up and took her hand in his, stroking it gently. She let him do so, all the while taking in his thinning hair, the double chin, the sensuality of his lips. She could never be attracted to this man. Eventually he spoke.

'Nina, if you come with me, then you will be all right. If you go to Thessaloniki ... well, things are getting difficult for people with your ... ideologies and inclinations, let us say. Don't go, Nina. Stay here or come with me. I warn you because I love you. I don't want to see you in trouble.'

She was astonished. 'What trouble, Niko? Are you talking about my political ideals? I'm not a communist, if that's what you're afraid of. I simply support democracy, free speech and care about justice. Isn't that what we all should do? In God's name, didn't we Greeks invent democracy?'

'Fine. And look what happened to Lambrakis, your hero. Run over in the street by a load of thugs while the police stood by and did nothing. You know what a mess our country's in just now. There are some who feel a firm hand may be needed to get things stable again.'

'Oh ... and who are these people?'

'Eh! ... people of power, people in the army maybe.'

'Don't tell me that young idiot, Constantine, plans some sort of coup. He's too weak and inexperienced to pull it off.'

'*Soppa*, shush, we don't need to talk so loudly,' said Nikos, looking around with disquiet. 'There are ears everywhere nowadays.'

Nina laughed in derision. 'Oh, Niko, grow up. This is England. There aren't spies everywhere.'

'This restaurant is a part of Greece,' he muttered. 'Nina, be serious. Heed my words. Stay in England or come to Greece under my protection. Or just wait for the moment till things sort out. You have plenty to do over here.'

'If I want to visit Greece, then I shall,' she declared. 'I don't fear anything. I have done nothing that could make anyone trouble over a little woman and her views. I know a lot of Greek men wish women hadn't been given the vote. And still see us as less useful than a mule, a mere male possession. Well, I'm not any such thing. I shall go to Greece whenever I feel like it.'

Nikos looked at her, saw the flash in her eyes and knew well how stubborn, headstrong and independent she was. He sighed and said no more.

Chapter 7

Thessaloniki: Where to go?

Max and Zoë walked down Angelaki Street in silence. He glanced across at the girl as she shuffled along beside him, head bent. His jacket looked strange on her slight form, the sleeves dangling down beyond her small hands. A few passers-by glanced at them curiously. They must have looked an odd pair, the tall fair foreigner and the small blonde-dyed Greek girl, her face a mess, wrapped in a man's jacket. Max still clutched his briefcase of papers against him to hide the bloodstains on his shirt.

He made up his mind to take her to his hotel room and pray they didn't encounter anyone of significance. He was not a coward but had no great ambition to meet up with an enraged Katsarakis and his henchmen. Zoë had said they'd been involved in the Lambrakis assassination. In what way he had no idea, but he did know how upset and distressed Nina had been when that terrible event took place a few years before. They tried to make it appear an accident at the time but she was convinced he'd been murdered. And as it turned out later, she was right. A judge had decided to investigate the case thoroughly and, despite a concerted effort on the part of the establishment, had brought many of the perpetrators to trial. But they had been the small fry. As always, the main culprits had been protected by a corrupt judiciary and wriggled their way out of the closing net. It seemed as if Katsarakis had managed to keep clear of the authorities, or bribed his way out of trouble – it all came to the same thing.

Once in his hotel room, he reasoned, Zoë could wash and

tidy up while he decided what to do with her. Perhaps Dimitri might have some old auntie in the country where they could send her for a while till things blew over. He knew how it was with women like this. They forgave their violent husbands and went back again for more of the same punishment, just as his mother had done. There was an odd bond between bully and victim that was impossible to fathom.

He steered Zoë into a quiet side street, away from exposure, until they came to the ancient, wide main road called Egnatia, a road built by the Romans that once led to Constantinople. Now busy with cars and buses and lorries, it took a little while to cross over and Max felt sure they were objects of some curiosity. With relief, they crossed at last and fled into the maze of streets that led to the Hotel Galaxio. Most of the other guests would now be at the Fair, dining at a taverna or in a nightclub up in the hills that surrounded the bay. It was nearly ten o'clock and early by Greek standards.

Max decided that boldness was the best approach and walked in, shielding Zoë in front of him, moving swiftly past the small reception desk at the entrance. As luck would have it, Anatolis, the young man who took the evening shift, was busy arguing with a friend on the phone and only caught a brief look at Max's back as he ushered the girl up the stairs. Anatolis had a vague notion there was a woman with him but it was of no interest to him what tart the foreigner brought to his bed. He turned his head away again and, cradling the receiver on his shoulder, returned to a vociferous and recriminatory conversation whilst trying to light a cigarette.

Once they had gained his room, Max sank down on the bed with a sigh of relief. Zoë threw off his jacket for the room was hot despite the open window. Max rose and opened the outside shutters to let in some air, though fresh would scarcely be the word for the foreboding atmosphere that slid into the room like thick treacle. All it did was make the sound of traffic more audible while bursts of loud, cheerful music came from the small open-air cinema across the road.

Zoë went to the window to look out. The room was on the third floor and she could see the screen quite well.

'It's Aliki Vougiouklaki,' she sighed. 'I love her so much. I wanted to see that film.'

'Well, you'll have to go another day,' said Max. He sat up and lit a cigarette. He felt the need of a large whisky and poured a shot into a small tumbler from the duty-free bottle beside the bed. Zoë watched him like a cat watching milk being poured into a saucer.

'You want some?'

She nodded and reached out a hand, drank it back, then choked and coughed till tears streamed down her face.

'Christ and the Virgin, that's awful stuff!'

Max laughed. 'What d'you usually drink?'

'Well, *ouzo* sometimes. Mostly *retsina*. Here, give me a cigarette.'

He gave her one and lit it for her. Her hands were trembling and he felt again that wave of tender pity. Her eye had swollen and was fast turning a dark blue but the cut lip had stopped bleeding at last. She looked a terrible mess, her blouse stained with blood and more blood congealed on her face.

'What am I going to do with you, Zoë? Look, take a shower. It's not a very brilliant shower but it's adequate. Then put on my bathrobe. I promise not to look while you change. I don't know what you can wear. I haven't any women's clothes here.'

'You haven't?' she said with a saucy look. Her fear had dissipated a little now she was in his room and felt safe.

'No,' he said shortly. 'Even though I'm a married man.'

'Where's your wife?'

'In England.'

'But *you* are in Greece.' She smiled a little and undressed while he turned his back and took up her pose, staring out of the window. She went into the little shower room but after a few moments poked her head out and said, 'I need to do pee-pee first. Where's the toilet?'

'I'm not letting you out of this room,' said Max. 'You'll have to do it in the shower.'

She seemed unperturbed by this and shut the door again. While she was in the shower, Max put on a clean shirt. The other shirt was ruined now, the bloodstains would never come off, so he might as well dispose of it. Rolling it up, he put it in his suitcase. Better not to throw it in the wastepaper basket or he'd have the maids gossiping, thinking he'd committed a murder or something idiotic.

He sat and smoked and drank some more whisky till Zoë came out of the tiny shower cubicle, unconcernedly naked, her hair wet and dripping. She took the robe he offered and began to towel her head vigorously, occasionally flinching and giving little yelps as she touched some sore spot on her face. Her clothes were flung on the wooden chair near the bed and once dry, she took off the robe and began to dress before him. She seemed as innocent about her nakedness as a child. He was horrified to see the bruises and welts on her back.

'Did Katsarakis do this?' he asked, sitting upright in dismay.

She nodded. 'He hits me with a belt or his fists.'

'The bastard,' muttered Max. It made him feel sick, almost physically so.

'I can't wear this blouse,' Zoë said sadly, turning now and handing it to him.

'Well, what am I to do with the damned thing?'

'I don't know.'

He put out the cigarette and stuffed the blouse along with his shirt in the suitcase.

'The shops will still be open,' he said. 'I'll just have to go out and get you something to put on. You're not going to be able to go anywhere with just a bra and skirt on. Stay here and don't move from my room and don't answer the door unless you hear my voice. Understood? I haven't figured out what to do with you yet but I'll talk about it with you when I get back.'

She looked up at him, her eyes wide and liquid with tears. Suddenly she prostrated herself and kissed his feet. He started back in surprise.

'Thank you, thank you,' she said with an almost religious fervour. 'You're my saviour, you're a good, good man.'

Max hauled her upright again. 'For heaven's sake! I'm not *that* good a man. I detest Katsarakis ... hate men who abuse women. But I'm not a saint, Zoë. You don't have to get humble about it.'

She shook her head. 'No one has been so good to me in my life.'

'Just don't budge from here, get that? There's some magazines from the aeroplane by the bed. They're in English but you can amuse yourself with the pictures.'

'I can watch the film from here.'

He looked over at the window. Walking over to it, he gazed down into the street below. No one would look up at this time of night but all the same, she might be seen if they did.

'If you want to watch the film then turn off the light so no one will see you. Okay?'

'Okay.'

He shut the door behind him with care and locked it. Safer that way. Then he hurried out into the night.

The shops stayed open later during the season of the Trade Fair and Max found one along Egnatia where he purchased some v-necked summery tops. He felt that Zoë's taste would run to soft pretty colours so he chose a pale pink and light turquoise. He also went to a *zaharoplasteion* and bought some delicious pastries and a bottle of wine. To save time he took a taxi back to the hotel. As he passed the reception desk, Anatolis looked up from an absorbing newspaper and bade him goodnight, his eyes resting on the bottle of wine tucked under Max's arm and the interesting bags in his hands. He had a slightly knowing look as he caught Max's eye but in return received an angry, unsmiling scowl so he said nothing. These tourists were all the same, he decided. Humourless and unpleasant.

Max made his way up to his room and gently called Zoë's name. Then he unlocked the door and went in. It was dark inside and he saw her silhouetted at the window as she leant out to watch the film across the road. She was quietly singing '*Karotsaki, karotsaki*,' to herself in tune with the pretty blonde screen star Aliki Vougiouklaki, whom she vaguely resembled … or tried to. Max smiled.

'Come away from the window now,' he said, 'then you'll see what I've brought you.'

She came away obediently. He put on the light and pulled the shutters closed. She peered inside the bags on the bed and opened them, exclaiming in delight.

'These nice tops are for me? And you bought *tiropites* and *bougatsa* too … . I love that! I'm so hungry. Oh, you're so kind, *Kyrie* Max, so kind.'

'It's all right,' he said hastily, not wishing for any more of her excitable adoration, a response he was by no means used to from the women in his life. He had to admit it was pleasing. Odd as it seemed, he felt no sexual desire for this girl, attractive as she was in a skinny kind of way. He felt sure she would make no objection to any advances he might make – but the need wasn't there, not a stirring of any kind. In a way this surprised as well as delighted him. Had the shock of losing Nina brought him to his senses at last? Maybe he was cured of women for ever; they had always brought him bad luck. He sighed.

Rinsing out the one and only glass, he said, 'We'll have to share it. You drink that side, I'll drink this side. Not the most elegant meal but I'm hungry too with all this drama and it's the best I could do.'

'I feel as if I was a queen,' she said, laughing and perching herself up on the bed like a child. She put on the pink top and plumped up the pillows. 'Come and sit with me?'

It was a narrow single bed but apart from the little rush-bottomed chair there was nowhere else to sit so he climbed up beside her. She was so slight she took up little enough room. For some time they ate and drank hungrily and in silence, then lit cigarettes. Max felt peculiarly peaceful and at ease with this young girl which also surprised him. She had overcome her terror now and appeared totally unaffected and natural. He looked at her, noting the darker roots under the thatch of long blonde hair, the upward curve of her green eyes and delicate features that looked more Rumanian or Hungarian than Greek. He wondered about her origins.

'What happened to your parents, Zoë?'

She looked distressed and her eyes filled with tears. 'All I know is that we came from a village outside Constantinople. My poor parents came here as refugees when the Turks took over. My father worked as a labourer most of the time and my mother sewed and made dresses for rich Greek women who treated her like dirt. They wouldn't let her in their smart drawing rooms but made her measure and fit them in the servants' bedroom. She was a clean woman but they acted as if she had lice. She used to send me over to them with the finished dresses to collect payment and I would stand outside waiting and sometimes they took the dresses and forgot to come back and I didn't know what to do. I had to knock on their door again and felt so ashamed. And they were mean! They haggled over everything and tried to bring the prices down so she hardly made a penny, after all that hard work, all those hours of stitching. There was a time when she cut a sleeve wrongly and didn't have enough material and she couldn't sleep for worrying about it. But she was so clever, she arranged it somehow and they never noticed.'

'Poor woman. What a life.'

'No fun, I tell you. Then when the war came, the Germans took over and there wasn't any work or any money or food. We all starved. Papa collapsed in the street one harsh winter and laid there and died. The Germans used to come round in a lorry and pick up all the dead; we never got his body for burial. Mum got tuberculosis and died a year later. There weren't any relations who wanted me, they were too starved themselves so I was taken to the orphanage and stayed there till the war ended. The Germans liked me because I was fairer than most Greeks and I had to entertain them sometimes. But I wasn't a traitor,' she added hastily, 'not a traitor, *Kyrie* Max. It meant I got some better food and gifts even, but I had to be careful as people thought I was one of them. As if I had a choice! Then *he* came and took me off and I've been with him ever since.'

'You mean Katsarakis?'

'Yes.'

'He married you?'

'Yes. The worst thing I ever agreed to do. I belonged to him then, no escape.'

'Are you going back to him?' Max hoped against hope that the answer was yes.

'How can I? He'll kill me now. How can I say where I've been? He'll kill you too. I don't know what to do. I daren't go back and I don't want to. He seemed kind at first but he tired of me after a while and got himself other women, brought them home even. Made me wait on them as if I was a servant. Or else tried to get us both in bed with him. And if I said "no" he'd thrash me. He just likes hitting people. It gives him pleasure. I've seen him do it to others, hitting them with a club or whatever comes to his hand. He's evil. Don't make me go back to him, *Kyrie* Max, please don't!'

'I won't, I won't. I have a few good friends here and they may know some place you can hide in the countryside. Cut your hair and grow out that awful blonde. It doesn't look right.'

'Okay, I will,'she said submissively. 'I'll do anything you say. You are very wise.'

She yawned a little and said, 'Where shall I sleep?'

'On the bed, of course. I'll take a pillow and manage on the floor,'

'No, no!' She looked shocked. 'I'll sleep on the floor at your feet.'

She insisted so much that he gave way and gave her a pillow and the top sheet. She wrapped herself in that after undressing swiftly. And while he lay awake contemplating his predicament for a long time, she fell fast asleep, snoring lightly on the floor at the bottom of his bed like a sweet little kitten.

Chapter 8

The Troubador Café, Old Brompton Road, London

The Troubador café was a hot spot for the young and liberal members of London society. The café was situated on the ground floor of an old Victorian house with a large window fronting the street. Shelves high up in the window were decorated with various coffee pots from around the world and plants trailed leaves and ferns in odd corners amongst the comfy chairs and tables. Nina often went there to mingle with the kind of raffish, amusing people whose company she enjoyed: journalists, writers and other creative people from whom she could pick up gossip, ideas and recommendations to help her in her journalistic aims. During the day she would often pop over for some good food and coffee and spend an hour or two chatting with those who gathered there. In the evening, musicians played varied styles of music in the windowless vaults below, fierce sounds that were new and different and suited her temperament. She had never been a lover of sweet sentimental songs, be they Greek or English.

She had just returned from a trip to York to interview a woman who had given birth to quintuplets. It was an amusing assignment, the photos of the babies were cute and it would fill up a column. But she felt that it was unworthy of her abilities and longed for something other than 'soft' stories, snippets of information, translating for foreign diplomats or interviews with women's lib demonstrators. She longed for something meatier that would really impress everyone. She knew Cousin Reggie respected her talents but he said that she should learn from the beginning, take things slowly, and keep her ear to the ground. All the same, he didn't mind her acting in a freelance manner, taking off when the mood suited her, which it often did. Thus she had begun to frequent the Troubador, making the most of the Bohemian characters there.

On these occasions, she would dress in a far more informal manner; jeans, simple tops. She kept her long, dark hair in a ponytail, a chignon or even a French plait. Nina was one of those people capable of blending in with any society and a master of disguise. Her father said she must have inherited this ability from her grandfather who had acted as spy for Venizelos during the First World War.

She seated herself in the front of the shop amongst the colourful old coffee pots and was quietly reading over some of her notes when a young man approached her table and smiled.

'Mind if I sit here?'

She looked up; he seemed vaguely familiar. Glancing around, she saw that there were plenty of empty tables at that time of the morning, but she shrugged and said,'Sure.'

He ordered coffee and a sandwich. After a while, he caught her eye and smiled again. 'You're Nina Hammett, aren't you?'

Surprised by this, she laid down her notes, picked up her coffee and sipped slowly at the cooling brew while regarding him. Now she remembered who he was. It was the young man who had greeted her in the Brompton cemetery the other day. He was a handsome young fellow, probably about twenty-one or twenty-two years old with neat regular features, warm and serious brown eyes and long dark hair swept back into a ponytail. He wore faded blue jeans and a denim jacket over a cheap white t-shirt. She wondered if he was one of the musicians from Earl's Court who often haunted this rather hippie café. She could tell he was a Greek.

'And you are?'

'George Praxiteles.'

'A fine name.'

'A fine family.'

Nina smiled at that. His voice showed pride.

'How do you know me?'

'Toby Johnson pointed you out to me. He's the Radio London presenter and said you sometimes contribute news items to his morning show.' Toby was a frequenter of the Troubador and Nina knew him well.

'Oh, right.' She relaxed. 'What can I do to help you,?'

He moved a little closer to her over the table, conspiratorial all of a sudden. He began to speak quietly in educated Greek. 'I apologise for troubling you, But I have heard that you are … a sympathiser.'

Nina looked at him and frowned. She wasn't sure she cared for this conversation. But he seemed a pleasant enough person and his deep brown eyes held hers with an air of truthfulness and directness that allayed her suspicions. Still, one had to be careful these days, as Nikos never tired of reminding her. She took out a cigarette. Praxiteles fished a lighter from his pocket and lit it for her a little clumsily. He seemed very young and awkward in some ways.

'Would you like a cigarette?' she asked. He accepted one and they both puffed away while Nina regarded him a little longer. She flung back a stray lock of hair that had fallen from her French plait and twirled it into place with her free hand. Praxiteles watched this movement in fascination. There was something sleek and cat-like about Nina that never failed to mesmerize men.

'I'm not sure what you mean … a sympathiser,' she murmured at last.

'You were concerned about the Lambrakis business and wrote a letter about it at the time; it was printed in the *Guardian*. It's common knowledge and many admired you for saying what you did. I admire you, Mrs Hammett. It inspired me to join the Lambrakis Youth when I finished my National Service. I think it's a marvellous cause though, as you know, it's dangerous these days to belong to such causes. But we need to fight for justice in Greece. You heard about Petroulas?'

Sotiris Petroulas was a young economic student, a member of the Lambrakides. He had carried Mikis Theodorakis through the crowd in order for the heroic musician to make a rousing speech against the tyranny of the government. Later that evening Petroulas was killed by a tear gas grenade that exploded above his head and his body was whisked away by the police.

'My friends caught some agents trying to bury Sotiris secretly but Theodorakis roused the local people and made them hand over the body. Then, do you know this, Mrs Hammett? … Hundreds of people accompanied the body from Athens Cathedral to the cemetery … hundreds! Theodorakis wrote a song in his memory and it was sung by the cortége. It was so moving. I wept and so did everyone else. My God, it was so moving.'

Nina leant back in her chair and stared at the floor for a long moment. 'I heard of it but didn't know the details.' Where had she been when this happened? Little escaped her attention when it came to Greek politics. Ah, of course, it was last summer. The time when she and Max had been in the process of re-considering their marriage. She had shouted at him like a fishwife, like a possessed creature. Was that dreadful harpy really her? Nina tore her mind away from the memories and the uncomfortable and guilty emotions they produced in her.

'I would have wept too,' she agreed, her voice low with feeling. 'But sadly incidents like that are no longer uncommon, are they? The government which the King has set in place without asking for any vote or referendum from the people is utterly corrupt; the plaything of the King and his Generals.' The young man nodded and looked unhappy. Nina smiled a little and briefly touched his hand with hers. 'However, Mr Praxiteles, I'm surprised – but happy, of course, to hear my little outburst helped to inspire a young man like you.'

'Not just me – others too. It was good to know people abroad cared about what was happening, supported our cause. My friends joined me in the Youth Movement. You can't imagine how exciting it is to be a part of it all, part of something new and useful. People in Greece are kept poor by the rich, it's always the way. People like Onassis and all those so-called Greeks who run their ships under a foreign flag and live away from our shores. They make use of us, they're not real patriots. They have one thing in mind – themselves, their power, their wealth.'

'I couldn't agree more.' Nina nodded her head. 'But why are you here in England?'

'After the incident with Sotiris, my family decided to send me to London. We have friends here, you see. I didn't want to leave when things were in such a mess. But they insisted and said I'd be able to help better if I came back with a qualification. And so I'm here. How different things are over here, how free! It would be so good to have such freedom of speech in Greece, to be able to talk politics without everyone reacting as wildly as they do back home.'

'Don't they say that paranoia is a chronic Greek condition?' shrugged Nina.

Praxiteles paused and smiled at her with warmth. 'You know, I wanted to meet you so much. They told me where to find you and Toby pointed you out to me one day. I had to get the courage to approach you.'

Nina smiled in return and tapped her ash into the ashtray. 'Who are They?'

'English friends at the London School of Economics.'

'Are you studying there?'

'Yes, I am. I'm taking a BA in Finance.' He paused and looked thoughtful. Nina offered him another cigarette and they called for more coffee. She remained quiet, wondering what was passing though his mind. Various ideas for articles were flashing through her own head. People always inspired her like this, inspired her with their fervour, their longings, their commitment. She wanted to champion them all against the injustices of the world. But that was madness. She alone could do so little. But at least she could write their stories and make others wake up to what was going on outside their sphere of knowledge. And what better than to wake them up to what was happening in her beloved Greece?

The coffee arrived and Praxiteles stirred in several lumps of sugar. He smiled at her and said,'English coffee! It's got no taste and I always like my coffee "*glyko*"'

'That's certainly very sweet now,' laughed Nina.'Do you miss home?'

He nodded sadly. 'I sometimes wonder if I'll finish this course. It's costing a fortune as it is. I know it's a very prestigious place and I'm grateful for the sacrifice my parents are making but we're not rich. I miss my friends; I long to go home again to Greece, to be in the thick of things. Maybe I should have gone for politics, that's more my thing. You know, my parents are good friends with Mikis Theodorakis. I admire him so much – such beautiful music, such inspiration, such a soul!'

Nina laughed gently at this youthful enthusiasm. Ah, to be young again and so full of passion! She sighed a little, feeling warmer towards the young man.

'He is indeed a wonderful person,' she agreed. 'A friend of mine, too. He has suffered so much, poor man. It's a long time since we met up. Is he keeping well?'

George Praxiteles looked solemn. 'As well as a man can when he suffers from Makronissos fever, tuberculosis and heaven knows what else.'

After the Second World War when anti-communism was at its height in the West, Theodorakis had been arrested and taken along with thousands of other left-wing protesters and partisans to Makronissos, an island south-east of Attica. Here the government intended to re-educate its citizens who had been contaminated by the 'red virus' of communism. It was at this time that Theodarakis contracted tuberculosis. He refused to enrol in the Army and was subjected to ten hours of beating with a baton, after which he was given over to a specialist in torturing bones and had his leg twisted and then broken. While he was unconscious, his hand was guided to a paper to make a cross on it thus ensuring his obedience to military service.

Nina and Praxiteles looked at one another, remembering.

'Why are our countrymen so inhuman to one another?' asked Praxiteles, his gentle brown eyes filling with tears. 'Why treat wonderful men like Lambrakis and Theodorakis in this way? All they are asking for is that we Greeks rule ourselves, have a proper democracy. First the Turks, then the British, now the Americans and a king who has no idea how to rule, who isn't even a true Greek. For heaven's sake, what has gone wrong?'

'It's the way men are and probably always will be,' sighed Nina. 'Men betray each other all the time. Love, power, greed – do these motivate mankind? No, because beneath all those lies the fear of extinction, the dying of the light. We hate because we are always afraid of something. And, above all, we hate change.'

At that moment, to their surprise, the sweet angelic voice of Nana Mouskouri began to sing'White Rose of Athens' on the radio. They stared at one another and couldn't help laughing a little.

'It's so amazing the way these things happen,' said Nina. She smiled tenderly at the young man. 'Life is so strange.'

'It's so good to talk to you like this,' said Praxiteles, looking at Nina with an adoring expression. She blinked a little. She had done nothing to deserve this. What comparison could she have to such great and brave souls as he had just mentioned? Could she stand up for the rights of her fellow men in such a way, put up with torture and suffering for the sake of a cause?

The café was filling up now as it neared lunchtime.

'Would you like a sandwich?' asked Nina. Praxiteles refused and glancing at his watch, looked horrified.'I must get back, there's a lecture in half an hour. I forgot the time speaking to you. You are such an impressive lady. Please let us meet again.'

They shook hands. He gave her a little card bearing his name and address.

'May I come and talk with you again, Mrs Hammett?'

'Of course, if I'm here,' she smiled.

'I'd like to keep in touch. Do you ever return to Greece nowadays?'

'Well, yes. I visit my friends and relations there.'

'You will always be welcome at our home in Athens. My parents would love to meet you. My father works for *Kathimerini* as a typesetter. I'm sure he would introduce you to Eleni Vlachou. She owns the newspaper.'

'Yes, I know,' said Nina with interest. 'That would be wonderful. I may well take you up on the offer.'

'Do. They would be happy to have you stay with them.'

He clasped her hand and then ran out into the street. She saw him hail a bus and just about make it on board before it carried him away into the depths of the metropolis.

Well, Nina reflected with some amusement. That was two invitations to Greece within one week. The Gods were trying to tell her something and maybe she should listen. She also knew which one she preferred. To meet Eleni Vlachou would be a real honour.

As she walked back home later that afternoon, Nina's mind turned again to Max and she wondered how he was coping at the Trade Fair. Was he making money, was it hot, was he staying with Dimitri or somewhere else? A thousand little questions came to her and yet there were no answers. Why was she even thinking of him, she wondered impatiently. But she knew why. She loved him so much and her heart swelled again with the misery of his betrayal.

She remembered the day they had taken a bus to his youthful haunts. He had been born in a miserable little terrace house in Bethnal Green and though those houses were long gone, the area was still run down and ugly to her eyes. Bombsites still lingered in some places and it was hard for her to imagine how terrible it must have been for the people of London during that inhuman war. Bad enough everywhere. Her mind turned to whole villages in Greece massacred by the Nazis. The madness of those men with their twisted Utopian visions of an Aryan race.

'You see how different we are, Nina?' Max's smile was sad.'You with your lovely home in the country, the green fields, the open spaces. Me with these brick walls and narrow streets? I was evacuated at the start of the war like loads of other children but East End kids weren't the ones they sent to nice places, we were considered too rough and dirty. I was pretty lucky – Mrs Tipton, she liked me a lot and she had a little smallholding in Shropshire. I used to love to help around the house and garden and even then I was interested in the tractors and asked Mr

Tipton all about them, looked at the engines. He even let me ride one in the field. I was so thrilled. Maybe that's when I first fell in love with machines. They had a dog called Lucy, a golden retriever. I'd never had a dog before. Lucy used to follow me around all over the place.' He had fallen silent for a long while, remembering those happier times.'I loved the freedom from home but all the same I wanted to get back to Mum. I was worried about her; she was a quiet sweet soul and the war affected her nerves a lot. She always said I was her support, her real pillar of strength.'

Nina looked up at him and clasped his hand.

'You're mine as well, Max.'

'Am I?' For some reason he looked sad as he said this and she squeezed his hand warmly.

'Of course you are!' She remembered looking around as they stood on the edge of an old bombsite; the houses at the edges scarred with half torn-away rooms that had once been someone's home. The area long since cleared of debris but left with that blank devastated effect in the streetscape like a gap in someone's teeth. 'Your father was at war, wasn't he … during all this?'

'Yes, he was, and I wish he'd never come back.'

'Really? You really thought that?' She couldn't imagine a life with a father whom she couldn't love, who was as hateful as Max's father.

Max added,'I loved living with Mum, just us two alone. I felt as if I was looking after her, protecting her. I was only a wee kid but that's how I felt. I was at school one day and when I came home the house was gone in a bombing raid and I didn't know where Mum was. I was so afraid, so alone in that moment.'

'You must have been! But she was safe?'

'Yes, she was safe; she'd gone shopping when it happened – one of those strange twists of fate. We went to stay with my auntie, three streets away; their house was still okay. And eventually we got a council house which was wonderful … until he came home.'

His voice sounded bitter and she squeezed his hand again.

In this moment his mind had been elsewhere and in the past and it wasn't a happy past. There was much he never told her about those years and she had a feeling she was better not knowing it: violence, misery, and fear were not a part of her youth. She had been loved, cosseted and spoilt. She knew that Max enjoyed the experience of belonging to a calm and peaceful family like hers. He always appeared free and happy when they visited Downlands. It probably reminded him of his happy time on the Shropshire farm. She in turn was fascinated by the hints of darkness and despair that lurked beneath his light exterior.

Although they were so different, she understood something about Max and it was the deep inexpressible emotion that lay in his heart but tried so hard to hide from others as if it was some form of weakness. She would always love him, be drawn to that shared ability to feel pain even while she felt anger and hurt at his foolish conduct.

Chapter 9

Thessaloniki: Rescue

Max awoke the next morning bathed in sweat, with a nasty taste in his mouth from all the sweetmeats eaten and the wine they had drunk last night. He had been too exhausted to wash his teeth or have a shower before dropping off at last into a deep slumber. Rising, feeling stiff as a board, he saw Zoë sitting quietly on the little cane-bottomed seat by his bed, turning over the pages of the magazines he had brought from the airport. She had evidently risen, washed and dressed while he had slept like a log, deaf to everything.

'*Kalimera,*' she greeted him. 'Did you sleep well?'

'No, I didn't,' he grumbled.'I'm worrying myself half to death wondering what the hell to do with you and here you are as cool as a cucumber after sleeping on the floor.'

She smiled a little. 'I've slept in worse places. But I *am* hungry, *Kyrie* Max.'

'We'll worry about that in a minute. I need to have a shower, I smell like a sewer.'

'You smell like a man,' she smiled. 'It's a good smell.'

He knew she meant it as a compliment and grinned. 'My wife wouldn't think so.'

She looked up at him, her eyes large and wondering as a child.'Is your wife beautiful?'

'Very.'

'I wish *I* was beautiful,' she said looking downcast. 'English women are always beautiful.'

'Some are, some aren't, like women anywhere. And Nina, my wife, is almost as Greek as you are.'

'But you said she was in England.'

'That's the irony of it,' he admitted. 'Her father lives in England and she works in London.'

'If I was your wife, I'd never want to be anywhere but beside you,' said Zoë.

'Hmm … well, it's just the way things are, Zoë. Marriage is a funny business.'

He had a wash in the bathroom down the hall and returned feeling a good deal more awake and intelligent.

'I'm going to go and phone a friend of mine,' he said.'She may be able to help you, have some idea where you can hide for a bit. She may even give us both some breakfast. I must try and get to the Trade Fair before it opens. If *I'm* not there as well, Katsarakis is sure to put two and two together.'

He went downstairs after locking the door to the room again and rather than use the phone in the hotel, looked for a nearby kiosk phone. From there he rang Athina. He had decided that it would be better to confide in her than Dimitri. Not that his friend would ever give him away but he would be bound to tell Yiota who in turn might let something slip out. Athina was as wise as her name and would have some idea what might be done. Plus Katsarakis knew nothing about the Petrakos friends and would be unlikely to mix in their social circles anyway.

'*Embros.*'

'Athina?'

'Max? Is that you? How good to hear you. But this is very early. Are you coming round to dinner tonight as planned?'

'Athena, I'm in a real fix. Not of my choosing, I assure you. Can I come round now? I need your help. Is Basil there?'

'Yes, he's still here. But he's off soon to sort out some difficulty at the shop in Kalamaria. Do you want him?'

'I think this problem needs a woman's help. Is it okay to come over as soon as possible?'

'I'm intrigued, Max. But of course. Come at once.'

Max made his way back to the Galaxio, ordered a taxi,

telling it to wait a few moments while he collected another passenger. He ran up the stairs as fast as he could and took what things he needed for the day.

'Come on Zoë, let's get out of here.'

Athina opened the door to them and stared in astonishment at the bruised and battered young woman. However, she made no comment but asked the unexpected guests in.

'Basil has taken the children to his auntie who lives near the shop. I thought you sounded so urgent it would be best to talk without them hanging around.'

'Thank you so much, Athina,' said Max with deep relief. 'The kids would have been awkward.'

'Well, I see that now,' she said looking at Zoë who was gazing around the elegant apartment with astonished fascination.

'It's not what you think,' murmured Max in English. 'Let the girl tell her own story. I'm just a pawn in the game.'

'I'm so hungry,' Zoë said. Her eye had fallen on the remains of the breakfast that still lay on the table.

Max looked at Athina and smiled. 'Neither of us has eaten yet,' he said.' We throw ourselves on your generosity.'

'But eat – eat what you want!' cried Athina. She waved to the table, still laden with fruit, bread, cheese and cakes. 'I'll make you English toast, Max. And your friend … ?' she queried.

'Zoë. This is Zoë Katsarakis. Not my friend exactly, but she came to me in despair asking for help and I couldn't refuse. It's rather a long story.'

Athina smiled and shook her head a little. '*Ach*, Max *mou*, always the knight in shining armour! Well, eat and drink first, both of you, then the story can be told. Come on, sit down. Eat, eat … *Kali orexi!*'

Athina bustled into the kitchen while Zoë and Max sat at the table and ate with an urgent appetite. Athina brought in coffee and toast and then a bowl of thick, creamy sheep's yogurt, the thick skin still unbroken.

'I got this fresh from the dairy this morning,' she said, 'I must have known I'd have guests.'

'I *love* sheep's yogurt,' said Zoë. 'You're so kind, *Kyria* Athina.'

'Now for the story, eh?' Athina sat at the table with them and regarded them one after the other.

Once the story was told, Max said he had to go and could he leave Athina to think what might be done to hide Zoë for a while till matters calmed down?

'No, I have to go for good,' said Zoë, who began to look fearful again. 'I have to disappear. You don't understand what Katsarakis is like. He'll kill me if he finds me. Please, help me to disappear. I'll do any work, anything.'

'I did think of taking Zoë to Mistres,' said Max, but even as he spoke he knew it would never work. Mistres was a village up in the Hortiach Mountains some way from Thessaloniki. There was a house in the village that belonged to Nina's family but it was seldom occupied unless Andrew visited it or Nina wanted to be alone. She loved that house, often telling Max it was where both she and her father were conceived. It would have been a good place to take Zoë but the neighbours would have been curious and there was never any telling when Nina might take it into her head to return there. It would *not* amuse her to find another woman ensconced in the place without her permission. She was always ready to think the worst. He felt sure that, knowing the circumstances, Nina would have been glad to help. But on the other hand she might assume he was lying and that Zoë was his mistress. So, no, not a good idea. Thus it was with gratitude that he looked to Athina for a plan.

Athina gave it thought. 'I have a cousin who has a farm out near Florina,' she said, 'maybe we can take you there. You can help on the farm, pay for your board and lodging that way.' She suggested they could eventually help the girl to get over the border to Yugoslavia or Albania. Zoë did not look enthusiastic about it.

'I speak Turkish,' she said. 'I could go back to Turkey.'

'My dear girl, that is not a good idea. Our relations with the Turks couldn't be worse just now, and you said yourself you no longer have people there.'

'There might be someone,' said Zoë obstinately, 'an old cousin or someone. It would be good to find my own people.'

Athina shrugged.'It's up to you, but to me it sounds a futile dream.'

The young girl lowered her head in submission. 'I will do whatever you say. I know I'm ignorant.'

'Poor girl,' Athina murmured to Max. 'I feel sorry for her. She seems so young and friendless. You're deep into it again,' she added with a smile, 'I just hope it won't land you in any trouble. She's fallen in love with you, you know.'

'Oh God, I hope not,' Max said with feeling. 'If anything happens to the machinery again, I'll be getting my walking boots on. They'll fire me on the spot.'

'But it won't be your fault. Anyway, they must have improved security at the Fair by now. They can't have incidents like that again. Surely it's bad for business all round?'

'Mmm ... things have improved and we've asked them to keep a particular eye on our stand. Dimitri has rallied some of his buddies. So ... yes, it should be okay.' But he was not quite as sanguine as he sounded.

'We'll change your appearance first of all,'Athina declared. She regarded Zoë with a little grimace. 'I'll get a bottle of black hair dye and we'll cut your hair, pluck your brows, make you up to look different. We're about the same build so you can have some of my clothes. We'll dress you to look simple and not too smart. You're going to a farm, you don't need smart stuff. I'll give Tasso a ring and see if he's happy with the idea. The sooner we get you away the better. But the problem is, Basil's got the car today,' she added frowning.

'Take her today if you can, Athina,' said Max. Frankly, he couldn't wait to get the girl out of his life. 'Look, here's the money for a taxi. You've got trusted friends you can ask. I need to get to the Fair soon.'

'Don't worry about the money,' said Athina, waving the cash aside. 'I'll ask Tasso. He's a good fellow and will do us a favour. He's trustworthy.'

Zoë's face cleared with joy. 'Thank you, thank you! It's so

good of you. God's good to me, leading me to you both.' She crossed herself devoutly as she said this.

'That's wonderful.' Max breathed a sigh of relief. 'Athina, I thank you from the bottom of my heart. I couldn't leave the girl but I don't want to be involved either. That bastard, Katsarakis, is not amusing. I really don't need any more trouble. My relationship with my manager back home is already at an all time low. I'm off then. Zoë, do everything Athina tells you and good luck, my dear. Here's some cash to keep you going.'

He put a wad of drachma notes in her hand and escaped before she could fling herself at his feet again.

Max took a taxi back to the Trade Fair which was by now in full swing with people streaming in at the main gate. Dimitri would be concerned that his boss had not turned up yet. Max was always punctual … very British, as Dimitri used to tease him. Max slipped in amongst the flow, quickly showing his pass to the men at the gate who knew him by sight, smiled and waved him on.

Dimitri was busy polishing the jeep when Max turned up at the stand and he greeted him with a cry of relief.

'*Vre, anthropi mou*!' he cried, flinging open his hands and dropping the cloth in his joy. 'My dear man, I was getting worried about you – where the hell have you been? Not like you to sleep in.'

'I didn't sleep in, I hardly slept a bloody wink,' Max replied, looking sour.

'Have to say, that's just how you look,' agreed his friend. Then in a lower voice, added,'by the way that bastard, Katsarakis, was asking after you earlier on.'

'Damn him!'

'Well, I agree. He looked pretty nasty. Is something going on I should know about?' Dimitri looked troubled.

Max thought swiftly. It was better that Dimitri didn't know what had happened. He reasoned that his friend might, just might, get into trouble. It mattered not for himself. He would be out of here in a few days' time and staying with Basil and

Athina in their little summer home at Halkidiki, having a relaxing week by the sea before returning to England. But he wanted to be fair both to Zoë and to whoever might elect to take care of her for the time being. So Max simply said, 'No, no, nothing to worry about. Katsarakis is just snooping around the machinery as usual. We really do need to remind Antonis to keep an eye on the stuff all the time. I feel half inclined to sleep here the night myself.'

'Are you mad? That's not a good idea at all. Big Bouros has lent me his boys and they're tough stuff. Just trust the boys, they're not fools. They know the likes of Katsarakis and his bullies. He won't try anything. He knows they'll find him in the end and he'll pay for it.'

'What was he after when he came by?'

'Just asked where you were and what hotel you were staying at.'

'Oh, he did, did he? Planning a little party for me, I suppose.'

'I told him you'd gone off for a pee and that he'd better bugger off before you came back as you wouldn't like his nosy questions one little bit.'

'What was his reaction?' grinned Max.

'Just scowled and said he'd speak to you later.'

'Well, he won't get the chance. I'm off to Basil's tonight for dinner. I'll leave a bit early – if you don't mind staying on a bit and winding things up.'

'Nope, you get off. And try and get an early night. What kept you awake, anyway?'

'Just worries. Life's always full of worries,' sighed Max. 'I'll be glad when the Fair finishes this year.'

Max manoeuvred his way through the day in a somnambulistic manner. The pleasure he used to have from being on the stand, chatting to people and the enjoyment of talking about his beloved machinery had fled from him this year. Everything in life was so wrong. The atmosphere everywhere seemed different and he wondered what it was. People still laughed and joked and enjoyed the variety of interesting things on show in the beautiful pavilions but … he couldn't put his finger on it … there was a sense of discontent, unease even.

However, he decided it was just a projection of his own disquiet. He saw no more of Katsarakis and hoped that he would never do so again. As for Zoë, with luck she would be far away by the time he got over to Basil's place. Athina had said she would take her that morning. She would phone her cousins and arrange to meet them halfway. They would take Zoë back to their farm in Florina, right up in the north of Greece.

When the main part of the day's work had been dealt with, he left the stand to Dimitri and friends and made his way out of the grounds. Standing at the main gate for a moment he looked up at the slender, imposing OTE tower, a truly impressive piece of engineering. As he lowered his eyes, he caught sight of one of Katsarakis' bully boys lounging by the tower smoking a cigarette. Their eyes met for a moment. Max turned on his heel and strode quickly out of the gate.

He walked towards the White Tower rather than straight to his hotel, just in case anyone decided to follow him. Sitting down on one of the red painted benches in the park by the Tower, he lit a cigarette and considered the situation. Was he being melodramatic? This wasn't a James Bond story, for goodness sake. All the same, the sense of unease persisted. It was still daylight, people emerging from their siestas and afternoon break. Nothing could happen. Yet they had killed Lambrakis in broad daylight, hadn't they? And Zoë said Katsarakis was vaguely involved in that business. She said he had supplied the weapons they used to beat the man to death. That was his trade, she said, supplying cars, weapons, even poison. He didn't kill people himself, simply aided the efforts of those who did so. That way he couldn't be blamed, he argued. He wasn't to know what purpose the items were used for, was he? Horrible man. He looked brutish enough to enjoy murder as a pastime.

Max ground the cigarette into the paving stones and rose. He looked forward to a pleasant evening with his friends in Karabournaki. But first of all, he needed a shower and a bit of a rest. His stomach felt bad after yet another foul hamburger with indifferent lager and he took some Rennies from his pocket and chewed them to calm the acidity down. Then he slowly made his way by a circuitous route to the Galaxio. Another man was at the desk tonight and Max nodded at him as he went by, telling him that he would check out tonight. He decided he would ask Basil if he could stay there for the latter few days of the fair. It would upset Dimitri, but that was too bad. It was obviously more comfortable to stay with Basil and he should have agreed to go there from the start.

He showered, changed into a clean white shirt and jeans and packed a case. He stood and looked at the case and wondered whether to call a taxi. But he didn't really want to cart the heavy case along with him this evening before he had asked if he could stay with his friends. He knew full well they would welcome him with delight but it didn't do to take people for granted.

'I'll be along for my case tonight, or tomorrow night,' he told the receptionist. 'I'll leave it behind the counter for now, if that's okay?'

'No problem,' said the receptionist. 'I'll put your name on it and leave it in the office. But you aren't leaving Thessaloniki already, are you? The Fair doesn't finish yet. Haven't you been to the Wine Festival?'

'No, not yet. Too busy,' Max replied. He didn't answer the question about leaving. Better this fellow knew as few facts as possible as well.

Nor was he in the mood for the scrum of catching a bus. Max went to the taxi rank and waited for a taxi which arrived at last.

'Take me to Karabournaki – Vassileis Olgas,' he informed the driver as he climbed in beside him, 'and don't pick up any more fares, if you don't mind. I'll pay you extra, just get me there.'

Greek taxi drivers had a habit of packing in any other passengers who might be going in the same direction. Max was not in the mood for all that either.

Chapter 10

Thessaloniki: Revenge

Max asked the driver to stop in the main road when they arrived at Karabournaki. He paid and walked the rest of the way. It was with relief that he clambered the stairs of the beautiful building in which Basil and Athina lived, scorning the lift. He rang the bell and was greeted by Basil.

'Good to see you! Come on in.'

The children ran up to him and Max was grateful for their interruption. He felt sure Basil would think him a fool to have got involved in this messy business but what else could he have done? He sighed and picked up Nitsa, carrying her into the *saloni*. She held him round the shoulders with her plump little arms and kept kissing his cheek as they walked along. It felt good, this innocent childish affection. It soothed his heart.

'We went to see the Fair,' she enthused when he set her down at last. 'Look, my auntie bought me a doll, see?' She thrust a frightful-looking frilly object under his nose and waved it about so much that its head looked ready to fall off at any minute.

'*Ftanei,* Nitsa! That's enough,' scolded her father and she subsided, looking sulky and annoyed.

Yiannaki came and sat down beside Max, giving him one of his shy smiles.

'Mamma's gone out,' he said, 'but she said she'd be back in time for dinner. It's all ready, it just needs to go in the oven. And I'm to put it in and make sure it's all right,' he added with pride.

'What's on the menu?' asked Max. He wondered if the children knew anything and looked over at Basil who shook his head a little as if reading his thoughts. That was a relief at least. Soon the Fair would be over and this unpleasant episode blown over. Hopefully that brute Katsarakis would turn to one of his other women and leave Zoë alone to get on with her life.

'It's *pastitsio*,' answered Yiannaki with a grin.

'My favourite.'

'Mmm, mine too.'

'But where has Mamma gone?' asked Nitsa.

'To see an auntie,' Basil replied.

'But why, which auntie?'

'Just go and wash your hands,' said her father shortly, 'she'll be back soon and tell you all about it.'

The children went off to perform their ablutions and while they were gone, Basil turned to Max and murmured, 'Some adventures, eh? What scrape have you gotten into now?'

'A pretty grim one,' sighed Max,'but with luck it will all fade away and we can go off to Halkidiki and enjoy a little peace and quiet. I could do with some sun, sea and rest. I'm worn out already this year.'

'It's been a difficult time for you.'

'Yes, it bloody well has.'

'I've had a busy day today.' Basil heaved a sigh. 'So many people still haven't had their rugs cleaned and made ready for the winter. Housewives aren't what they used to be. They had everything done at the proper time when I was a young man. A lot of them are working these days as well as running a home and that's a problem. A real problem. Women should stay in the home and keep things running well, shouldn't they?' He grinned. 'I wouldn't say that to Athina, she'd tell me women ought to get out in the world as well. But thankfully *she* seems content to be at home with the kids for now – though she talks about helping in the shop when they're both at school. That would be okay by me; Athina knows the business pretty well but my cousin helps me out and she does fine, plus she needs the money, she's a widow.' He paused and shrugged his shoulders. 'Eh, well, that's how it is these days, women interfering in everything, never satisfied.' Basil sipped some wine and shook his head sadly. 'Anyway, there's been a sudden rush now the weather is cooling down. A woman came in today and wanted to dye her rugs dark brown. That's good, it means she'll make more use of them. They were quite stained. Now they'll have a new lease of life.' Basil and his brothers' dry cleaning firm was renowned in Thessaloniki for their ability to dye clothing and rugs.

'It sounds as if business is doing well.'

'Yes, everything does fine during the Trade Fair. It brings us tourists, shops can stay open longer, it's the best thing that's happened to Thessaloniki. Long live Nikolaos Germanos.'

Max smiled at his friend's enthusiasm. 'Who was Nikolaos Germanos?'

Basil raised his shoulders and opened his arms wide. 'But, my friend, he was the founder of the TIF!'

Max grimaced comically and looked suitably ashamed of his ignorance.

'Yes, he was from Halkidiki and a great intellectual, a clever man who had vision. He persisted with his vision even when others called him a fool. That's the sort of man I admire. Men who build our country and help it advance, not rioters and anarchists and communists who do all they can to bring us to ruin. What is it they hope to achieve, what do they want from life? Or are they just jealous of those of us who work hard and keep a stable community? I get sick of these fools who go round smashing out shop windows and creating trouble.'

'I suppose they're expressing something, sort some of anger.'

'Against what? Against poverty? Then let them find some work. We were refugees from Constantinople, we started from nothing. It can be done with hard work. They prefer not to work. They're lazy scum.'

Max shrugged,'It's true that there are people of that sort in every country,' he said, 'and I don't know anything much about Greek politics and aspirations. You'd have to talk to Nina about all that.'

Basil remained serious, his eyes always slightly unhappy as if life was constantly difficult. Max wondered why this should be when his friend was comfortably off, had a lovely flat and a happy family. Yes, it was indeed due to his hard work and the work of his father before him and there was no reason for their thriving business to fail in any way. It seemed to Max that those who had plenty were always fearful of losing it.

The children now returned and Yiannakis, with careful consultation of a new watch his father had bought him that day, decided it was time to put the *pastitsio* in the oven. The huge dish of pasta layered with lamb mince went into the oven and soon delicious and appetizing smells began to arise. Beside the sink was a tomato salad, already prepared. The children began to lay the table and took a delight in performing these tasks. Max watched them with a smile, thinking how blessed this family was.

As if on cue, just as Basil pronounced that the dish was ready for consumption, Athina arrived and the children greeted her with exuberant joy.

They ate and chatted about general things until it was time for the little ones to go to bed. Athina had fobbed them off with a story of taking things to a far-away auntie who was ill.

Basil poured out another glass of wine and held it out to Max. The two men took their wine outside onto the veranda and smoked and chatted until Athina joined then.

'I'm simply exhausted,' she said, sitting back and moving her shoulders up and down to free them from tension. It had been a long journey.

'Athina, thank you so much for helping,' said Max with a rueful expression. 'I'm really sorry to have landed you with this.'

'You'll have to tell me the whole story,' said Basil, looking from one to the other. 'I only know a little of it which Athina hurriedly explained before she set off for Florina with this girl of yours.'

'She's *not* mine,' said Max tersely.

'No,' said Athina. 'Why should a girl always belong to

someone? She is her own person and she's trying to escape an evil man. It's okay, Maxaki *mou*, I don't mind being tired at all. We drove her halfway to Florina and my cousin came to meet us in his truck. Zoë sailed off with him, perched up in the cab. She looked so happy and free. I was glad to help. But tell Basil the story. I can see he's dying to know.'

'Gladly,' said Max . He explained how Zoë had come to him in despair and how he had helped her to escape, keeping her in his room for the night.

'I couldn't think what else to do, and no, there wasn't any funny business so you needn't look at me like that, Basil. She's a pretty little thing but she's young, frightened and vulnerable. I'm not the cad Nina seems to think me. She has an air of innocence about her, that poor girl. I felt really sorry for her. She seems to have had a sad life.'

'First time I've heard of you behaving so well,' grinned Basil.

'I'm a much misunderstood man,' said Max grumpily.

'Hmm … all the same, and being really serious now, Max, take care to avoid that guy, Katsarakis.'

'I will, don't you worry. In fact I've checked out of the Galaxio just in case one of his pals followed me there. I saw one watching me when I left the grounds today. Basil, Athina, would it be too much to ask to stay here for the last few nights of the Fair?'

Basil flung open his hands, palms upwards. 'You could have stayed all the time, *vre* Max, but you insisted on being near the Exhibition Park and your damned machinery. Come by all means. You're more than welcome.'

'Yes, yes, come,' said Athina with enthusiasm. 'You can help with the packing when we to go to Halkidiki next week. Won't it be wonderful? We're all looking forward to the break.'

'No joke, I am *really* looking forward to it. Like you, I feel pretty exhausted. Business-wise it's been successful here but emotionally, I feel like a wrung-out rag.'

Later, Athina showed Max his room.

'I always keep it ready for guests,' she smiled.

'You're an angel, Athina.' He gave her a hug.'I'm deeply grateful. I'll have to go and get my things from the hotel, though,' he added.

'What things? No, no, get them tomorrow. Basil can lend you pyjamas, a razor, a toothbrush. What else would you need for the night?'

'Okay, I'll get them tomorrow evening on the way over here.'

When he had showered and bid everyone a good night, Max settled down on the cool pillows, listened for a while to the distant sounds of traffic and fell into a deep, dreamless sleep.

It was a busy day at the Fair and the weather was sultry again. Large drops of rain fell, sending people scurrying for shelter. Dimitri was put out to hear that Max was going to stay at Basil's place.

'You should have come to us, we're nearer,' he grumbled.

Max shrugged. 'Look. it's better to be further off, just now,' he apologised.'I feel a need to distance myself a bit. I'll be really glad when all this is over, Dimitri. I've lost heart in this business. I reckon I'm going to resign from my job when I get home.'

'But what the hell will you do? Machines are your talent, your life.' Dimitri was astonished. 'We've sold all our stock, got plenty of orders for your bosses and I've gathered a whole new clientele who'll use my workshop. Tinos, my lad there, says he's had callers coming all week to get repairs and buy the odd motor. What more could you ask?'

Max shook his head. 'I don't know. Perhaps I just feel a bit depressed at the moment. Maybe I'll feel different once I'm home, eh?' He looked at his little friend who was peering at him with a worried look. 'It's okay, Dimitri, I'll be fine.'

After the stand was closed for the day, he walked to Aristotelous Square , his mind on many things, not the least of which was Nina. He experienced a sudden longing to have her there beside him, walking together along the promenade, looking at the glorious light shimmering over the sea, feeling the gentle breeze on their cheeks. He wanted to smell the perfume in her hair, feel the softness of her body as she bumped into him occasionally, take her to bed … God, it didn't do to go there. It was too painful.

I need you Nina, I need you, he groaned to himself.

Just ahead of him he suddenly saw a slender, elegant woman walking along with the swinging graceful walk of his wife and for a crazy moment, he was convinced it was her. He hurried up to the girl who turned to him in surprise, her face that of a stranger.

'*Me sihoreite, despinis*. Sorry, so sorry. I thought you were my wife.'

That sounded mad. He was definitely going mad, imagining he saw his wife everywhere. He decided to visit a bar, have a coffee or maybe a few glasses of *raki* till his nerves steadied themselves.

He sat on a rush-bottomed chair next to a small table outside a little *cafeneion* and ordered *raki*, tossed it back, ordered another, then a cup of black coffee. He didn't feel hungry though he had eaten little that day. If anything, he felt a faint sickness. It troubled him, this morbidity that had suddenly seized his soul. He wasn't a man often given to depressions or moods, but when such a state of being approached, he knew from experience it would hit him with a vengeance, making life dark and pointless. Max was no coward. But this inner darkness was a terrifying place.

The twilight was deepening fast, intensifying all the night sounds, the distant rumble of traffic, the chatter of voices as people ventured forth into the fresher air of the evening and the cafés and eateries began to fill up. Music was playing in the restaurant next door and the cheery sound of the bouzouki could be clearly heard. It was so different to the kind of pop music that was becoming popular back home. He was too old to appreciate the wave of new sounds like the Beatles and Elvis Presley and all the other singers and bands of the day. Something about the bouzouki was peculiarly timeless. It would always sound like this, he thought. The lilting music always made him want to move, to dance. He had been given lessons by Dimitri and Yiota but could never quite get the hang of the complex steps; his feet would become twisted and put everyone else out of line and they would laugh good-humouredly. He always became annoyed at himself. Why couldn't he relax and let go and not be so British and stiff! After several attempts, he would give up trying and content himself with watching and saying '*Opa*' every now and then.

As he sipped his coffee, he saw a woman stop with a few friends outside the restaurant. She was plump and middle-aged but attractive in a tight fitting sleeveless pink dress. Listening to the music, perhaps a favourite song, she began to smile and click her fingers and then with the encouragement of her friends who began to clap, she started to dance. Her movements were slow and graceful and rhythmic, arms twining like graceful snakes over her head. Max watched in fascination and envy. Such lissom naturalness, the twist and turn and flow of body movement; the woman was suddenly a sensual goddess, a dancing nymph, exquisite and free and alive. People stopped on the sidewalk and joined in the clapping till the music finished and the woman, laughing and not even out of breath, moved on with her friends.

He loved being here, loved the oriental atmosphere of the place. The freedom, the simplicity of the woman's spontaneous dancing impressed him. Perhaps he *would* resign when he got home. He might even come and live here for a while, help out Dimitri or Basil in some way, have a quiet, simple life amongst his good friends. There was nothing for him in England any more. He was free, wasn't he? He was his own master, no one else to worry about. Maybe go to the States. Or Australia. Anywhere to flee himself.

He wondered what had brought on this fit of depression so suddenly. Was it something to do with seeing Zoë cowering against the tree, so terrified of that brute of her husband? It had revived all those unpleasant childhood memories locked in the basement of his mind. The hatches which he had battened down on all those inner devils had burst, letting them escape, and now they were raging around him, phantoms, ghouls and vampires of the heart. It was a good thing his father had died of kidney failure when Max was in his teens or he would have killed the bastard himself.

For a brief moment his mind slid back to the narrow terraced street of his childhood. All he could remember was the darkness of the house, the shadowy, twisted stairs which filled him with an anxiety that had to be faced every night on the way to his tiny bedroom overlooking the street. The night noises became magnified in his childish ears into wails of misery and despair. Despite missing his mother, his brief stay in Shropshire was like a revelation of a life so different to the mean streets of his birth. Returning to London was a blow at first and he was torn by a longing to go back to his foster parents and the wonderful open spaces of the countryside. But his mother missed him and wanted him back once the first panic was over and he, in his turn, was delighted to see her again. To this day he remembered coming home from school to find those old East End houses blown away and lost forever. The huge hole and pile of rubble suddenly giving space and light amongst the cramped darkness was exhilarating and exciting. They eventually moved into a three bedroomed council house which was large and airy and pleasant. He had been so happy with his mother, just the two of them alone.

Then *he* had returned. His father, by now a stranger and unwelcome. A man cold, self-absorbed, frightening, cruel.

Max pulled himself together, smoked a last cigarette and clicking his fingers, summoned the waiter and paid the bill. It was still early and he wanted to keep moving, walking, just anywhere, tire himself out and resist thinking and longing through the constant movement. He walked up Aristotelous to Egnatia till he reached the Arch of Galerius. For a brief moment he stopped to admire the beautiful carvings on the old Roman arch and wondered at the vanity of a man who needed to record his exploits in this manner. Here stood the triumphal Arch while Emperor Galerius was long gone, just a name in a history book. It reminded him of the walks he and Nina used to take in the old Brompton Cemetery and how she had once said that names on the gravestones were all that was left of us when we died. She was right. The thought saddened him even more. It made everything seem so pointless and meaningless. Where was that foolish Emperor now?

Lighting another cigarette, he turned back along Egnatia, plunging into one of the side streets that led to the Modiano market. The stalls were all covered or deserted and the area dark and quiet. Light shone from a small cinema along one of the streets but over it all loomed the huge tobacco factory, its high wall rendering the place dark and forbidding. Normally Max would have enjoyed a walk around these silent and eerily empty labyrinthine streets. It looked so different at night to the daytime of commerce, trucks bringing in produce, vendors calling out their wares, goods spilling out onto the pavements. Now the darkness struck him as sinister and strange. A strong sense of unease made him turn back.

Retracing his steps again, he walked back in the direction of the church of Agios Georgios and turned off toward the Hotel Galaxio, glancing upwards at the old shuttered buildings, now made into flats, remnants of the days of Turkish occupation. Even around here the streets were quiet, most people busy indoors, wives cooking suppers and seeing to the little ones. Others had already set off to eat and drink at the tavernas. He heard the occasional wail of a child, the laughter of some woman from an open window overhead. Here and there a radio was blaring out the wailing music of the latest favourite singer.

Se kath' iliovassilema, to lathos mou thimiseis
Pou mes'apo ta heria mou, tha'feisa na mou figeis

So true, so true, he had indeed let her slip away, slip from his hands into the sunset.

He strolled along, in no real hurry, glad to hear these normal human sounds pull him a little from the darkness of his grim and foolish thoughts. Athina said she would be at home with the kids when he returned. His heart was gladdened by the idea of being with these cheerful, welcoming people tonight. It would lift his mood, liven him up to have good friends, good food and wine. They might even make it to a nightclub, to 'Kounies' up in the hills, pick up Dimitri and Yiota on the way, have a good time.

A sudden prickle of the hairs on the back of his neck made him turn swiftly. No one seemed to be in sight apart from a couple of middle-aged tourists strolling along on the other side of the street. He walked on, his nerves on edge now, his ears alert to any unusual sound. He was nearing the Galaxio, passing by some narrow side streets, when a man's voice called his name. He stopped, irresolute, and hearing another sound, turned just in time to see a dark figure emerge from the shadows. Before he could defend himself, he was felled with something rock-hard and unyielding against the side of his head that sent astonishing colours and sparkles of exploding light though his skull. He felt blood spurting from his mouth and pouring down his neck. He was going to die and he didn't want to die.

'Nina!' he cried as he fell.

He felt himself dragged across the ground into the shadows. The figure of a large beefy man stood over him and booted him several times in the side as he lay motionless and fast losing consciousness.

'Fuck Nina!' the man muttered, then laughed. 'Too many bloody women in your life, you bastard Englishman, and you have to take mine as well.'

Dimitri finished for the day and, after making sure everything was locked and put away, decided that he would walk home rather than catching the bus up Georgiou. He had been sitting in the little office for some time and felt the need to stretch his muscles. Yiota had promised to make him his favourite beef stew tonight and he felt hungry just thinking about it. Yet, he lingered a little as he left the Exhibition Park and lighting a cigarette, stood looking around him at the passing crowds as if searching for something but with no idea what he was looking for. He felt very uneasy. Just after Max had left, he spotted that brute, Katsarakis, walking past their stand looking bullish and enraged; a dangerous, unpredictable creature. Why was that man hanging around so much? What did that bastard want with Max anyway?

Something had happened and Max was keeping quiet about it, but it was sure to be something to do with a woman. Dimitri knew his friend. He was an unmistakable magnet for the ladies and always in hot water. Half the time, it wasn't his fault at all.

A man given to instinctual feelings, Dimitri had a very bad feeling just now. Max was in trouble. Maybe he would just walk to the Galaxio and check if his friend was still around, have a little chat and a beer and warn him about Katsarakis again. He did feel a slight resentment that his friend was so taken up with Basil Petrakos this year when usually Max visited his own family more often. Yiota had grumbled at him for not bringing him back for a meal. 'Have you made him angry?' she asked.'Why won't he come?' But in fairness, Max had known Basil from long before, when they were students in England. Petrakos was a wealthy, educated man while he, Dimitri, was not. Max was bound to be drawn to someone of his own class.

He realised he knew little about Max's background. All he did know was that his friend held down a good job with Ford's at Basildon, was comfortably off and that his in-laws in England had a fine house and a farm with several acres of land. His wife, Nina, was a beautiful, clever and a respected lady. Her Greek grandfather, Costas Cassimatis, had fought bravely in the First War and died some years ago. He had been a well-known figure in Thessaloniki, came from a good family. Nina was a lovely woman. Max was lucky.

Dimitri had been sorry to hear of their separation. Yiota knew that her husband played around a bit but she tended to shrug and turn a blind eye. She knew he would never leave her and the children. It seemed that Nina had English ideas and refused to tolerate Max's escapades. Max had sworn that the little lapse with his secretary had been the only time since they where married and that she had practically thrown herself at him – but Dimitri found that hard to believe. Perhaps if they had children, things might have turned out different, who could say? Nina might have been more forgiving.

He walked along the road towards the Galaxio, lighting up another cigarette as he went. The air felt cooler now that darkness had fallen which was a relief. An old acquaintance passed by and they nodded, stopped for a brief chat.

'I must move on, got a friend to see,' Dimitri said and hurried his pace a little. At this rate, Max would have checked out of the hotel and be with Basil Petrakos. It was probably a waste of time going at all, yet he felt impelled to do so by some inner disquiet that refused to go away. Yiota would grumble if he was late for dinner, but that was too bad.

He stopped at the corner of the street where the Galaxio was situated. He could hear the faint bursts of sound from the open air cinema along the road, a familiar sound for him. The streets here were narrow and mean-looking. It was such a dump. Why had his friend chosen this place? He should have insisted that Max stayed with them, but the foolish man wanted to be alone. Englishmen were strange creatures. Why not stay with friends, have a laugh and plenty of excellent food? He'd get used to the kids and the noise. This was a city, for heaven's sake, what did he expect? Being alone was not healthy. It was unsociable and morbid.

Few people were around here at this time of the evening. He stared at a foreign-looking middle-aged couple who passed him by. They looked like Germans. Oh, well, the past was the past and Germans now brought in revenue as tourists. More Greeks spoke German than French or English now. And why not? That's where the money lay; get something back from them after all they'd taken from the Hellenes in the last bloody war.

He stopped again and crushed his cigarette butt into the ground. Looking up, he felt a stab of horror. A huge looming shadow seemed to emerge from a side street and throw itself across the wall and pavement like a demonic being. For a moment he froze in his tracks and automatically crossed himself. But it was a trick of the lamplight; the shadow shrank and the figure of a large man moved out of a side street and just as quickly crossed the road, disappearing into an alleyway beside a small block of dilapidated old Turkish style apartments. He knew it was Katsarakis. No one else towered as huge and menacing as he did. It was like watching a Boris Karloff film.

Shit. That bastard was up to no good, skulking around the Galaxio. He'd have to warn Max about this. Hopefully Max had long gone and was now in Karabournaki. Dimitri strode quickly towards the hotel whose neon light spilt a bluish glow on the pavement. He stopped at the side street where Katsarakis had issued forth. Something made him walk along it a little way, receding further from the faint musical bursts of song and dance at the cinema. It was a silent, empty street.

Pah, nothing here … I'm going crazy tonight, he told himself.

Turning swiftly on his heel, he was about to leave this oppressive area when he thought he heard a faint moan. He stopped. Shook his head. Maybe he imagined it. Too many horror films. He looked around, nerves tightly strung wires ready to break. But it came again and he followed that sound until he saw a crumpled human heap in a dark doorway and ran towards it, heart beating wildly.

Chapter 11

Downlands, Gloucestershire – Where is Nina?

Andrew Cassimatis leant back in his swivel chair and stared out of the library window at the rolling lawns that led down to the blue-grey surface of a little lake. A swan glided across and disappeared from view under the thick hanging branches of the alders and willows that half-surrounded the perimeter of the waters. Those old bent willows he had so loved in his youth now looked gnarled and ageing. Perhaps it was time to cut them down. But he hated changing anything . Downlands looked much as it had done before the First War, let alone the Second, and he liked it that way.

He let his mind drift back to those far-off days when, as a lad, he came here during school holidays to stay with old grandmother Clarke. She had been parsimonious in the extreme, never letting the lamps be lit till it was almost too dark to see. Plus a regular stickler for time-keeping; no tea if he wasn't there, hands washed, as soon as the bell had rung. She had loved him in her own cold manner but he was never too sure whether she approved of his 'foreign blood'.

Amazing that she had bequeathed him Downlands. He knew that it was partly due to the sense of guilt she had felt in betraying his mother, by interfering in her relationship with his father. Grandma had never approved of her daughter's love for a foreigner, never approved of anything Dorothy did. And especially had not approved of an unmarried daughter arriving home pregnant and unrepentant.

However, the real reason for his windfall was due to the fact that Grandma Clarke knew he loved the place far more than his elder cousin, Reggie, who had no interest or desire, other than a pecuniary one, in the old house and gardens. Surprisingly, Reggie had borne no ill-will nor fought him over the matter of his disinheritance.

'You went and fought in the war and I didn't, old chap. I just wrote newspaper articles. I was a black sheep in old Gran Clarke's eyes. A regular black sheep. Sums it up, really. Still, she left me some useful cash just when I needed it, so she was fair in her own peculiar way.'

'You never wanted to live here anyway, did you, Reggie?'

'Not on your life! Neither does Mother. A crumbling old heap like this. It'll cost you every penny you earn to keep it going. I'll end up richer than you, old boy.'

This prophecy had to some extent come true. Reggie's entry into journalism, before the war had broken out, had led to a meteoric rise in a well-known daily newspaper. He had since joined the board and was doing very well for himself in various other areas in the City. Andrew, on the other hand, had left the Army and returned to finish his abandoned studies at Oxford then went on to study medicine. He now had a fairly successful practice in Gloucestershire but no ambition to rise further in this profession. It was true, Downlands did eat up most of his earnings. But he had no regrets over that. He loved the place with a passion.

His wife entered the room at this point in his reflections and smiled when she saw the half-drunk cup of tea beside him. She had brought that and a plate with three digestive biscuits at four o'clock, an ingrained habit with Andrew since the days of Grandma Clarke. She had never know this old lady but her presence and her habits still seemed to brood over the place. Helen never felt as if she was truly mistress of this house. It would always be that cranky old lady, now long gone.

'You've let your tea go cold again, Andy,' she jokingly complained, 'don't know why I bother bringing it in to you.'

He pulled her towards him, encircling her with his arm.

She allowed herself to be held there reluctantly, never fond of shows of affection. It amused him that she was very like the old lady in this respect. 'I always feel grateful when you do,' he said, looking up at her with a smile.

Helen disengaged herself, walked over to the window and followed her husband's gaze over the damp autumnal garden.'What were you thinking about just now, Andy? You looked very far away.'

'I'd floated off into the past. Thinking of the time I was told that Gran Clarke had left me Downlands. I couldn't believe my luck. And thinking of the day I came back here with Mum after the war and walked through the rooms feeling thrilled and exhilarated to know it was all mine. She was pretty chuffed too. I mean it was hers as well, as far as I was concerned.'

'She still thinks it is sometimes,' observed Helen dryly.

'Oh … no, no. Let's be fair. She knew it was mine and was happy for me. She's never interfered in any of our decisions, now, has she? Anyway, she stayed in Salonika once we found Dad again. She didn't come back here till after his death in'55.'

'How did Nina feel when she first came here?' asked Helen curiously. 'She must have found a dark old place like Downlands pretty odd after living so long with her grandfather in Greece.'

'I think she hated it,' said Andrew, looking sad. 'I don't think she cares for it even now. Mum and I seem to be the only ones who love old Downlands. I'm never too sure what *you* feel, my enigmatic lady. You never grumble or run anything down. But I know you'd rather be in London.'

Helen made no reply, just kept staring out at the lake, watching the calm progress of the swan across its waters. Suddenly the bird arose with a majestic flap of its wings and took off into the fields beyond.

'I'm not worried,' she said eventually. 'I'm always pretty content wherever I am.'

'You *are* too, old thing, you're such an easy-going girl. I know I take advantage of you.' Her husband took her hand, trying again to draw her towards his lap, but she pulled her hand away with a faint smile and walked towards the door.

'Are you coming to supper or do you want it brought in here?'

'Oh …' he rose and stretched himself, shrugging back his shoulders to ease their stiffness. 'I've had enough of writing my perishing memoirs. I'll come. I meant to pop down to Cottersely's Farm this afternoon but time seems to fly by some days.'

'Time spent dreaming, Andy,' Helen observed.

'Well yes,' he admitted,'I was always a dreamer. Anyway, I'll go in the morning.'

Andrew enjoyed a pleasant morning down at Cottersley's farm the next day. He and Dorothy had bought the place after the war at a cheap price because the farmer, Jim Turnbull, had died in action and his widow wanted to move away and stay with her children in Hereford. It had many happy memories for both Andrew and his mother. Both of them in their turn of childhood days at Downlands would walk the lane to the farm to purchase milk and eggs. Dorothy used to go with her brother, Richard, who later died in the First War. Andrew walked that way in his own youth during the twenties.

Cottersley farm was now managed by a young family called Braithwaite. It was good to see young children running about the place and enjoying the fields and hedgerows as much as he and his mother had once done. The farm was doing well: fruit orchards, some dairy, a couple of pigs and plenty of chickens. They were discussing the new idea of growing fruit and vegetables that could be picked by people for themselves. It was a fast-growing and lucrative business that saved a good deal of work for the farmer and was fun for the customers.

As he walked back home accompanied by Sam, his border collie, Andrew realised that the countryside had altered very little since those early days at the turn of the century. The land that wound down to the farm was still full of primroses in spring and dog rose and honeysuckle in summer. Now it was autumnal and old man's beard fluffed in the hedgerows, the fat grey cushions of seed softening the rusty-looking leaves and dark twigs. Andrew loved the English countryside. Despite his paternal Greek blood, he felt as if he belonged here. He had never quite taken to life in Greece although he knew that his father's blood stirred in him now and then, particularly when he was with his daughter Nina. She was so very Greek, his beloved Nina. Not only in looks but in mannerisms and attitudes. When she played Greek records on the gramophone, he felt truly transported back. He wanted to dance, to move as he had once done in his youth.

Nina had once brought him a recording from the States of some rebetika music. This had been banned in Greece, as too subversive, first by the Metaxas regime and then during the war, but it had always managed to flourish underground as plants will do during the winter months, waiting for the moment to spring forth again. Hearing this music played once more had reduced him to tears. The sound flowed through him, needling every nerve in his body.

'It brings back memories of your mother,' he told Nina. She stopped the record and hastened to comfort him. He was trembling and she was shocked.

'I didn't mean to upset you, Papa.'

'It just brings back vivid memories, my darling. I don't think I can listen to it any more. It's too painful.'

Anna, his one true love, had been a refugee from Smyrna along with her father and brothers. They had lived in a tumbledown house in the old abandoned Turkish quarter of Thessaloniki. Amazingly, the houses were still there. These wooden houses had survived the Great War, the devastating fire that had swept Thessaloniki in 1917 and the German occupation. He had gone back some years after the Second War and was pleased to see the homes being renovated and becoming habitable again. They had scarcely been so in Anna's time when the roof had dripped rainwater into a bucket and whole families were forced to use the same latrine.

Andrew would never forget Anna. His first love, his last real love. Helen was a marvellous wife and he loved her dearly, but it was a different feeling. In many ways, he knew she suited him better than the wild and spirited Anna Manoglou would have done. Anna was a free spirit. She would never have made a good wife. Nina was much like her mother in character. The same brave, foolish, freedom-loving, stubborn nature.

Andrew came into the hallway at Downlands just as the phone rang. He heard Helen's voice and her tone made him pause for a moment as he took off his muddy outdoor shoes. Patting Sam on the head and bidding him off to the kitchen where the dog greedily lapped at his water bowl, he went into the hall and looked enquiringly at his wife.

'Oh, he's back now. Here's Andrew,' said Helen. She put a hand over the mouthpiece and said, 'It's a call from Greece for Nina. They can't seem to get hold of her in London.'

Andrew frowned and took the call.

'What's the problem?'

A Greek voice with a heavy accent sounded in his ear. 'Doctor Cassimatis? This is Basil Petrakos here. I'm a friend of your son-in-law, Max Hammett. We try to find Nina, your daughter, but with no success. She's not at her London flat. She told us many times that she and Max come and stay with you in the country and we remembered that she was a Cassimatis before her marriage. We managed to find your number that way. I am sorry for troubling you but Max is badly hurt and in hospital right now.'

'Max hurt? What on earth's happened? Was it an accident with the machinery?'

'No, I regret he was attacked by a local thug. It is a complicated story. Is your daughter there?'

'No, she left here last week, went back to her London flat. As far as I know, that's where she's supposed to be. Have you tried her employers? She's an independent journalist but she does a lot of work for *The Daily News*. You can ask my cousin Reggie Patterwood, as he's employing her.'

He gave Basil the phone number and asked again, 'What's poor Max got himself mixed up in now? Who is this thug? Have the police got him?'

Basil told him that Katsarakis had conveniently disappeared;

no one had any idea where he was. And the police didn't seem too bothered about finding him either. He told Andrew that they meant to take care of Max when he came out of hospital, take him off to their little holiday home in Halkidiki to recuperate. But Nina needed to be told and they hoped she would come along to visit her husband.

'His jaw's been broken; he can only whisper but he asks for her,' said Basil. 'He was close to death for a day or two. He lost a lot of blood before his friend found him and called the ambulance. We were really worried. But he's pulling through.'

'Good grief! This sounds terrible. What the devil provoked such an attack on the poor man?'

'It's a long story, Doctor. But the police have been informed.'

Andrew didn't like to say that this was scarcely reassuring. Greek police were noted for their ability to be bribed or to turn a blind eye to certain crimes. He paused and then said, 'It's immensely kind of you to offer to take care of him, Mr Petrakos. I'll come over with Nina and we'll fly him back home as soon as we can. He can stay here and my wife and I will nurse him, we're both qualified to do so.'

The whole thing sounded crazy. What was Greece coming to when thugs wandered about attacking men in broad daylight? Nina was always saying that things were bad over there now. He had lost touch with the happenings in his father's country and frankly hadn't much cared. The seaman's strike and the state of the economy here in Britain were a lot more interesting and newsworthy.

Now he wondered where on earth Nina had gone. How was it that she wasn't at her flat? Perhaps she had gone visiting a friend or was off on some assignment for Reggie. His cousin told him that Nina was turning into an excellent reporter with a keen nose for a story. 'She's determined to make us a real scoop,' he said, 'and I believe she will. She's got courage and charm and is very determined.'

Andrew knew his daughter. She was certainly determined.

Chapter 12

Downlands: A need for action

Andrew tried several times to contact his daughter at her flat. There was no reply. He rang Reggie at the newspaper offices. While he waited for the switchboard to put him through to the great man, he tapped a pencil on his desk in an impatient manner.

'Where the devil's Nina, Reggie? She's disappeared from the face of the earth.' Andrew snapped at him.

'Hello to you too, old man,' responded his cousin amiably. 'She went off on an assignment and I've not heard from her for a few days. She just gets on with it and sends in the report when it's all finished. She works for me but does a lot of freelance stuff as well. I'm not her keeper.'

'Sorry, Reggie, bloody rude of me to shout at you. But the fact is Max, her husband, has been attacked in Greece – had his skull smashed in or something pretty bad. She should know about it and get over there to see him. The poor fellow may be at death's door.'

'Good grief, how the dickens did he get into that sort of trouble? Sounds like a good story though. British citizen attacked in Athens.'

'Salonika, as it happens. And what the hell are you talking about, a good story! You newspapermen are the limit. Where's my daughter, is more to the point.'

'She's her own person, you know. Anyway, I thought they were divorced.'

'No, they're just separated while they sort things out.'

'Sorry, Drew, old chap, no idea where she is at this precise moment.'

'Well, as soon as she rings in, let her know how things are. Tell her I'm on my way to London tomorrow and will book a flight to Athens, then to Salonika. I want her ready and packed. I'll be staying at the Portland Hotel for a couple of nights.'

He gave Reggie the number and address and put down the phone, feeling exasperated and frustrated.

'The trouble with Nina,' he informed his wife, 'is that she likes to be mysterious and do things her own way. In the end, I'll just have to go on my own and she'll have to follow on. Poor Max. He sounds in a bad way.'

Later that day he had a call from Reggie. 'It seems Nina left a message with my secretary yesterday morning to say she's following up a story in Greece. She's already over there, as far as I can tell.'

'What! Why didn't the damn secretary inform you of the fact sooner?'

'Busy,' said Reggie briefly. 'Look, we're all busy, Andrew. I'm sorry, but it's the sort of thing Nina does, going off on her own tangents, and frankly, she always comes up with something interesting. I just let her get on with it. That was our agreement when I hired her. She said she didn't want her wings clipped.'

Andrew smiled a little at this. 'Hmph! That's my daughter, all right. But haven't you any idea where she's gone? Hasn't she left some forwarding address?'

'She said she was going to Athens for a few days. Staying with some friends there to see how the land lies. That's what she said. Then she's off to that house you have in the mountains. She gives a phone number for someone called Aris Praxiteles if I need to get hold of her. Apparently he's something to do with *Kathimerini*, the Greek newspaper in Athens. Says she should be back in a week or so.'

'She never told *me* she was going to Greece,' said Andrew, disgruntled by this daughterly omission,'but then, she never does say what she's up to half the time.'

'I'm supposed to be her boss and she doesn't tell *me* anything,' said Reggie. 'Anyway, here's the phone number of this Praxiteles character which she left as a contact.'

Andrew wrote the number down and said, 'She must mean to stay at Mistres when she goes up north.'

'Sounds like it. I hope you get hold of her, anyway. Let me know how things go. When are you setting off?'

'Tomorrow morning. I just heard again from Max's friend, Basil. He assures me that Max is comfortable and no need to rush over as they're taking care of him. I do wish I could get hold of Nina, though. She really should be with him.'

'Depends if she cares or not.'

'She cares. I know she does, despite all she says.'

Thessaloniki: General Hospital

Athina looked at Max as he lay in the hospital bed. He was sleeping now and looked pale and thin. His head was partially bandaged but the doctor assured them that his skull had only sustained a small linear fracture and would slowly heal on its own. Most of the blows received had caught the side of his face, breaking the jaw cleanly in two places. This was now wired shut in order to let the breaks heal. At first there was concern that his hearing might be impaired. But he was young and fit and they were hopeful all would mend in a couple of months. The doctor had told them this morning that Max's ear drum looked sound, no permanent damage. He had been incredibly lucky. Athina felt ill just thinking of what might have happened.

Dimitri popped his head in and saw her sitting there, a book open on her lap, studying their friend.

'Eh, Athina *mou*,' he said coming up to the bedside and regarding the sleeping invalid. He spoke softly, afraid of waking Max, his usual bounce and merriment much subdued. 'In God's name, what a terrible thing to have happened. I feel ashamed that a *xeni*, a foreigner, has been treated like this in our country.

What's happened to everyone? The world's going mad. There's no feeling, no respect or moral fibre any more.'

Athina shut her book and nodded in agreement. 'I'm so angry that that despicable Katsarakis got away. And though Basil has made a fuss with the police a dozen times, nothing seems to be happening. They don't appear to care about law and order at all. It almost feels as if they're on the side of these thugs. He's useful to them somehow and they're protecting him. I agree with you – what the hell *is* happening to this country of ours? The man from the Embassy – Mr Wright, I think he's called – he promises to make a real fuss, I can tell you.'

'They always say that.' Dimitri curled his lip. 'Officials, they're all damned useless. And the British … they won't do anything to upset our King. It will all get quietly forgotten, like a lot of other things that happen nowadays. I reckon I'll go look for that bastard myself. Make some enquiries. I know people who can help.'

'No, don't, Dimitri,' begged Athina, 'these men are gangsters. Don't get involved. You've got a wife and kids. Max said he didn't want us to get into trouble.'

His face lit up at this. 'He spoke to you today?'

'No, no, *o kaimenos*, the poor man. It tires him to try and whisper so he writes on a pad. We have it by his bed so he can 'speak' to us. He's going to be a very silent man for some time. His eyes always show me how glad he is to see us here,'Athina laughed a little. 'Ach, Dimitri, it's thanks to you he's survived. If he'd stayed any longer on that stinking doorstep, he'd have bled to death.' Athina stopped and her voice trembled. Dimitri came and put an arm around her. 'We were so scared he might die,' she murmured.

'Our good Virgin took me there,' said Dimitri, crossing himself vigorously. 'Then I saw that bastard running away. Thanks to God, the streets were getting busy again and he couldn't hang about too long or I feel sure he'd have hit Max more than he did. And that would have done for our poor friend. They reckon he used some sort of thick wooden club. It was like Lambrakis, eh? And some say Katsarakis had a part in that as well. Pah! ... these men aren't human beings, they're monsters.'

A nurse and doctor came in at this moment and the friends were shooed out while an examination was made of the patient. Dimitri and Athina walked in silence down the white, impersonal corridors towards the entrance and the bright sunshine outside. They stopped on the hospital concourse, lit a cigarette and inhaled both smoke and fresh air in equal thankful gulps. Hospitals were depressing places. As they parted, Dimitri asked, 'But where's his wife. Where is Nina? I'm surprised at her. She should come.'

'Her father is coming from England. He says Nina is in Athens on some business assignment and no one quite knows where she is. But she's coming over to Thessaloniki later. Hopefully we can contact her then.'

'Women should be at home, not gadding about all over the place,' said Dimitri angrily. In her heart, Athina agreed. She too was annoyed that Nina was nowhere to be found. What sort of woman was this, leaving England without telling anyone, not even her father, where she was? What sort of inconsiderate person was she? And her poor husband in such a state.

Later that evening, Andrew arrived at the General Hospital and found Max sitting up in bed and with some difficulty sipping what looked like *avgolemono* soup through a straw. His face lit up when he saw Andrew, his eyes following on from him as if seeking another figure and he mumbled incoherently through half closed lips.

Andrew shook his head gently. 'Nina's in Athens, Max, old fellow. But she'll be here as soon as she can. Poor chap, look at the state of you. It's okay, I know you can't talk too well. I can see it's not easy.'

He didn't dare to show how shocked he was. The discoloration of Max's face was mainly hidden by bandaging but what showed was like some florid purple growth. The hows and the whys could wait till later. Time enough for that. It was obvious he couldn't be moved but appeared comfortable enough here and receiving competent care from the staff. All the same, Andrew wanted to get Max home to England as soon as possible. He also was determined to make enquiries with the police and the Embassy. Was nothing being done to find the cause of this attack?

He had questioned Basil and Athina but, of course, it was Dimitri who supplied most of the answers. In that gentleman's opinion it wasn't about robbery, as everyone assumed. It was due to some jealous revenge over a woman. Andrew sighed. If Nina knew that she would probably just turn round and go away again. Why couldn't Max keep his trousers zipped up, for heaven's sake!

Finding his daughter had proved a trying and almost impossible task. The girl was like a bird flying from perch to perch. When would she leave whatever she was doing in Athens? He had rung the Praxiteles apartment and a rather dim-sounding young girl informed him that Nina was out 'somewhere.' He left a message for her to contact him at his hotel if she came in early enough that evening. He waited up till midnight but there was no call and he felt angry and disquieted in turns. He rang again the next morning and this time a quiet, well-spoken lady answered the phone.

'I'm Stella Praxiteles,' she informed him. 'I apologise, Doctor Cassimatis, but your daughter Nina left us early this morning to stay with Eleni Vlachou for a day or two and said she would ring you when she came back. She is very interested in *Kathimerini*, the newspaper that employs my husband, and hopes to write some articles for them. She was so excited by the idea of meeting Vlachou. It is such an honour, you know.'

'Didn't you tell Nina that it was urgent?' said Andrew, doing his best to hold back his annoyance.

The woman paused. 'Well, no – Lexi, my daughter, didn't mention that there was anything urgent. I'm so sorry. Lexi isn't always too sensible. I hope it isn't anything bad.'

'It's bad enough.' said Andrew shortly. 'Her husband is in hospital.'

'Christ and the Virgin, that's terrible! He's in Athens?'

'No, in Thessaloniki, which is where I am also.'

'I'll give you Vlachou's phone number. I'll go and get it.'

'Don't take the trouble, Mrs Praxiteles. Let us not interrupt my daughter's scoop for anything,' said Andrew with some bitterness. 'Tell Nina I shall be at our house in Mistres when she returns. And tell her to come quickly. It's urgent.'

Mistres: a mountain village near Thessaloniki.

Andrew went to Mistres the next day. He hired a Volkswagen and drove northwards towards the Hortiach Mountains and the little village where his father had inherited a house during the thirties. Now the family used it whenever they returned to Thessaloniki. Andrew never ceased to have strong and vivid memories whenever he came back here. Not only had his own parents conceived him here, he too had made love here to his beloved Anna and conceived Nina. It was a special and important place for him emotionally. The passage of time had scarcely altered the little village or its inhabitants nor dimmed the associations of pain and pleasure in his heart.

He walked down the dusty main street, no longer an open sewer but still no better than a dirt track. The crazy half-wild dogs that used to strain at their chains and bark with ferocious greeting were no longer in evidence. Those few dogs still kept were in kennels at the back of houses now though several mangy cats crouched on walls and drifted furtively into the shrubs as he approached, staring out at him with twitching tails and wild wide eyes. Hens still wandered about in the gardens and strayed into the road or flapped their way to the top of a wall, venting their feelings of joy every time they laid an egg. A cockerel strode proudly amongst his harem and occasionally shooed them all into a group as if to demonstrate his domination.

The houses were patchy and tumbledown but Andrew knew that they were clean and beautifully kept inside by proud matrons. A few half-built new structures appeared amongst the older ones, waiting to become some young girl's dowry. Hiding all the tumbled masonry, the empty petrol cans and poverty, bougainvillea clambered over ancient walls, covering them with an amethyst layer that nodded and trembled in the breeze.

Andrew was greeted on all sides by friendly faces and voices and responded with pleasure. It always felt like a homecoming when he was here: that other side of him that was Greek resonated to the language and the cheerful, weather-beaten faces of the villagers. He had known many of them since he was nineteen years old. It was before the Second World War that he had made his first visit to his homeland; a reuniting with his lost father. The father he and his mother had believed to have died in the First World War.

'Eh, Doctor, *kalosorizate!* Welcome, welcome!'

Women with shrill, excited voices bustled up to him to ask about his health, his family and he made the usual smiling, polite replies but nothing else. It wouldn't do to tell these kindly gossips his business.

'Are you here on holiday?'

'Yes, yes, just a short holiday.'

'Is your daughter coming too?'

'Yes, she'll be coming soon.'

'Have you any grandchildren yet?'

'No, no, not yet.'

'Why not! What's the matter with the girl?'

'Oh, *yiatre mou*, Doctor Andreas, you're sent from Heaven. I pinned a silver hand by the *Panayia's* ikon in our chapel just yesterday! Can you come and look at old Anthoula later? She's not been well at all.'

And so on.

It took a while to reach his front door but he made it there at last and entered the soft cool atmosphere of the house, closing the door firmly behind him. The villagers knew his ways and didn't resent this shutting everyone out. He was from England, what did one expect? He had English ways now. But he was still the son of Costas Cassimatis. He was one of them too.

Flinging his jacket over a chair, Andrew went into the kitchen to get himself a glass of water. The small fridge was stocked with bottles of water, some milk, bread, unsalted butter, feta and a tub of yogurt. Even the little votive candle before the ikon of *Panayia*, the Madonna, had been lit, casting a welcoming warm light in the corner of the room. One of the women, the sister of the local priest, came in every week to open the shutters and air the rooms, dust them and clean them. He had contacted the priest before coming and arranged for Roula to put a few items in the fridge and thankfully the message had been passed on. He would get her to do some more shopping when she came in tomorrow morning.

Old Xanthi, who had looked after his father for so many years, had died long ago. Her crocheted lacework and beautiful embroideries still remained, adorning the tables and chest of drawers. Andrew fingered them gently, his mind hearkening back to the past. He could almost hear her voice and deep, hearty laughter, hear her calling him to eat her wonderful *moussaka*.

'What is the first thing you say when you come to visit here, *Kyr* Andreas? You say, "Where's your *moussaka*, Xanthoula *mou*!"– and here it is.'

But no longer was anyone there to cook for him and he would have to make shift for himself. After drinking a large glass of water and unpacking his few clothes, he went out again. The village sported a little *cafeneion* where the men sat outside on brightly painted blue chairs playing *tavli* on wooden tables with chequered cloths. They greeted him affectionately and patted a chair next to them for his use, while the proprietor bought out the best *raki* and some bits of olives and feta on a plate for Doctor Andreas. His father had been much revered in this village. To them he was a hero of the old days, a Venizelos man, a patriot. Not like these rubbishy men from Athens with their neo-Nazi leanings. Pah, they would send them packing as they had always sent traitors packing.

'Has Mrs Ioanna any *tiropita* left?' asked Andrew hopefully. He loved those triangular little cheese pastries. Thoma, the proprietor laughed and said,'Of course! I'm sure there's some left. If not, she can make you an omelette.'

'Or both, I'm famished,' said Andrew.

Food was soon brought and he enjoyed every bite, eating out in the fresh air of the mountains. His mother had once said that his soul would always be in Greece because he was conceived there. And it was true. Here he was a Greek, a Thessalonian to boot. Something fell away from him when he was at Mistres. He smiled and thought how much freer and simpler and more natural life was here. He went to bed that night feeling a little the worse for wear after drinking *raki,* an unaccustomed habit. These days it made his head ache. But, he reflected, not half as much as poor old Max's head was aching.

It was just after siesta time two days later when Andrew heard the barking of the dogs and the sound of a taxi drawing up at the door. He was busy in the kitchen making himself some toast and boiling a kettle to make a cup of Nescafé. He quickly opened the front door and there at last was Nina, paying the taxi driver. As if on cue, villagers came tumbling out of their houses to see who the newcomer was and were now surrounding her and calling out welcoming greetings. She looked over at her father standing in the doorway before responding to the clamour around her. After a few moments, she came to greet him and murmured quietly, 'Papa, what on earth are you doing here in Greece? You haven't left Helen, have you?'

'I've left her at home, certainly,' he said.'Come on in, I need to talk to you in peace … yes, Maria, we'll pop in to see you and Christos later … Nina, where the dickens have you been? We've been trying to find you for ages.'

Nina pouted at him just as she used to as a naughty child. 'Why are you so cross? What's so important, for goodness sakes? I'm sorry I didn't ring back but I really had to go when Eleni Vlachou asked me. It's such an honour and she's a busy lady, Papa.'

She came in and put her light travelling bag down in a corner, took off her jacket. Andrew shut the door quickly and the shrill voices of the women ebbed away into the distance. Nina shivered a little. The weather had begun to change now and the rains had fallen, cooling the atmosphere. It would soon be time to lay the thick rugs back in the rooms and put on the calorifer. Their house was considered to be a rich man's place. It had belonged to a wealthy aunt who had left the house and its splendid olive groves to her nephew, Costas. The olive groves had long ago been sold off; Andrew hadn't the time or inclination to harvest them. But the well-built stone house remained, with its cool marble floors and pleasant shuttered interior. It even boasted a bathroom and a less primitive toilet than most. Many of the other houses in the village still housed their animals inside at night while the family slept upstairs in the loft or up on the flat roof when it was too hot.

'God, it's so much cooler up here in the mountains,' Nina said and went into her bedroom to retrieve a cardigan. 'Let's light the *jaki,* Papa. Shall we?' This was one of the few houses that had a large fireplace in it with chopped logs neatly stacked up at the side.

Andrew looked at his daughter in silence. She looked so beautiful, her long, lustrous dark hair tied back in a simple ponytail. Just like her mother. His heart was squeezed in pain. This place would always remind him of Anna. Remind him of the day she came to him here in Mistres and told him she was leaving to join the *andartes.* That was the night Nina had been conceived. He had never seen Anna again.

'What is it, Papa?' asked Nina, catching something in his expression.

He shook himself mentally. 'Oh, nothing, my love. Just living in the past as always. But the important thing is the here and now. Look, come and sit down for a little, I'll make some coffee first. I have bad news. That's why I've been trying to get hold of you. It's been like chasing a butterfly from flower to flower.'

'Oh!' Nina's face crumpled, She looked so like the young child she had once been. 'Oh, what is it?'

He remained silent while he made some coffee on the stove, and Nina sat down and looked up at him expectantly, all attention now.

'It isn't Helen?'

'No, not Helen, nothing at home.' He brought over the coffee and she sipped at it slowly, watching him, her eyes anxious. 'It's Max. He's been attacked by some thug and is in the AHEPA hospital right now.'

Nina went white. She raised her hands to her mouth. 'Oh God, is he alive, is he all right?'

‘Thankfully his skull wasn’t damaged badly, just a linear fracture which will soon heal. But his jaw is broken and a rib or two cracked where the bastard kicked him.’

‘My poor darling! Do they know who did it, have they caught him?’

‘We know who he is, Dimitri saw him running away. It was Dimitri that saved Max, found him lying in a heap in a shop doorway near his hotel. He swears he saw the man who tried to destroy their Exhibition stand last year, remember? Katsaki or something. It seems he has some grudge or dislike of Max, though I think it’s more likely the Ford thing. Some people here hate anything to do with the Americans. Who knows. Maybe it’s just mindless violence.’

‘It’s nearly always political these days,’ said Nina grimly. ‘But have they caught this fellow?’

‘He’s disappeared into the depths of Ano Toumba or some village network in the mountains. Who knows. He’s nowhere to be found, anyway.’

‘Or the authorities don’t *want* to find him,’ Nina said bitterly. ‘These bullies are useful to do the dirty work, though in the long run the men at the top will always sacrifice the small fry to protect themselves.’ She sighed and moved tense shoulders a little. ‘Oh, Papa, I really want to go and see Max right now – but I’m so exhausted. I couldn’t face another long journey tonight, I really couldn’t. It was a hectic coach journey from Athens and really foggy in the mountains. The crazy driver was whizzing round hairpin bends like a maniac. With a sheer drop on the other side. My nerves are in shreds. But we must go and see him tomorrow. First thing.’

‘Yes, we’ll drive there in the morning. He’s in good hands and comfortable. Have a rest and we’ll eat in tonight. Roula promised to bring something over later. Then you can tell me what you’ve been up to and why you hopped back to Greece. And tell me who these Praxiteles people are you’ve palled up with.’

‘They are such a superb, hospitable couple: Alex Praxiteles and his wife Stella. I met them through their son, George, who contacted me when I was in London. He's a very nice young man, a member of the Lambrakis Youth Movement, but he's studying in London just now.'

'Right. But I hope you're being careful where you go, who you interview. There's always been undercurrents of intrigue and all kinds of undesirables round Athens and Thessaloniki.'

'You're so English, Pa. I suppose you'd think Mum was an undesirable if you met her now.'

'You shame me, Nina. Yes, we do seem to change our opinions as we get older, become more conservative and critical of others. But believe me, your mother was always desirable.' He smiled a little and Nina looked up at him searchingly, for Andrew seldom joked in the way Max did. She saw that his eyes were sad as he said this. At such times, she realised exactly where the intensity of feeling came from that drove her. It was in her blood.

'She was thrust into the unhappy life she led,' Andrew went on. 'She was a baby when she and her father and brothers escaped from Smyrna. They were wealthy, educated musicians before that.'

'It must have been such a difficult time. *I kaimeni i mama mou.* My poor Mama,' said Nina. Her heart often ached because she had no real memory of her mother and had never met her uncles or her other grandfather, Old Manoglou. The only one that had escaped the Germans was her uncle Savvas who had fled into Albania and never been heard of since.

'Anyway,' she said, after a while, 'you needn't be worried, I have a nose for undesirables and do my best to avoid them if I can. But sometimes they have the best stories.' She thought briefly of Nikos Galanis. Yes, he was certainly undesirable. 'You needn't worry about young George. He's a charming boy, his parents well educated, middle-class people. I don't think his mother is too happy that he's got involved with Theodorakis and the Youth movement which is why they've packed him off to England. They think some of these young folk are a bit wild, a bit anarchic. But George assures me that's not the case. It was Aris, his father, who introduced me to his boss, Eleni Vlachou.

She's a powerful person and runs the *Kathimerini* and *Mesimvrini* newspapers. It's unusual for a woman to have such power here in Greece and I so admire her. I have some ideas for an article I want to write both for them and for Cousin Reg. She's a most interesting, attractive woman, Pa. It was an honour to meet her. I'd love to work with her some day.'

'You'd live in Greece permanently?'

'I haven't ruled it out.'

Andrew looked downcast. Nina smiled and patted his arm,'You want me to go back to Max and have us settle in the Cotswolds, don't you? I know you do. But I'm not sure that will ever happen. I do love him – I love him dearly – but I'm not sure I can ever settle anywhere for long. And Max is restless too, though in a different way. He wants new experiences all the time as well – but they tend to be with other women.'

Andrew nodded and sighed. 'Well, that's the way of it. Anyway, we'll arrange to have Max flown to England as soon as he can be moved. We'll take him to Downlands, Nina, take him home with us.'

'Yes,' nodded his daughter, 'we'll take him home and nurse him there. My poor darling Max. How does he manage to get mixed up in all this when he's the sort of man who tends to mind his own business?'

PART TWO
IMMOLATION

Our mind's a virgin forest of murdered friends
And if I talk to you in fables and parables
It's because it's more gentle for you that way; and horror
Really can't be talked about because it's alive
Because it's mute and goes on growing:
Memory wounding pain
Drips by day, drips in sleep.

'Teleftaios Stathmos' George Seferis

Chapter 13

Downlands. March 1967

It was a sunny spring day at Downlands; the sun had at last triumphed over the grey obscuring clouds of the last few weeks and a burst of warmth after so much rain brought out the vibrant yellow daffodils and the youthful green of trees and hedges. Max and Nina walked arm in arm round the gardens of Downlands, breathing in the fresh, sweet air. The little lake glinted in the sun while a few amiable ducks toddled downhill in a row, quacking cheerfully, bent on getting to the water for their early morning bathe. A large magnolia tree at the side of the lawn, popping with fat baby buds, was ready to open its waxy pink and white flowers.

They stopped for a moment and looked about them with delight. Both felt at peace with the world and with one another. Max felt as if a huge darkness had rolled away from him. He shook his head a little. Extreme movement still gave him twinges of pain but he was otherwise mended and glad of it.

'It's good to feel normal again,' he said.

'I quite enjoyed it when you couldn't say a word back to me,' Nina teased. Max grinned, put his arm about her shoulders and they walked on in silence, feeling close and loving with a tenderness that had been absent for so long that it felt totally new. It was new – it was borne from the deepest understanding and pain and like nothing they had ever felt for one another before.

Max kept looking down at Nina and wondering how he

could have succumbed to another woman and such a woman as that girl in the office. He couldn't even remember the damned girl's name … Sheila? Yes, Sheila … as if it mattered, as if he wanted to remember her name or his shame and sense of betrayal and degradation. What the hell had come over him that her crude advances so easily aroused him at the time? The girl was attractive enough; she had the type of looks that certainly used to attract him once upon a time: slim, blonde, big-breasted, happy to do anything required, no holds barred. Sheila flattered him, adored him, and made him feel good again. And he needed sex desperately. She was up for it whenever and wherever, though mainly in her little flat in Dagenham. She favoured weird positions and liked to be held up against a wall or bent over the kitchen table dressed in nothing but high heels. It all felt deliciously exciting and squalid at the time. Perhaps he was seeking some kind of revenge. Nina would never indulge in this kind of sex. She was quite conservative and had been particularly cool and distant for some time, both sexually and emotionally. That was his excuse and assuaged any guilt he may have felt. But now he told himself he should have made more of an effort, tried to woo his wife back again, break through her defensive barriers – as he had done when they first met.

The 'affair' had lasted all of a couple of months. He then tried to break it off, feeling bored with the sex, tired of the vapid comments and possessive attitude of the wretched girl, who seemed to enjoy the arrangement of being a mistress. She told him he was quite safe with her, she didn't want to marry anyone, she liked being single and free – but she *loved* him, she loved him so much she would stay with him forever. *Forever!* The word alone struck notes of horror in his heart. Angry at his failing, angry at the stupidity of it all, he told her it was a mistake, it was all over.

Sheila said nothing at the time. She stood and stared at him for what felt like an age. He had lowered his eyes back to the papers on his desk to dismiss her. He knew he'd put it badly, that he'd been cruel to deal with it in his office, of all places. It had just come blurting out that day, a bad day when all was going wrong and his mood was irritable and miserable. She shut those full red lips together tightly, grabbed her coat and bag and stormed out of the building. She didn't return again and everyone wondered what was going on. It probably provided gossip for weeks. Max, however, had breathed a sigh of relief and thought, that's it ... it's over, never again. But it wasn't that easy to get away. Sheila phoned his wife in a fit of wounded spite and landed him in the worst row he had ever experienced. He was amazed at Nina's reaction. She was so enraged, he'd thought for a terrifying moment she would have a fit.

Even remembering that terrible day upset him. The way Nina had run out of the door and over the road into the Brompton cemetery as if to seek solace amongst the dead. That was two women who'd run away from him that week! He followed her over there and tried to speak to her but she refused to listen.

'Go away, don't ever come back!' Nina shouted at him and he knew she meant it. She would never forgive him and he would never forgive himself. He had seized some things, packed and left at once, full of dismay and fear. Anger, too. Anger with Sheila, who'd proved to be a spiteful bitch and not the easy-going person she'd pretended to be, anger with himself for his stupidity, and anger that Nina would not listen, would not forgive a human error. He was damned if he would beg for forgiveness any more, though, and so he coldly left her alone.

After that, they had spoken once or twice on the phone, voices strained and distant like strangers ... worse than strangers. They exchanged the occasional bitter letter but not seen one another again till the day Nina walked into the hospital in Thessaloniki.

He had felt his heart leap with such joy and gratitude that he knew – as if he had not always known – that there was no one as beautiful and unique as his wife. She was his, she didn't belong to anyone else. He was totally certain she hadn't lain with anyone else since their separation, because it was not in her nature to do so. Which made him feel all the more ashamed and sad that he had deceived her. The thought often crossed his mind ... suppose she had found someone else? Loved another man? He knew he would go mad if she did so and, in that at least, understood her own feelings of possession and sense of betrayal. The intriguing result of it all was that he no longer felt any desire or interest in another woman, whereas at the start of their marriage his mind and eyes had occasionally strayed; an old habit hard to break. Now he simply knew that no one on this earth could be like Nina. No one. Not for him anyway. He had missed her so much, life had become a void; an ache in his heart, soul and body that was indescribable in its pain.

Nina had received a terrible shock when she first saw her husband in the General Hospital, wired, bandaged and bruised. What little she could see of his face looked awful, a mass of yellowing bruises, blue eyes bloodshot and tired. His genuine delight at seeing her made all the old feelings of love rush back and she had run to his side, taken his hand and kissed it fervently.

'Oh, my darling, my darling!'

He couldn't even smile but his eyes said it all. Tears gushed from them and she wiped them away tenderly with her fingers.

'Don't cry, I can't bear you to cry. I'm here now. I'm not going away. I promise. Oh, Max, Max, how did this happen?'

She still had no real notion of the events that had transpired before the attack on her husband. Dimitri had explained that one of the men at the Trade Fair had become angry at their success and because he hated foreigners he'd discharged his anger on Max. She remembered about the damage last year so the story made sense. No one made any mention of Zoë or the part she had played in the story. Best Nina didn't know or she'd be sure to jump to the wrong conclusion. Dimitri was so happy that the couple had been brought together again.

Like others, she demanded to know whether the attacker had been caught and furious at the typical stalling bureaucracy of the Greek police. But she was more concerned about Max. She wanted to get him home to Downlands. For once, her English home seemed a haven of peace and tranquillity. For once, she was ashamed to be Greek. Her father shared her anxiety about Max and they flew him back home as soon as it was safe to do so. They both thanked Dimitri profusely.

'You saved my husband's life,' Nina said. 'You're a wonderful friend, Dimitri.'

'He's like a brother in my eyes,' Dimitri replied, 'a brother. I just thank God I got to him in time.'

There was always something vulnerable about Nina's husband despite his toughness and a careful detachment from life which at times made him seem shallow or indifferent. She had always sensed this wounded side to him. It brought forth a motherly part of her own nature – which wasn't a side of herself that she knew well or was even comfortable with, but it came naturally when she was with Max. And just lately, he'd really needed her, she knew that. She was prepared to let everything else in her life slide in order to be with him, reassure him, take care of him.

Max's good friends in Greece were desperate to make up for what they saw as a blot on Greek honour and *filoxenia*. But Andrew insisted that they brought him back to Downlands. Nina knew that Max was glad to get back to the peace and security of dear old England. It was some time before he felt well enough to do anything normal but the good nursing he received, plus the fact that he felt relaxed and safe at Downlands, made his recovery speedier. Max was not a person to feel sorry for himself. He made great efforts to get up and move, to put the past behind him. Above all, Nina knew that he was happy to be with her again. Her heart relented. She loved him, he was a good man.

They walked on towards the little lake, wrapped in their own thoughts but companionable nonetheless. Stopping by the water's edge, they watched the ducks for a little while. There was a sense of deep peace in their silence. Max gathered Nina a little closer. It was good to look up and see his face handsome and almost unmarked again.

'Does the jaw still ache?' she asked, her voice tender.

'Most of me aches,' he said, smiling down at her. 'But I don't care. Katsarakis cost me my job, but, frankly, I meant to resign anyway. Above all, though, he's given me back my wife. So all in all, the pain inflicted was worth the result.'

Nina laughed and squeezed his arm. 'That's true. We owe him our gratitude. But it's a terrible way to make a couple reunite!'

There was as yet no news of the Cretan's whereabouts and the general opinion was he had made it back to Crete and was hiding somewhere over there. Neither of them cared any more, nor sought revenge. He was far away now; it was just some bad dream.

'I've learnt my lesson, you're far too precious to lose,' Max said and bent his head down for Nina to kiss him. Nina did so and they hugged gently. Max stroked her face and hair and looked at her for a long time. The Sunday church bells were ringing in the distance and the pleasant softness of the air, the special feel of an English spring made his heart swell. Unbidden, he found coming to his mind fragments of a favourite Walt Whitman poem:

I heard you, solemn sweet pipes of the organ, as last Sunday morn
I pass'd the church …
Heart of my love! You too I heard, murmuring low, through one of the wrists around my head.
Heard the pulse of you, when all was still, ringing little bells last night
under my ear.

He traced the fine blue veins in her arms; he kissed them, kissed the pulse in her wrist, turned her hand over and kissed it in a moment of intense effusion and longing.

'I so want to make love to you,' he murmured. 'I'm up to it now, so be warned. Nothing wrong with that bit of equipment.'

Nina smiled and stroked his cheek. 'Abstinence has made our love all the sweeter, eh, Max?'

'Waiting is a regular aphrodisiac in itself.'

'Waiting for anything makes a change for you,' she declared, 'you're such an impatient man as a rule. Well, good comes from everything. Come, my love, it's getting chilly, let's go indoors. Helen is waving to us so it must be time for lunch.'

After a delicious piece of roast beef and all its Sunday trimmings, cooked by Helen, who excelled in good English cuisine, the four of them sat about in the lounge reading. Nina glanced over at Max. He looked unusually contented of late. The enforced rest had calmed him down a good deal; he was less restless, tense and anxious. She, however, felt more so. It was as if they had exchanged energies. She longed to get back to Greece and finish off her interviews. She had busied herself of late with small jobs in the local area, commuting to London now and then to help with some translating or interpreting work. But she had a strong instinct that matters in Greece were in a bad way and that something was going to happen soon. There were distinct rumours that the King and his generals had something up their sleeve and people were convinced that the he had consulted the CIA. It was well known that many influential Greek-Americans were members of or otherwise involved with that organisation, yet another bitter pill for the ordinary Greek patriot to swallow.

She had been there last January when Constantine had given his New Year address in which he managed to accuse seventy percent of the population of being communist. As far as he was concerned anyone who wasn't royalist, or who didn't toe his right wing party line was bound to be a Red. Everyone suspected everyone else of being a communist. It was crazy. Well, what else to expect? The King's mind was distorted by his elders. He was just an inexperienced young man, a puppet in the hands of a domineering mother and his own generals.

Because of this speech, the brilliant music of Mikis Theodorakis had been banned on Greek radio. It made no difference. Records were still sold and the ban ignored. It reminded Nina of the stories her father had told her about her mother Anna singing her forbidden rebetika songs in secret smoky dives in Thessaloniki. That music had been banned by the prime minister of the time, Metaxas, because it told of pain and suffering, deadened briefly by smoking hashish; spoke of the torments in prisons and the gnawing of hunger in the vitals.

Spoke too of the ancient homeland, Smyrna, a land now lost forever to the conquering Turks who had driven them literally into the burning sea. But the truth always came out in the end and people woke at last to the reality and not the enforced ideal. People wanted freedom to think for themselves.

She wanted to be there in the thick of it, seeing for herself what was happening. She could stay again with the Praxiteles who lived in the Zografou suburb, or even with Eleni Vlachou at her apartment. Mrs Vlachou had promised to give her a tour of the seven storey newspaper offices in Omonia Square.

'Max, what are your plans for your future?'

He raised his head at this and frowned. '*Our* future, I hope, Nina.'

Andrew raised his eyes from his newspaper and regarded the couple intently when he heard this question. Nina regarded her two beloved men and felt a tide of impatience rise up in her. She knew her father still hoped against hope that now the couple were reunited, they would settle down with them in Downlands. As if Max could ever become a farmer or be idle all day. As if she, Nina Cassimatis, could ever be a placid housewife like Helen, happy to cook roast dinners and walk the grounds with the dogs.

'Yes, yes, our future. But what I mean is, have you decided what to do, what job to get? You *can* still go back to Ford's. They've kept the job open … or *a* job anyway.'

Max shook his head. 'I don't want to go to back. I'll think of something else.'

'You know you can stay here as long as you want,' Andrew said hopefully. He laid down his paper, ready to enter the argument he sensed might be coming. Helen continued to knit placidly, glancing up now and then to read the expressions on the faces before her but without any apparent interest in the outcome.

Max smiled.'Thanks, Andrew, but no, that wouldn't suit either myself or Nina. I know I speak for her too.' He glanced at his wife, who nodded vigorously.'The fact is I did have some plan in my head even before all this happened. The events at the

Trade Fair, the general state of things at Ford's just now have all led me to feel it's a peculiarly timely event. Unpleasant but timely.'

'So what's your plan?' asked Andrew in a tone of resignation. 'It's a bad time here just now, constant strikes, unemployment, recession looming. Wilson keeps trying to stave off devaluation but he'll have to give in eventually. Basically the country's in a mess. What will you do if you don't go back to Ford's?'

'I thought it would be an interesting experience to join my friend, Dimitri, in his little repair workshop. He always says he could do with a good mechanic. One of his guys left a short while ago and he'd be glad of the temporary help. Or maybe working for Basil in some way. I'm pretty good with accounts and stuff. Don't know anything about dry cleaning but I'll soon pick it up.'

Nina looked at him in surprise. 'You really want to go back, you want to live in Greece?'

'Well, not permanently. But for a year or so, perhaps. I love Thessaloniki. I'd love to go back there and be with my friends.' He sighed. 'But that's all changed now.'

'Why?' she asked eagerly. 'Why should it be? I also need to return to Greece, especially Athens where Aris and Stella live. You remember I told you about George Praxiteles? He's an economic student but he wants to go back home and finish his course there. His parents sent him over to London to keep him safe from this Fascist menace which they feel is always hovering in the background of Greek politics. But he's a brave boy. He wants to go home and help his friends in the Lambrakis Youth to carry on their work. It's becoming increasingly difficult for them but they are truly dedicated people. Oh, Max, the young are so vital in Greece! I admire their spirit. They are the only answer to those old men who are stuck in their ways, stuck in the past. The writer, Vasilis Vasilikos, you remember… . the one who wrote *Z* …He was right to call them "dinosaurs". They are. Men who want nothing to change at all and who see anything new as some sort of threat against them and their traditions, comforts and desire for power. They want to keep people stupid and poor.

That way they can recruit scum like that Katsarakis to help them, forming a sort of thuggish defence movement against democracy.'

Max's face showed some anxiety. Nina was always fighting causes. He too yearned for her to 'settle down' but he knew she never would any more than he ever would. It was in her blood, all this. Both her mother and grandmother had been the same, full of zeal, independent, untameable, unconventional. It was what he loved and hated about her.

Andrew also spoke now, his own face showing concern. 'Nina, this doesn't seem to me to be a very good time to go to Greece on missions. If what we hear from our friends is true, things are in a complete constitutional mess just now: constant riots, demands for elections and unrest everywhere. If you must, go as British citizens for a brief while. But don't get involved or start trying to get scoops and all that stuff. Reggie can do without it and lump it.'

Nina looked at him and pouted. '*Ade, Papa mou*! According to you it's always a bad time for anything. And you're the one who skipped Oxford to go to Greece almost as soon as you'd left school.'

Andrew smiled. 'You always win an argument,' he conceded,'by reminding me of my youthful folly.'

'But you don't regret it, right?'

'No, how *could* I regret it?'

He didn't add that then he wouldn't have met his Anna, conceived their beloved daughter. Not in front of Helen. But they all understood and for a moment silence reigned. Helen looked up again and her eyes narrowed as she regarded her husband. Max wondered what her true feelings were. She never showed any emotion over anything, always neat and precise and calm.

'But you promise to take care, both of you,' said Andrew after a little while during which they all listened to the steady clicking of Helen's knitting needles.

Nina smiled. 'All right,' she conceded. 'We'll just go over there and enjoy Greek Easter and see how the land lies. I promise to be good.'

'I'll make sure she is,' smiled Max and Andrew nodded but his face looked anxious.

Chapter 14

Thessaloniki: March 1967

'My feeling is that bastard Katsarakis is hiding around Toumba somewhere,' Dimitri said to his wife.

Yiota looked up from her ironing and stared at her husband. 'So what? Let him lie low. Who cares? Max is in England now and safe from the man.'

'I want to find him and have him turned over to the police,' said Dimitri. His dark stubbled chin was set in the intractable look Yiota knew by heart.

'You know very well the police are more likely to turn you in. He has friends in high places, like all these crooks. Leave it alone, Dimi. Types like him get their come-uppance in the end. Don't get involved.'

'I have friends too. And if the police won't sort him out, they will.'

Yiota put the iron down with a bang. 'Dimi, please!' she pleaded, 'don't get into this. It'll be dangerous.'

'Maybe. But what you women never understand is that this is a matter of honour. Max is a *xeni*, a foreigner, a guest. We can't have him treated like shit by a low criminal like Katsarakis. Men like this need to be shown up if there is any sort of justice in this country. I agree there isn't much. But even our crooked lot of police must know this could become an international incident.'

'So – they'll hush it up, you idiot. You won't get justice here.'

Dimitri shrugged and capitulated. 'Okay, true. But I feel bad. My blood calls for revenge.'

'I feel bad too,' said his wife, much relieved by his sudden change of tone though still doubtful. 'But what can we do? That's how it is. We need to keep out of trouble these days. Things are getting worse, not better.'

Dimitri walked up to a gate set in a tall, stolid wooden fence. It had a strong security lock but he knew the combination and after he tapped it in, the gate swung open and he walked through. Once inside, he found himself in a yard littered with car parts and other pieces of machinery. Round the back in what had once been a garden filled with fig and almond trees, were rows of shiny, well-cared-for vintage cars. The high fence ran around the perimeter of the house and garden, keeping prying eyes away and certainly not welcoming any intruders. He went up to the house, turned the handle of the glass door with its rusting ironwork grille and walked in. Somewhere in the house a voice on the radio was wailing a song against a strident bouzouki. Not one of his favourite singers. He liked serious stuff, the sort that composers like Theodorakis wrote. Like '*Epitafios*', that sublime poem by Yiannis Ritsos, set to music, written to commemorate the dead heroes. He liked music that meant something and moved his heart deeply.

Big Bouros was taking a shower in the cement floored room beyond. Dimitri hadn't seen the man for some time and was appalled to see how enormous he had become. Always large, the man's flesh had now expanded on all sides, the drooping folds of his belly hanging right down to a huge scrotum the size of a large orange. On top of this monstrous body was a small head, the hair now thinning and grey. Big Bouros turned and grinned when he saw Dimitri.

'Eh, my friend, I wasn't expecting you just yet. Getting ready for my girlfriend, she'll be round soon as she can get her husband out of the way for a bit. Go into my office while I dress. I won't take long.'

Dimitri obeyed and sat down on a large empty wooden box that served as a seat, contemplating the idea of the sort of woman who would want Big Bouros as a lover. It was hard to imagine. He looked around at the office which was piled high with boxes, spare parts, and stacks of papers. Dimitri was a tidy man and the muddle and chaos offended his sense of rightness.

After a brief while, Bouros came into the office, dressed in loose trousers and a large grey cotton sweatshirt, rubbing his ears and hair with a towel. He flung the towel aside and sat in the one decent chair at his desk.

'Good to see you, Dimitri! How's things with you?'

'Eh, good enough. Business is picking up despite the political uncertainty about these days. No one wants to commit themselves to anything let alone a new car so they're flocking to people like me to glue together their old bangers for a bit longer. And you?'

'Well, I do fine. People always want to have the sort of cars I specialise in. They're status symbols. Collectors want to have'em and show off. I love my cars. Hard to part with them. But needs must.'

Bouros specialised in American cars and fixed them with the help of a couple of young men he had rescued from the streets. The two men lived at the back of the house and shared a room. They also shared the cooking between them but mainly went out to a *cafeneion* to eat. Dimitri asked how they were getting on.

'I've trained them up,' Bouros told him.'They've proved to be good lads, loyal to me. And they're talented too – become great mechanics now, the pair of them – and they keep an eye on things. I've had a couple of break-ins but they soon sort out anyone stupid enough to try anything on. Just as well, I'm not up to all that rough stuff any more. My health is crap.'

Bouros was a kind man and despite the suffering he obviously felt in his joints when he moved, his face was always cheerful. Dimitri felt sorry for him. His condition was strange. He had begun to pile on weight like this after an asthma attack some years ago; it was certainly not due to greediness over food. The poor man scarcely ate anything in an effort to keep his weight down.

'They say it's oedema,' he sighed. 'I retain fluid and those damned doctors put me on diuretics. It made me pee every ten minutes, drove me mad. But I lost eight stone.'

Dimitri viewed him with amazement. He'd lost eight stone and still looked massive. Poor fellow. It was a marvel he could move at all.

'You want a beer, a coffee?' Bouros asked. 'I can send one of the boys for something.'

'No, no, don't trouble. I wanted a word with you, that's all. Bouros, I need your help,' said Dimitri, 'you know a lot of people, all sorts of characters. I need to try and find Manos Katsarakis. Can you ask around and see if anyone knows anything.'

Big Bouros looked at Dimitri with a shrewd eye` . 'He's the one who nearly murdered your English friend. You want the bastard killed?'

'Well, no …' admitted Dimitri, 'but I'd like to give him a regular beating. Teach him a lesson.'

'He'd make mincemeat of a little chap like you, no offence.'

'Maybe I'll surprise you. I want to get a boot in at least, the first blow,' said Dimitri grimly. 'Your boys can break his legs for him. But we have to find him first. Thing is, where?'

Big Bouros gave it thought. 'His *koumbaros* might help with a little persuasion. His best man is bound to know where he is, eh? A brother in all but blood, one's *koumbaros.* Glad I never married, myself. No desire for a blood brother or any other sort of brother.'

'It's a thought. Can I leave it with you?'

'Sure. We'll ask around and let you know.'

'Okay. I'll leave you to your … girlfriend, then.'

Big Bouros' face broke into a happy smile. 'She likes big men, she does; likes feeling squashed and having her head rammed against the bed head – so she says.'

'Right,' said Dimitri. He would have preferred not to have this image to take with him but still, he was glad someone was prepared to give the poor fellow pleasure. Even the girls up the Monastir road would have had second thoughts. Bouros had little enough besides his cars and his money. The house was a tip; it looked like a half-constructed building. Dimitri remembered that it was once a neat little dwelling when the widowed mother was still alive. And Bouros was a good-looking, slim young man. Life played some nasty tricks on people.

It felt good to be back in Thessaloniki. And it was even better now because this time Nina was here with him. Max savoured his happiness and found himself like a young lover again, constantly looking at her, wanting to touch, make love to her. They were staying with Basil and Athina at the moment but intended to rent a little apartment in the city as soon as they could.

'I love being with our friends but it would be nice to have our own space,' said Nina as they walked along the promenade one afternoon. The sea breeze ruffled her loosened hair and she shook it out into its teasing playfulness and laughed with joy. 'Oh, I love it here; love the blue of the sea and the sky. Love the light and the shadows. Just look at those birds, Max!'

An enormous flock of raucous white gulls came flying high over the housetops and circled about the bay several times before disappearing again in the direction of the docks. They stopped and watched them, then joined hands again and walked on.

'I love it all too, but I love it most that you're here with me, my little Nina,' Max said, swinging her hand up and down as they walked along.

'We're like children again,' Nina laughed. 'But don't you agree, Max? It will be nice to have room to write and read in peace, eat when we want and eat what we like. I need to gather my ideas and it's not easy with two youngsters, lovely as they both are, constantly wanting to be amused and noticed.'

'They're only kids. Yiannakis is no bother. He's a quiet lad.'

'Neither of them is a bother, I love them both. I just want us to be together on our own.'

'Ah, with that I agree.' He stopped and turned to face her, gather her in his arms. 'Nina, my darling, you can count on me.

I never want another woman but you, ever again. Playing around was a habit, I guess, having been footloose and fancy free for so many years. But losing you was terrible. I realised then how much I loved you and needed you. I don't want to lose you again.'

'I don't want you to be *too* possessive!' she laughed. 'But I'm so happy to hear your promise. I was terribly jealous. I never thought I'd feel that way. It's frightening how quickly that nasty feeling arose, choked me almost, made me blind with rage. That scared me. I always thought myself a rational being. And it's been miserable without you. I missed you so much.'

'I hope so. I hope you missed me even half as much as I missed you. Never again.'

They kissed for a long time, much to the interest of other promenaders who were strolling along. Then they went on arm in arm, feeling contented.

'I'd love to live in an apartment here,'said Nina, 'somewhere overlooking the sea. But it will be expensive. Athina's promised to help me find something tomorrow. Any preferences?'

'I'm not bothered. You find a place you like. As long as it's not too far from Laladika.'

'You need to be near Dimitri's workshop?'

'If possible.'

'But that's near the port.'

'I mean – don't go miles out to Karabournaki or Kalamaria.'

'I'll find somewhere nice and cheap and near the centre. Neither of us is earning just now. We'll have to cut our coat accordingly.'

Athina and Nina went apartment searching the next day and found a beautiful top floor apartment to let. It was in the old and famous Agia Sofias square, one of the large blocks of old flats that faced the ancient church. It had large French windows that opened onto a balcony overlooking the street below and was high enough to see right over the rooftops to the sea itself. Max was glad to see how happy Nina looked as she pottered about the flat, rearranging furniture, setting out her little office with a typewriter and a stack of paper and carbons. She meant business, he could tell. In fact she seemed quite enthused about the stories she meant to write.

'I really want to go to Athens soon,' she said, 'I want to talk to George Praxiteles and his family and some of the boys and girls who belong to the Lambrakides. I want to tell the world how they are helping to mould a new Greece, fighting against tyranny, injustice and oppression.'

'Must you go so soon?'

'Of course, now is the time. I feel something in the air but can't put my finger on it. Something is going to change, hopefully for the better. But I want to be in the thick of it. I've chosen to be a journalist, Max dearest. I have to follow my nose for a good story. Plus we need some money,' she added with a laugh.

'I know, nor would I want to stop you. You're very talented Nina, I'm proud of you. I'm enjoying helping Dimitri at his workshop but he can't afford to pay me any official wages..'

Nina nodded. She knew that Max couldn't obtain a Citizen's Certificate which would enable him to work. But Max had his driver's license and passport as ID which was something.

'It's a problem,' she agreed. 'They're hot on that sort of thing here. It's a damn nuisance about that £50 limit on taking cash abroad, How on earth will we manage?'

Max grinned. 'I brought four £50 notes hidden in the hollow heels of my shoes.'

'You didn't!'

'I certainly did. It's my money and to hell with Harold Wilson and his idiotic policies. Plus, Basil has offered to lend us some cash till we can move our money abroad again. I have some savings put by for the moment; it'll last the year. And you'll be earning a bit with your articles and stories which we can save in our account back home for when we return.'

Nina laughed. 'You're getting good at this,' she remarked. 'You'll be joining MI5 at this rate. It is annoying but things are tough everywhere. And there's always something miserable going on in Britain. At least, here in Greece, we have the sun, the sea and cheerful company. A little *psaraki*, a little *raki* and we're happy. Hopefully we won't need to go back too soon, eh, Max? We both love it here so much.'

'I love it as much as you, Nina, but we can't stay forever. You could, I suppose. But you don't want to abandon me again?' He smiled as he said this, half-joking, but Nina sensed his anxiety. She drew him to her and hugged him. 'Never, ever again, Maxaki *mou*!'

His face cleared and he smiled with his usual cheerful manner. 'We can always return again, rent a place when we come back, spend half our time here. When I'm back in England, I'll think of something to do, maybe open up my own garage workshop. It's good to mess about with cars again like I used to so … I hated the sales manager role. I like to get my hands on good bodywork.'

'So I notice,' said Nina dryly.

Max gathered her in his arms. 'Especially such glorious female bodywork. Put that damned pen down. You're always clutching a pen or a phone. Put it down and kiss me instead.'

Nina laughed and obediently let the pen she was holding fall to the floor. It was followed by her dress, then her undergarments, until she stood naked and exquisite before him and he laughingly picked her up and carried her towards the bedroom to investigate the bodywork.

Chapter 15

Thessaloniki: Problems from the past

Dimitri was busy at his workshop, polishing up a Volkswagon that a client had brought in the other day for servicing; a very up-to-date, beautiful blue notchback. He stood back and regarded his shining handiwork with pride. He could see what Big Bouros meant when he said it was hard to part with a real beauty of a car. He would love to afford a car like this, take the family out on excursions to the countryside. They could all pile in there, with room for *yiayia* too.

His young trainee mechanic, Tinos, was working at a bench and gave him a shout. 'Someone's coming, boss!' Dimitri looked up as a young man appeared at the workshop entrance and looked around for him. He recognised him as one of the young fellows that worked for Big Bouros. Putting down his buffer and wiping his hands on his overalls, he came over to greet him. Thankfully Max hadn't come in to help today but was round at Basil's place. He didn't want his friend to know about his search for Katsarakis. It was far better that he didn't.

'*Kalimera, Kyrie* Dimitri.'

'*Kalimera,* Savva. What news have you got? Have you found him?'

'Oh yes. We found him hiding in a deserted old building near the dump where Yianni Fotos, his *koumbaros*, lives. Seems Yianni sends over his wife, Eleni, with food every night and she cleans his clothes and stuff. But as they always do, they've become careless. They think things look safe and Katsarakis has been seen round his old gambling haunts and favourite tavernas again. None of his cronies are likely to report him to the police – who've washed their hands of him anyway. Especially as the Englishman hasn't pressed charges.'

'No, but Cassimatis made a fuss all right.'

'He may have done. But it's all forgotten, isn't it? More important things for the police to worry about just now with all these riots and protests.'

'Just as well. It suits us if they don't bother about him. Let's go round tonight and surprise our friend Katasarakis, shall we? If the police won't do anything, we'll mete out our own justice. Give him as good as he gave my friend. Let him have *his* jaw and ribs broken.'

Some days later, a young woman with short-cropped curly dark hair, large sunglasses, wearing a tight, black knee-length skirt and simple white top came up to the garage door. Dimitri looked up from his work in surprise.

'Can I help you, *Despinis*?'

She stepped into the cool darkness of the shop where smells of oil and petrol mingled in a delightful mixture. Delightful to a mechanic anyway. The young woman wrinkled her nose a little and made a little noise of disgust as she picked her way towards him through discarded tyres and bits of machinery that lay on the cement floor. She looked slim and attractive and Dimitri eyed her appreciatively.

'I'm looking for *Kyrie* Max Hammett. A friend told me he works here with you?'

'He comes and help me now and then. He'll be here tomorrow.'

'I need to see him today. I have to go back home tomorrow. Where's he staying?'

'He's renting a place on Agia Sofias Square.'

'Can you give me the address?'

Dimitri hesitated. Who was this woman? He couldn't see her eyes screened by the smoky sunglasses but he felt one of his prickles in the nape of his neck that told him something wasn't right.

'Well, I'll give you his phone number. You can contact him and tell him your business, *Despinis*...?'

She didn't give her name, just smiled. Something about her was vaguely familiar but Dimitri couldn't place her at all. Was this some secret mistress that Max had omitted to mention? Dimitri grinned at the thought. Best not let Nina find out. She'd murder Max.

'All right. Let me have his number. Is he here for long? '

'Well, just for a while. Like a sort of change – a holiday. He's been through some unpleasant experiences.'

The woman's face fell. 'What ... what sort of unpleasant things?'

'He got beaten up by a stupid brute who broke his ribs and his jaw. For no fault of his own. That sort of thing. The nice things that happen in Greece these days.'

She put her hand to her mouth. 'Christ and the Virgin! The *poor* man. Let me have his number, let me speak to him.'

Dimitri went to his office and wrote the number on a piece of paper. She followed him and, looking around her almost fearfully, said, 'Can I use your phone, ring from here?'

It came to him then in a flash. 'You're Zoë Katsarakis!'

She went very pale and snatching the piece of paper from him, shut the office door and said, 'Shhh ... don't say that name. No, don't even say it! I'm Zoë Georgiou now. *He* may hear ... I swear he's a man who knows everything.'

Dimitri leant back against a filing cabinet and surveyed her.

'He's not going to bother anyone for a long time, *Kyria* Zoë,' he said softly, 'just now he's stuck indoors with his beloved *koumbaros* and his wife, nursing his own broken ribs.'

Zoë took off her dark glasses and stared at him. She was prettier now that she had rid herself of the straggly locks of dyed blonde hair and pasty make-up: plumper, healthier, less anxious and hollow-cheeked than before.

'Did Max beat him up?' she asked with great satisfaction.

'No. As a matter of fact, I did.'

'You?' She surveyed the small wiry man before her with disbelief.

'Eh well, with the help of a couple of friends,' Dimitri admitted. 'You know what Englishmen are like. Max didn't want to pursue it. For your sake mainly. He didn't want to start any more trouble. Best to let it go, he said. But I wasn't going to do that. It's *filotimo*, you know … honour. Max is my good friend.'

'Then I thank you, *Kyrie* Dimitri,' said Zoë simply. 'I thank you for avenging your friend and my saviour. You're a *palikari* – a good man. Please let me use your phone.'

Dimitri shrugged. 'Use it if you must. But take care, his wife's here in Greece with him now. She doesn't take kindly to other women, a jealous lady. And don't tell him about my work on Katsarakis. I don't think he'll like it.'

'I won't. I just want to speak to him, to thank him again.'

'Hmm … well, make it snappy.'

As good luck had it, Nina was out shopping when Zoë called. Max was amazed to hear that Zoë was in the city and not too pleased either.

'What the hell are you doing here? You know it's not safe to come back.'

'Oh, *Kyrie* Max,' she quavered, 'You've no idea how boring it is up north. Florina is beautiful but I miss the city, you know, I miss the city life, the streets, the cars. I longed to see a couple of my friends.'

'I thought you didn't have any friends?'

'I have one or two girl friends from way back. They're good girls, they won't give me away.'

'I hope you didn't tell them where you live now.'

'Not really. I sort of did. It's all right. They won't say a word.'

'I wouldn't trust anyone if I were you. You're such a foolish girl, Zoë.'

'Please don't be angry with me.'

As always his heart softened towards her. 'I'm not angry, Zoë. Just worried you'll get in more trouble with that lovely husband of yours.'

'I was a bit scared at first but thought it would be okay as someone said he'd gone back to Crete. When someone said he was seen back here, I was terrified but, thank God, he can't bother me for a while now he's been seen to.'

'What d'you mean? Have the police got him?'

'No, no …' she checked herself, remembering her promise to Dimitri. 'I mean… I hear he's been beaten up, that's all.'

Max was not surprised by this news. 'He's bound to get his comeuppance some day from one of his enemies. Men of his sort always do. Where is he? In hospital?'

'No, he's lying low with his *koumbaros* in Toumba.'

'Let's hope he stays there and doesn't cause more trouble. Anyway, you sound well. Better get back to your farm, eh? Before Katsarakis resurfaces and someone gives you away.'

'But I wanted to see you again. Can't we meet for a coffee? I could come to your apartment.'

'Are you mad? Not a good idea, Zoë. My wife will be back any minute and she doesn't take to my having coffees with unknown ladies. Forget me. Go back to Florina and keep away from the city.'

'Oh, just a coffee, *Kyrie* Max. Anyway, I don't have the fare back to Florina.'

Max sighed. 'Ah, I see. You're after some money, are you? And I thought it was my fantastic good looks.'

Zoë giggled. 'That too. I *would* so like to see you. But yes, I do need some money for the bus fare. I swear I'll return it as soon as I earn again. Just a loan, you know.'

'Yeah, yeah. So why couldn't your friends help you?'

'They're always stone broke, like me,' she sighed.

'You're hopeless, Zoë, you really are. Okay, we'll meet so I can lend you some cash. Stopping for coffee is too dangerous. We'll be spotted by someone nosy for sure. *Don't* hang around this city. Katsarakis may be out of commission but he has friends who'll recognise you and tell him. Especially if they spot us together. That's my advice, You're real trouble, you know that? And don't get in touch with me any more. I have no yearning to get my jaw broken again. I'd rather you didn't, Zoë.'

'But I'll be sad if we never meet again,' she replied with a little catch in her voice. 'I will be so sad.'

'Sometimes you just have to let go of the past, let go of people,' he replied, 'however much you like them and want to keep them in your life. People accumulate like possessions. And frankly, Zoë, you and your fellow are not possessions I want to keep in my life. Where are you speaking from now?'

'At your friend Dimitri's garage.'

Max was silent for a moment. 'How did you know I might be there?'

'*Ade kale*, everyone knows Dimitri and know he is a buddy of yours. Maria, my good friend, said she'd seen you helping him at his workshop so I knew you were back in Thessaloniki. I was so glad.'

'Your friends should mind their own business,' said Max grimly. 'Meet me at the Agia Sofia church, in the garden, and I'll give you the money, anything to get rid of you. I'll give you half an hour.'

It was one of those peculiar synchronicities that makes one feel some sadistic god has been reading a Thomas Hardy novel. Nina was not especially religious but, as she began to walk home from her little shopping expedition down Tsimiski, she came to Agia Sofias Square and felt a sudden wish to enter the cool interior of the beautiful old church. She remembered pictures her grandfather had shown her of the time when this venerable building was made into a mosque under Turkish rule. Thessaloniki was then called Salonika and was an important thriving city, mainly run by the Jewish population. The Turks had tolerated their religion as 'people of the book' and the Jews fleeing from Spanish persecution in the fifteenth century came there to settle, flourish and prosper, found libraries, schools and synagogues. Fifty five thousand of those poor souls had been lined up in this very square in 1942, publicly humiliated, then taken away by the Nazis to be gassed in Polish concentration camps. Very few Jews lived here now and that kindly harbour for Hispanic Jews, the 'Pearl of Israel' was no more. Agia Sofias

Square was the place where the service of thanksgiving was held when Greece was at last liberated from the Germans on November 2nd 1944. The area resonated with history.

Now, the minaret had long been removed and the old church almost restored to its former beauty. It was said to be even older than the great Agia Sofia in Constantinople and had been badly damaged by a fire in 1890, mauled in air raids, earthquakes and other disasters. Yet the church still stood there, its little garden filled with pines and palm trees, retaining its peace and beauty despite everything modern man could fling at it. There were still frescoes and mosaics to be found beneath the whitewash that covered the damp and ancient walls but progress seemed slow and only a few had so far been uncovered.

Nina was surprised at her sudden urge to go inside and look around. She wanted to light a candle and make a little prayer. As she did this, crossing herself devoutly, she thought with a smile that these things instilled in childhood were buried deep and never quite went away. Innocent, gentle rituals. Making the sign of the cross over one's chest brought attention and consciousness to the heart. Thinking with love of others, praying for their good. Greece was said to be the first European area to become Christian and was still a deeply religious country. The old Orthodox ceremonies and rituals marked the passing of the year, instilling a rhythm to life that was lacking in many other more secular countries. In England nature was fast being abandoned in favour of industrialisation. It would become the same here no doubt.

She loved both her countries. But she was more Greek than her father. She had been born here and lived in Thessaloniki till she was about seven years old, whereas he had been born and brought up in Gloucestershire till he was well into his teens. It made a difference. Besides, he was more English by temperament, being closer to his mother. She was definitely more Greek. Interesting that she had never wanted to marry a Greek though. Englishmen on the whole made better husbands. Much more courteous and considerate.

Having lit her candles and made a prayer, Nina sat for a

little while in silence, looking around her at the remnants of geometric patterns around the arches, left from the Muslim days. Ikons gleaming with silver filled the nooks and walls and huge chandeliers swooped down from the curved dome still covered with whitewash. But she knew that below that pallid covering was a vibrant image of the *Pantocrator* looking down upon her from His heavenly vault encircled by the apostles, just as there was in other Orthodox domes. Here He was hidden from mortal view but He was there all the same. It seemed symbolic, somehow. She felt an incredible sense of peace and love.

In a little while, she rose, collected her bags and began to make her way out into the bright sunshine beyond. For a moment the light dazzled her and she stopped to put on her sunglasses. She then paused, astonished, wondering if it was a mirage. There was Max strolling through the gate into the gardens laid out before the church where he now was looking around him. Her heart leapt. How did he know she would be here and at this time? How amazing!

She laughed aloud with joy and was about to call out to him when a young, slim girl wearing large sunglasses and a wide brimmed sun hat, arose from her seat on a low wall and walked towards Max. They began to talk earnestly and she saw Max slip something into the girl's pocket. Nina moved herself out of their vision and watched from behind a large bush. Just in time it seemed, for now her errant husband glanced up and looked around with a furtive air, as if afraid of being seen. The girl rose on tiptoe and kissed Max on the lips and for a brief moment, he responded. Then after a few more words, he moved away and walked swiftly out of the gate. The girl looked after him. He turned a little and she waved but he did not wave back.

Nina was stunned. Who was this girl? What was Max up to and what had he just given to her? A phone number?

The girl had seated herself down on the wall again and was calmly smoking a cigarette. Nina walked over to her and sat beside her.

'Who are you?'

Startled, the girl jumped in her skin and stared back. She seemed afraid.

Maybe she knows who I am, thought Nina. *Good.*

The girl made no reply but instead dropped her cigarette and rose to leave.

'Oh no, you don't,' said Nina, laying a hand on the girl's arm and restraining her. Her tone was stern and commanding. The girl sat down again and Nina saw that she was trembling.

'Who are *you*?' she whispered.

'I am Nina Hammett. *That* was my husband you just met. He gave you something. I want to know what is going on between you two.'

A look of relief came over the girl's face. 'Oh, Max's wife, eh? It's okay. Nothing is "going on". He's helping me, that's all.'

'Indeed?' said Nina, her voice cold as ice. 'In what way?'

'Giving me money,' said Zoë simply.

'Money! For services rendered, I suppose?' Nina was furious. All her peace and love had disappeared the moment she saw Max greet this girl. She wanted to strangle the creature. Young and pretty. Obviously desirable. Obviously a tart.

Zoë's mouth puckered into a pout of dislike at Nina's scathing tone, full of the assumption that she was some cheap call girl. Her own face hardened now and her little chin went into the air.

'Yes!' she said angrily. 'Yes! If that's what you want to believe. For services rendered. He took me to a hotel and we spent the night together. Make what you will of that, Mrs High and Mighty. No wonder he wants to leave a bitch like you.'

She now rose and made good her escape while Nina sat there, stunned and ashen.

'But why? Why are you leaving for Athens right now? What's happened?'

Max was in shock. Nina had burst into their apartment and was now flinging her clothes into a suitcase, gathering up her papers, camera, tape recorder and other items. She refused to speak to him.

He went up to her and tried to take her by the arm but she flung him aside with such a look of fury and contempt that he recoiled. His heart sank. Somehow she had found out about Zoë and was thinking the worst. What else could it be?

'Look, Nina, would you just stop for a few moments and tell me why you're so mad at me? Maybe I can explain.'

'*Explain*! Oh, you can always explain things, Max, always use your charm and your lies. But this time it won't work. I *saw* you with this woman. She told me you were lovers. So nothing's changed and all that stuff about loving only me, always being true to me from now on … it was all rubbish. All lies.'

Damn Zoë. He knew she'd be trouble. What the hell had the stupid girl being saying?

'I don't know how you and Zoë met …'

'Oh, Zoë! That's your tart's name, is it?'

'Her name is Zoë Katsarakis. She's the wife of that bastard who nearly killed me.'

Nina paused now and stared at Max for a moment as this registered. Her face stormy, she resumed her packing. 'Frankly, I don't blame him. Now I understand, now I see what all that business was about. I thought it was strange, a random attack like that. But mess with a Cretan's wife and you're asking for it. You're so stupid, Max.'

'Look.' Max was desperate and he took her forcefully by her arms now and turned her to look at him but she refused to look. Refused to meet his eyes.

'Zoë was being beaten up by her husband. I tried to defend her. She came running to me one evening covered in blood and asking my help. I couldn't refuse and let him kill her, Nina, could I?'

'Why not? It was their business,' she said stubbornly. 'You're always interfering.'

'For goodness sake! Have you no compassion … no feeling or pity for another woman in terror? I've told you before. That's how Dad treated my mother. I won't, can't stand by and see a woman mistreated.'

'Then let me go. You're hurting my arms.'

He let her go and turned away in despair.

'Nina, Nina. Don't do this to me again. I messed about with just one woman since we married. I said I was sorry. I swore I wouldn't do so again. And I haven't. Why can't you believe me?'

'She said you took her to a hotel room. You wanted your payment, I suppose, your payment for helping her. That's all men ever think of – how they can get inside a woman's knickers. That's all *you* ever think of ...' She was white with fury and totally unreasonable. It was useless. It was never going to work. The rational, warm, wise Nina could turn in these moments to a fiend of cold jealousy and hate. Max sighed and leant his forehead against the door post.

'If you can't trust my word but believe this girl instead, there's nothing I can say or do,' he said. 'I sometimes think you have no heart, Nina. Greece is all you care about. Abstract ideals ... not human beings with all their muddle and complexities and failings. You are above us all.' He walked out of the room and left her to her sullen packing. Slamming the door behind him he went off for a walk, anywhere, he didn't care. Anywhere. It wasn't the first time. But it *would* be the last.

Nina paused in her packing as the door shut behind him. For a moment her heart stopped. She wanted to run after him and say she was sorry. But then the memory of that girl in Agias Sofias came back to her, the memory of the one in London too, that girl's hateful voice telling her all about their tawdry love affair in every salacious detail. And she hardened her heart again and turned back to the suitcase on the bed.

Chapter 16

We have a sick patient here. We must decide how soon he will be able to walk and when we should remove the plaster cast. But if we decide the patient needs more plaster, we will give it to him.

Colonel George Papadopoulos' remarks on Greece in 1968

Athens: 3.00 am April 21st 1967

Something was very wrong. She woke up and listened intently. There it was again, the sound of heavy solid wheels rumbling in the distance, but what wheel made a noise like that? Nina looked at the clock by her bed and the luminous hands said 3.00am. She sat up and stared into the darkness, broken only by the faint light that crept through the slats of the shutters. Her heart was beating with a mixture of alarm and excitement.

She rose, her throat parched and dry. Swallowing some water from the glass by her bed, she made her way over to the window. Pulling back the thickly pleated net curtains, Nina threw open the shutters and leant out into the coolness of an April night. Just a few hours earlier she had been chatting in a café with some friends; a normal and peaceful Athenian night. Now a strange atmosphere gripped the city, a sense of panic, anger and dismay. Shouts, strident voices and shrieks floated on the night air. She needed to find out what was happening. The commotion was round Vassileis Sofias, a main road some way beyond where the Praxiteles family owned a small block of apartments in a quiet back street in Zografou.

Stella and Aris Praxiteles lived in the ground floor flat. Their son,George, who had now returned from England, had vacated his own room for her as she was an 'honoured guest' and was sleeping on a sofa bed in the dining room. Above them was an apartment let out to a young couple and above this was another apartment in the process of being built, steel girders sticking up in the air and rubble and masonry everywhere. A typical sight on the Athenian skyline. This was to be the dowry of the Praxiteles' daughter, Lexi.

Hurriedly Nina dressed, flung on a jacket and seized her Leika camera. She had no idea what was going on but her instinct told her that the unusual hubbub was due to some major crisis. A fire? No, not that – there were no fire alarms or church bells ringing the tocsin. It sounded for all the world as if huge vehicles such as tanks were rumbling along.

It had long been rumoured in political circles that the King intended to enforce some kind of military law and disband his Parliament. Greece had been filled with unrest for so long. First the war with Turkey and Bulgaria, then the First World War, so soon followed by the Second War when Greece was occupied and half starved to death. Then the Civil War and the interference by the British and Americans. The foreign powers treated Greece as if it was of no account except as a buffer against the Red tide they saw sweeping them all away.

What was this deep fear in everyone's hearts? Yes, there were communists in Greece and many others who veered to the left like herself, but they were small in numbers; nothing like the threat imagined. But fear is like a virus, spreading to everyone. Stories of communist terrorism, half-imagined, became reality in the minds of the comfortable middle classes, fuelled by the propaganda of the extreme right who spread tales of *paidomazoma* – the supposed kidnapping of children for brainwashing into communism – tortures, massacres to strike fear and loathing in people's hearts. Nina knew that old Queen Frederica believed all these stories as did so many other people.

And the Queen influenced her son, Constantine, all the time, a powerful, stubborn woman who believed in the supreme right of the monarchy to do as it would. Imaginary enemies seemed almost a necessity to human beings. Perhaps it stemmed from some ancient sense of anxiety when men walked like apes and the nights were full of unknown terrors. But surely now, a little civilised rational thought, a little toleration would be so much more effective than this horrified gut reaction towards anything new and different.

If she could take some pictures, what a scoop that would be! She would take them straight round to the *Kathimerini* offices in Socrates Street where Aris Praxiteles worked as a typesetter. He was there now, working through the night to get the morning papers out in time. Then she would cable the news to Reggie in London.

Throwing on a light coat and her sandals, Nina slipped out of her room, made her way to the front door and out into the marbled entrance hall to the flats. She ran silent and swift towards the source of the clamour. At the corner of one of the streets that led into Vassileis Sofias, she stopped in sheer amazement. Huge armoured tanks were rolling past. So she was right, that *was* the noise she had heard. There seemed to be armed soldiers everywhere, shouting commands in deep, harsh tones, stopping cars, pointing guns at ordinary, unarmed people as if they were involved in a film, in a mock battle. It was all pretence, surely? It couldn't be real. Not Athens on a quiet night before Easter? There had been no warning at all, nothing of late to indicate that simmering beneath the surface were plots and counter-plots and discontented, power-hungry individuals ready to enforce their own version of the law. She snapped away with her camera, taking care not to be seen. Those soldiers looked unpleasant and she didn't want to get mixed up with them.

She tried to make her way to Syntagma Square but it was obvious that she would never get through. There were no taxis in sight and the roads were swiftly being blocked. The police stood around looking bewildered, unsure what to do. They made no resistance because, on the face of it, it was the Greek army in control and presumably set in motion by the King himself. So they stood passive and waiting. Those few people who argued or demanded to know what was going on were pushed aside and roughly handled. Suddenly the individual was of no consequence or importance. It was as if a huge grinding machine was set in motion that crushed down in its monstrous path any foolish souls caught in its cogs and wheels.

A soldier with a gun in his arms turned and stared in her direction. She hastily slipped back into the shadows, praying he wouldn't come looking for her. It felt frightening all of a sudden and her heart pounded in her chest, knees shaking a little. This was the first time she had been faced with anything as menacing as this in her sheltered life. Aghast, Nina slipped back to the Praxiteles apartment as quietly as she had gone. As she entered the front door, she met Stella Praxiteles in her dressing gown, fumbling for the light switch in the hallway.

'What's going on, Nina?' she asked fearfully.

'I have no idea. There are army tanks and cars and soldiers everywhere. They're pushing innocent citizens out of the way and I've heard shots. No idea who they are shooting or if they are simply warning shots. I couldn't even get down to Syntagma, I was too scared to try. I suspect it might be the King making his much threatened coup.'

'A coup? In the middle of the night? Tanks, soldiers? This is Athens. Haven't we had enough unrest and trouble! Why does the King want to do all this? What does he hope to achieve?'

Lexi appeared now, rubbing her eyes and looking bewildered.

'Why are you all up? Has something happened to Papa?'

'No, my child, Papa is at work, he's fine. But Nina says that some sort of *putsch* is taking place.' Stella put her arm around her daughter and hugged her tight. Lexi was a nervous young woman of eighteen who was prone to hysterics when she was afraid. Her lips quivered now. Nina also hastened to reassure her.

'It's nothing to worry about, Lexi. It all looks controlled and no one is doing anything crazy. It's just so weird, so organised and sudden.'

'I wish Aris was home,' said Stella. 'Shall we wake up George?'

'No, better leave the boy alone. He's probably sleeping through it all like a lot of people. They'll be in for a big surprise in the morning. I'm such a light sleeper that I immediately picked up something odd about the usual night sounds, something different in the atmosphere. I could hear the rumbling noise in my dreams though it was some way off.'

Lexi began to shiver with cold and they sent her back to bed with reassurances that all was well and she was not to worry at all. The two women made themselves cups of coffee. As they sat down in the kitchen, silent and uneasy, they heard George in the hallway. He put his head round the door and stared at them.

'There's something peculiar going on,' he said. 'I thought I heard you all up. I was woken by a lot of shouts. Any idea what's happening?'

'I was just going to ring Aris at the *Kathimerini* to see if they have some news ready,' said Stella. 'They're sure to know what's going on out there.'

She went into the hallway to do this while George poured himself a cup of black coffee and strode around the room with it. He looked troubled.

'When Mother's finished on the phone, I'll try my friend Alekis. He may have heard something. He's a good friend of Theodorakis and has been helping with the newspaper they send out. He will know what's going on.'

Stella came back. She looked worried. 'I can't get hold of the newspaper offices. It's as if the line's not available. Do you think they've cut the lines or something? Oh, Nina, I'm afraid for Aris. I hope they're not in trouble over there.'

'*Kyria* Vlachou will be there, I'm sure,'said Nina soothingly. 'She's a really sensible, calm lady who doesn't panic. I expect they're working very hard to get the paper out with all this news. I feel so frustrated not being able to run over there to talk to someone. I took a lot of pictures though,' she added with satisfaction. 'Soon as I get the chance to get out safely, I'm sending them to London. I'll try Reggie later, when we get some more news from Aris. Even if he is in bed. It will be such a scoop!'

George went off to ring his friend Alekis and was away a long time.

He returned after a while and sat down, staring at the floor.

'What is it, George? What news have you heard?' Stella asked, pouring him another cup of coffee. He stirred in sugar and drank it absentmindedly. Looking up at last he said, 'They've taken some of our leaders away and cut their phone lines. No one really knows about Alekis being involved so he's okay for now but he plans to hide somewhere till it all blows over.' He looked up at them, his face young and frightened. 'Alekis says it isn't safe for any of us any more. He thinks they'll beat our friends till they talk about us all. Theodorakis is on the run. Oh God ... what should I do?'

'Surely they won't arrest you?' said his mother but her hand trembled so much that Nina took the cup from her and set it on the table.

'Oh, they will,' said George bitterly, 'if they're on the King's side, they will. His mother loathes Lambrakis and all who represent his movement. Remember when Lambrakis tried to talk to her when she was in London on a visit, that stupid visit? He wanted to speak to the woman, ask her to release all those prisoners held since the war. She took it all wrong, thought he was attacking her or something idiotic. All our problems began then, I swear.'

He began to pace around. 'I'll have to go; I have to join my comrades.'

'I told you not to return here, we knew it wasn't safe for you,' wailed his mother.

'I know, Mother, I'm sorry. I don't want to get you and Father into trouble as well. I'll wait till he comes home and see what he says.'

'Why must you get involved in all this?' cried Stella, her voice full of despair. 'Why not settle to your studies, find a nice girl, live a normal life? What's the matter with all you young people nowadays that you have to keep fighting everything? There isn't a war on, for God's sake!'

George stopped his pacing and confronted her. His face was serious and Nina, watching, felt a wave of empathy towards him; he was far more mature than she had thought.

'Listen, Mother,' he said quietly, 'I mean no disrespect to you or Father or your way of life. But all the fists raised in defiance by the young, this is the proof of change, this is the true power. It's the people that have power against tyrants and greedy corrupt men who want us to stay quiet and stupid all our lives so they can grow fat and rich while we stay poor. People don't realise they have this power, they're content to be lulled by what they take for peace; the pointless repetition of things, the rut of everyday existence. The Romans had circuses, now we have foolish American films to amuse us and make us forget what's happening under our noses, forget that our freedom is being taken away from us every minute of the day. It's a crazy cycle of meaninglessness. You're wrong, you see, wrong to think your way is best. You want us to grow up, marry, work, have children as if this cycle should go on forever and ever, no change. As if that brings peace and contentment. Has it? Children grow up and then we worry about them and there's no more peace anyway. Just worry, worry. We younger ones don't want to follow the age old ruts, the comfortable, secure paths trodden by generations. Those paths are worn now, they lead nowhere. You have to trundle on them back and forth like machines, like a conveyor belt going round and round – because if you follow them to their end, they lead to the edge, the very edge of the cliff. Then where to go? Over the edge to destruction. People turn a blind eye to so much around us that is like an illness, a canker of the Greek soul. We have to make new paths, new challenges or we sink into apathy and stagnation. Freedom or Death, remember?'

His mother remained silent for a long while and George, almost shaking with the feeling this speech caused in him, lit a cigarette and began his pacing again.

'Ach, my God! I still don't understand,' his mother said helplessly, 'I still don't see the need for all this talk, this fighting your elders and wiser men. Freedom and Death was when the Turks had us by the throat … yes, freedom from that. Freedom from the German occupation, yes. We all fought for that. You talk nonsense, son. You're just children still. You play games. You can't right the world like this. It's never going to change, can't you see that? Why not follow what we've done for centuries; we have been happy with the measured old ways. It's when things are all stirred up like this that no one is at peace, no one happy. You can't change things – a few boys and girls like you.'

George shook his head impatiently. 'You don't understand, Mother. Don't you remember that Kazantsakis says "A person needs a little madness, or else they never dare cut the rope and be free".'

Stella shook her head. Tears gathered in her eyes but she said nothing. Nina also kept silent but she secretly agreed with the young man even though his words meant anarchy. She had never believed in the comfortable rut either. The sort of rut her father had chosen to live in. To her also it spelt death, not freedom. The young were eagles that wanted to fly above it all and she wanted to soar up in the ether with them.

Dawn broke. Stella moved automatically to open the shutters and let in some daylight. It was still chilly and she shivered a little. Nina slipped her cardigan about her friend's shoulders and Stella gave her a wan smile in return. They made some more coffee and George and Stella both sat staring bleakly at the floor, unsure what to do, where to go. Everything had now fallen silent. No more sounds of shooting, cries or rumbling wheels. It was eerie, as if the city held its breath and waited. But waiting was not Nina's forte. She was always one for action rather than despair. By now it was about 6.30 am, time for the radio station to broadcast news and music.

'Let's put on the radio,' Nina suggested. 'Maybe there's some sort of announcement.'

Military marches mixed with old folk songs filled the air.

'I suppose Theodorakis music will be banned again,' said George with resentment in his voice. 'These people always do such stupid things.'

'They'll still find a way to spread Theodorakis' music,' Nina declared. 'He's too well known and admired abroad, too famous. They can't suppress genius.'

George was fretful. 'I'm worried what will happen if they catch him again,' he said. 'I can't bear to think of it! He got tuberculosis last time they subjected him to all that torture and misery. *Kyria* Nina, you will have to report it as soon as you can. The world needs to know what's going on here.'

'I want to get out and wire my photos to London, I want to ring Reggie,' Nina tapped her fingers impatiently on the dark polished table, glancing at the clock. Was it safe to venture forth? She longed to move, to do something. 'Maybe we'd better wait for your father to come home and find out what exactly is happening.'

A voice came on the radio now and declared: '*In pursuance of Article Nine of the Constitution, We, Constantine, King of the Hellenes take the decision to suspend Articles five, six, eight, ten, twelve, fourteen, eighteen, twenty, ninety-five, and ninety-seven of the Constitution throughout the territory of Greece, because of dangers which threaten the order and security of the country.*'

'What the hell does all that mean?' asked Nina, astonished.

'It means that they can arrest anyone they like,'said George. 'It means they can arrest anyone of any rank or title if they think they're a 'threat' to whatever regime this is. And if it's the army and the King's doing, it's going to be pretty right wing.

'You see now, Mother, do you see now? Don't you see the grip we're in? How these Fascists have got us by the throat? The King clings to his throne like a fool hanging onto a sinking ship. He'll drown if he doesn't watch it. What the devil's he up to, I wonder. What's going on right under our noses? He's got us ensnared by his army. Isn't that like the Nazi occupation? Don't you see that means we aren't free to say what we want, write the music we want, help our fellows as we want? If we dare say or do anything different to what they think is right, we're all Reds in their eyes.' George paused and threw back his long hair like a rearing horse, took a deep breath then continued bitterly, 'But it doesn't mean we can't try. Slowly, bit by bit, each generation will change something. I have to believe that or die.'

Aris turned up at about seven o'clock that morning. He looked tired and fed up. 'No, nobody really knows what's happening,' he replied to the frantic questions of his wife and son. 'Look, give me some coffee and toast. Things are mad today, all rush and confusion and I haven't had a drink for hours. We're trying hard to get something out in the morning paper. Luckily, *Kyria* Vlachou managed to get over from her flat to the newspaper offices near Omonia with her husband and could direct operations. Our reporters on night duty were filtering news to us and we got together a last minute edition … to think earlier on we were wondering what was to go on the front page. Everything has been so quiet of late.'

'The calm before the storm? It's unbelievable,' said Nina. She was writing down notes as he spoke. 'Tell us more, what news have you got so far.'

'They've arrested Kanellopoulos.'

'What? Arrested the *Prime Minister*?' Everyone was aghast.

'I tell you, the reporter came in looking really upset. He's a tough one too but he said he couldn't believe his own eyes. He, and many others, saw armoured cars arrive outside the Prime Minister's little apartment and block off the roads. Then they saw him being carried out, forced into a car, yelling "You are all traitors!" His poor wife came down sobbing and wailing and said these men came banging at the door and told him his life was in danger and they wanted to help him get away. When Kanellopoulos tried to stall, they tore out the telephone wires, dragged him away as soon as he was dressed.'

The listeners looked at each other in dismay.

'But it makes no sense,' said Stella, 'Kanellopoulos is right wing, he has good friends in the army. Why would they treat him as if he was a criminal?'

'I have no idea,'said Aris grimly, 'no more idea than you. It's a madhouse just now.'

'I'm off to phone the news to Reggie,' said Nina and dashed off into the hall, relieved to be able to do something positive at last. At least the phones round here hadn't been cut. Only those to *Kathimerini* and perhaps other newspapers and government offices. It transpired that no one in any of the overseas Press Offices had even thought to listen in to the Greek news. Like everyone, they were taken by surprise. Reggie was delighted with the scoop and phoned his own editors straight away.

'It's real luck you were on the spot, Nina,' he said. 'Good girl, you said you thought something was brewing.'

'I didn't think it would brew this fast,' she said, 'or so silently and sneakily. I bet we see a regular uprising by the afternoon.'

'Just take care.'

'I've got to get these photos to you, Reggie. But there's no way just now. Aris says there's soldiers with guns everywhere and they're not being sweet and nice.'

'It doesn't matter,' his voice held a trace of regret at losing such a scoop and Nina almost smiled. 'Your safety is more important, remember that. Take care and don't put any backs up. Your father will blame me for letting you go off on your own like this.'

'Of course, he won't! He knows how pig-headed I am. I'll take care. Anyway, I'm here on my British passport, thankfully and I'll wield that at them. It's my friends here I'm worried about. Especially George. I'm really afraid for the boy. He's determined to fight and I feel he's in real danger.'

Chapter 17

Thessaloniki: morning of April 21st 1967

Opening a sleepy eye, Dimitri looked at the clock and groaning, rolled over in bed. He hadn't slept well that night, waking up almost every hour, lying staring at the flickering darkness. The film in the cinema across the road was playing its third showing of *The Thirty-Nine Steps* when he went to bed and crazy images of cars tearing along empty roads, bleak scenery in Scotland, men with guns and screaming women tumbled about confusedly in his head. He swore he knew the actors' lines off by heart now. The night was silent at last and even the roads were hushed with the heaviness of sleep.

Maybe it was worrying over the bills he had to pay. Always bills, bills. He owed a couple of months rent to his brother-in-law for the workshop premises near Laladika. He knew Nikos wouldn't fuss too much but the man had a family of his own to keep. How had he managed to get so behind with the rent? It worried him; he'd never owed much in his life. It was his principle to pay debts as soon as he could, his philosophy being that other ordinary people needed their cash as much as he did. It was different cheating the tax man; cheating the government was a natural occupation amongst all of them. But then business was so slow of late. There were always repairs, of course, and these kept him going but the real money was in used car sales and nothing was shifting despite all his best efforts.

Then there was Max. His friend worked as hard as ever, worked too hard. He refused to go home to his flat sometimes, preferred to spend the night under a car or taking a truck to pieces. Dimitri knew what that was all about. It was Nina. Max pined for Nina, he always had done, despite his apparent indifference. His friend had gone back to acting his light, witty, detached self but he, Dimitri Cosmatis, was not fooled for a minute. Max was a deep-feeling man; he just covered it up with layers of cotton wool, soft, soft ... you sank in and never seemed to touch the hard, unhappy bit beneath.

He fell at last into a deep, strange sleep. When he woke, he lay for a moment or two, his arm under his head, then glanced at the clock by the bed. Almost half past six. He was usually up by now but everywhere was so quiet, so hushed and he strained his ears for the sound of a bus or passing car.

Yiota now stirred beside him and raised her head.

'Haven't you gone to work yet?'

'All in good time, don't nag me.'

'You've usually gone by now,' she said, sitting up and surveying the alarm clock on his side, 'not like you to be lazy. What's up?'

'I don't know; just didn't sleep well.'

He rose and put on the wireless they kept in the bedroom while he was dressing. Instead of the usual programme some strident martial music was playing. He twiddled the knobs. But it was the same on all the stations. That was strange. Then a deep serious voice announced that Athens was calling from the Army radio station and an important announcement would be made. This was followed by another burst of marching music. Yiota sat up again, the sheet falling away from her, and stared at him. 'What the hell's going on?'

'Shut up and we'll find out.'

Dimitri sat down on the end of the bed, one sock on and one in his hand. Yiota arose and putting on a dressing gown over her pink nylon nightie, sat beside him and brushed her hair as she listened.

'Because of an abnormal situation that developed after midnight endangering the internal security of the country, the Army has taken over the government of the country ...' the voice went on to enumerate the various Articles that had apparently been suspended due to this unknown 'threat' and ended saying that it was 'signed by Constantine, King of the Hellenes, the Prime Minister and Members of the Cabinet.'

Yiota looked puzzled. 'I don't understand it.'

'Better you don't. It sounds bad. Make me a coffee and keep the old woman away from the radio in case it upsets her. Just get on with things as usual, take the kids to school and all the rest. I'll go out and see what's happening. I'll let you know when I come in for lunch.'

'Your mother won't be upset; she's a tough old thing, as you well know.'

'True,' admitted Dimitri, 'she and Papa saw no end of troubles in the war. She'll just shrug, I suppose.'

'She won't blink an eye, that old bat. Besides I can't see what there is to have hysterics over … it sounds like some idiotic move by the government. What's new about that? Anyway, I need to go shopping. *Kyrie* Manoli will be sure to have the latest gossip. I'll know long before you do.'

Dimitri swallowed some coffee, dipping in a rather stale *koulouri* left over from the day before. It stuck in his throat and he wished he hadn't bothered.

'Get some decent bread,' he shouted at his wife as he left, 'and stop buying the kids cheap *koulouri*. You fill them up with rubbish sometimes.'

'It's your stupid mother who buys it, not me!' Yiota shouted back indignantly but the door had already slammed.

There was an eerie quiet everywhere. Dimitri headed for his little Vespa motorcycle parked in the side street. He started off on it but as he approached the intersection of Tsimiski and Stratou, he saw a row of armed soldiers in the road. They stopped him and told him to go back.

'No work for anyone today, no school for the kids. If you have any, keep them at home.'

'But what the devil's going on?' demanded Dimitri.

'Don't need to know. Just do as you're told.'

'I have work to do, cars to mend, I can't sit about at home,' he protested.

'Look, just get home.'

'But I need the money, don't you understand! I need to deliver some cars today … I promised the owners.'

The soldier looked angry and motioned with his gun. 'If you don't turn and go back now, I'll shoot you in the leg. Then you'll have to mend yourself.'

Dimitri began to boil with rage.

One of the soldiers stepped forward and motioned to his comrade to step back. He looked familiar and Dimitri recognised him as one of his previous clients. He would understand! But the soldier shook his head at him and said quietly, 'Look, *Kyrie* Dimitri, there's a curfew for today. Things will sort out by tomorrow, for sure. Keep out of trouble. Get back to your wife and kids and just stay in for now.'

Dimitri threw his hands up in the air. 'This country's gone raving mad,' he declared. But he turned round and headed home to give the news to Yiota who stared at him in disbelief.

'Can't I even go shopping?'

'There's no shops open to go to. We'll have to make do with what we've got.'

There was no keeping it from the old lady now. On hearing the news that some sort of coup had happened, no one had a clue by whom, she crossed herself and shook her head. 'Eh, what do you expect?' she declared. 'The country's ruled by fools. It always has been.'

The only happy people were the children who were to miss school for the day.

Agia Sofias Square

Max stood on his balcony and looked down into the silent street below. The peculiar quiet out there had made him wake early, wondering if it was Sunday and he'd got the day wrong or slept for years like Rip Van Winkle. Then, on hearing a curious rumbling noise, he went idly over to the window, looked out and then looked again. Now he saw two tanks rolling by with soldiers standing in the turrets holding guns. What the devil was going on?

While he was shaving, he listened to the incessant military music and occasional announcements on the radio. Like everyone else in the country, he wondered what was happening. Nina had often declared that something was about to occur. She was certain the King would try something, anything to prevent the elections taking place which were sure to bring in the more moderate Papandreou and give power to his vociferous and energetic left wing son, Andreas. So, it looked as if this was it. The King had made his move.

He went downstairs and wondered if it was worth trying to get over to the car repair workshop. But he soon realised it was useless. It was evident there were no buses running, no taxis on the road. And though he often walked the distance, he felt sure there would be road blocks of some sort. He gave Dimitri a ring at his home, wondering if he had managed to get in to work. He wasn't surprised to hear his friend's irritated voice.

'Any idea what's happening, Dimitri?'

'Are you kidding? Even the soldiers don't know, no one has a clue. I tried to get over to the workshop but they sent me back. Yiota's terrified and my mother is just resigned … says she's seen it all before. The fellow downstairs, who does a nightshift, said there were tanks outside the Ministry for Northern Greece really early. They were waving guns around and he came home fast, I can tell you. It's all very well but I need to earn a living. I've no idea when we're even going to be allowed to go to work!'

Max grimaced. 'Well, there's not a lot we can do. Just wait and see. They can't keep folks indoors forever. They're just staking their positions. It's obviously a coup of some sort. Very neat and quiet. In the middle of the night and, as far as I can tell, no bloodshed either.'

'It looks that way. But Max, I don't like the sound of this. It's all very right wing, very dictatorial. I don't like it. I feel trouble in my bones for some of us.'

'But you're not involved with KKE, you never were.'

'You think that makes a difference? As far as these loonies are concerned, anything from Centre to Left is a threat to their idea of how things should be run.'

'Look, you've never been politically active. I can't see you need to worry,' Max said. 'We'll just get on with the work we have to do and keep your head down, if it's really as bad as you say.'

'I feel it in my bones,' said Dimitri, 'I feel something is really wrong. But I daren't let the women and kids know.'

Karabournaki

Basil Petrakos was eating his breakfast serenely. Athina had got Yiannakis ready for school and sent the lad off with a pat on his head and his little satchel filled with lunch and few school books. They hadn't put the radio on until then because Basil preferred peace and quiet while he ate and considered the day ahead. Now it was nearing Easter, there had been a good deal of work to do while everyone spruced up their clothes and homes for the holiday ahead. Many had brought in their winter rugs to be cleaned and made ready to roll up and put away during the warm summer months.

He enjoyed it when things were busy – liked using the skills he had acquired since boyhood working with his father and two brothers in the dry cleaning shops around the city. Each brother ran a shop and there were three in all. Basil supervised and was in charge of the business as befitted the eldest son but they were basically independent and what they earned in each shop was up to them; they maintained their own families, paid their taxes and rates and on the whole lived in reasonable comfort from the proceeds. He could afford to rent a pleasant flat and run a car and put food on the table for his family. He was content.

Basil liked his life to be regular and orderly. He took care of the paperwork and made sure there was no dodging from any of the brothers of what was legally due. People saw him as a man of honour and merit. He was not a shark, his prices were fair, his work and that of his brothers' exemplary. He took a pride in maintaining the excellent standards begun by his father, who had come to Thessaloniki from Constantinople during the exchange of population which had been imposed by Kemal Ataturk. His father brought his business skills with him and, helped by his careful and pragmatic wife, set up his shop and in no time expanded into a second one. It had given him great pleasure to send his eldest son to England to learn more skills. Basil regretted that he hadn't finished his studies over there. But at the same time, it was satisfying to be in charge. In the end, skills were learnt through work and experience and not in a college.

The shops that belonged to the Petrakos family were his pride and joy. Nothing had upset him more than the sheer insolence of some of the recent strikers and rioters who took to the streets in constant protest and thought nothing of slinging stones or bottles through shop windows just for the hell of it. People became frightened and stayed indoors and that was loss of business. His shop on Angeliki always seemed to be in the forefront of the problems. He was tired of finding things in a mess after such incidents. There was little to loot from a drycleaners but clothes were sometimes torn from hangers, flung upon the floor and trampled on and even the dry-cleaning fluid stored in cans sometimes taken off, for what purpose he had no idea. No doubt to start a fire somewhere but he wouldn't put it past some of them to drink it in place of spirits.

Everyone was upset by the eternal grumbles and bad behaviour of these dissatisfied, lousy Lefties. Where did that sort of thing get these fools? Did they think it cost nothing to replace glass windows, re-clean or replace damaged clothing? Didn't they understand that time spent having to sweep shop floors and the pavements outside of broken glass and detritus was time wasted? To the Devil with them all! They were envious of anyone who worked hard and made a decent living with the sweat and toil of many years and whose fathers had worked so hard before them. The trouble with these Lefties was that they had Right pockets. Oh yes, they wanted the same standard of living all right, but not by working for it like any other decent citizen. Half those bums preferred to hang about the streets and *cafeneions* playing *tavli*, drinking *raki* and talking politics. If they could wrest a decent man's money from him by violence, that was okay. It made him so angry he wanted to go and round up the lot of them and make them clean out the palace latrines.

Basil now switched on the radio and listened to the music and announcements with a smile.

'Have you heard the news, Athina,' he declared cheerfully, 'it looks as if our good King has made a move at last. There's some sort of takeover by the palace going on and with any luck this may mean some order will be restored in this country at last. Thanks be to God.'

At that moment, Yiannakis banged on the door and came bursting in full of excitement.

'There are soldiers out there, Papa! And a big tank. They told me to go home there's no school ever again! They had real guns.'

Basil looked annoyed for a moment but then his face cleared. 'Fine, son, but it's just for today. Go and do some schoolwork in the kitchen … you needn't think you're going to play with your sister all day.'

Yiannaki's face fell. 'Can't I go over to Bobby's house? Please, Papa!'

'Later, maybe. But do some work first. Life isn't about play all the time. Order will be restored tomorrow, wait and see.'

Chapter 18

Downlands, Gloucestershire, England. Evening of April 21st 1967

Back home in England the news had made the front page of the *Evening Standard*. It was nothing compared to Reggie's headlines in his paper the next morning:

EYE WITNESS ACCOUNT OF THE KING'S COUP IN GREECE; DIRECT FROM OUR REPORTER IN ATHENS.

But Andrew Cassimatis had not as yet seen this story and instead read out the brief account in the evening paper over supper to Dorothy and Helen.

' "The King's Men seize power in Greek coup; Premier seized and forced to sign a decree".' There's talk of shots reported in Athens and tanks and troops patrolling the streets. Heavens above, what on earth's going on?'

'Another coup?' said Dorothy wearily. She had seen a few in her time and it meant little. 'I expect this will start some fireworks. I do hope Nina is safe in Athens with those political friends of hers.'

'Oh, she'll be having the time of her life, I expect. She'll be running round getting photos and wiring stuff off to Reggie. After all, she's right there in the middle of it and can let him know what's going on in detail. It's probably a boost to her ego.'

'All the same,'said Dorothy, 'you should give her a ring, don't you think? We can't be sure if it's peaceful or not. It seems to me that it's all a bit of a *fait accompli* but the Greeks never take anything lying down.'

Andrew ate his toast thoughtfully. 'Yes, I agree, I'll ring her right now.' Deep down, he was afraid that, knowing Nina's love of involvement in all things political, she might well get herself into trouble.

It was impossible to get through to anyone in Greece that night. However, the next day things seemed restored to some normality. Andrew was able to ring the Praxiteles and was relieved to hear Nina's voice sounding cheerful and excited.

'I've managed to get to a Press Office earlier on today and wire through more news to Reggie. Reporter on the spot, aren't I? Did you see my report; Reggie said it was out in their morning paper? I wanted to send the pictures I took during the night while it was happening but a nasty-looking policeman stopped me on the way to the office and took my camera away. Can you believe that? I was furious! They would have been fantastic shots, a real scoop. I told him I'd report him to the embassy and the press but he didn't give a damn and said I should be careful I don't get myself arrested. As it was, as a *xeni*, a foreigner, I was told to go and see the police this morning. They questioned me for ages. I had to switch on all my feminine charm and it worked. "Oh well, you may be a journalist, but you're a Greek, you're really one of us," they told me at last and let me go. They suppose like fools that I'll be on their side and put over their warped viewpoint. Movement was restricted for a bit, lots of phone lines cut and yet today it's as if nothing has happened at all. It's all quite strange really. The populace act as normal and seem totally unaware that thousands are being arrested and taken off to secret places and may never be seen again. It's the apathy that scares me most, not the coup.'

'But what is this so-called threat? Has there been any sign of a communist uprising?'

'Well no, that's the weird thing. No sign of anything at all. That's why people are so taken by surprise, so dumbstruck by the whole thing.'

‘There were certainly plenty of signs of trouble in 1944,’ said Andrew. ‘Everyone knew what was going on – the whole world, not just Greece, was afraid of a swing from right to left. Everything was in the balance. You say there’s been no signs of this?’

‘Earlier in the month there were just the usual demos and stuff from the Workers Union and the students. They’re always protesting about something or other. But nothing out of the ordinary. Aris feels sure it’s all to do with the forthcoming elections. These extreme right wing types are scared stiff that Papandreou and the Centre Union will win and *they’ll* be accused of being involved in right wing plots and thrown in jail. They’re trying to save their own skins. The King just seems to be a bit of a pawn in their game at the moment.’

‘I’m worried for you, darling,’ said Andrew, ‘do take care.’

‘Oh, everyone keeps saying that,’ said Nina breezily, ‘I’m fine, really I am. I’m rather enjoying the adventure.’

Andrew put the phone down and felt a deep sense of dissatisfaction and anxiety.

Helen looked at him and frowned. ‘I take it that wasn’t a very satisfactory conversation.’

‘No, it wasn’t. Nina seems oblivious to any danger. That girl is so stubborn once she’s set on a path.’

‘Maybe I’m getting my own back now,’ murmured Dorothy.

‘What do you mean?’ he asked sharply.

Dorothy looked up from the book she was reading and regarded her son. ‘There was a time when a certain stubborn son of mine came and informed me he wasn’t going to go up to Oxford but over to Greece, come what may,’ she said. ‘Now perhaps you know what I felt.’

Andrew lowered his eyes as memories flooded back to him of that time so long ago. He sighed deeply. ‘I know, Mother. But I don’t regret what I did.’

‘Hopefully, neither will Nina.’

'George. You'd better hide, you'd better get out, son.'

Aris spoke rapidly. He had returned to the newspaper offices for work that afternoon and stayed on there in support of the boss and staff. When the sun had set, a curfew was announced on the radio and Aris learned that he wouldn't be allowed to return home till next morning. One of the editors in an office upstairs called him up urgently to witness something so horrifying that he had felt in a panic for the safety of his son, but it was impossible to use the office phones as the lines were cut. He ran downstairs and looked out. Police were guarding the entrance to their offices and soldiers were standing up in the turrets of their tanks and shooting bullets up into the air as a warning to anyone who ventured forth after the curfew. An earlier announcement had warned the citizens that anyone who was out after sunset would be shot. He was stuck and it made his blood boil, his heart ache.

However, Aris was an Athenian born and bred and knew the backstreets and alleyways of that area very well. Under cover of darkness, he slowly and carefully made his way home like an alley cat, sliding along walls, pausing now and then in the shadows for breath, his heart thudding with fear and excitement. It was a long way and a long time before he made it at last and by then he felt a nervous wreck. Slipping over a wall at the back of their little garden full of lemon trees, he banged on the back door and a startled George answered it.

'What is it, what's happened, Papa?'

Aris came into the kitchen where he sat down heavily. Stella and Nina came hastening from the *saloni* to see what was going on. Poor Stella's eyes were wide with terror. She was sure the police had come for them all.

Aris asked for a shot of whisky, which he drank neat. Then he calmed down at last and said, 'My God, I don't believe what my own eyes have seen! They're like animals, they're tearing the offices of the Lambrakides apart.'

These offices were on the fifth floor of a building opposite the *Kathimerini,* which was located down a narrow street. From the newspaper office they had all been able to observe what was going on over there. Switching off their own lights, they had stood in the darkness and watched as soldiers, aided by the police and others, had entered the building and ripped the place apart, taking out files, books and anything else they could lay their hands on. What frightened him most was the peculiar fury and passion of the marauders who had smashed furniture and files and ripped down curtains as if they were attacking some hated and unseen enemy that resided in the very fabric of the building. What sort of people were these? Why so filled with hate over a bunch of young people whose only aim was to do good and help their fellow citizens?

'George, you must go. They've taken files and things. They'll find your names and addresses there. You boys had all better hide till this thing calms down.'

'I'll go,' said George, 'I don't want to get you and mother in trouble.'

'Where will you go?'

'Best you don't know. I'll find somewhere to stay; somewhere we Lambrakides can work out a plan of action.'

'No, no, stay low for a bit. They've closed all the airports, all the borders, wouldn't even let any trains and buses in from Turkey. You'll be arrested at once if you try to get out of the country. You'll have to think of something.'

'We told you to stay in England, we told you,' said Stella, sobbing.

'Mama, I didn't know this was going to happen, none of us did.' George gazed sadly at the hand-copied bulletin from Theodorakis and his militant band of comrades.

TO THE GREEK PEOPLE

Fascism has struck our country. The king, his generals and the CIA believe our people will be reduced to silence by violence and terror. We call upon all honest officers, soldiers and patriots to stand beside the people, to say no to violence … .no to dictatorship and fascism.

Greek democrats, this crime will be the beginning of the defeat of our enemies of freedom. Organise yourselves, fight and resist the dictators of the junta.

People of Athens, demonstrate in the streets! Patriots, meet in Constitution Square! Forward to the liquidation of the enemies of the people and the country. Fascism will not be victorious! Long live democracy! Long live Greece! Long live the Greek people!

'Houses are being searched even now,' George said, 'phones are cut and people dragged away. What I can't understand is, who's behind it all? One of our friends said they live opposite the King's aide-de-camp and saw soldiers breaking down his door and carting him away. If it's not the King, then who is it?'

'I have my suspicions,' said Aris. 'We've been hearing rumours about a group of extreme right wing officers who are scared of losing their power, their pensions, their standing in the community if the Centre takes over. They're not the King's generals, just a few hubristic peasants who've risen in the ranks and don't baulk at torture and violence. They thrive on it, they've been known to use it. One of them, a guy called Pattakos, a mere brigadier in the tank corps, is a relative of one of our editors who spoke about him some time back. They're scared – and so like all scared beasts, they're striking first.'

'Did you hear the announcements at work, Aris?' said Stella. 'Did you hear that the King has now appointed Constantine Kollias as head of the new government? He says the country is on the edge of an abyss and the elections would have made no difference.'

'Kollias … that fool! He's just a puppet of the King. He meddled in the whole enquiry over Lambrakis.' said George bitterly. 'Fools, all of them. And the King too. What are they playing at? Now people will do nothing, they'll think it's all legal and proper and just accept another tyrant in the place of the ones we've had before. We have forgotten Metaxas.'

'But he did do good as well,' his mother pleaded, 'it didn't affect us that much.'

'No, but it wasn't democracy either.'

'I agree,' said Aris, 'the press was throttled and kept in order. We couldn't speak our minds, say what we really felt. They banned different forms of music, set up youth groups that were like Hitler's Jung and just about everything else. No Greek wants to live under those conditions, Stella. *We* may have been comfortable and unaffected because we're not part of KKE, the communist lot. We've kept our mouths shut and have never become involved in politics. But thousands were affected, we know that now. They were taken off to those island prisons and tortured. We have friends who remember it.'

'Isn't that what I've been trying to tell you, Mama *mou*? Everyone seems afraid to do anything,' said George miserably. 'I have to go and join my friends, see if we can rouse some sort of protest. I'm not running away. I mean to fight.'

Tears rolled down his mother's face but she went to fetch him some food to take with him. He grabbed a few toiletries, shirts and underwear and stuffed them in a bag.

'What about the curfew though? How safe is it to go now? Papa, you were so brave to make it home. You were so brave,' George hugged his father.

'Do as I did, take the back ways to your friends. The way things are going the security men may come looking for you any minute. Go out by the back door into the little garden and over the wall,' said Aris. He pushed some money into his son's pocket and hugged him again while his mother clung desperately to her boy for a few moments.

'Take care, Giorgaki *mou*.'

'I will, Mama. I will. Don't say a word to Lexi. She'll just be scared and scream and cry all night.'

'Where the hell *is* Lexi?' asked Aris, looking around as if suddenly aware his daughter was missing.

'I've sent her to visit her friend, Toula. She's staying the night there.'

'Thanks God, for that,' said Aris. 'That child is so nervous. Keep her away from home as long as you can.'

George turned now to Nina and hugged her. 'Goodbye *Kyria* Nina. I hope I haven't got you in trouble too.'

Nina shook her head. 'It's okay, George, I'm quite safe. They can't prevent me from leaving Greece – and I have my foreign journalist's card. Thank God I used my British passport this time. I wish I could smuggle you out with me. Maybe we'll think of something.'

'Thanks, but I'm better on my own,' he said.

He slipped forth and disappeared over the wall into a little alleyway beyond. Stella burst into tears and sobbed on her husband's shoulder.

Chapter 19

Thessaloniki: April 23rd: Dimitri is worried

Dimitri found Max already in the workshop, hammering out a big dent in a rear door. He looked as if he hadn't even shaved. Dimitri sighed to see how haggard and neglected his friend looked.

'You look as if you've been here all night,' he said.

'I have.'

'We'll have people complaining if you're banging out car doors too late!'

'I don't do *this* at night! I just polish or spray paintwork or do some paperwork. I suppose I must have dropped off in the office at some point.' Max put down his tools and wiped his hands. 'We've got to get this panel-beating finished, door sprayed and ready by this afternoon when the owner comes over to collect it.'

'True enough, and we need the money, so let's get on with it. I'll see to the Volvo with the broken rear lights. You finish off this old Merc, you're doing a good job.'

The two men worked silently and as hard as they could to catch up with the neglected work. The customers would understand but Dimitri disliked letting folk down.

Before going home that night, Dimitri went into town and decided to get some fruit and vegetables from the Modiano market … and maybe some nice flowers for Yiota. He seldom shouted at her but he'd been feeling fragile this morning and they'd had a blazing row, not helped by his wretched mother's interference. She hated her daughter-in-law and always liked to get her oar in. Women! He couldn't even remember what it was about now. But he had left Yiota in tears and he hated to do that.

On the way to the market, Dimitri passed by the offices of the *Macedonian News*. Over the entrance a teleprinter was flashing the news that the world was about to be saved from some terrible communist take-over by virtue of this brilliant move on the part of the King. People were talking excitedly, shouting, gesturing and blocking the pavements. A policemen came up and told them to move on. 'You'll all find out soon enough,' he said. Someone who knew the man called out, 'Eh, Spiros, what do you think of all this? Have you had orders from the King?'

'What orders?' the policeman said truculently. The truth was he didn't know either but wouldn't admit it. Dimitri stared at him, then looked away as the man glared back. He didn't hang around but moved on swiftly through the stalls of bright-coloured fruit and vegetables and flowers in the market place.

Things seemed eerily normal. People went about their business as if nothing had happened. Shops were opened as usual, buses and cabs ran, people sat in cafés eating pastries, sipping drinks and chatting, gesticulating, carrying on as always. Yet an air of uncertainty hung over the city and even in the countryside.

April 27th, Holy Thursday

Dimitri went out on his little Vespa to see a farmer who had bought one of their tractors at the Trade Fair and was talking about buying a new truck. It was Good Friday tomorrow and he knew he'd better get some business done before the shops closed down and the bells began to toll throughout the day. It was a day that always gave him the creeps. The incessant Passion plays on the television, the mournful sound of the bells and the sense of something having died. He wondered at times what it was all about, what it really meant. Stopping for a cigarette, he leant against a tree and watched an old woman in the fields. She was standing stock still, surveying the field and wailing aloud with grief. He had seen this sort of emotion before, women sobbing over the *Epitaphios* on Good Friday as if they really mourned Christ's death.

Grinding the cigarette into the earth, he went up to the woman and asked her what made her so unhappy. She paused for a moment, her eyes streaming with tears, and crossed herself vigorously.

'Are you a fool?' she cried. 'Don't you understand anything? If Christ doesn't rise on Sunday, we shall have no corn this year.'

He didn't dare ask her if she really believed that. He knew she did. He knew that this was something very ancient, this belief in the risen god, the bringer of life and light and joy, something close to the pagan Greek heart. Part of him mocked it. But another part felt stirred by something deep and meaningful. He smiled at her and said gently, 'Christ always rises. Have no fear, old lady.'

He got back on his Vespa and set off once more. The cool breeze whipped at his hair as he bombed along the silent and almost empty road which took him through small villages that felt almost uninhabited compared to the ceaseless bustle of the city. Occasionally an old man would plod by on a donkey or a thickset young man, almost blackened by the sun, would drive by on a muddy battered old truck or a cart. An occasional open-roofed car would flash by and disappear in clouds of milky dust. On the way across the plain he saw some women, wrapped in their black clothes and headscarves, setting off to work in the tobacco fields, which glistened green in the early sunshine and stretched for miles. Poppies splashed their scarlet vividness along the roadside and other wild flowers were scenting the air like heady wine. All seemed so normal, so serene and simple as it always had been. Centuries of ancient activity still took place and the peasant people were little changed at heart or in their customs. It soothed his spirit to be a part of this, yet he felt that a sombre cloud, a miasma of darkness hung over everything that would soon blot out the sun.

What nonsense! It was all in his fancy and he shook his head to clear it. Maybe it was nothing after all. Maybe things would be better, who could say. How backward Greece was compared to other countries. Max had told him a good deal about the world; he was a well-travelled man, a man who had got about – not like himself, an ignorant, ill-educated clod. He had never been outside Greece. He had taken Yiota to Halkidiki for a honeymoon trip and once to Athens and that was all. He too was ignorant, they all were. Stuck in their little worlds, their everyday comings and goings, their petty worries, the food they enjoyed, the family rituals and timeless activities, unchanged for centuries. Life was so different elsewhere. What would it be like to live in Italy or Spain or Germany? One of his cousins had gone to work in Germany and said it was a great place. Regulated, orderly, lots of business and good money. England sounded a good place too but he'd never stand for the weather … all that fog and rain!

He wondered if he could ever persuade Yiota to move to Germany with him. But she'd never agree. She still had a hatred for the race because they had killed her father during the occupation, shot him in cold blood. And her elder sister had died of tuberculosis, the whole family starving and cold during a terrible winter that had blanketed Europe; bodies had lain in the streets all winter till the snows melted, just like in the Great War.

He felt a sudden yearning to have sex. Yiota showed little enthusiasm these days and it was the only way he knew to relieve his sense of anxiety and unease. He needed a good fuck with a girl who'd do whatever he asked. Yiota was such a prude and refused to take her nightie off, even on their honeymoon. He had hardly ever seen her naked; she still covered herself up when he came in the bedroom and undressed in the toilet. She was affectionate enough but as soon as he became sexually amorous, she'd shake him off and give a nervous little laugh as if she was a teenager on a first date. She'd had two kids, for heaven's sake! They weren't virgin births! But he knew that a lot of women were like this. He wasn't alone. Yiota's mother had always had a village mentality and brought her daughters up this way. It wasn't her fault.

On the way back to the city, he stopped at a little two-storied house on the Monastir road. There wasn't another dwelling around for miles. It stood solitary, tucked a little way from the main road. He parked the bike under the shade of a huge plane tree and went in. It was warm that day and when he had chosen his favourite girl, Marta, he asked to go up on the terrace with her. The terrace was open to a cooling breeze at the sides, partly covered by a roof made of plaited straw. Here the couple twisted and writhed and made plenty of noise, working themselves up into a sweat that dripped off them as they rolled about on the bed. Dimitri finished at last, withdrew his satisfied penis with a little shake, and arose. Marta lit them both a cigarette and they sat there, puffing contently like an old couple. Then they went downstairs and while Dimitri availed himself of the primitive earth closet, Marta fetched him a jug of water and a bowl for a wash. The proprietor of the house brought over a Fix beer. Nobody spoke much, there was little to say. He didn't come here for conversation but relief.

'I needed that, thank you Marta,' he said in simple gratitude. He felt a man again, not a quivering jelly. He thought of Max. Time he brought him here too. It would do the man good. He kissed Marta lightly on the cheek and left, contented and relaxed and rode off to find his client, the farmer, humming an old Sofia Vembo number that his mother used to sing.

After the Easter ceremonies were over and things had returned to normal, Dimitri went over to see his *koumbaros*, Petros, to check on their beloved whippets. He and Petros enjoyed going hunting on the occasional Sunday, shooting rabbits and tiny little black birds, *mavropouli,* or any other game they could find up in the mountains. It was a favourite sport and good to get away from the grime and smoke of the city, up into the wide open air. Up there beyond the Sai Sou forest, the wind blew fresh and cleared the brain. Good to get away from people and their demands: Yiota, the kids, his mother in law, customers, tax men, you name it.

Petros was a thin, tense man but he was one to be trusted, straight, honest and honourable. However, he was also very fiery, full of intense feeling and strung-up nerves that often exploded in anger which did his ulcers no good. He made good money selling quality hand-made carpets in the Bezesteni market and wasn't a man to throw his cash around on drink and gambling like some of the fellows from these parts.

Dimitri would have liked to go hunting every Sunday but he knew Yiota would make a fuss so, for the sake of peace, he limited it to once a month. Petros went as often as he liked; his wife seemed pleased to be rid of him. Their house was in the suburb of Kalamaria, a small, one-storey whitewashed place with a red tiled roof and a huge fig tree in the front.

Petros and his sister Merope would argue about who had planted the tree. Merope insisted their father had done so but Petros stubbornly maintained he himself had buried an uneaten, ripe fig there one day and the tree had grown from this act.

'He's daft,' Merope said. 'What an imagination!'

'I'm telling you the facts,' Petros would yell at her but she, a stolid, sensible, immoveable woman, would just smile at him and shrug.

Dimitri had come from round these parts and he and Yiota had married in Agios Nikolaou, the small church near the seafront. His mind went back to that day, the bells ringing happily, the beauty of his young bride in her virginal white dress as she came shyly towards him. The crowning ceremony had made tears come to his eyes. He thought of the village children running around greedily grabbing at the little bags of almond comfits that were being doled out from a huge pile, prepared by his aunt, Julia. Petros was such a handsome young man then, unmarried at the time. He and Dimitri had been schoolboys together, joined the army together. Now Petros was a nervy man who smoked far too much and looked permanently worried and anxious. Being up in the mountains with his gun and the dogs was the only way to calm his troubled nerves. For Dimitri, it was the whorehouse. Each to their own.

Dimitri drew up outside their house, parked the bike by the

roadside kerb, then stood for a while smoking and staring up at the fig tree, now grown to huge proportions and shading the hot, dusty road. His mind sped back to long-ago summers when Petros' wife, Fi-Fi, would climb the tree barefoot, a basket slung round her arm, to collect the juicy, plump figs that melted in your mouth. Figs were an erotic fruit; first the slow sensuous peeling of the covering layers, the exposing of the pink ripe inside, the fig now an open vulva. He thought of Marta and smiled. Then of his pretty wife Yiota whom he loved dearly but no longer desired. Life was a strange business.

A grapevine wound itself around a fence, the young fresh leaves glistening in the evening sun. It was a good time of year when everything still looked new, alive and vivid. Later it would all be dusty, dried up and tired. Dimitri felt a bit that way himself just now. Shaking off this unaccustomed malaise, he walked round to the back where the slender, streamlined whippets recognised his whistle and came bounding out of their kennels, straining on their chains and barking furiously. He patted them in turn and spoke to them with tenderness, feeding them some tit-bits he had brought with him in a bag. Petros now emerged from the house and came to embrace him while Fi-Fi poked her head round the door and waved a ladle, then returned to her cooking.

'*Re*, Dimitri, where've you been lately? The dogs are pretty glad to see you too, you stranger!' Petros bent down to one of the dogs and gave it an affectionate rub on the head, pulling its ears gently. It looked up at him with its intelligent brown eyes and gave a short bark in response to his greeting. 'You staying to dinner? Fi-Fi is cooking *dolmades* with *avgolemono*; the young vine leaves are delicious this time of year.'

'No, I can't stay, Petro, though I'd love to try the *dolmades*. Yiota expects me home soon and apparently I'm to take them all out to a *psarotaverna*. I came to see the dogs are okay and ask you if you've heard what's going on in the city. Also, there may be a curfew, another reason to get home.'

Petros looked about him as if ears were on every corner. There wasn't a soul in sight but nonetheless he drew Dimitri into the house. They went into the little *saloni* and sat down. Fi-Fi appeared as if by magic with a couple of Fix beers and some glasses.

They lit cigarettes and Petros spoke, even then his voice was subdued. He picked in his nervous manner at a frayed purple thread in the embroidery on the table. It was a highly coloured impression of a bunch of grapes spilling out of a basket. The embroidered grapes began to unravel a little but he picked away and Dimitri watched him, distracted for a moment, almost amused at the thought of what Fi-Fi would have to say when she saw the damage.

'It's bad, Dimitri. I hear they've carted off some off our old friends already. They're busy rounding people up as if there was a war on. I can't make it out at all. Some say it's the King and his generals but those in the know reckon it's another lot altogether.' He lit up another cigarette and then went on, 'some say it's been planned for a long time. We'll soon see who emerges and then we'll know what's what for sure. The King has made some speech telling us that Kollias is taking over as Prime Minister. He doesn't give any reasons why Kanellopoulos has been given the push. My feeling is the King's been duped or is scared of his own life. I wouldn't be at all surprised if we see him running out of the country with his little Danish wife and his pesky mother Frederica in tow. Though where he'd run to, heaven knows.'

'To England, like as not. They take in all the ex-kings.'

'Hmm ... well, these are his problems, not ours. He's got plenty of money to live on. We have our own troubles.'

'Will they come for you? Are you afraid?'

'Who knows,' said Petros grimly. 'They know my leanings are towards the far left. Someone will denounce me when they start to use their old tricks, the *falanga*. What man can stand having the soles of his feet beaten with iron rods for hours? I would denounce the world.'

'You really think it will come to this, people taken off to those bloody island prisons again, tortured? You remember that evil house where they took the "dissenters" and used to rev up their motorcycles to drown out the screams of their prisoners?'

'I most certainly remember. And they're at it again. Thank God, I was too young then but I knew of uncles and cousins who just disappeared for good. Their bodies never turned up, God knows what they went through. Sounds as if it's going the same way again. When will the Russians come to our aid, Dimitri, when?'

Dimitri tilted up his chin and threw up his hands, 'Are you still so blind, *re* Petro! The Russians don't give a toss about us now, despite the old ideas we once had that we're all Orthodox Christians and should stick together. They've banished religion over there anyway. They couldn't care less what we get up to over here. Anyway, there's no threat, there's not enough commies in this country to start a bonfire let alone a real overthrow of the country. Why do you still believe in the Russian idea?'

'They've banished religion, it's true,' said Petros, looking grim and stubborn, 'and I can't say I blame them. Religion is a lot of rubbish and priests stir up more trouble than anyone. Look at that pesky Archbishop Makarios in Cyprus and his supposed union, his "*enosis*". Where's all that going to get us? We loved the British during the war, they were good comrades. But now look at it all. We hate each other where we were once friends. They won't let go of that wretched island and they're siding with our ancient enemies the Turks. Well, that's a turnaround, isn't it? Who can you trust? That damned priest will bring us to a war with Turkey the way things are going. That might get this lot of our backs, though. It might be a good thing.'

'What are you talking about, *re malaka*?' demanded Dimitri in disgust. 'What good did war ever do? We don't want to start another European war, for God's sake.'

Fi-Fi called from kitchen that dinner was ready.

'Sure you won't stay?' asked Petros.

Dimitri shook his head. 'No, thanks, I'll be off. But keep me informed of what happens and if there's any more arrests.'

Chapter 20

Athens: 28th April, Greek Good Friday

It turned out that the King's coup with his generals behind him had been planned for the 23rd and a group of unknown colonels had cleverly taken the initiative to 'save the country' as they put it. Little about these men was known as yet and the country waited and wondered. Meanwhile many had no time to wonder. They were rounded up in their dozens, taken away to island prisons or to the Security Police headquarters at 18 Bouboulinas Street in Athens to face torture, false trials and imprisonment. As yet, the rest of the population knew nothing of this. It was Easter and time to celebrate the joyful rituals of the Orthodox Church.

The Colonels triumverate – Pattakos, Papadopoulos and Makarezos – prepared a 'feast of the resurrection of the Greek Orthodox civilisation. The country will rise like the fabled phoenix,' they declared. 'It will rise like Christ and be reborn.' The phoenix amidst its flames became their symbol, their flag of renewal and power. To no one's surprise, the Americans quickly came round to accepting the new regime while the British, ever cautious, waited a day or two before doing the same. Rumours flew about CIA plots and heaven knows what else. But no one knew for sure and there seemed little could be done to resist.

Not everyone was as passive as this. Theodorakis had come out of hiding and a meeting was held for those Lambrakides who had so far escaped arrest. They decided to publish a resistance newspaper to be called *Nea Ellada* … New Greece. This paper would tell the truth of what was happening, not the lies fed to the other papers who had to publish what they were told or be shut down. Many offices had already been torn apart. The only newspaper that stuck out and refused to publish under such restrictions was Vlachou's papers *Kathimerini* and *Mesimvrini*. Life was not being made easy for Eleni Vlachou, but she was not to be budged despite all the threats. She would not print lies, she declared. Fortunately for her, she was too well-known a figure internationally to be carted off to prison. Even the colonels weren't that stupid. They wished above all to appear in a good light abroad.

George was sure to be amongst the rebels that followed and aided Theodorakis in spreading his rebellious words, and Nina prayed for his safety. Aris had told his son not to ring home in case the phone was being tapped. Police had already called upon them and turned the place upside down searching for incriminating material.

'Where is your traitor son?' they had shouted at Stella who simply wailed and sobbed and they had left her alone in disgust. Thankfully, Aris was out at that time at a meeting with his employer, Vlachou, and other newspaper colleagues.

They seized several of the books they found on the shelves, some of which belonged to George.

'Why are you taking those books?' Nina asked in amazement.

'All big books are communist books,' said the policeman.

'But that's Shakespeare – and the one in your hand is Aristotle … don't you know our own classics, man?'

'They're filthy communist trash!' the man yelled and Nina took a step back at the fury in his voice. These men were ignorant fools. It was impossible to believe this was really happening.

'Don't you have to have a warrant to come barging in here to search a private citizen's house?' she demanded.

The man sneered at her. 'Lady, we don't need warrants. These are grave times. The country is under threat and we have full permission, don't you worry.'

'This would never happen in England,' she said angrily.
'Then return to England, madam,' was the cold response.

Thessaloniki: Basil's shop

Easter Day was now over and Christ had risen yet again to proclaim His Majesty. The faithful had taken home their lighted candles, protecting then so that they would not blow out and bring bad luck. On reaching their various homes, they marked their doors with the sign of the cross in candle wax and crossed their breasts before re- entering their homes and their lives, refreshed and renewed by this holy event.

Now there was plenty of work to be done as suits and dresses were brought in for dry-cleaning. Thank God, business was as usual and the city back to normal. Basil raised his head wearily from a pile of papers and files and took a gulp of water from a glass on the desk. He rose, stretched and went out of his little office into the shop beyond and for a while watched his widowed cousin, Agatha, ironing by the large window. It was a hot day and she wore a thin cotton sleeveless blouse and a flowered cotton skirt. The sweat dripped off her as she moved the iron back and forth, tucking it into the crevices, flattening the seams, frills and collars of the garment she was working on. Then she hung the dress on a hanger and added the finished article to the long aluminium rail at the back of the shop. Here stood a large machine with a flat broad top. Her son, Sotiri, a lad of fourteen, was working on this, rolling forth embroidered damask tablecloths and crisp heavily-starched white sheets.

At the door, chatting to Agatha, was Tobias, a middle-aged fellow who had set his cap at the young widow. He was quite a wealthy merchant and had a flashy white Mercedes. Agatha rather liked to be seen around in this car by her neighbours who in turn loved to gossip with delight about her wicked goings-on. But there was nothing in it, she simply used the poor man as a glorified chauffeur, making him think she might, just might be interested in him, despite his ugly face and over-flowing figure.

Today he was posing in the doorway in an astonishing sky-blue suit with white socks and shoes. The terylene material of his suit was so thin that his underpants were visible. It was all Basil could do to prevent himself from laughing but Agatha took it all in her stride and even seemed impressed.

Fanning himself with a sheaf of papers, Basil called young Sotiri over.

'Get us some *limonada*, Sotiri, there's a good lad.'

'All of us?' asked Sotiri, looking at his mother's admirer, still posing in the doorway.

'Of course, all of us. Bring a big jug and some glasses.' He gave the boy a drachma note and went back into his office after a perfunctory greeting for Tobias. He couldn't stand the man. A low, ill-bred sort; flashy, stupid. He hoped against hope that Agatha wouldn't be lured by the fellow's money and smart car. Women could be so easily bought. The thought of being at their wedding and seeing that ugly, thick-lipped fellow kissing his cousin made him feel ill.

A familiar voice outside brought him out of his office again. It was Hadji-Stavros, their local policeman, popping in with some shirts to be washed and ironed. He was a decent enough man. Why couldn't Agatha take to him instead? He was also a widower, a good god-fearing man who took care of his mother and two small children on a meagre policeman's pay. The man was good-looking too, well made with strong, brawny arms, his hair soft and dark and he had really vivid violet blue eyes. He would be a good husband to her, not a bully like that cheap crook she was chatting and smiling with now. However, if it was money she wanted, then Hadji-Stavros had little hope.

'Good afternoon, *Kyrie* Vasili,' the policeman called when he saw Basil emerge from his office, 'how's things?'

'Well enough. And yourself?'

'Eh, the same!'

'What's the latest news about this coup that's going on?' asked Basil. 'No one seems to make head and tail of it.'

'You think I know?' said the policeman rolling his eyes. 'We never get to know anything. But I do know this. It's a very good thing for us Greeks. We need taking in hand. We need a firm hand. Things have been going from bad to worse in this country, believe me. Those commies are responsible for a lot of trouble, a lot of trouble.'

Basil nodded in agreement. 'You really think this will improve things?'

'Oh yes, they've started rounding up the troublemakers already. No more looting and rioting for those bastards. What *they* want is anarchy so they can take control. What we decent citizens want is a little law and order, a little peace and quiet. How can the economy ever recover when you have idiots like this constantly getting on their hind legs like a load of braying donkeys? What are they after?'

'I've no idea,' Basil sighed. 'They rage and grumble at those of us who work damned hard for a living. It's sheer envy half the time.'

'That's the way of it,' agreed Tobias, Agatha's admirer. 'Sheer envy, as you say, *Kyrie* Vasili. Some rotten little shit scratched my Merc the other day, scratched a huge mark along it just for spite. It was my bad luck I had to go to Toumba for some orders. That's where all these low-life characters hang out. Round them up, Officer Hadji-Stavros, round them all up, I say. Frankly, I'd string them all up from the walls of Seven Towers like they used to in the old days.'

'Well, I wouldn't go that far,' said Agatha, piping up now and looking at Tobias with some disgust. 'But they do need to realise the police won't tolerate their misbehaviour; make them a little afraid. That's the best way. They need jobs too. Jobs that can help them feed their families. But there are never enough jobs to go round all these refugees and immigrants. It's all a worry.'

'Ach, they're just lazy half the time. They don't want to work, those sorts. Well. For the moment we're rounding up the worst of them, the real trouble makers,' said Hadji-Stavros. He smiled at Agatha who smiled back as she took his shirts and handed him a receipt. 'Tomorrow?' he asked her.

'We'll have them ready for you tomorrow,' she agreed.

Sotiri arrived at this moment, bearing a tray with tall glasses and a large jug of lemonade, clinking with ice. Seeing Hadji-Stavros, the lad's face fell and he said, 'I haven't brought enough glasses, uncle.'

By now, Basil had brought out a couple of chairs to the front of the shop and invited the policeman to sit down for a moment or two. Tobias took in the scene and hastily said, 'Don't worry, my boy, I have to get going. Important business to do in town. Let the officer have my glass. His is thirsty work,' and he grinned ingratiatingly at Hadji-Stavros. It was a good idea to keep well in with the police, especially these days.

Hadji-Stavros gave him a brief, dismissive nod. Tobias looked at Agatha with hope. 'I'll come back and give you a lift home,' he said.

'It's okay, I've got shopping to do,' she said, her eyes on the handsome, blue-eyed policeman.

'*I'll* see you home,' said Hadji-Stavros. 'There are a lot of hoodlums still about. Especially where you live. We intend to make every area safe to walk in, if it means carting off the whole of Ano Toumba.'

Tobias slunk off, looking like a dog with his tail between his legs. Basil smiled to himself. Good man, that Hadji-Stavros. What a relief it was to have law and order at long last.

Young Sotiri poured out the drinks and they sat out on the pavement under the awning where a cool breeze was at last stirring. Two pretty young girls in very short mini-skirts went past and Sotiri strained his neck after them and whistled. Hadji-Stavros looked after them with deep disapproval.

'I've a good mind to go and tell those two little tarts to get home and put some decent clothes on,' he said fiercely. 'It's disgusting the way girls dress now. And what goes with that? No respect for their parents, for their husbands, for the church.'

'They look nice,' protested young Sotiri. 'Anyway, they're probably foreigners.'

'That may be so, but it doesn't take long for these things to be mimicked. There's no respect any more, that's what I'm saying. Our chief has spoken to us and told us that it's time to get things back on the straight path again. We need to rescue our Hellenic-Christian civilisation. That's what he said. These commies have no religion at all.'

'Did they really kill people with the jagged edges of tin cans in the war?' asked Sotiri, his eyes wide with fascinated horror.

'They certainly did, my boy. And you'd better believe that they'll do it again if they're allowed to gain even a tiny foothold in our country.'

'Karamanlis said Greek communists were the most aggressive in Europe,' agreed Basil. 'My father fought them during the Civil War. But to be fair, there were atrocities on both sides.'

'Obviously. We have to fight back. And the only way is to use their own methods and weapons against them.' Hadji-Stavros rose now, donned his hat and gave Agatha a winning smile. She looked up from her ironing and smiled back. Despite the fact that sweat poured off the woman, she looked plump and attractive.

'Would you like me to come and escort you home when the shop shuts tonight, *Kyria* Agatha?'

Agatha fluttered a little. 'Why, that would be so kind of you, Officer.'

It was two thirty in the afternoon and Basil was closing the shop for lunch and siesta. Agatha had finished the day's ironing and was washing her face with cold water at the little sink in the back of the office while Sotiri pulled down the blinds and shut the windows. The phone rang and Basil paused. He didn't want to get involved with a client just now, he longed to get off home for a shower and a hearty meal. However, he picked up the phone with a sigh. To his surprise Athina was on the other end, her voice full of tears, almost shrieking into the mouthpiece.

He held it away from his ear for a moment. 'Calm down, calm down, what the devil's the matter?' It was so unlike his wife to be in a state of hysterics, it made his heart jump and race with fear, 'What's happened?' he asked anxiously.

'Basil, come home, come home at once. Some young thugs

have attacked our little Yiannaki. He's shivering and shaking, my lamb, my baby! One of the old women upstairs found him in the hallway, bleeding. Oh God! My poor baby!'

Basil was horrified. Such a thing had never happened before. Especially in their smart neighbourhood. Where was all this marvellous law and order that Hadji-Stavros had boasted about? He shouted to Agatha to hurry and briefly told her the news as they left together.

'My Virgin Lady!' she exclaimed. 'What's this country coming to?'

'Take the keys and open the shop later if I don't get back. Ask Hadji-Stavros to come by our place as soon as he's dropped you off home.'

She took the keys and wished him well. He ran to the back of the shop where his car was parked and drove like a maniac till he got home, panted and puffed his way up the stairs, forgetting the lift in his haste. Athina was waiting at the top of the stairs and he followed her into the flat.

Yiannakis lay on the sofa, his face deathly pale with shock. Someone had chopped at his beautiful brown curls exposing red raw and bleeding patches on his head as if tufts had been pulled out or cut too close to the scalp. Other than this he seemed unhurt apart from a few vivid bruises where his arms had been held.

'What happened, son? Who did this to you?'

Yiannakis opened his eyes and stared at his father, then burst into tears. 'I tried to fight, Papa, I really did.'

'Yes, yes, son. I'm sure you did. But who were these people, how many of them?

'There were three of them. Boys of fifteen or more. I never saw them before. I think they're from Aretsou. They got hold of me as I was coming home from school and started to laugh ... they threw my satchel away, Papa ... I don't know where it is. My teacher will be so angry if I lose the books. Then they started to cut at my hair with big scissors like the barber uses. They laughed at me and said I was like a girl and that long hair wasn't allowed any more in our new Greece. They said men had to be men and they'd teach me a lesson while I was young. They'd teach me …' the child's voice wobbled as he recalled the terror he had experienced.

Basil smoothed his child's face with both hands and held back the rage he felt. It was true that there had been cases of young men being stopped and having their hair cut forcibly in front of everyone, shaved to the scalp like criminals. But that thugs should attack a young child, here in Karabournaki! Hadji-Stavros had better deal with this at once, see the police commissioner straight away, see someone who could deal with it. Make sure that this sort of criminal business was stopped.

'We'll find them, son, don't you worry. I'll have them put in jail faster than you can imagine. We'll find them and I'll beat them personally.'

'But, Papa, you will look for my satchel?'

Basil almost cried. He bent down and kissed his son tenderly, an unusual gesture for him. 'I'll go look for it now,' he promised.

Chapter 21

Downlands, Gloucestershire, May 1967

When Andrew spoke at last to his daughter, she told him about Eleni Vlachou, the owner of the newspaper *Kathimerini,* who had bravely made the decision to stop printing her paper.

'It's sending shock waves amongst these bastards,' Nina told him, 'they've threatened to put her under house arrest. They tried to coerce her but there's nothing they can do. It's her paper, privately owned, and if she refuses to publish all their lies, that's up to her. It seems to astonish them that she, a mere woman, has this power. I believe they imagined that the State owned the paper and, as you know, it's the most influential in Athens, the biggest circulation, so it's a blow to their image. They want people to believe they are doing all this for the sake of Greece, freeing Greece from some dreadful scourge, when in truth the unseen enemy is within themselves, in their mediocrity and power-hungry hearts, and they're terrified of it.'

'Should you be saying all this on the phone? I thought you said it might be tapped?'

'I don't care! Let them hear what I think! They can't do anything to me. I'm a British citizen, after all.'

Oh, so now it suited her to be a British citizen. Andrew couldn't help a sad little smile. 'What of your friend who works for the paper? How's he managing?'

'Aris? He'll manage somehow. He refuses to go to another newspaper. All her staff are solidly behind her. They're so brave. You've no idea what's going on here. Early this month the colonels published their list of banned works. Can you imagine...they've banned a Bulgarian-Greek dictionary! For some reason they don't like classical tragedies either. And they've dissolved the Lambrakis Youth movement and are hunting them down savagely as we speak. There have been some dreadful developments but well, you're right. I shouldn't speak much about them on the phone. I'm writing up a real, stinging article, one that the censors here won't get their hands on but which will lay the truth bare for the world to see. I have a few plans of my own. I'm determined to get this stuff through to Reggie in London.'

'Nina, take care. I worry about you.'

'You have no need to, Papa *mou*,' she answered coolly. 'I can take perfect care of myself.'

Her father wasn't so sure about that.

Athens: Nina writes Polemics

Nina sat at the old mahogany desk in the *saloni* of the Praxiteles apartment and rattled away at the old Underwood typewriter until her arms and shoulders ached. Words flowed like water and she poured out her feelings into a polemic article that she felt sure would make the world sit up and take notice, make people come to the help of the Greeks.

These new rulers, these despots, liked to make out how patriotic they were. And yet their first act had been to forcibly arrest the lawfully elected Prime Minister, Kanellopoulos, a statesman of unimpeachable character, dragging him away like a criminal. She was even beginning to feel sorry for poor Constantine, a victim of crafty, bullying men. They had used their power to force the young King into signing their declarations, arresting his one good friend and all his advisors so that he stood alone and without friends in this moment of crisis. It was this original agreement to the situation that was Constantine's downfall. People believed at first that he was 'with' the Army coup and that all in all it might be a respite from all the fury and controversy over the forthcoming elections.

Nina wrote about the bravery of Mrs Vlachou who remained defiant of the strong arm tactics and threats of the new regime. The staff had been dispersed, journalists told to find jobs elsewhere for the present. The machine rooms fell silent, the offices were emptied and the huge building on Socrates Street echoed eerily with just a skeleton staff keeping the machines ticking over and busily dealing with legal problems.

Aris Praxiteles had no work now and was obliged to manage on a small pension.

'It's impossible to find work, anyway,' he said gloomily, 'we're being discriminated against. Our best journalists have been taken on by other newspapers then suddenly sacked for no reason. It's obvious their employers have been got at. They've tried to get us all to sue *Kathimerini* and some people have done so because they're afraid not to. But I refuse and so does most of her staff. We're loyal to Vlachou and loyal to what she believes in. Freedom to say what must be said, not publish all the lies that are fed to the other papers. Now, they all sound the same because they've all been given the same copy to print. May as well have just one paper and be done with it.'

After a couple of hours of hard, passionate outpouring of her ideas and information, Nina stopped typing and gratefully accepted the coffee Stella brought her. Sipping it, she said, 'I'm going out tonight, Stella. A friend of *Kyria* Vlachou has asked me over to their place for dinner and there'll be one or two Scandinavian journalists there. They're the only people who seem to be taking some interest in what's going on over here. I want to gather as much information as possible about her situation as no one is allowed to ring her or communicate with her any more. She's virtually under house arrest. I have a feeling she will try to get out of the country at some point and work from Paris or London. I may join her and other Greeks who are fleeing the country. Eleni thinks we can do more to help from abroad, spreading the word about what is going on over here.'

'Nina, you must take care. If the CIA is behind this, don't let anyone know your plans – don't be too … bold.'

Nina smiled. 'Foolish is what you meant to say. And I know

there are risks. But this is what a journalist has to do, take risks. The truth has to be found out, Stella, and told to the world. I'm not afraid of these bullies.'

Stella appeared unconvinced. Deep in her heart, Nina had qualms too. But as she continued typing her article, she glanced now and then in moments of thoughtfulness, at a photo by her typewriter. It was the only photo she possessed of her dead mother. Her father had taken it with an old box camera one day when his beloved Anna was unaware.

'She would never have let me take a photo of her, she hated cameras,' he told Nina. In the small black and white photo, Anna was caught washing clothes at the little sink in the hovel where she lived with her two brothers and her father, Old Manoglou. She had turned towards Andrew when he called her and he'd captured her open-eyed stare of surprise, the thick tucked-up mane of hair falling about her face in heavy tendrils. She was truly beautiful. Nina tried to see her resemblance to her mother. Her father often said she was the image of his Anna. But she herself couldn't see it at all. Her mother was far lovelier, almost a goddess to be worshipped.

'I want to be brave and wise and sacrifice myself for our beloved Greece, just as you did, Mama,' she whispered, pickling up the photo and regarding it with love. She kissed the picture tenderly and set it back. It was her ikon, her *Panayia* in human form. If only she had her mother's courage, her mother's principles. She loved Greece with all her heart and soul, loved its past, its ancient history and monuments. But above all, she loved the brave deeds and heroism shown by its people. The great names; Pythagoras, Pericles, Sophocles, Aristotle and the more recent names of Kolokotronis, Bouboulina, Mavromichalis, Lambrakis … so many that had died rather than see Greece taken over by tyrants. What had happened to them all? What sort of men and women lived here now and calmly let themselves be taken over by men a hundred times worse than the lazy Turks or the brave but dictatorial Metaxas?

Nina gathered together her papers when she had finished. She wanted to publish it and distribute it here in Greece but she knew that even small printing presses had been seized and if she was to buy too much paper, that would be reported by some sneaky shopkeeper and cause trouble. Somehow, Theodorakis was still managing to print out his own polemics and these were being circulated everywhere by those Lambrakides who had so far escaped capture. She had no idea where Theodorakis was at present. He was being moved from house to house and she had heard from a reliable source that he was still composing his music, sending it out of the country somehow. She smiled with deep satisfaction. Thank God for some brave men, for fighters who were fearless!

Her other option was to smuggle her article out via one of the foreign journalists who still managed to have an interview with Vlachou. Even they had been astonished at the fact that things seemed so quiet and normal, hardly believing that anything untoward had occurred. It was only when the stories began to filter out of tortures, beatings and the arrest of hundreds of innocent citizens that they began to wake up.

She, Nina, would make things known. She would beg the world to sit up and help them. Where now were the British and the Americans in their real hour of need?

Chapter 22

Thessaloniki, May 1967: Max has a visit

Max was beginning to feel tired, hot and sticky in the damp and oily pit underneath the old Fiat he was working on and was contemplating the idea of a cool drink from the little fridge in the office. He heard someone come into the shop. Dimitri had gone to deliver a reconditioned truck to a client in Mihaniona and young Tinos, who came in to help with re-spraying and general repairs, tidying up and errands, was taking his kid to the dentist so Max was on his own for a few hours. He popped his head out, expecting to see one of their customers. To his amazement and dismay he saw that it was none other than his arch enemy, Katsarakis, standing in the open doorway, looking around.

'Eh, you English shit, come out from under that stinking hole, come out and talk to me,' the Cretan growled.

Max climbed up the steps and scrambled out, grabbing a rag to clean the oil from his hands. He took his time and kept a wary eye on the intruder, wondering what he could have to say, sensing danger with every fibre of his body.

Katsarakis was dressed in a dirty white vest and a pair of baggy Cretan-style trousers. His hair was cut far shorter, accentuating the heavy, stolid, square features. He moved slowly and limped a little and Max wondered what sort of a fight he had got into that had actually caused this huge brute some damage for a change. Folding his arms, Katsarakis leant his great bulk against the door post, regarding Max with an amused smile. 'So, you English coward, you prancing, pretty man, you can't revenge your own quarrel but you get your little Greek friend to sort it out.'

'What the hell are you talking about?' Max was bemused. He had never been told about the saga with Big Bouros and his boys.

'Don't pretend you don't know. Your friend had me out of circulation for a bit and no one does that to Katasarakis. You pretend that wasn't your idea, eh?'

'First I've heard of it, but if it's true then I wish I'd been there to punch your filthy face in,' was the heated reply. 'You smashed my jaw, you bastard! I don't take that lightly either. If a fight's what you want; I'm more than willing.'

The big Cretan snorted in derision, then laughed, 'Pfff! I'd make mincemeat of you in no time, you're made of thistledown. My last little effort was simply to teach you a lesson for messing about with my woman. I don't take to that kindly. And that's what I came to find out. What have you done with her, where are you hiding her?'

'Which woman are we talking about? As far as I know, you have half a dozen.'

Katsarakis made a threatening move toward him but Max picked up a heavy torque wrench and stared him in the eye. 'Don't come any nearer,' he said. He looked calm and determined. Katsarakis stopped in his tracks and said angrily, 'You know damn well, *re aliti*, you know where my Zoë is and I want her back! Tell me where she is or you'll be sorry for it.'

'What makes you think I know where she is?' demanded Max. 'Why have you got it into that thick skull of yours that I'm interested in her? The girl is nothing to me.'

'You've been seen with her, so don't lie to me!' roared the man. 'You took her to your hotel. I know all about it, so don't lie!' His face had flushed a dull ugly red and he looked intimidating and dangerous. Max braced himself, ready to inflict some damage of his own if the fellow attacked him. Katasarkis seemed to realise this instinctively and drew back, his face slowly losing the red flush but twitching now and again like that of an enraged bull.

'I'll find her, if it's the last thing I do,' he muttered.

Max felt a shadow pass over him at the mere thought that this foul creature might find poor Zoë and prayed that she had got the hell out of the country somehow. Katsarakis was unlikely to have a passport of any sort. Few ordinary Greeks did.

Katsarakis, with his tuned-in animal instincts, seemed to read something in the look that crossed Max's face. 'Oh, yes, I'll find her and teach her a lesson,' he grunted. 'Give her to my boys. She won't walk again after that, she won't go running anywhere. And I'll deal with you lot too. I'm well in with this new mob now. They like good patriots, good citizens like me. I'm friendly with the big boys, do you know that? Thanks to me, they've rooted out a load of commie bastards and sent them off to have a little treatment on the islands. I know where they're hiding; Katsarakis knows everything, got ears everywhere. Tell that to your little friend when he gets back, yes, tell him that. Tell him his pal, Big Bouros, is facing a few awkward questions.'

He gave a laugh that chilled Max's heart and then turned and limped off from wherever he had come from. Hell, as like as not. Max put down the wrench and taking a solitary, battered, rush-bottomed chair from the back of the shop, he placed it out on the pavement outside the shop, found himself a cold beer then sat and lit one cigarette after another, thinking over what had been said and feeling very troubled. After a while, with a leaden heart, he went back to his work.

Dimitri exploded in wrath at the news. 'That bastard, that piece of filth, that devil! What does he mean he's "in with the big boys"? What big boys? I can believe it though; people like him change their allegiance by the hour as long as they can save their filthy hides. He's the sort they used to have on the islands, you know. The sort who enjoy torturing men and women and even children. You don't know the half of it, Max, thank God. You don't know what some of my older friends went through during the Civil War. Some still can't walk properly, can't breathe as they used to.'

Dimitri's heart was full of grief and pain. Big Bouros! What chance did that poor fellow have if those crazy butchers really had got hold him? His heart would give way in sheer terror. Dimitri felt that it was his fault he'd got his friend mixed up with Katsarakis. Pity they hadn't finished him off and buried his carcase somewhere. But Katsarakis had a gang of roughnecks who followed him. They would have wreaked their revenge anyway.

Max followed him outside after a while and they both stood and smoked in silence, watching the cars speeding by, the late night buses crammed with passengers going home or off to the nightspots.

'I don't get it,' Dimitri said aloud, 'I don't understand why people were marching, demonstrating and screaming their heads off a short while ago about various stupid things, just as we always do. Then this … this happens and everyone is silent. As if it never happened and the 21st of April never occurred. As if it was a dream they had in the night and now the day is here, it can be forgotten, life can just go on as normal.'

'Perhaps they're afraid?'

'When were Greeks ever afraid? Didn't we get together, communists and right-wingers and resist the Nazis together? But as soon as the war was over, they chose to forget how much the commies did; suddenly they were the enemy and all those mother-fucking collaborators got let off. Yes, the Reds did do bad things but most of the stories you hear are crap, all right-wing propaganda. There's always bad things in wars on both sides, no one plays nice.'

'That's true,' admitted Max. 'We Brits have had our share of it. We haven't always played nice either.'

'Seems to me, life is dirty,' said Dimitri bitterly. 'That good man, a doctor, an athlete, an intellectual, that hero Grigoris Lambrakis, began a peace organisation and look what happened to him? Killed right here in the streets of Thessaloniki by yobs in the pay of the police. The police, who are supposed to guard our liberties and our cities. Now this. And we just take it on the chin. People have turned spineless.'

They shut up the workshop and went home to Dimitri's flat in Vassilis Georgiou to have supper. Yiota greeted them and chattered on as always about the local gossip. The two men ate in silence and after a while she stopped talking, occasionally giving her husband an anxious glance. The children shouted and fought and played up even more than usual as if aware that their father was too preoccupied to yell at them in his normal fashion. Yiota's attention was taken up by them till it was time for their bed. They went off amidst noisy protests and exclamations and she was obliged to follow them, screaming at their antics. Max sighed. The noise, as always, was deafening.

'*Vre* Dimitri, can't you tell these boys of yours to behave?' Yiota complained.

'I'm tired. You see to them. You're their mother, for heaven's sake! Just sort them out,' was the cross response. During all this, the old grandmother sat crocheting quietly in a corner without comment. After a while she said, 'What's wrong with you two men? You're like a morgue tonight.'

'Tired, *mitera mou*, that's all,' said Dimitri. He sounded and looked tired and she shrugged and said, 'Well, you've a family to keep, after all; you do work hard, my boy,' put back on her spectacles and went back to the *Romanzo* magazine and her knitting.

Later that night when Max had left them and returned to his flat near Agia Sofias Square, the children asleep at last and the old lady snoring in her room, Dimitri sat out on his little balcony opposite the cinema, smoking a last cigarette before turning in. He stared at the flickering screen of the cinema opposite, casting its unnatural light on the trees and the walls that surrounded the area, listened to the tinny music and the foreign voices. This week it was some stupid Italian film where everything would end up fine, the baddie caught, the good bloke kissing the girl. It was all unreal, this life in flickering images, sugar-coated, stupid and meaningless. How could people go there, sit in the darkness stuffing their faces with food and watch all that rubbish? Life wasn't like this at all. He still trembled with rage at the thought of Big Bouros being taken away, God only knew where.

Putting out his cigarette, he undressed swiftly and climbed into bed with his wife. She turned over and touched his face, her expression worried. 'What's bothering you, Dimi? I'm scared. Something's happened.'

'They've taken Big Bouros, Yiota. And I'm scared for our *koumbaros* and for myself too.'

'But why take Big Bouros? He's harmless and sick. He's not a Red.'

'He's left wing, that all that matters. I heard the other day that they arrested a bus driver just because he complained about something the new lot are doing. He had the courage to stand up and say what he thinks and that's the result. They've rounded up anyone who opposes what they say. It's a dictatorship of the worst sort and no one seems to get it. They don't see their liberties have disappeared overnight.'

'But surely people will protest? There'll be marches and all the rest of it? People don't take things lying down, not here, not in Thessaloniki.'

'I don't know,' he said wearily, 'I don't understand it either. All I know is, you'd better get things ready just in case I have to do a moonlight flit. Max will take care of the workshop, they daren't do anything to him.'

Chapter 23

This road has no end, has no relief, however hard you try
to recall your childhood years, those who left, those
lost in sleep, in the graves of the sea,
however much you ask bodies you've loved to stoop
under the harsh branches of the plane trees there
where a ray of the sun, naked, stood still
and a dog leapt and your heart shuddered,
the road has no relief…

'Epiphany', George Seferis

Asphalia Headquarters, Bouboulinas Street, Athens, June 1967

He had tried to escape. Tried to tear free from his captors as they led him every other day to be interrogated, only to suffer the more because he struggled and refused to be pushed up those stairs again. Those hateful stairs that led to the terrace and to torments beyond description. Then flung into a dark, cramped isolation cell in the basement after beatings he had never thought possible to bear, denied food and water, exercise, cigarettes or even a blanket to cover himself with at night. He used his shoes as a pillow and slept on the hard cement floor, amazed that he could sleep at all. As he sat against the wall of his cell, he had all the time in the world to wonder what he could have done to avoid capture.

When George fled home, he had stayed for some time with his best friend Alekis. Then Alekis was caught distributing leaflets for Theodorakis and taken away. The security police came to Alekis's place to search for incriminating evidence but by then George had escaped and made his way to another young friend, Lakis Tarlantzis. However, they were not welcomed by Lakis's father who loudly berated them for getting into trouble with the authorities.

'It's time you kids grew up,' he shouted. 'Took some responsibilities in this world. It's not about playing soldiers and spies and being brave and stupid. Just go to the police and tell them you're not going to be involved in this stupid Youth movement and then we'll have a bit of peace and quiet.'

'Are you mad, Father!' Lakis shouted back. 'Go to the police? They'll shove us in jail as fast as they see us. They won't believe anything we say. Is that what you want, you want us in jail?'

At this, Lakis' mother began to wail and beat her breast and ask what was the world coming to.

'Now you've upset your, mother, you selfish boy. You'll bring trouble on us all with your nonsense. Go away till you calm down, don't come back till you do.'

'But where can we go?'

'Ask your friend Theodorakis. He seems to be lying low well enough. They haven't caught *him* yet. If you ask me, he's out of the country by now, saving his own hide. Think he cares about you lot? I doubt it.'

Lakis had been so angry that he had walked out of the house and made his way to his waiting friend, George, lurking in the garden.

'We're not staying here now, not if my father begs us,' he declared. 'He cares about nothing but his own safety. He's just scared, a fucking coward.'

'I don't blame him for being scared, Lakis. I'm scared. I certainly wouldn't stay anywhere near my parents' place. I don't want them in trouble as well.'

Lakis calmed down a little and glanced back at the house. His mother was at the window, her face streaked with tears. 'No, I don't want them in trouble either,' he admitted.

His mother came out and hastily stuffed a small roll of drachma notes in her son's pocket. 'Don't tell your father,' she whispered, 'it's a little I put aside. Take care, my son, take care.' She scuttled back indoors. Lakis felt the notes in his pocket and his eyes filled with tears but he brushed them aside and said angrily, 'We'll find somewhere. I have a good idea. There's my Zo-Zo … she knows everyone. She's a real brave girl and I feel sure she'll help us. Come on Giorgo … let's get the hell out of here. I'll never come back again. I swear it.'

'Better not to swear such a thing,' said George crossing himself fearfully, 'God may hear you.'

'I don't give a shit about God.'

George remembered that terrible day in June when they had found him and Lakis hiding like hunted animals in an outhouse at the bottom of a garden in the suburbs of Nea Smyrna. The owners, friends of Lakis' father, were away for the summer months at their place up in the hills and Lakis said it was a safe place. His girlfriend, Zo-Zo, brought them food and took their clothes away to wash each day. They knew that they couldn't stay there forever and planned how they might make their way to Piraeus and get a boat from there to Italy. But Zo-Zo berated them and said they were cowards.

'You're going to leave the country,' she hissed, 'leave your comrades – who have already been rounded up – leave them in the lurch. Run like dogs with your tails between your legs! What sort of Greeks are you? What would Lambrakis say of you, or Theodorakis? Those men are heroes. Lambrakis was ready to die for Greece, Theodorakis is hiding and printing out stuff for the Party all the time. He's trying to rouse the youth of this country. And you want to run away.'

She put them to shame. They knew they must make a move, try and join other members of the organisation and put up some sort of resistance, distribute leaflets, maybe plant a few bombs in factories here and there, cause some sort of disruption. It would cause them all such joy to blow up the Esso-Pappas oil refinery, that symbol of American dominance over Greek finances. That damned Papadopoulos – they knew he'd been trained by the CIA! So yes, do anything rather than allow the colonels to tighten their grip of fear on the populace.

So they changed the escape route and decided to try and make their way to Thessaloniki instead. Zo-Zo brought them a map and said she had a contact, a friend of her father, who could hide them in his lorry taking produce up North from Piraeus. They had to make their way to the port somehow even if it was on foot and meet him coming off the ferry boat from Crete.

'Theodorakis' music is banned,' she said, 'but people still play the records. They refuse to take notice and it's dangerous. But who cares! I'm going to play it as loud as I can when you've got away safely. They can arrest me. I don't give a damn. We'll show them who counts in this country! We'll show them, I tell you.'

The two young men listened in awe. Women could be so strong. It made them feel inspired, ready to do defiant acts of their own. They were ready for their next move and packed their bags and gave Zo-Zo cash to get them food. Going by Metro made them too nervous in case they were recognised round Syntagma Square. They would take themselves to Piraeus, hitch lifts if they could. Then off to the North to carry on the good work.

A day or so later, they heard soft footsteps outside the shed door and their hearts lurched. Someone tapped three times. Was it okay to open the door?

'It's me, brothers, it's Savvas.'

Savvas, a gentle lad of eighteen, was the younger brother of Alekis. Relief flooded over them. They opened the door and let their friend slip in. He looked around the hideaway and shook his head.

'They'll find you here, you've got to move. They're searching all sorts of places … not for small fry like us, they're looking for Theodorakis. He's hiding round here somewhere. Not the best place for you to have come to.'

'We know that. But where else?' said Lakis. 'We're going to

get out of here and go to Piraeus. Zo-Zo knows a lorry driver fellow who'll give us a lift to Thessaloniki. Giorgo has a cousin there who may find us a place to hide out, be incognito. But it looks like we're going to have to walk to Piraeus.'

'I'll see what I can do,' Savvas promised, 'I'll get you a lift, someone to take you to Piraeus in the back of his car. Isn't easy, there seem to be security police everywhere just now, they're catching us like fish in a net. But once you're away from here you should be safe. I'll let Zo-Zo know what I've arranged and she'll see you tomorrow. Just hang tight.'

Their hopes rose and they began to feel impatient, anything to get out of this enforced idleness. They were both students and Zo-Zo had managed to bring them a few books which they sat and read and studied, wrote essays and played chess and *tavli* to pass time. But now they wanted to do something, be active. Zo-Zo was right. It wasn't good or manly to sit around waiting to be snared like helpless rabbits.

The next morning they listened out for her footstep, her three knocks on the door. But no one came. They looked at each other in alarm. Where could she be? They were fearful of the truth. God forbid that brave girl had been arrested. They sat in silence and made up their minds it was time to try and slip out, walk to the city centre and maybe get a taxi, just get away while they could.

They shaved, washed their faces in the cold water they had brought in at night from an outside tap. They hadn't bothered much of late but if they were to mix amongst the crowds at Syntagma, it wouldn't do to look different or untidy.

'I'll cut your hair,' said Lakis. 'I've heard this new lot hate anyone who looks like a beatnik. We don't want to draw attention to ourselves at all.' Regretfully, George allowed his friend to take scissors to his head and shear off his long locks.

'Come on, said Lakis, 'I have a bad feeling, Giorgo. A bad feeling.'

They threw their few belongings into the rucksacks. But it was already too late. They heard shouts and the sound of men in the garden. Terrified, they cowered down in a corner but there was nowhere to hide and they dared not run out and be shot.

Shooting would have been a good thing, George realised now. He wished they *had* run. They wouldn't have shot them; those bastards wanted them alive for their own amusement.

The shed door was broken in and they were dragged forth, flung on the ground and their hands tied high up on their backs. It felt as if the bones would break and the pain rendered them speechless. One of the men booted George in the kidneys and he howled like a dog with pain.

'Filthy communist brats!' their captors snarled. 'Let's see what a little talk with Inspector Lambrou will do to persuade you to change your minds and be good Greek boys.'

'It was your girlfriend gave you away. How about that, eh?' grinned one of them as they hustled them into waiting cars. 'Never trust a woman! Foolish boys.'

They both knew that Zo-Zo would never have given them away unless they had tortured her beyond endurance. Their hearts sank. She must be captured too. They were later to learn that the security police were fully aware of her activities but had allowed her free movement in order to lead them to any other Lambrakides still in hiding.

George and Lakis were flung into the tiny basement cells at The Asphalia Security headquarters. Here they were kept in solitary confinement for three days, not even allowed to go outside to the toilet. The place stank like a urinal. Damp was creeping up the whitewashed walls and paint flaked off on their back when they leant against them. There was scarcely any light in the cell. It was narrow and low, like some mediaeval prison – so hot and airless one felt ready to faint. A small grid was the only way some air could enter. It was inhumane.

The next day, George was shoved up the stairs that led to the terrace roof. They came to one of the shower rooms at the far end. His heart was beating in fear. He had heard about this terrace and how the beatings and tortures took place there in the old days. The mere thought of what might lie in store for him made him want to wet his pants but he held on. He would not shame himself no matter what they did. He would be brave, somehow, he would be as brave as other men had been before him.

In the shower room, a large window was boarded up and long pieces of wood were stacked against an old copper boiler. He was stripped naked and these were now used to good effect upon his person as he was subjected to two hours of interrogation, his head banged against the wall till he was dizzy, his genitals beaten till they were swollen. So far they didn't use the *falanga* but he knew it would be coming. He said nothing, nothing at all. He was dragged back down to his cell. This treatment was repeated for three days.

'Tell us the names of your friends,' he was ordered. 'Tell us where Theodorakis is hiding and you can go free. If you don't help us, don't prove yourself a good patriotic Greek, your family will suffer, you hear? We'll shoot your father and mother.'

One day they told him they had his father downstairs. 'You want him to be killed?' they asked. 'He's going to be shot today if you don't tell us about Theodorakis. Where is he? Where's he hiding?'

These threats were the most terrifying of all. He wanted to kill himself. He had brought shame and fear upon his family. But he prayed they were bluffing and held his silence. In another interrogation in Inspector Lambrou's office, his head was banged against the desk and he was repeatedly hit with rulers and whips and even threatened.

'We'll throw this obstinate communist bastard out of the window, shall we?'

'Let's do that,' chorused the others.

And so the psychological torment went on. Frankly, George didn't care if they did throw him out of the window. It would end the pain at least. He was now asked to sign a statement denouncing his past, swearing loyalty to the new regime and denouncing his friends. He refused.

Next day they brought up Lakis to the terrace as well and forced George to watch them beating the soles of his friend's feet with the *falanga*. Lakis began to scream and a urine soaked rag was stuffed in his mouth while any other sound was drowned out by the sound of a guard banging on the lid of a copper boiler with a metal pipe. George was to find out later that a sound like a motor cycle engine would also be revved up to drown out the sounds. If any of the neighbours inquired, they were told the screams were from the women in labour in the maternity hospital across the road.

'Beat me, leave my friend alone,' George begged but they laughed at him.

'Your turn will come, don't worry. You can save yourself and your friend if you sign your statement.'

He wanted to do anything they asked then. But he knew Lakis would not allow it and so he kept his silence. Would poor Lakis ever walk again? His shoes, which had been left on to increase the pain as his feet swelled up inside, had burst and the toes looked broken. George went back to his cell in the basement and sobbed bitterly. He was so sickened that he couldn't eat the little that was given to him. He knew his mother had sent food and a blanket in for him but he had not been allowed to have any of the food and they had taken the blanket away again. The cell crawled with bugs and he felt filthy, inhuman.

Then miraculously, a day after the terrible experience of seeing Lakis beaten, they took him out of solitary confinement and to one of the cells on the fourth floor which were larger, had some ventilation and some company. Too much company at times as there could be as many as five or more sharing the tiny room. But it was better than being alone, a comfort of sorts to be able to talk to others. They said that he would be allowed reading matter, writing materials, some exercise in the courtyard and showers and a toilet. George wondered if it was some new way to lull him with a false sense of security.

'Have you had coffee on the terrazzo?' others would ask him. It was the code of the prisoners meaning had one been taken to the terrace – but apart from this no one discussed their tortures. What was there to say? They all suffered. They knew what went on. Although fear dominated the atmosphere, there was also a sense of stoic calm as if they were determined not to be cowed. But it was almost breaking point for George when he was passed on the way to the toilet by no other than Zo-Zo with her escort guard. She was a pitiful sight, her clothes hanging on her body, her face full of terror and pain. She was weeping silently and didn't even look at him as they passed. George stopped for a moment. He wanted to speak to her but his guard hustled him on. He felt sure the meeting had been staged on purpose.

Lakis, unable to walk now was not seen in the exercise yard or shower rooms and George wondered where his friend was and if he was even alive. Surely no one could survive such beatings for days on end. He had heard of many whose heart had given way and had to be taken to the prison hospital. When he asked, a relatively friendly guard told him that Lakis had been transferred to Dionysos, a military camp outside Athens where he would be 'educated' – in other words brainwashed – before being released. 'Bleached' into a good White Greek.

Chapter 24

Athens June 1967: Nina is defiant

It was impossible to get anyone to talk about what they felt. They were all too frightened. It made her blood boil. Why this terrible atmosphere of fear? Greeks never used to be like this. But people murmured that they dared not speak, there were informers everywhere and you really couldn't be sure who to trust these days. Fathers gave information on sons and sons on fathers. Anything to save their hides.

She returned to the Praxiteles place after her interesting dinner at Maria Constantinou's flat near Plaka, filled with the urge to go and write up her diary and a report. As she paid the taxi driver, she looked over at the apartment block and wondered why it was all so dark. No warm welcoming lamp shone its diffused light behind the flowing net curtains of the ground floor window. Even the hallway was unlit. A sense of foreboding gripped her. She entered the dark, marble floored hallway and put on the light. As she went to put the key in the lock, she realised the door was slightly open. It swung back suddenly into the flat, the shock of it making her heart leap within her. Hastily, she felt around for the light switch. The chandelier in the centre of the ceiling now flooded the room with bright light and she looked about her. She called out for Stella and Aris but there was no reply and as she looked over at the desk where she had left her typescript, she saw that it had gone, the last page, left in the typewriter, angrily ripped out with just a small piece of paper left jammed in the roller.

This was frightening. Had they arrested poor Aris? And for what crime? Why take Stella as well? She sat down on a chair and looked around her, uncertain what to do. Her head began to nod after a while and lolled forward into sleep. But she was immediately startled awake by the sound of the front door opening. To her relief, Stella came in, her face ashen, her hands trembling.

Nina leapt up, went to her friend and led her to a seat. 'What is it, Stella, what's happened?' she asked urgently. 'Where's Aris?'

Stella wrung her hands and began to sob. 'Nina, Nina! They're still talking to him at the security headquarters. They say they have George, they say they found him and some of the other Lambrakides hiding out in an old hut in Nea Smyrna. They're accusing our boy of all sorts of crimes and don't believe us when we say we didn't know where he had gone. And they didn't like your article when they found it. They said George had written it and that he's a traitor to the country and the Government. Oh, Nina, I'm so afraid. What are we to do?' Stella raised her voice in deep grief. Her cries unnerved Nina for a moment, making her shake with fear. But she recollected herself swiftly. She couldn't show fear or even anger now. She had to console her friend.

'If they've let you go, then I'm sure all will be fine. And George is not a criminal. They can't keep him. They'll just scare him and then let him go.'

'My child, you have no idea what they do to people. Just for the fun of it. The stories I heard during the Civil War, the way people just disappeared. You've no idea.'

Nina shuddered. 'Why do evil men come out of the woodwork at such times? Men who enjoy torturing others, get pleasure from it? Where have you sent your Lexi? They won't come and arrest her as well?'

'No! … ach, *Panayia mou*, Blessed Virgin! Thank God, she is staying with her cousins in Piraeus in their summer home. She doesn't know anything about it and we mustn't breathe a word to her. She'll be so upset, so ill. She's always terrified even in normal times. This will really send her into a fit.'

Nina poured out some whisky for them both and they drank it neat.

'That's warming,' said Stella gratefully. 'I feel cold inside, my heart is frozen in fear, Nina. I'm so glad you are here.'

'My heart isn't much better,' said Nina, patting her friend's hand. 'Stella, I'm troubled that my wretched article will get George in trouble. I'll wait and see if Aris comes home soon. If he's not back by the morning, I'll go to the police myself and claim the article and tell them it's mine. I'll see if I can help to get George and Aris free somehow. I do know a few influential people who might help.' She had suddenly thought of Nikos Galanis and wondered if he really had the influence of which he had boasted while in London. She knew that he had returned to Greece. He had phoned her before leaving and given a contact address. Surely he would help her.

'No, no! They may arrest you too. That won't help anything. Say nothing, Nina! It may make things worse.'

'I can't say nothing,' cried Nina, 'I wrote the article and what's more, I want it back. I'm a journalist, I am bound to write reports and state what the true situation is. It's not going to be published here. They can't detain me. I came in with my British passport, so they can't stop me returning home.'

'Yes, but they may never let you back again. And you certainly would be stupid to come back on your Greek passport. Your article is very strong, very angry. You're showing what a wicked lot they are, these colonels. They don't want that. They want to present an image of patriotism and solidarity in the country. They want other countries to accept their side of the story.'

'Well, I'm going to risk it,' said Nina stubbornly. 'But I'll wait for the morning. God willing, Aris will come home again, safe and sound. Come on, Stella, let's try and get a little sleep and make our plans in the light of day.'

'I can't sleep without my Aris in bed next to me,' Stella fretted. But she went and washed her face and lay on her bed and quite suddenly fell fast asleep fully clothed, worn with exhaustion and misery. Nina also lay on her bed but her mind whirled with thoughts and plans and ideas. She was angry with herself for having left the article lying around … how stupid of her! But she had never dreamt that the police would come and arrest Aris. Something must be done. She felt afraid, of course, but also challenged. What would her mother have done in these circumstances? She would certainly have done something. She would never have sat back and let injustices remain unrevenged or unsolved.

Nina glanced around at the dreary grey filing cabinets and office furniture. On the wall was a large portrait of Constantine and his pretty little Danish wife, Anne Marie. The place stank of sweat and stale cigarettes.

Inspector Alkis Papanikolas sat opposite and stared at her.

'*Kyria* Hammett, you do realise that if, as you claim, you are the writer of this ridiculous article, you have committed a great offence against our country?'

Nina studied Papanikolas for a few moments. She looked into eyes that were soft brown, long lashed and almost sweet in their expression with thick dark eyebrows which curved over in a perfect arch. She could swear he plucked them. No man had eyebrows as perfect and symmetrical as that. Papanikolas was not a handsome man but he was attractive. He must have been about fifty yet his hair was still rich and dark, short cropped and stubby with just a hint of silvery grey at the temples. His suit was immaculate and the small square gold cufflinks at his wrists were carved with the head of Apollo. A natty dresser. She decided he was a homosexual. Her feminine wiles would not avail her with this man.

'I'm a journalist,' she replied. 'Of course I write articles – and I write the truth, as all journalists should.'

'And as they do,' was the reply, 'as all our newspapers do.'

'They do nothing of the sort,' she said scornfully, 'and you know it. They publish what's given to them by the colonels and *that's* all lies.'

'You are being very foolish.' The Inspector leant forward and lowered his voice. His tone was sweet and gentle, yet it held a menace that made her flinch. 'People here have been arrested for less than this. They've disappeared, *Kyria* Hammett. It's well in my power to make you disappear if I wish to.'

'I think not,' she said, keeping his gaze unflinchingly. 'I have many contacts in England who are very powerful. My boss runs a highly esteemed newspaper and you think he won't make a big stir? That would really give your little game away. You know perfectly well that it would create a big international incident. And that's just what you people don't want.'

Papanikolas leant back again in his chair and studied her face in turn. He was angry that a mere, slight woman should have the power to make counter-threats. But he didn't show his anger; he remained sweet and gentle in the way that he always did, a manner which terrified his victims whenever they were brought before him for they knew full well that next to Inspector Lambrou, he was one of the cruellest men in Athens. Nina, however, seemed calm and undeterred. And this annoyed him.

'So, will you please return my article and let Aris Praxiteles and his son free? They haven't committed any crime. I can vouch for that.'

'You can vouch for that, can you?' sneered Papanikolas. 'And I'm to take your word for it; a traitorous Greek woman who has turned against her own country, married abroad, forgotten where her place is and how to behave. Running about all over Athens instead of caring for her husband, home and children. And where is your husband, may one ask? He's not even with you, and like all Englishmen obviously hasn't a clue how to keep his women in control. I've heard all about your grandfather, you know. He was a Venizelist liberal and he fell from grace in his day. If he was alive, we'd have had him in for questioning like a shot. He fell from grace as all these leftist liberals do because they are not true patriots. As for your mother, she was a communist for sure and the Germans rightly hanged her.'

Nina's face flushed and she leapt from her chair. 'Don't you dare speak about my mother and my grandfather like that, you bastard! Costas Cassimatis was a real patriot, he almost died fighting for his country. He was an invalid for the rest of his life because of that horrible war. And my mother died fighting with the *andartes*, fighting to free people like you, bastards like you! Let me tell you, I *am* a true patriot, a Greek first of all even though I married an Englishman. And the English understand democracy a hell of a lot more than people like yourselves. I believe in keeping that freedom our parents fought for not handing it to tyrants like you.'

Papanikolas smiled his sweet smile. *Now* she was aroused, *now* she had lost her *sangfroid* and he gloated at having stung her where it hurt. But he also knew that he dare not inter her in one of his pretty little prison cells or send her to be pleasantly interrogated at the Security headquarters in Bouboulinas Street. Pity, he would have loved to throw her into a cell there where she would be unable to lie down properly or wash herself, where she would soon crawl with lice and stink. Where she would scream in terror and wait to be raped daily by the guards.

Nina caught something of his thoughts and fear rose up in her like a wave of bile but she refused to show it. He dare not touch her, she was sure of that. But would he let her friends free? That was looking less and less likely. She sank back in her chair and tried to restore her calm once more. It didn't do to lose one's temper with men like this. It wasn't the way to go about it at all, but she would never plead. That would give Papanikolas such pleasure, she could see it in his eyes.

'Please let Aris and George Praxiteles go,' she asked again, voice steady now but her cheeks still flushed with feeling. 'What can you want with them? They're innocent citizens.'

'So innocent that the boy was caught hiding with other well known offenders. That's innocence, is it?'

'Oh come on, Inspector, he's young and stupid. He just got caught up in something beyond his understanding. You know very well his father has never been involved in politics.'

'All newspaper men are involved in politics and they're all Reds at heart. They have to be restrained, kept in order, don't you see that, *Kyria* Hammett?' The sweet voice, the sweet smile, the soft brown eyes; Nina shuddered as she listened to him. He sounded so reasonable, so pleasant. She wished he would storm and shout as most Greek men did, especially men of power like himself. His exquisite manners were terrifying in these circumstances. She had heard of Nazi officers who had been like this in the war and wondered if he modelled himself on one of Goering's men or if the world simply produced such travesties every now and then. Men with beautiful exteriors and evil hearts.

Papanikolas went on, his head a little tilted and his hand gracefully waving a lighted cigarette as he spoke. He could have been addressing a row of little schoolgirls as he spoke in his gentle tones. 'Nothing can ever be done for this country when people are forever thinking they can say and do as they please, challenging authority and the church. There are no more morals, no respect for authority, no respect for religion. We need respect restored, *Kyria* Hammett. Surely you can see that? We are bringing order. This is for the *good* of the people.' He paused and looked at the papers before him on his desk.

'George Praxiteles is simply being questioned at the Security headquarters for now. We need to discover the ringleaders of this local cell and he will help us. I'm afraid he and his friends will be brought to court. But if, as you declare, they are so *innocent* … then they have nothing to fear, have they? You see how lenient we are? It doesn't hurt the boys to be a little scared, you know. This way they will learn the error of their ways. This is for their own good and for the good of the community at large.'

'And Aris Praxiteles?'

'He is also being questioned. But if we find him free of the "Bulgarian" taint, we'll release him.'

'I think I shall pay a visit to your headquarters at Bouboulinas,'said Nina, her face flushed and angry. 'I shall ask for Lambrou, your deputy head, himself. Is George being treated fairly? I doubt it.'

'Why trouble Lambrou? Why should there be any doubt about Greek justice?' asked Papanikolas. 'It's true we aren't soft like your English friends. We Greeks are used to a little – let us say – coercion. But it's necessary at times. Greek men can be stubborn and uncooperative.'

'And what is this "coercion"?' demanded Nina. 'Haven't we all heard tales of beatings with the *falanga*? For God's sake. It's brutal. Can his mother visit him, yet? She's sent money over for his food but they won't let her visit. How can we even be sure he's being fed or that the blankets she has sent get to him? I don't trust you people.'

Papanikolas smiled his sweet smile. 'What nonsense, dear lady. Of course, the boy is being fed and cared for. His mother may come along soon. We still have some legal formalities to deal with and then he'll be ready for a visit. Remember, Giorgos Praxiteles is an avowed member of a party that has been banned and deemed to be a threat to National Security. He will undergo trial along with many others. And we shall be merciful and send him to our military camp Dionysos. He will be well treated there, of course, merely trained to be a good citizen.'

Nina cast her eyes down. She was deeply disturbed by what she heard and what she read between the lines of all this false talk of justice and coercion. But what more could she do?

'Don't forget that I am a friend of Eleni Vlachou,' she stated at last. 'I know you are refusing access to her now but I'm in touch with foreign journalists who know her and know the true situation. News of all this is finding its way out already. Foreign opinion will turn against you and there will be enquiries made eventually by the Commission for Human Rights.'

'They will find nothing to report if that is the case!' snapped Papanikolas. For once he lost his urbanity and seemed visibly discomposed. He calmed down swiftly and added, 'Do your worst, madam. I'm afraid that *you* meanwhile must return to England. People like yourself are unwelcome here. I suggest you pack your belongings and take the next flight home. You will not be welcome in this country again. You have chosen England, so stay there and write what you will. It can do us no harm. People will see how much better the country is being run under our new government.'

He stood up now, his attitude cold and dismissive, but the smile and tone of his voice as pleasant as ever. Nina rose and walked out, slamming the door behind her.

Papanikolas watched her walk away through his office window then put a call through to Lambrou at the Asphalia headquarters. He reported the conversation.

'She threatens us with that arch whore, Vlachou,' he said, 'and she means to return to England and write her filthy lies. I have her report here. Can't we arrest her?'

'No, it would cause too much trouble,' Lambrou replied. 'She's a journalist and has contacts in Britain and of course there's Vlachou to consider. We know people abroad are keeping an eye on her situation. Have this stupid woman tailed to see what she does and make sure we deport her as soon as we can.'

'We could arrange for her "disappearance", couldn't we?'

'It's always a possibility. But just shadow her for now.'

Chapter 25

Thessaloniki 1st June 1967: Dimitri flees

Max listened to the radio and to the latest army orders banning Theodorakis' music and dissolving the Lambrakides. All to cleanse the country of the evils and the passions aroused by this 'wicked' man and his music! These new developments worried Max. There was the official version, the stuff they put out over the news and there were the versions he kept hearing from his friends who were fluttering about like so many startled, frightened birds caught in a cage, the door of which was slowly and inexorably being shut. They felt trapped and there was nowhere to fly, nowhere to turn. Letters were now subject to censorship: every citizen, high or low, could be tried by a special court martial if they did not entirely agree and endorse the new government that had been formed. Pavlos Zannas, the director of the Trade Fair had been arrested for the offence of translating a foreign news bulletin from the BBC and circulating it. Dimitri said that many of his EDA friends had been rounded up and taken heaven knew where. They simply disappeared in the night. Every day, Dimitri expected to hear bad news coming his way and Yiota was always pale with terror every time the doorbell rang.

The latest news was that Petros, their *koumbaros,* had gone into hiding and Dimitri was seriously considering joining him up in the mountains.

'He and his friends are busy printing sheets condemning the coup,' he stated with pride. 'Someone has to do something, eh Max?'

'Don't get involved, Dimitri.'

'I must get involved,' his friend said stubbornly. 'I've stuffed a few leaflets under doors and in people's pockets myself. You have to take risks. If I have to make a run for it, then I will. But I can't sit by and see our country ruined by these buffoons. Petros has taken the dogs and the guns. He knows people in the mountains and these bastards will never dig him out. Fi-Fi has gone to stay with her sisters in Kallithea. If I hear a whisper of danger, I'll follow him up there. You'll take care of things, won't you, Max?'

'Of course, I will. If they let me. If they don't send me packing back to England. I've reported to the police and they seemed very dubious, asked me endless questions. Asked about you and your politics. I told them you were a true blue member of the Greek Community, not a red shirt in sight. But they didn't seem too convinced.'

'Well, I'm not a Red. You're right enough about that. But they know my leanings and I'm wondering why they haven't rounded me up yet. It troubles me.'

'It troubles me too,' said Max. 'Especially since our charming friend Katsarakis made his threats.'

They were both busy in the workshop next day. Tinos, the young mechanic, had taken a car out for a test drive round the block. Max, straightening up from scraping at some oil and refuse in a carburettor, saw a dark black car draw up a little further down the road and remain there. He had seen this car before, hovering around the area. He felt a flutter of disquiet.

'Dimitri,' he said, 'get down into the pit under that big truck. I'll drive it over and hide you. Stay down there.'

Dimitri raised his head and looked alarmed. 'What is it?'

'Just do as I say.'

His friend obeyed with no more need for words, climbing down hurriedly into the damp, evil smelling pit full of sump oil and grease. Max started up the large Ford truck brought in that morning for a service and positioned it over the pit, hiding anything below from sight. He got out, raised the bonnet and tinkered with the insides while watching the dark car outside with its occupants. One of the men in the car had meanwhile emerged from it and was surveying the road, looking up at the signs above the varied warehouses and factories. He was a large, frowning, humourless-looking fellow with a thick moustache and dark glasses that made him look like a Hollywood version of a Mexican bandito. After a while he crossed the road, sauntered up to the door of the garage and peered inside. It took him some time to adjust to the gloomy interior. Max had switched off the lights in the little office and turned on a small spotlight to illuminate the area he was supposedly working on.

The man came up to him. 'Are you the owner here?'

'No. I just help out now and then.'

The man frowned even more on hearing a foreign accent.

'Are you an American?'

'What business is it of yours?'

'It *is* my business,' the man snapped in reply. He surveyed him for a few moments. 'What are you, then … German?'

People often asked Max these questions. His fair hair made them assume he was German or Scandinavian. He felt irritated but knew he had to remain calm and polite.

'English,' he replied with an affable smile but the man just scowled back at him.

'You speak good Greek.' The man's tone was suspicious.

'Thanks,' said Max turning his head away and rolling his eyes. So that made him a spy? These people were so dumb.

'Where did you learn to speak Greek?'

'I have a Greek wife.'

The man considered this then asked, 'So is this the workshop of Dimitri Cosmatis?'

'Yes.'

'And where is he now?'

'Taking a tractor to … Mihaniona.'

'When will he be back?'

'Oh … not for a day or two. He usually stays there with some relations for the night.'

'I see. I see.' The man didn't see, luckily. Max prayed young

Tinos wouldn't come back and give the game away. The intruder cast one more look around the scruffy workshop with an air of distaste. 'This place stinks,' he said and blew his nose into a spotless white handkerchief. 'Poof! How can you stand it.' He looked at his cream-coloured trousers and his smart suede shoes and then at the oil patches on the floor and backed away a little.

'I get used to it,' said Max and turned away, resuming his apparently absorbed inspection of the engine as if to finish the discussion. But he flicked a filthy rag about in an absent-minded fashion that appeared to alarm his visitor even more. The man watched him for a little while from a safe distance, the permanent frown deepening to a scowl of anger.

'I'll be back in a couple of days,' he said at last. 'We are ordering Dimitri Cosmatis to be here. We need to question him about a few things. Just a few questions, you understand. No need for him to be alarmed. We're looking for a few criminals and he may be able to help us as to their whereabouts.'

'Who shall I say wants him?'

'Security Police. If he's not here, we shall be obliged to search the premises.'

'I trust you'll have a warrant.'

'We don't need a warrant. We act under government orders. Just make sure he's here.'

Max waited until the man returned to his car where he stood chatting to his companion and smoking a cigarette for a few moments, still staring about him and up at the sign above the garage as if memorising it. When at long last the pair had taken themselves off, Max moved the truck and let Dimitri out of the pit, his red overalls now covered with even more grease.

'What did you make of that?' said Max. The two men went into the little office at the back and stood staring at each other in dismay. Tinos now arrived, whistling cheerfully. They were both deeply thankful he hadn't come sooner, as he was a good Christian lad and inclined to be truthful in all circumstances. George Washington wasn't a patch on him. If he had been questioned by those police agents or whatever they were, he would innocently refute all Max had said.

'What are you doing, boss?' Tinos asked in surprise as he stared into the office where the two men still stood in the dark.

'Having a break,' said Dimitri shortly. 'Just get on with it.'

'Okay,' said the lad, shrugging. He went over to one of the cars, opened the bonnet and took a look inside, whistling away and occasionally bursting into song, little phrases from popular tunes.

'I have to get the hell out,' said Dimitri under his breath as they watched the lad.

'Suppose someone's still around watching?'

'Have to risk it. I'll go home and pack a few things and speak to Yiota. She'll be so upset, damn it! But better she doesn't know where I'll be. Better you don't either. Max, keep things going while you can. Otherwise it's up to Tinos if they pack you off home. Whether he can manage the place alone, I don't know, just have to pray he can. I'll leave you to fill him in on what he needs to know. Just act innocent if they grill you. I hope the bastards don't try to arrest either of you.'

'Me too. Take care, Dimitri.' Max hugged his friend and felt close to tears. He guessed Dimitri would make his way to join Petros in the mountains. As for himself, he began to wonder just how long it was safe for him to remain round here. These characters seemed to make their own rules now. He wondered if it might be an idea to go to Mistres, Andrew's home in the mountains, and rusticate for a bit. He was still in touch with his father-in-law and felt sure Andrew would have no objection. He could find another lad to help Tinos and take himself off.

Max still rented the flat in Agia Sofias Square. Dimitri had often said he could stay with him and Basil had made the same offer. But somewhere in the back of Max's mind was the vague hope that Nina might, just might return to Thessaloniki, see the error of her accusations. It was a foolish thought and he knew it.

Dimitri had occasionally slipped him a wad of notes for his work which had been more than adequate to pay the rent and save a little. Max wanted few things. Clothes were of no interest and he always ate with Dimitri or Basil and spent little beyond the necessities. Thus he had saved some cash which would serve him till he was able to return home. He had money in his English bank but just at present it was hard to organise a money transfer due to economic problems in Britain where the recession was sending the prime minister, Harold Wilson, into a paddy as to what to do to retain his credibility. And organising anything in a Greek bank was a waste of time in itself. One could spend the morning there drinking coffee and chatting while clerks rushed around trying to sort things out and getting nowhere.

Greeks never paid in cheques and they never trusted banks which had a habit of disappearing overnight with their entire client's cash. Most of Dimitri's hard-earned money resided in a box underneath the marital bed. Max knew that Yiota was well provided for and could manage for some time on these savings.

He was troubled over Nina. He could never feel really separated from her. It was as if, despite all their differences, they were indeed of one flesh and one heart. She was his wife and always would be. One day he was determined to woo her again, explain things to her, tell her that they should never be apart like this; it was like cutting each other in half.

Andrew had spoken to him on the phone the other day and told him that she was still in Athens and getting mixed up in the politics surrounding the rebellious Vlachou newspapers. This worried him now. He knew his wife, knew she would never sit by and keep quiet, or better still, return to London. He wondered if she thought of him at all. He had heard nothing from her since the day she had packed her bags and stormed out of the flat. He felt deeply saddened that she had never given him a chance to explain himself. He longed for her, his body ached for her. Did she even think of him?

With all these whirling thoughts in mind, he returned to the Ford and began to do some real work on it.

Dimitri's first port of call was to the house along the Monastir Rd. He had packed hastily and flung a few things into a duffle bag. He then tied his gun to the side of his Vespa, covering it over so that it wouldn't be obvious, climbed on the machine and roared away from his home and his life as so many Greeks had done in the past – off to the freedom and safety of the caves and retreats of the Hortiach Mountains. He had kissed his wife goodbye and said he was off to make a long delivery and she wasn't to worry. She understood what he meant and began to weep silently.

'Stop that!' he said, tears welling up in his own eyes. 'I have to go and best you don't know where I am. All will be well, this lot can't last forever. Sooner or later someone else will come along, some bigger boss – or the British and Americans will put their foot down and restore democracy. But I'm not hanging around to be carted off to one of their blasted island prisons, no thanks.'

She knew he was going away to join Petros, leaving them to manage as best they could just as her father had done in the last war, off to that high, difficult, stony refuge, amongst the gods. And may the gods keep them all safe! Back to the 'government of the Mountain' as they used to call it in the old days. Would these things never end? Wiping her tears, Yiota, helped Dimitri pack a few shirts and pants in his bag and put in a little pack of fruit, olives, *haloumi* cheese and a hunk of bread.

'I'll find a place to get a drink,' he said. 'Don't worry, stop fussing. Kiss the children goodbye for me.'

Now he was sitting drinking Fix beer with Marta. He'd relieved his feelings of despair and anger with a good roll on the bed upstairs on the terrace. Marta understood and gave him extra time to get it out of his system. 'I'm not watching the clock, *palikari mou.* You're a brave man, you needn't pay anything,' she whispered.

'Of course, I'll pay, Martaki *mou*,' he sighed, 'you're a working girl. And you're the best.'

She smiled and patted his cheek. Dimitri was her favourite too. He was a thoughtful lover who actually cared enough about her as a person to make her enjoy their encounters as well. She lit him a cigarette which he took gratefully. He then drank the beer in great gulps. It might well be his last beer but he was too thirsty to savour it.

'Did you know Big Bouros has been released?' she said. It was Bouros who had first brought Dimitri here many years ago. Bouros was a good deal slimmer and fitter in those days, not the flabby wreck of later years. He had even supplied a few Albanian and Yugoslavian girls to the proprietor and the girls had no complaints. Bouros insisted they were well treated and taken regularly to the doctor for check-ups. The girls were all fond of the poor man and pitied him.

'No! Where is he?'

'They dumped him in the hospital when he got too sick to mess around with any more. But his boys went and got him out at night and he's being looked after by his sister in Kavalla. He's a mess, Dimi, a mess, the poor man. What they've done to him. Oh, my god!' She crossed herself hastily.

'The bastards! Did they give him the *falanga*?'

'I'll say they did. He told us that it took three men to get him up on the table, poor sod. Whenever he passed out, they threw a bucket of water over him to wake him up and started again. They had no pity. He'll never walk again, his feet are a mess, unrecognisable. It made me feel sick. Some of us went to see him in the hospital and he was a wreck, his skin hanging in folds where he'd lost weight. The nurses had shaved his face and done their best to tidy him up but he was pitiful. If he lives, it won't be much of a life.'

'If I only knew who did it....' Dimitri swore.

'What can we do?' said Marta. 'We have to wait till it's the right time to strike back. There are always these beasts, every country has them. We used to think it was just the Nazis but every country has men who delight in torture, get a sexual thrill from it. They want to come and have sex after; it turns them on so much.'

'Do you know any of these men, Marta?'

'I know a few,' she said. 'I make a note of their names, if I get a chance. When they go for pee-pee, I take a quick look at their identity cards.'

'You're a clever girl. We'll make a list and those men will live to regret it.'

The torturers were one thing, but Dimitri knew full well who had betrayed Big Bouros and made sure he was arrested. It was the same person who had betrayed him, so that he was forced to flee for his own life, leaving his beloved wife and kids behind to fend for themselves. He'd definitely get that bastard, Katsarakis, if it was the last thing he did.

He rose, kissed Marta on the cheek and fondled her ample breasts for a moment with regret, then, slinging his bag on his back, roared off again down the highway and climbed the dusty roads in his little Vespa; roads that led higher and higher into the Hortiach mountains. On the way, he would hide his bike in a cave he knew and set off on foot over old, long forgotten tracks and passes till he reached the stronghold of the eagles.

Chapter 26

Athens: Nina finds a way

Nina walked home, deep in thought. She had heard so much about the treatment men and women had faced during the civil war and she knew that the same was likely to be meted out to those taken to the headquarters in Bouboulinas Street. She felt sure that George would resist to the end, as would the other Lambrakides. She shuddered at the thought. And Aris, poor man, he was innocent and yet he too had been snatched from his peaceful, ordinary life simply because his son had chosen to uphold democracy and freedom. Aris had never caused trouble, a quiet, inoffensive person who did his work and cared for his family as best as he could. She knew that Aris had been taken away because of her damned article and a deep sense of guilt pervaded her for unwittingly bringing more troubles upon these good friends.

She wanted to help them with a passion, but what could she do? There was so little time left. The police would come round in a few days, maybe even today, take her to the airport by force and send her back to England. Certainly she would do all she could to make known the cause of her friends and others like them if she was forced to return. But first she wanted to aid George and Aris and Stella.

There was one avenue left, though she wished she didn't have to take it. She must try to see Nikos Galanis and see if he could speak to someone in authority perhaps, make a few waves. She dreaded the idea but knew that he had always been attracted to her. She would have to use this to the best advantage. What else could she do? Using womanly wiles was not her normal style though it had its uses now and then! She was an honest and straightforward person but there were times when a woman's beauty and charm were strong weapons and in a war with powerful men, they had to be used.

As she walked along, she felt instinctively that she was being followed and looked behind her. There were people milling about the pavements as usual; no one looked especially sinister. The feeling persisted, however. She decided to go into a church and pray for a little, sit in the cool and peaceful semi-dark and try to figure what she would say to Nikos. She entered a little church in Zografou. The cool interior soothed her body, while the golden glow of votive candles trembling in the darkness wrapped her round with the warm embrace of a welcoming mother. It reminded her of the day she had spent in Agia Sofias in Thessaloniki, that tremendous uplifting of the soul … only to come forth into the bright foolish world and see Max kissing that horrible girl, that slut.

Her heart ached again at the sense of betrayal. She realised then that he was always in the depths of her heart though recent events had made thoughts of him disappear beneath layers of worries, ideas and plans. Now his face came to her vividly and she yearned for his arms about her, comforting her, listening to her troubles and suggesting sensible things to do. She yearned for his light, funny comments, his ability to lift her spirits when they were down. Once she had seen this as flippant when to her, life was so serious, so intense. Now she saw it as a way of lovingly shifting her immense burdens and sense of duty … duty to who? To what? To her unknown mother's memory? She bowed her head and sighed.

She cast a glance about her as she walked down the aisle. The church was fairly empty, just the usual old women crossing themselves with fervour, kissing the ikons, muttering their prayers. A young woman was tying a silver foot near the ikon of a favourite saint in the hopes that a cure for some loved one might be found, someone who had injured a leg or foot. If only she still had that sweet simplicity of belief. Like most people, Nina had lost it along with her childhood, though something still persisted in her. The church still gave her comfort and repose but she could not kiss an ikon now. However, she made the sign of the cross three times while a fierce-looking old lady stood next to her, watching her intently. Nina smiled to herself a little. Perhaps the old woman thought she was an Italian Catholic and might summon up the Devil by crossing herself incorrectly. Lighting a candle, she set it in the tray. She thought of her friends. *May God help to preserve them*. She thought of Max who, for some reason, had come to her mind and heart so vividly that she almost felt as if she might turn around and see him standing near her. For a moment she looked up and stared into the dim lit apses of the church. Then she lit a candle for him too. *May God take care of you, my love.*

When she left the church, she glanced around. She was sure she had seen that man before. He was standing by a shop smoking a cigarette, apparently absorbed in the radios and gramophones on sale there. He didn't turn around when she came out and she swiftly slipped down a little street next to the church and made her way to Syntagma Square. Looking behind her as she entered the large square, she saw the man again. He was ambling along but she surprised him by her sudden turnaround and caught him staring at her. His eyes swiftly slid away and he paused as if to light up a cigarette. Her heart lurched. That damned Inspector was having her shadowed. She would have to give this fool the slip somehow.

As she approached the bus stop she saw a bus waiting to go and jumped on board. To her relief it set off before the man had finished lighting his cigarette and she had the satisfaction of seeing him drop it and make a run for the bus but it now sped into the traffic and off in the direction of Omonia Square. Would it be wise to take the metro from Omonia, she wondered? Probably not. Maybe a passing taxi would be best.

At Omonia, she got off the bus and quietly walked off in the direction of Plaka and headed for Monostiraki station. However, instead of entering the metro station, she flagged down a taxi instead.

'Take me to Psihiko,' she said. She knew this was where Nikos Galanis still lived, in the pleasant villa which had belonged to his parents. It was a fifteen-minute journey and the taxi driver picked up two more fares en route, one an elderly woman who also wanted Psihiko.

'It's okay, you can drop me off here,' she told the driver and paid him, scrambling out by a crossroads then waiting till he had turned and driven away with his other passenger. She walked swiftly along searching for a street called Iraklion. It was a long time since she had visited this place and things had altered a lot in that time; more houses had been built there and it was all unfamiliar. However, an old man directed her and she found the house with its wrought iron door and marble steps. Pots of geraniums sat on the entrance steps making a splash of vivid red against the whiteness of the walls. It reminded Nina of her grandfather's house in Mistres. He'd been fond of geraniums, loved the sharp, pungent scent they exuded in the heat and he would often stop to lift a flower head and smell it. Geranium oil was good for the skin, he had told her. Old Xanthi, their *doula*, had rubbed the oil into her hands and feet when Nina was small and it had soothed her baby cries. Stooping to smell the flowers now, she felt a wave of comfort come over her but also one of sadness. How long ago it all seemed.

She had lived with her grandfather Costas till she was seven years old, knowing that she had an English father but never sure that she would ever meet him. He was away at war, her grandfather explained. One never knew who might come back from the war or who might be lost forever. Then one day, after the terrible war was over, her father and Dorothy had turned up at Mistres and taken her away to England.

She had hated it at first. Hated the damp and the cold and the unemotional, calm precision of the English people. But eventually she realised that beneath that apparent unruffled composure lay kindness and care and good common sense. They were rational and reasonable people who disliked demonstrations and fuss. Nina was passionate but she preferred self control. Irrational emotion was foolish and childish and too many Greeks seemed prone to a good deal of screaming and shouting about nothing in particular. But she had to confess to herself with regret that she too, was capable of irrational emotions, especially where her husband was concerned. She half smiled … after all, she was a Greek. And her heart stirred with a violent mixture of joy and grief, strange ancient grief that mourned something lost and intangible whenever she was here in her homeland.

Now that she was here – standing before Nikos' house – she paused and felt that same heart flutter with panic.

'Mama, would you do this?' she wondered. 'Must I go and see this man I loathe and beg a favour of him? What sort of price will he demand of me? God, I'm so afraid. I wish I was brave.'

The leaves on the lemon trees in the garden rustled gently like a sigh. The perfume of the blossom came dancing on a sudden little wind and wrapped about her and for a moment she felt a sense of peacefulness. All these glorious scents she was inhaling made her think of the exquisite perfume that was said to have emanated from the tomb of Agios Dimitrios and she wondered if her mother was a saint now, if her unknown tomb in some mountain village gave forth a sudden sweetness mistaken for the scent of mountain herbs wafting in the breeze. She felt uplifted, sure that her mother was with her in spirit and that she must go ahead no matter what the consequences.

Marching up to the door, Nina rang the bell. The sharp peal echoed inside the hallway, bouncing on marble, carpetless floors and echoing from the walls. It felt in her heightened state of nerves like a death knell but she held her courage and refused to turn and flee. The door was opened clumsily, as if the owner was unused to visitors and had forgotten where the latch was. Nikos stood before her. He had his carpet slippers on, baggy old trousers and a brown woollen pullover that did little to hide his paunch. In his hands he held some papers and his reading glasses were perched on his head. She was startled to see how old he looked. He stared at her, amazed. 'I never thought I'd see *you* here, Nina.' His face flushed with sudden pleasure. '*Ella, ella mesa, paidi mou*. Come, come on in, tell me what brings you to see me.'

He ushered her into the house. It was still furnished in the traditional style with old sepia photos of his parents on the wall, heavy old furniture, lots of embroideries everywhere draped on seats, tables, and sideboards. But they lacked the crisp neatness and the care his mother would once have given her beloved trousseau. Now they were all a little moth-eaten, dirty and crumpled. She knew his mother had left to live with her daughter now; no old lady came forth to greet her. Her mind went back to the few visits made with her grandfather a long time ago, when Nikos was a young, skinny lad of thirteen or fourteen and she a small child. Even then he had eyed her with that narrowed gaze of his as if undressing her. She had felt afraid of him then and she felt afraid now.

It saddened her to see the neglect of and disinterest in his childhood home. It was clean enough. No doubt some *doula* came to cook and clean. He had told her that he had inherited everything including some olive groves outside the city. He had a sister but she was now married and lived comfortably in Piraeus.

'Sit there, I'll bring you a glass of wine. Sit there a minute.'

He seemed suddenly aware of how shabby he looked, glancing at himself in the mirror near the door with some dismay. He took off his glasses and pushed his hair back with his hands. 'I wasn't expecting anyone,' he said as if in apology.

She wanted to refuse but thought that a glass of wine might relax both of them, make her task easier. So she smiled and nodded. He disappeared into the bedroom and re-appeared, his hair brushed, a pair of slacks and clean shirt on.

'I apologize for my appearance, I didn't expect visitors,' Nikos said again as he handed her a glass of chilled white wine.

'*Pos*! ... come on, I'm the one to apologise! You were relaxing at home,' she said.

He sat back and regarded her with curiosity. There was something in her voice that made him suddenly alert.

'Nina, I don't feel that this is just a social call,' he murmured.

His eyes fastened themselves upon her and moved over her from head to foot, a slow lingering expression like a child savouring a delicious treat, half expectant that it might be taken away at any moment. Nina drew a big breath and composed the sick feelings that arose inside her. Part pity, part disgust. Did this man really think she had come to him of her own volition? Out of desire for him and his company? She had never shown him anything but a mild friendship – because he was a fellow Greek, because she had known his family when she was a young girl. She knew perfectly well that *his* feelings for her were lustful; it couldn't be called love. It didn't *feel* like love. He was always polite, attentive, kindly even. But something in her always knew that his eyes were unclean, revealing unclean thoughts. She understood lust, ardour, desire ... had encountered it in many men, felt it herself. But Nikos was tainted in some manner by a heavy, sensual darkness and she didn't like the feel of it. She prayed now that his good nature would make him want to help her without asking for anything in return. But she held little hope on that score.

'*Ohi*, Niko,' she said and tried to smile, 'no, it's not a social call, I'm afraid. And I don't have a lot of time here in Greece either. I thought of you, you're an old friend. I need your help, if you can give it.'

'What sort of help? Are you in trouble with the authorities?'

'Yes, I am. I wrote a rather polemic article which their wretched security police got their hands on while raiding a friend's house ... raiding it for no good reason! ... and they intend to deport me. I've managed to buy a little time, given their watchdogs the slip – at least, I hope so. I don't want to get you in trouble too. But you said you knew people, helpful people in the new regime. At any rate you implied you knew somehow what was going to happen.'

He smiled briefly, gave a little nod, but said nothing. After a moment's pause, Nina went on, 'It's not for me, Niko. I'll leave Greece if they insist. I can wage war, so to speak, from England.'

He interrupted her. 'You don't, I gather, like the new government?'

She thought before responding. She was uncertain quite where Nikos stood with these so called 'saviours' of Greece. Was he with them? He had always seemed to go along with her opinions about Lambrakis, her horror at the way he had been assassinated. He knew her leaning was to the Left. Thinking about it all, she realised she had never been sure where his allegiances and opinions lay. Little comments that escaped him occasionally had made her aware that he tended to the Right politically – but was he in agreement with this new government or was he just playing along with it like so many others in order to save his skin?

'Don't be afraid,' he urged as if sensing her dilemma, 'I won't betray you. How could I do such a thing? Anyway, it sounds as if you have already betrayed yourself. You always were an impulsive, outspoken woman, Nina. I admire it in you. But at the same time, I've always thought you were foolhardy. That's why I offered, that's why I said I'd take you under my wing. I can still look after you, even now. Make sure you're allowed to stay. They'll leave you alone, they won't send you back to England. But you won't be able to write articles for your newspapers, not even on the sly. You can't do that. You'll have to conform, you know that.'

'It's not about staying in Greece, Niko. Anyway, I couldn't live quietly under this regime. How can I? I'm a lover of freedom, freedom of speech especially and there's no such thing at the moment. Surely you know that? I'd *have* to fight and then I'd really land myself in trouble. No it's better that I get back to England. I can probably do more good from there. I've already said, it's not about me. I've come to see if you can help my friend.'

'What friend?' his voice hardened.

'A young man, a follower of Lambrakis. They've arrested him and taken him to Bouboulinas. Oh, Niko, you know what that must mean!' her voice trembled.

'What's this young man to you?'

'His parents are friends of mine – his father, Aris Praxiteles, works for Vlachou and her newspapers. They're questioning him too, but he's no communist. They think everyone's a communist, this lot. You've only got to walk on the left side of the street! Thankfully I think Vlachou managed to put in a word for him, even though she's under suspicion herself. They daren't do too much to her because she's always in touch with the foreign press. I'm praying Aris will be freed but his son, George, they won't let go. They want to get him to sign some paper, some sort of declaration. He's a brave and stubborn boy, he won't recant in order to get away. He just won't do it, I know he won't.'

'And what do you think I can do?'

'Well, do you have any influence at all? Do you know anyone who might help? When we were in London, you said that you knew people …' her voice trailed away miserably. She rose. 'I'm wasting your time, aren't I? It was just talk, all that. You don't know anyone at all.'

He was stung by this. 'As it happens, I *do* have influence,' he said, 'a lot of influence. I know our Prime Minister, Colonel Papadopoulos, very well. He's related to my family through my mother who came from his village. I know I can speak to him whenever I want. I've already spoken to him to declare my allegiance to all he and his men stand for. He owes me a couple of favours. He's a good man, he won't have forgotten. And there are a couple of other officers that owe me too. I helped their wives with any … let us say, family problems … as well as any burdens their mistresses may have presented them with along the way.'

Nikos smiled a little as he said this. Nina stared at him. 'Abortions?'

He made no reply, merely shrugged and pursed his lips. His fingers drummed on the tabletop beside him. He lifted his glass of wine and sipped it slowly while watching her over the rim. She also sipped her wine and gazed at the floor.

'So,' Nikos went on, 'it's possible I *can* speak for this boy – but if he is stupid and refuses to play along with any scheme, then it will be for nothing. You know that. And he sounds stupid, frankly, getting mixed up with those gangs of people who go round the villages, spreading all their propaganda.'

'Oh, Niko, you don't believe all that right wing clap-trap! You *really* support this unelected Government?'

'But of course I do. So should any right-minded person. We've needed someone to get to grips with this country. Look, the King has made a hash of things so far and it won't be long before he flees the country, you mark my words, Nina. He's planning a counter-coup but everyone knows about it … it's doomed to failure already. Freedom, democracy, these are words that are forever abused. Now and then we need a strong government to make things right again, bring the country back to some morality and sort out the economy which, you must agree, is in a dire state. Greece is ready to rise and be reborn under the guidance of these brave and wonderful men.'

'They probably thought that about Hitler,' Nina blurted out. 'Yes, Hitler got the economy together, he brought order for a while. He fooled everyone for a bit. Is this really what you believe in?'

'My dear girl, what kind of comparison is that? Papadopoulos, Pattakos and Makarezos are hardly Hitler. For a start there are three of them, not one mad tyrant. They are sane, civilised men. They want to restore Greece to stability and calm. We have had to re-discover ourselves as a nation and not under the imposition of foreign kings thrust upon us by Britain and America. It's time a good parent came to restore peace in the nursery. Greece is still a young child politically, after all those centuries of torpor under the Turks.'

'You'll never persuade me that killing people, torturing them, refusing free speech of any kind can be deemed as good? You know full well that there's a mass extermination taking place of anyone who even faintly disagrees with the new regime while everyone talks your talk and pretend nothing's happening. So long as it doesn't affect their comfy little lives, it's not happening. Is this really what you believe in? I can see you can't or won't help, Niko. I'm sorry I troubled you. I don't see how I can help George and I feel terrible about it, just terrible.' Nina rose and a sob broke from her. She picked up her bag and prepared to leave.

Nikos also rose and came over to her.

'Nina, Nina,' he murmured and took her arm, drawing her to him and gently rubbing her back in a soothing motion. 'You misunderstand me. I *will* help you. How can I not help an old friend – a lady I love so much? I can get the boy out, but he needs to keep his mouth shut, that's the problem. I know those sort of boys ... they think they're heroes, they think they're the new Achilles and Ajax. Common sense they don't have. I'll think of something, trust me. You know I'll do anything for you, anything.'

He pulled her to him more strongly now and kissed her hair and her forehead. She allowed him to do so but closed her eyes tight.

'You're all tense, all tense. Let yourself go, Nina *mou*. Come on, come on, let me kiss you ... I'll help, I promise.' He was stammering now in the intensity of his desire and he began to kiss her lips, letting his hand wander to her breasts which he grasped firmly.

'Let me go, Niko!'

'Come on, *agapi mou*! You know I adore you! You know I do!'

'No, I can't do this, Niko. I'm still married!'

He held her away from him for a moment. '*Ade*, you've left the man, we all know that. He's a milksop Englishman, not a hot-blooded Greek. Not the man for a woman like you, Nina. Forget him. You can soon get a divorce. Look, I swear I'll help with this boy. Give me all the details and I'll help. And I mean it, I promise it on my mother's name. Do you believe me?'

Strangely, she did. 'Yes, I do.'

'Look, I know you don't love me, Nina. You still love that stupid Englishman. But you're a modern woman, a woman of the world. Give me one night of pleasure with you. That's all I ask in return. One long night. Then go back to England and wage your war of words. Believe me, I can give you pleasure too. I know how to treat a woman. You may even come back for more.'

She was silent. He grasped her by the chin roughly and lifted her face.

'Will you?'

She couldn't see what else to do. It wasn't as if Max was faithful to her. And it wasn't from love but expediency that she would give in to Nikos. One night was all he asked. Nobody would know. Could she do it, even for George's sake? Go against all her principles, her belief in what was right and wrong? She thought of the boy, a good innocent boy and what he was suffering even now and knew she had to do it. One night. It wasn't the end of the world. It was just her body she was giving, not her heart and soul. That would always belong to Max, whatever he had done to her. He had probably already found someone else to share *his* bed. She nodded.

'I'll think of something today,' Nikos said. 'I promise. It may take a day or two to arrange. Come back tomorrow and I'll let you know what's happened. Unless you want to stay tonight?'

'I'll come in a day or so, Niko. I'll ring you. Make sure you've kept your side of the bargain.'

'And then you'll stay the night? You'll keep your side of the bargain. You promise this on your mother's name?'

'When I say "yes", I mean it,' she replied, and he nodded.

'I believe that. You're a Cassimatis.'

He kissed her again, a long slow kiss which she endured as best she could. Finally he let her go and she walked out into the fresh air, walked swiftly away down the street and away from him.

Chapter 27

Thessaloniki: Max prepares to leave

Max knew his position was delicate. It wouldn't be long before they returned to ask where Dimitri Cosmatis had gone. He was working here unofficially and could only stay in the country for a short while longer before he would have to return to England. He decided it was time to prepare himself and so he gave his landlord notice, packed his few possessions. He would take them round to Athina and Basil's place and carry as little as he could with him. The landlord wasn't too pleased. It seemed no one was pleased with him just now, Max thought wryly.

His plan was to tell everyone that he was going back to England. Better everyone thought he had left the country. He would, in fact, go to Athens. He had discussed this on the phone with Andrew, who was deeply worried about his daughter.

Max had long ago explained in detail how the situation of their parting had yet again arisen and Andrew had begun to think his daughter was reacting unreasonably. His son in law wasn't anything like the devil she had painted him to be. He was glad to turn to him for help and wished with all his might he could reconcile the two foolish lovers.

'We haven't heard anything from her in a long while, Max. Please see if you can find her, talk some sense into her and get her out of Greece. It's dangerous for someone in her position and you know full well Nina likes to poke her nose in where she shouldn't. She hasn't any real experience of political matters or even as a journalist. Reggie is getting worried. I'm afraid for her life. Curious people have been known to disappear in Greece for less.'

Max was alarmed. 'I'll try, Andrew, but I doubt she'll listen to me. She thinks I'm a dyed-in-the wool rogue. She's convinced Zoe and I are lovers and refuses to listen to me.'

'I have such a stubborn, headstrong daughter,' Andrew said despairingly, ' my God, but she's like her mother! Can't make these Greek women see sense. But do try, Max. She may listen if she thinks you've come after her specially. Women do like that, you know, for all their tough stance, they like to feel protected.' He gave Max the address of Nina's contacts in Athens. 'Find her, Max, do your best to overcome her stubbornness. If you can.'

'I'll get her home if I have to tie her up and put her on the luggage rack,' said Max grimly.

He spoke next to Yiota and told her he meant to leave, that he had to return to England. She was frightened and upset.

'Who will run the garage now? How will we live, Max?'

'Tino will keep it going. I'll speak to him and try to sort something out.'

'Ach, it's bad enough Dimitri has abandoned me, now you, Max. I can't bear it!'

'Dimitri will be back soon, I feel sure of it. You'll manage, Yiota.'

Dimitri's mother, Theodora, accepted the situation. Her husband had joined the resistance movement in the mountains during the war and she had little sympathy for tears and fuss; she was made in the Spartan mould.

'*Kyrie* Max has his own life to lead,' she said, '*he* has a country to return to. And stop worrying about Dimitri. He also knows where to go. He knows what to do. Petro and others are up there with him, he's not alone, Yiota.'

'He'll be sleeping rough. I can't bear to think of it. *Ach … the-e mou*! Ach, my God! My poor husband!'

Yiota refused to be consoled – her bed was empty and she was crying herself to sleep. She was in fear of being arrested herself to prise out the whereabouts of Dimitri and Petros but, thank God, no one had troubled her so far.

'He's small fry, my son,' sighed Theodora when Yiota expressed this fear. The old lady crossed herself in gratitude and waved her hand dismissively.' He's not as important as he thinks.'

'How can you say such things?' Yiota cried. 'Your son, your only son has had to run away. God alone knows when he'll be home again.'

'Tears won't help him,' stated the old lady. 'You young women are all the same. Got no guts, can't begin to do the things we had to do in the war. Pull yourself together and think of the children.'

'I am thinking of the children!' shouted Yiota. 'They may become fatherless. It's no help having you reading the *Romanzo* day and night. I'm half inclined to take the kids off to my mother's in Mihaniona. But then I worry that Dimitri may return and no one will be here to greet him.' And she began to weep again. 'Why must you go too, Max?'

He took her hand and patted it awkwardly. 'The police came round again the other day looking for Dimitri and they didn't seem too amused to find me working there. I feel worried that they're going to tell me to go back any day now. Officially, I can stay as a visitor another month but obviously I'm not meant to be working. I told them I was just helping out, not being paid for my work but they wouldn't buy it. Someone work for nothing? Not even a mad Englishmen would do that, they said. Mad Englishmen do things like that all the time, I told them, I'm not a greedy Greek.'

'That will have pleased them,' said Yiota, smiling a little through her tears.

'Yes, that made them ecstatic. I am definitely losing friends fast round here. That bastard Katsarakis also came calling again and he's furious that Dimitri has slipped away. Now, *he* has no regard for international law or any other law but his own. He's likely to slug me and finish me off one dark night. Well, I'm not hanging around waiting for that to happen.'

'So you'll really go back to England?'

Max hesitated briefly. It was better to keep Yiota in the dark.

'Yes, that's the best thing to do for now,' he nodded. 'Greece isn't very welcome to me just now. Plus I don't want to take any more money from Dimitri's share, you need all he has in his savings for now. And I can't ask Basil Petrakos for another loan. I'm running out of money fast and though my father-in-law would willingly send me some, our government in England have imposed a ban on taking out more currency from Britain because we're in such a pickle back home with strikes and depressions, you name it. Things are bad everywhere it seems. I'm not returning to a happy place back home, I can assure you.'

'The world is a mess, what can I say. Thank God, Dimi saved a fair bit of money. It was meant to be for a new car for us all,' sighed Yiota. 'But we'll need it to live on now. I'll ask Tino to take over the repair shop but I don't have much faith in him. He's a good boy but not that experienced. There's only one thing to do. I'll give up the flat, take the kids and go to my mother's.'

'What about me?' Theodora demanded. 'Are you going to abandon me? Nice thing, I must say.'

'You've got a daughter in Aretsou, go and stay with her. What else can we do?'

The old lady didn't look too pleased. 'My daughter won't welcome me. She's out at work all day. And her house is tiny.'

'This flat's tiny, but you've managed on the bed settee for years. You can manage on hers.'

And so the matter was settled and after a hasty meal of fried *okra* and bean soup, Max went to the workshop and spoke to Tinos of the plan to leave.

'You're going back to England?' said Tinos. He looked ready to weep. 'How will I manage on my own? I'm not that good yet.'

'You know enough to manage, Tino. Haven't you a friend or relation who can help?'

Tinos stroked his chin and considered, 'Well, there's my *koumbaros*. He has a brother who knows a fair bit about cars. He'd be glad of some extra cash.'

'That's okay then. Only take on the work you feel you can cope with. Yiota will probably be leaving soon, she plans to go to her mother's for a bit. Draw your wages and expenses, put aside the rest so Yiota can ask for some money to live on and keep a good eye on the place. If any unpleasant-looking characters seem to be hanging about, then tell the police.'

Tinos looked worried. 'What sort of characters, boss? You're scaring me. First Dimitri goes off, now you and Yiota. What's going on?'

'Dimitri has made a few enemies,' Max explained. 'Some roughnecks. They denounced him to the authorities and he's had to go into hiding. Best you don't know anything about it, Tino. Stay ignorant, just do your work and if people come asking, tell them you have no idea where he's gone, he just upped and went and the Englishman has got fed up and gone home and told you to look after the workshop. All of which is true and all you need to know.'

'Okay, boss,' said Tinos, shaking his dark curly head and looking worried as well he might. 'But I don't like the sound of it. I've got a wife and two children and I don't want anyone threatening them. They may think I *do* know what's going on and try and get it out of me by force. I know those sorts. How did Dimitri get mixed up with that lot? I bet it's something to do with Big Bouros and his boys.'

Max remained silent. If Tinos knew what had happened to Big Bouros, he'd be terrified.

Tinos' frown deepened. He looked about the workshop and shook his head. 'I don't like it. I may want to go and work somewhere else. What then?'

'You'll just have to lock the place up and leave it at that,' said Max with a sigh.

'I'll give it a go, boss, but if things get troublesome, I'm off. I've my own family to think of.'

Max nodded. 'Okay, that's fair enough. Make sure that truck you've been working on is delivered to its owner. We promised it would be ready tomorrow.'

'What about that old truck of Dimitri's?' Tino asked, indicating a battered old Ford at the back of the garage awaiting attention.

'Oh, leave it now. It's not important and will have to wait.'

'Dimitri wanted me to change the tyres on it.'

'Well, do that then. But that's all. It's the other truck that's important. Look, Tino, I've a few things to finish off here myself, then I'll return to my flat and pack. I'll be leaving as soon as I can. You may as well go now and I'll lock up. If Yiota leaves soon, she'll let you have a spare set of keys, okay. Keep them till she returns if you do decide to pack it in and just pop in and keep an eye on the place now and then.'

'What about the cash?'

'Take your wages, of course, and anything left you can sort out with Yiota. She'll leave you her new address or some way to get hold of her.'

Tinos nodded and then embraced him.

'I'll be sorry to see you go, boss.' he said. 'Safe journey to England. At least you can get the hell out of this mess. You're lucky.'

'Things are in a mess back home too.' But, Max reflected, nothing like the frightening state of affairs here in Greece. The troubles in Britain would all blow over eventually and there would never be the sort of coercion or latent sense of fear that he felt here. No one could tell how long the situation in Greece might last. It could go on indefinitely.

'I'll miss you,' said the young man mournfully.

'I'll miss Greece,' said Max, looking around him with a smile, 'even this grubby old workshop and being with you and Dimitri and all my friends. Thanks, Tino. Good man. I'm sure things will be okay and you'll be able to carry on.'

When the young man had gathered together his things and gone, Max looked about and considered what he would do next. The undigested beans jumped about in his stomach so he sat down for a while to try and relax. His mind ever on Nina, he pondered whether to take the train or the bus to Athens as the cheapest option. He decided on the bus and after shutting up the workshop, returned to his flat to sort out his belongings and plan his journey.

Chapter 28

Athens: Nina makes a decision

Nina was unsure how much to tell Aris and Stella. It was important to let them know where she was going and why but at the same time she was afraid to raise their hopes over George. Nikos Galanis might well turn out to be all hot air. Had he really helped out Papadopoulos and co at some point in his life? It made sense and he seemed confident enough that he could help to get George freed. She knew she would have to trust him. The price to be paid overwhelmed her. She was not a woman lacking in courage but this trial ahead of her made her tremble and feel ill.

A woman of her word, Nina had never made love to any other man but Max since her marriage nor had any desire to do so. They might be separated but they were still married in the eyes of the law and, more importantly, in the eyes of God. Divorce did not enthuse her. It was messy and wrong. She loved Max and always would love him, despite everything. She tried to console herself with thoughts of his own unfaithfulness but it no longer roused her ire as it had done in the past. As if seeing everything in a new light due to the circumstances she now found herself embroiled in, she gave thought to what had happened.

The girl she'd seen with Max outside Agia Sofias. How else was she supposed to view that episode? Yet, something in her heart felt uncertain. Maybe it wasn't what she had immediately assumed, maybe there really was an explanation for the incident.

She hadn't let him explain, hadn't allowed him a word in his defence; simply construed the worst, torn by that terrible jealousy that arose in her whenever she thought of Max with another woman. How could she be so unreasonable and irrational?

None of this inner questioning helped her present predicament. She had given her word to Nikos that she would spend the night with him, come what may. And she was obliged to keep that word. She would have to admit it to Max one day and it would be interesting to see if he felt jealous in return. She hoped he would. Suddenly, an overwhelming longing for her husband came over her. She wanted him here, wanted his advice, his support. Nikos wouldn't have dared ask such a thing if he knew Max was back with her. Sometimes she was just too truthful. It would have been wise to say her husband was in Athens too. She wished she could get hold of Max but had no idea where he was now. It was possible he was still with Dimitri but equally possible that he had run out of cash and returned to England long ago. And anyway, she didn't know what to say. She hated apologies.

Should she ring her father? That was out of the question. Her pride forbade it. But what then? Nikos would never offer her any help from sheer philanthropy. He was a greedy, unpleasant man and mixed with greedy, evil, power-hungry men. Her mind went to George in some foul cell in Bouboulinas Street never knowing if he would be freed again or left to rot as so many prisoners were left to do since the war, despite all efforts to have them freed. He was so brave, that boy, and she loved him like a son. No matter what had to be done, she would do it to help him, she had to do it however distasteful. The mere thought of Nikos taking her to his bed made her flesh crawl but she put the thought from her mind.

Now she knew how a prostitute must feel: obliged to shut off feelings and heart and simply perform like some animated puppet.. A sudden wave of pity for her less fortunate sisters made her heart soften. After all, her father had made no secret of the fact that her own mother had sold her body to help keep her brothers and ageing father from starvation in those terrible days in old Salonika; those days when the people of Smyrna had been driven from their homes by the Turks. They had fled to the 'Mother of the Poor' as Salonika liked to call itself then. Their welcome was scarcely maternal and less than generous, plunged into poverty of a crippling kind.

Nina returned to the Praxiteles apartment with a heavy heart. No one answered her repeated knocks and she began to feel some alarm when at last she heard a shuffle behind the door.

'Who is it?' came a quavering voice.

'Stella, it's me, Nina!'

Stella flung open the door and embraced her with joy. 'Nina, *agapi mou*, my dear one! We've been so worried. Where have you been? You went dashing off to the police station and we were convinced you'd been arrested or worse. Thank God, you're back.'

They shut the door and Aris came out of the other room to greet her. He looked tired and drawn but didn't seem to be bruised or beaten.

Nina surveyed him, 'Thank God you're okay, Aris.'

He grimaced a little and opened his shirt. There she saw the marks of beating, bruises and welts on his body.

'They're all over him,' said Stella, her face a mask of misery. 'I've been bathing them to remove the dried blood.'

'They were very careful not to mark my face,' said Aris. 'They are crafty bastards.'

'Where did they take you?'

'To Bouboulinas. Inspector Lambrou came to see me in an office and there were about another four men there too. He seemed most affable and pleasant to begin with. He told me not to worry, I would be freed, it was just a little co-operation he wanted. But I didn't know *what* they wanted. I told them I was never involved in politics but they said I was an employee of Vlachou and she was a communist. That all newspapermen were the same.'

Nina shook her head in disbelief. 'These people are mad.'

Aris continued, 'They took off my shirt and beat me with anything to hand in the office, rulers, pieces of piping. Yes, you're right, they were like madmen, cursing, swearing, insulting me and my family, saying crazy stuff. But in the end, they let me go and said I was lucky to be free.'

'I think they're afraid of Vlachou's influence,' said Stella.

Nina agreed. 'I think so too. Did you see George at Bouboulinas, did they allow you to see him?'

Aris raised his chin in denial. He began to tremble. 'Not a sign of my poor boy. I asked where he was and they laughed at me. Said he was being well cared for downstairs and I wasn't to worry. He would be freed when he had finished helping them and signed a paper of some kind. I was on the fourth floor in an office there. Lambrou's office, I think. I could hear screams from upstairs, it was terrifying. And there were strange sounds as if someone was banging an empty tin all the time. Maybe it's some form of torment for the poor bastards in the cells beneath. I was sure they were going to throw me in a cell … but they just let me free. I feel dazed. But I want my son, Nina – I want my son freed too!'

'We all do!' she exclaimed. 'Aris, you poor man … how helpless you must have felt.'

'Nina, it's impossible, it's just impossible.' Aris sat down in a chair and clasped his head in his hands.

'I'll make us some coffee,' said Stella, looking at her husband with troubled eyes. She disappeared into the little kitchen.

'Not impossible, Aris,' said Nina, sitting down next to him and patting his arm.

Aris looked up and his eyes beseeched her. 'Is there something you can do, Nina … you have contacts. You know people. Can you help?'

'I'm going to try and do whatever I can to help get George out of that hell hole they've taken him to.'

She dared say no more. What if it was all to no avail? Nikos might try – but would they listen to him, would they really do him a favour?

'My boy won't come out of there alive or if he does, he'll be a broken man. My God, I can't bear it. I asked them to let him go and take me if they must have sacrificial victims for their altars. But they said it was the young who need to understand, the young who had to be reformed and scourged from the evil of communism. I told them George is not a communist. He's just an idealistic boy who wants to help his fellow men, who wants to help his country be free and democratic and not be indebted to the Americans.'

'That's probably the worst thing to say,' said Nina grimly. 'Everyone's convinced the Americans are behind all this. At any rate, they're certainly not stopping it.'

'I have nothing against the Americans,' said Aris, 'they have put a lot of money into the country, helped us a great deal. But then there comes a point that they feel that they can dictate to us as if we are nothing but a troublesome child. Greece is like an undisciplined teenager in their eyes, always wanting to be independent and free but incapable of managing alone or having much common sense.'

Nina smiled a little. 'I think you're right. I'll quote you on that, Aris.'

Stella brought in the coffee and Aris got out a decanter of brandy. Nobody felt hungry but Stella warmed up some left over pasta from lunchtime and they ate in a half-hearted manner.

Aris kept looking up and shouting, 'He's not a communist. My boy is not a communist. He's a patriot, a true Greek!' – as if he was still under interrogation. Stella and Nina looked at one another, speechless and troubled.

At last, Stella banged down her fork suddenly. 'Oh, Aris, wake up! It's all very well but Giorgo adores Mikis Theodorakis. And everyone knows that Mikis is an out-and-out Party member who used to think Stalin was a god. All the Lambrakides are tarred with the same brush. They'll never let our boy go, never, never!' She began to sob, huge loud, tearing wails of sound that even the callous, unfeeling gods on their mountain peaks must have heard. The listeners felt their entrails being torn out with the pain of this primeval sound of grief.

Stella calmed down after a while and went to wash her face. Aris said no more but looked at Nina in despair. She still didn't dare to say anything about her hopes. Better not. She had steeled herself to what lay ahead but felt tomorrow would never come. They spent the evening listening to the radio without talking, all with their minds elsewhere. Minutes crawled by as if Time had grown wings of lead and was incapable of flight.

Nina still slept in George's room. Lexi, who usually slept in a small room at the back, looking out over lemon trees and small gardens, was still with her relations. Aris had told the girl not to worry, all was well and she was better off with her auntie and out of the city.

'I couldn't stand having her fretting and worrying every minute,' he said wearily. 'Things are hard enough. She loves it by the seaside so let her be there. She doesn't know the worst. I pray she'll *never* know the worst, poor child.'

They all smoked a last cigarette and turned in to attempt some sleep. Stella took a couple of aspirins. Her headache was killing her, she said, her eyes red-rimmed and the anguish still visible on her drawn, ghost-white face. Nina hugged her and let the older woman sob for a while on her shoulder.

'Stella, I'm going to go and see someone tomorrow,' she told her, 'I may be away for a while so don't be alarmed. But I have hopes I may be able to help in some way.'

Stella looked up and touched Nina on the cheek with a trembling hand. 'You're so brave, *agapi mou*, so brave. But I don't want you to be in danger. This is our trouble, not yours.'

'It *is* my trouble,' said Nina firmly, 'I'm a Greek, aren't I? And I love my friend George dearly. You think I won't try to do whatever I can to help him, to help you all?'

She went to her room and as she undressed, looked around at the paraphernalia of a young man. The room had been searched by the security police and turned upside down but Stella had tidied up again and things looked fairly normal. All the forbidden records of his idol, Mikis Theodorakis, which George had secretly kept and played had been taken away and no doubt smashed to fragments. Nina thought of the beauty of that amazing man's music, the poetry and fervour and feeling. What was so evil about that? She wondered yet again at the wilful madness of humanity, the strange fear and enmity that one group of people held for another – when all could and should work in harmony and wisdom.

The walls looked bare. Several posters had been ripped away, harmless pictures of the young man's favourite film stars.

'They said they were obscene,' Stella had told her, shaking her head in disbelief. 'I mean, you saw them. Were they obscene? A couple of pretty girls in swimsuits? He's a young man, for God's sake. Who are these people?'

Who indeed? And what had turned others who until now had appeared perfectly normal, ordinary citizens and upholders of the law into frenzied brutes?

Nina lay in the young man's bed and thought of him and prayed with all her heart and soul that Nikos would do something to help, no matter what it cost.

Chapter 29

Thessaloniki: Confrontations

Max hoisted his small duffel bag on his shoulder. In it he had the mere necessities of civilised life: an electric shaver, toothbrush, torch, cigarettes and lighter. He had also put in a few socks, a change of underwear and a couple of shirts. He'd have to buy more when he was in Athens but for now, this would do. Best to travel light and unencumbered. The rest of his luggage remained at Basil and Athina's home.

Much to his irritation, he was now obliged to go over to Laladika and have a last look around Dimitri's workshop before he caught the bus from the station. Yiota had rung to tell him she was leaving with the kids that morning and that Tinos had already decided to pack up the job. He was too frightened, she said, and she didn't blame the boy. He was young, he had a family. Could Max just make sure everything was delivered, paid for and sorted out, no angry clients likely to ring and say they'd still got one of their cars in the garage. She had taken what money there was, hidden in various places on her person and even a wad in each of the children's knickers. The keys were with *Kyrie* Manolis across the road. Somehow she would manage. But she sounded tearful and afraid.

'We'll have to live on herbs and greens,' she said, trying to joke, 'like all those peasants do.'

'Maybe you can find a job to keep you going,' he suggested. 'Mihaniona's a decent-sized town.'

'Eh, yes, but what! Cleaning houses or slaving in a shop? That's all I'm fit to do,' she grumbled. 'But I'll try. I'll have to.'

'Good luck, Yiota.'

'You too, Max, safe journey to England.'

'Thanks.'

He resented having to take time to go back to the workshop but he couldn't let the poor woman down. Cursing Tinos for a chicken-hearted bastard, he took the bus to Giorgiou. Yiota had told him she would leave the keys to the garage with Manolis who owned the electrical shop opposite her flat. Manolis had his radio on at full blast blaring out cheerful love songs, and lilting bouzouki music. Rather than lifting his spirits it made Max sad and full of longing. He felt troubled and apprehensive and prayed he'd find Nina safe and well, persuade her to see reason and return with him to England – return to their lovely little flat in Brompton where he had taken her as his bride, carrying her across the threshold and pretending to stagger under her slight weight. His wife who was like feather down in his arms! Start again, try again, be lovers once more. For some reason, he had a fleeting vision of them walking along the shady, tree-lined paths of the Brompton Cemetery on a summer's evening, talking about their hopes and plans. Nina had really loved that place. He smiled sadly at the memory.

He walked to the workshop, taking the route along the seafront towards the port where Dimitris had his workshop.. It soothed him to see the blue, calm sea stretching before him. He longed to take a train and be back in England. Greece wasn't the place he once loved so much. But he berated himself for such thoughts. Did one only love when things went well, were pleasant and fun? No, one loved for always, just as he loved Nina despite all that had come between them. And he loved Greece the same way. He wanted to help, but how could he?

He shut the workshop doors behind him as he went in; he didn't want any nosey neighbours popping in to find out what was going on. He looked around. The cars and the farmer's truck were all delivered to their varied owners, the area silent, empty and quite tidy. The battered old Ford truck belonging to

Dimitri was still standing at the back of the workshop. Dimitri always intended to do something with it and sell it but the spare parts had never manifested or he simply had never found the time to do anything with it. It wouldn't be worth much even if he did make it roadworthy. He'd be better selling it for scrap. Tinos had swept all the litter into a corner and put the tools away on the shelf. That was something, at least.

Max went into the office and prepared a notice to put on the door announcing that the garage was temporarily closed. He then boiled up some water on the little gas ring, made himself a cup of black Nescafé coffee and sat and looked at the account books. They all appeared in good order, all the customer bills paid in and nothing owing to any one. The safe was empty, all the money taken to Yiota. No one should bother to break in and if they did, good luck to them.

There was nothing else to do. He sighed at the waste of time. That was it. Now he would go and catch the bus that would take him to Athens and his beloved Nina.

He took a last look around the little office and went to switch off the light. A sound at the front of the shop made him spin round, his nerves ever in a heightened state. Someone was rattling at the door. He sighed in annoyance. Should he pretend there was no one there? Suppose it was the police after Dimitri? Well, he had no idea where his friend was and they were unlikely to try and arrest him, especially if he told then he was now leaving Greece. He opened the door and stared in astonishment. It was Zoë. Or what could be recognised as Zoë. He opened the door and helped her in and quickly looked around. Thank God, no one in sight. He shut the door again.

'Zoë! What the hell are you doing here?'

She stood motionless, then slowly began to shuffle towards him. She could barely walk – in fact he thought she might fall at any moment. Max took hold of her arms and guided her to his office. She sat down painfully on a chair. Her clothes were torn, her face bruised and marked, turning purple, a livid hue that spread across her eyes and down into her neck. When her blouse fell open he saw the purple and black bruises on her small breasts, breasts that had been twisted and bitten and marked with cigarette burns.

He brought over some water and tried to apply a handkerchief to the wounds. Zoë waved him away.

'No, don't touch, Max. It hurts, it hurts.' Her little whimper was like that of a wounded animal.

'Zoë, how the hell did he find you? Why did you come back, you utter little fool!'

'I just felt lonely, Max,' she said with a little sob. 'I wanted to see my girlfriends. I wanted the city lights.'

'You stupid girl!'

'Don't be angry with me. Not you. *He* was so angry, the bastard! He took me to his place and beat me, then he said I wasn't worth fucking and turned me over to his'boys'. They had me there for hours, over and over again. Oh God! I'm in such pain. I think I'll die.'

'You won't die. But you may need to go to a hospital. Come on, I'll take you in a taxi.'

'I daren't go to a hospital. I don't want to. I'll put some stuff on when I can. Max, please take me away from here. Take me to England with you.'

'How did you know I was going to England?' he demanded. Was nothing a secret round here?

'I don't know. I just hoped you'd had enough. I heard Dimitri was gone, Manos said so and swore he'd find him. But he knows he'll never find him if he's in the mountains. He'll get killed himself. He's not that crazy. It's just talk. Then Toula told me Yiota and the kids and the old *yiayia* had all left and you were sure to go. So I meant to come and find you. But Manos found me first. Someone saw me and recognised me and followed me to Toula's flat. They beat her up and left her unconscious. My poor, poor friend, they might have killed her. I don't even know. They dragged me off to Manos and I was terrified. Take me away, Max. Please.'

'And what happened after … I mean, they just let you off after … after … they just let you go away?' Max felt himself seething with fury. The stupid, stupid girl!

'They threw me out in the street.' She began to sob now, tears rolling down her cheeks already blotched with mascara and bleary make up. He felt for her pain but he was still angry. She would not listen, she just would not listen. The girl was crazy as well as stupid.

'Has it occurred to you, that Katsarakis knows full well you'll come crawling over to me? That that's just what he wants you to do? He's probably out there now waiting to make his entrance.'

She put her hand to her mouth. 'Oh, no … no, surely not. No one followed me, I swear. I walked here, it's taken me an hour. I walked. No one followed me. I did look.'

'I'm surprised you can see at all with your eye half closed up. Oh, you poor stupid girl. Listen, Zoë. I can't take you with me. It doesn't work like that. I can't take you, I don't want to take you. I'll give you some money … and I don't have a lot of that either. Get a taxi, take yourself off to the train station and get the hell out of here. I have to get a coach.'

'Where are you going then, if you aren't getting a train yourself or a taxi?' she asked. 'The coach to where?'

Damn, he should have been more careful. 'I have some business to see to in Athens.'

'I'll come with you to Athens.'

'No! You will not come with me. Can't you understand that simple fact?'

'I love you, I want to come with you!' she wailed.

Max sighed in exasperation.

'I thought as much,' said a deep growling voice. They looked up and saw Katsarakis at the garage door. He pushed it shut behind him and advanced upon the office. They were trapped inside it like rabbits. Zoë began to scream but Max put a hand over her mouth. 'Be quiet, let me deal with it.'

He walked to the door of the office, refusing to be caught inside, and shut the door on Zoë. Her look of abject terror smote his heart. It was the look he'd seen on his mother's face when his father began to slowly unbuckle his brass studded belt, swinging it in his hand and staring at her. It made Max feel sick to the pit of his stomach as well as enraged.

He had been a reasonable boxer once but was no match for this huge man and he knew it. Some sort of cunning was needed. He had taken a spanner from the office desk and held it in his hand but it wasn't a large one and he felt it would do little more than graze the huge forehead of the Cretan. But it might stun him long enough so he could grab the long, heavy wrench from the workbench and really knock him out.

Katsarakis sneered. 'Pah! You won't even make me bleed with that thing. Put it down, *re malaka,* you useless piece of shit. I'm really going to finish you this time. Nothing between you two, eh? Yet she comes running to you every time. And she says, "I *lo-ove* you", like a silly schoolgirl, that whore. But I promise, she won't want a man inside her again. Not for a long time. She's had a good time with my well-endowed boys. Proper Greek sandwich she made. It was fun to watch. You think we forced her? Never – she wanted it. She's a whore.'

'Shut up!' seethed Max. He couldn't bear to hear the man. He was evil to the core. And he knew full well that the Cretan wouldn't be happy with simply breaking his jaw this time.

As if reading his mind, Katsarakis laughed, 'So, my little shrimp, I'll break every bone in your body. I know how to do that beautifully. I used to break the legs of the communist bastards when we had them in prison on Makronissos. They taught me how to do it. I was just a lad and that was the only way I could save myself. Oh, they tortured me at first but then I became one of them. Got good at that sort of thing. You understand. I'm a kind man at heart. I'm a kind man. But that's what life does to you. You have to join them when you know you can't beat them.'

'You think I'm going to swallow that sob story?' snapped Max. 'You just love torturing and bullying. It's in your nature. Don't give me that shit.' He remained poised, ready to make a move, maybe dodge the brute and catch him by surprise. But he had little hope. Katsarakis was like a steamroller.

However, as the man lunged at him, his face smiling and gloating, Max sidestepped quickly and surprisingly did catch him off balance for a moment. Using the larger end of the spanner he hit him on the neck just at the back of his head. Enraged, the Cretan spun around and punched him so hard, Max went sprawling on the floor. He lay in a daze for a moment.

'This is it,' he thought. He had a vision of Nina and held it firm. He would die with her on his mind at least.

Katsarakis gave a laugh and moved to pick him up like a rag doll. But at that moment, Zoë came flying out of the little office. She found wings despite her pain, forgetting all in the moment of despair. She would not see Max killed. He was the only man in the world who had ever been kind to her. She loved him! That pig would never get away with it.

She had found a metal paper knife in the office. It was a mere toy, really, decorated on the handle with a carved *Evzone* shoe, but it was quite long and came to a sharp pointed end and was surprisingly strong. She flung herself on Katsarakis and pushed the blade into him as deep as she could. It entered the fleshy part of his back and had the effect of stopping him in his tracks. He growled and turned and grabbed her instead of Max, shaking her hard.

'You bitch!' he shouted. 'You little whore!'

But his attention was now distracted from Max who rising clumsily, ran to the workbench and seized the long heavy wrench. Holding it in both hands, he swung it hard and hit Katsarakis on the head with all his might. This felled the man who toppled over like a huge tree and lay senseless on the floor. Blood now poured from his head and seeped from the knife wound Zoë had given him … it was still sticking in his back and looked almost comical, like a little pin in a huge pincushion. Max stood and stared at him, wondering if he would recover and rise again. Zoë, however, went wild. Sobbing, she grabbed the wrench from Max's hands and hit Katsarakis on the head and back over and over again.

'You'll never hurt me now,' she screamed. 'Never again! Nor anyone else.'

Max woke himself up and grabbed a hold of her, pulling her back.

'For God's sake, Zoë! You'll kill the bastard.'

'I hope I have!' However, she calmed down a little and gazed at the battered body with deep satisfaction. 'I hope I have killed him. I don't care what happens. I've rid the world of an evil man. God will forgive me.' She crossed herself and turned away.

Max felt the man's pulse. He was certainly dead now. Was it his blow or Zoë's that had done it? It scarcely mattered in the end; they both preferred him dead. His heart sank. What the hell to do with a dead body that was as heavy as an ox and a clinging woman enfeebled by her injuries? It was amazing how she seemed to have forgotten them in her enraged state.

Like it or not, he owed her his life. That was a fact. He *had* to help her get away.

'Zoë, you saved me,' he said quietly.

'I saved us both,' she said and began to sob hysterically. He allowed her to do so for a little then took her and made her sit down in the office and gave her a glass of water.

'We have to think of a way to get rid of this body.'

'I don't know how, I don't know what to do,' she said, fearful now.

He went out into the garage again. It was horrible to have to look at the body, the head now battered and almost unrecognisable. But despite these injuries, everyone would know whose body it was. There was no disguising that huge man. Everyone in Thessaloniki knew him.

Max looked over at the old truck in the corner of the workshop. It was just about roadworthy. Thank God those flat tyres had been changed. There was a kind deity somewhere, after all. There used to be a can of petrol hidden away in the garage somewhere, Dimitri always being cautious enough to keep one around in case of a strike or some other shortage annoyance. Max hoped that Tinos hadn't taken it away for safety's sake.

After a short search, he found a full can of petrol in a cupboard in the office and thanked his lucky stars. Tinos had overlooked it. He filled the tank and tried to start the engine. It spluttered a little like a grumpy old man woken from a nap but eventually he coaxed it into life. It sounded terrible. The exhaust looked ready to fall off any moment but it would carry them for a few miles ... but where to go?

The coast was the best bet. He would throw the body over some cliff and it would eventually be washed out to sea. By the time it came ashore he and Zoë would long be gone.

But what a body to move! How the hell did butchers manage those huge carcasses of beef? He felt as if Katsarakis was no longer human – just a piece of meat to be heaved and shoved. Getting a large rag, he wrapped it around the bloodied head of the corpse. Then slowly and with immense difficulty began to drag the body towards the truck. Zoë roused herself with a groan, the pain of her limbs having re-manifested now the excitement was over. He waved her away. 'It's all right, I'll manage.'

She insisted. 'No, I'll help.'

Between them they heaved the body into the back of the truck. Panting, they stood and looked at one another when this was at last accomplished.

'Get me a drink of water, Zoë,' said Max. Sweat poured from his forehead. He would have preferred a large whisky, a bottle if there was one. But the glass of water revived him a little and he splashed his face and arms with it.

He covered the body with a piece of old tarpaulin. Then there was the floor to wash. He boiled up a saucepan of water on the little paraffin stove, filled a small bowl and began to rub away the bloodstains from the concrete. Then he spilt a little motor oil over the area and scrubbed at it again with a rag. It now blended in with all the rest of the oily marks and grime of years that coated that floor. No one would notice it.

Max looked over at Zoë who was watching him.

'For God's sake, give yourself a wash, Zoë,' he said, 'try to look as normal as you can. We seem to be forever steeped in blood, you and I,' he added ruefully.

'Blood unites us, Max,' she said, her little face crumpled with pain. 'We are bound by it and it will always unite us now.'

They stared at one another for a few moments. There was indeed a strange bond between them.

'Who can understand *Moira*?' said Max almost to himself. 'Why did she choose us?'

'I don't know,' the girl said simply. 'I only know I felt love for you from the first moment I saw you. And I have brought pain and unhappiness to you. Max, I am so sorry.'

He smiled a little and took her hand. She seized his and kissed it then went to do his bidding and wash herself at the little sink in the office. Meanwhile he took off yet another bloodstained shirt which he wrapped in a ball and stuffed under the tarpaulin together with the rags used for the floor. It was an ordinary cheap shirt from the market and not identifiable. He would bury these rags or throw them over with the body. His departure was definitely delayed and he groaned inside. He so wanted to get to Athens. Taking another shirt from his bag, he put it on then drew out the other one and gave it to Zoë.

'You'll just have to wear this,' he said. She looked at him and half smiled. He tipped up her chin a little and studied her face. Nothing could be done about the livid bruises and swollen lips and eyes. Anger boiled up in him again at the way that brute had treated her. Max felt no regret about Katsarakis' death. He had it coming to him. It was his life or theirs. Amazing little Zoë! He felt real admiration for her spunkiness in that moment. She saw the look in his eye and unspoken warmth flowed between them as between two comrades.

'Just keep your face turned away towards me, keep it in the shadow. Come on, get in the cab.'

She obeyed meekly. He helped her up into the truck, then put his duffel bag in the back next to the lump which was the erstwhile Katsarakis. He opened the big double doors of the garage, drove the truck out and then went back, pulled them together and locked up. He prayed that Katsarakis had come alone and none of his boys were hanging about waiting for him. It was evident that Katsarakis had meant to kill them both and leave them to rot in the garage. A nice surprise for Dimitri when he came home! So it was more than likely he had come alone. Max's eyes swept around anxiously but only a few passers-by were in the street. Nobody gave them a glance; there was nothing unusual about a truck leaving the garage for delivery. Plus, it was siesta time now and to his relief most of the shops were shut.

They drove out of town and through the suburbs. The roads were fairly quiet and he followed the back street route. Taking the Monastir road, he drove along almost empty highways and then turned off onto a dirt track that led through some fields towards the coast. Eventually he reached a small and pleasant little area on the top of the cliffs where he had sometimes picnicked with Dimitri and his family. The fields were silent and deserted under the autumn sky. A late crop of watermelons were lying fat and ripe upon the ground waiting to be harvested. Praying some irate farmer would not come along, he drove the truck into the dusty field and beyond until he came to the cliff edge. From here there was a glorious view of the blue sea and sky stretching for miles. It was a still, peaceful, undisturbed vista. Not a soul in sight. They got out of the truck, lowered the flap at the back and began to haul out the huge body.

'I keep feeling he may be alive,' said Zoë fearfully, 'that he will suddenly awake and roar with anger and kill us both.'

'Zoë, he is dead,' said Max grimly. 'You made damned sure of that.'

'Oh God, I killed someone.' Her voice quavered. She crossed herself several times.

'Don't lose your nerve now. He deserved it. You saved my life, remember?'

She set her little chin at that. 'Yes, and I would kill him again for that.'

They hauled the body towards the cliff edge and looked down at the sea below. Shame to spoil its calm beauty with this monstrous burden. Max removed the tarpaulin. They would bury that elsewhere. With a huge shove, he pushed the body over the cliff. They watched it tumble downwards, the arms and legs flailing outwards like some strange puppet.

'*Karagiozis,*' said Zoë, as they watched. 'A puppet, a shadow now.'

The body splashed into the sea. Its heavy weight propelled it downward into the deep but in time it would float up and be washed elsewhere. But bodies were often washed up these days, the new regime had thrown so many in the sea. Who would know or care who had killed Katsarakis? He had many enemies.

Max now had a new problem. What was he to do with Zoë? He felt that it would be impossible to take her to Athina and Basil. She would be seen by some gossipy neighbour and they would be in trouble. It took little enough to get arrested nowadays. After burying the ragged shirts and tarpaulin in a deserted spot, he sat and smoked in the truck with Zoë and thought about it hard. He remembered Dimitri telling him about a house along the Monastir road. He'd often shown it to Max when they drove by and told him he should go try the girls there.

'They're good clean girls,' he said. 'You could do with a bit of fun, Max. Stop acting like a monk on Mount Athos, shunning all that's female. It's not natural.'

Max had never had the slightest desire to take up this offer but he remembered the place now and when their cigarettes were smoked, they set off for it.

'I don't want to stay in a whorehouse,' said Zoë indignantly.

'Have you any better ideas? You can stay there till your bruises and wounds heal. You can't return to your friend in the city – if, as you say, she's even still alive. Katsarakis' men will be on the lookout for you. *They're* bound to suspect us two of killing him even if the police haven't a clue. You must go back to Florina again – if they'll take you back. You keep hopping off. Or find a job elsewhere. Start a new life, Zoë.'

'You won't take me with you?'

'Zoë, I am married. I love my wife. I was just about to go and join her in Athens to take her back to England with me when you and your wretched boyfriend came bumbling into my life again. I want to leave this country now. I've had enough. It will never be the same again.'

'I'm sorry, Max,' she said again in a low little voice.

‘It’s how it is. It’s happened. But forget me, Zoë. I’m nothing special and I’m not a hero. You are young and pretty. You’ll find a good man. You’re free of that fellow now. Go your own way.’

He drove into the little yard beside the house and took Zoë inside. The girls stared at them in amazement and fear to begin with but when Max told them that he was a friend of Dimitri, Marta smiled at him and nodded.

‘Then you’re a friend of ours too,’ she declared, taking Zoë by the hand and holding her close beside her in a motherly fashion. ‘*I kaimeni*…the poor girl, just look at her. What fuckster did that to you!’

Max had decided to simply tell them that Zoë had been beaten up by a nasty lover and that she was afraid to return and had nowhere to go. He had told her on the way that she must never mention Katsarakis or think of him again. No one was to know of their connection. The proprietor listened to their story and surveyed Zoë with some distaste.

‘I don’t want to take her in – who knows what she is?’ he announced. However, the other girls who had come to hear the story shouted at him.

‘We want to help her,’ they chorused. ‘Aren’t you ashamed, *vre* Antoni!’

He looked put out. ‘Who’s to pay for her board and lodging,’ he asked truculently. ‘She’s not going to earn her keep looking like that.’

‘I’m not going to stay here,’ Zoë declared, ‘to be insulted. I’m not a whore! I don’t earn my keep like that.’

The girls laughed and took no offence.

‘*Skotistika!*’ Marta yelled, ‘we don’t always have to open our legs to work, you old pimp. She can cook, she can clean and sew. She can earn her keep that way, eh?’

Antonis looked annoyed but he was obliged to agree, faced as he was by the rebellious expressions on the faces of the girls. Max gave Zoë some money and she followed him outside slowly and painfully.

‘I’ll never see you again,’ she said. Tears rolled down her cheeks.

‘No, Zoë. You’ll never see me again. Find a good man someday and take care not to say a word, remember. Stick to your story.’

‘I will, Max *mou*, I will.’

He got in the truck and set off back down the Monastir road to the city without a backward glance.

Chapter 30

Athens: Averoff Prison

Doctor Nikos Galanis did his rounds of the prisoners. He usually dealt with the women there and had to admit to himself that conditions in the overcrowded prisons were horrific but he dared not voice any sympathy. One pregnant woman had been so badly beaten that she had begun to bleed and he had just had her taken away to the Alexandra Maternity Hospital.

'Have I lost the baby, Doctor?' she asked pitifully, clutching at his hand.

'Have faith. It may be all right,' he assured her. But he knew full well that she had miscarried and sighed. It wasn't good to treat a pregnant woman like this. She told him she had showed her tormentors the doctor's certificate but they had ignored what it said, taken it away and never returned it.

He liked women and it was one of the reasons he had chosen gynaecology as his special branch of medicine. Easing their suffering, both emotional and physical, had always been his aim and his special brief in his new position was to keep an eye on the pregnant women in the prison, deliver any babies that had either come to term or been born prematurely.

Nikos told himself that, after all, these women were anarchists and communists or they wouldn't have been arrested; they deserved all they were suffering. Their minds had been turned by dreams of impossible Utopias. These babies would become evil people like their parents, so losing them was probably a good thing. Thus reasoning and hardening his heart and soul, he set about his work in the varied security prisons around Athens and remained aloof and dispassionate from what he saw. All he could do was help the women to bring forth the children they'd spawned and if the babies were taken elsewhere, he cared not where or what happened. If anything he felt proud that he had been chosen for this position. He worked hard, making good use of his contacts in order to be well in with the new regime.

However, he had promised Nina to help get out the boy, Giorgos Praxiteles, and whatever his faults he was a man of his word. It was true that he knew Colonel Papadopoulos, had met him once and helped a cousin of his to have an abortion. But his buddiness didn't extend as far as he liked to make out. He would have to think of some way of getting the boy out. He could try speaking to Doctor Kioupis, who was the favoured doctor working at Bouboulinas St. Doctor Kioupis ran the medical station there and visited the prisoners, ostensibly to ensure that the hygiene and so forth was adequate, but his real task was supervising the tortures and beatings to make sure that they didn't go too far and attract bad publicity.

Kioupis owed Nikos a favour or two and could use his influence on his behalf. The only way to get out the Praxiteles boy was to concoct some story and ask that the boy be sent to some local hospital for treatment. Soon, some of these Lambrakides were to be transferred to Dionysos, the training camp near Athens. Once there, beyond his jurisdiction, there was no way he could get to him.

He spoke quietly to Kioupis when he encountered him that day at the Security HQ in Bouboulinas St. 'You owe me a favour, Kioupis. Remember when I saw to your niece's little problem? And with that medicine you wanted brought from Britain?'

'I remember,' the other doctor replied, looking annoyed at this reminder of his family shame. 'What's the favour, then?'

'I've been asked to check up on a Giorgos Praxiteles,' Nikos said. 'The young man is a friend of a foreign journalist I know and she swears to make a fuss if I don't help get him released. Any ideas?'

'Those cursed journalists are a thorn in our side,' said Kioupis angrily. 'Why can't you tell her to go to the devil?'

'She's an old family friend from way back but she married an Englishman and she can make a lot of trouble for us when she returns. She's well in with some of the big papers over there. This little gesture may make all the difference to her attitude. She either gets the boy out and promises to keep quiet, or she loses him. It's up to her.'

'Hmm … that makes good sense. Yes, very good sense.' Kioupis smiled. 'You're clever indeed, Dr Galanis. Yes, I remember that boy, he was taken to isolation in the basement at first but lately he's been removed to the fourth floor and allowed a little more freedom. He's a stubborn one and resists all we ask of him so he's been … administered to a little. They're waiting for his face to improve before they let his mother see him. Or *she'll* go running away shouting her head off about it. Women are such tiresome creatures. They don't understand what has to be done.'

Nikos looked at Kioupis and couldn't help a slight shudder passing over him.

'Did they give him the *falanga* as well?'

'No. For some reason he's been spared that. He's been lucky so far, just beaten about, nothing that won't heal in time. So your journalist can't say too much because, once the wounds heal, no one will be able to tell. They tend to hit the fleshy parts of the body so there will be no lesions. It's his word against ours if he does talk. He may be sent to Dionysos or Averoff prison soon. Most likely the former as he's one of these young Lambrakides.'

'What's his condition?'

Kioupis considered. 'It's true he's had a bad bronchial cough of late. But I don't think he has bad bronchitis. However, I can maybe get him into the hospital, tell Lambrou he's not fit to stay in his cell, tell him that it might affect the others in there with him. If you want him out of the hospital, it's up to you from there. He'll have a guard with him. But maybe we can sort something out. I'll see if I can get him a reprieve. I don't promise. Depends what mood Lambrou is in. Frankly, the boy hasn't told us anything useful and I doubt he has much information. One of his friends has spilt the beans though. He did have the *falanga* and Praxiteles was forced to watch. It didn't make *him* talk but the friend was a lot more useful. I don't think this young fool Praxiteles is a very active member of the communist party.'

'Okay. Can you see to this matter soon? It's vital I do something soon.'

Kioupis looked at him curiously. 'I'll go and see the boy later today. We'll transfer him to hospital tonight.'

The next day Nikos went to the hospital and asked to see Praxiteles. The young man was lying in bed asleep. Probably the best sleep he'd had in a long while, thought Nikos as he surveyed him. He was handsome once, he thought, and a faint wave of pity came over him but he brushed it aside. His looks would recover in time.

He woke the boy by shaking his shoulder. George started awake in terror, looking wildly at him, his arms flailing.

'I'm going to check you over again,' said Nikos and took out his stethoscope, putting it to the boy's chest. He was indeed a mess. His face was puffed up, tongue swollen, front tooth missing, eyes dark and hollow with lack of sleep. In his opinion the boy's breathing *was* restricted and Nikos felt he probably did have mild bronchitis. Maybe he had saved his life by getting him out. Nina couldn't fail to be grateful.

The young man looked up at him. He seemed to see something in the doctor's eyes and looked at him again. 'Haven't seen you before,' he mumbled.

'I'm not the regular doctor. But I have been told you have symptoms of bronchitis and that's why Doctor Kioupis sent you here. Listen to me now – you will, however, seem better today as I mean to discharge you. Do you understand what I'm trying to say? Just nod in reply.'

The boy's face fell. He sat back, exhaled a long breath and then began a fit of coughing. He shook his head. 'This is some trick, a new torture.'

'It's not anything of the sort. I'm here to help you.'

'What then … I go back to Bouboulinas?'

'I've arranged it that you are to be freed. You have no further information for the Security Police and they are dropping the charges against you. You'll be sent home today but the hospital has to assume you're fit to leave now.'

'You're sending me home?' whispered George. 'Why are you doing this, Doctor?'

'Because your friend, Nina, she asked me to help.'

'Nina Hammett? God bless her.'

'I've no doubt He will,' said Nikos dryly.

But I shall have my thanks from her first, he thought – and smiled to himself.

Athens: at the Praxiteles apartment

Before leaving her friends, Nina sat down and wrote Nikos's address on a sheet of paper. Just in case she should disappear en route and no one know where she had gone. She felt sure she was being tailed and though her shadow was a stupid fool, easy to outwit, she was afraid that someone a little more intelligent may be sent to follow her today.

In the back of her mind, she wondered if she had fallen into a trap of some sort. But, no, he wouldn't give her away. She was sure of that. He'd always wanted to get her into his bed since he was a young man and had simply seized an opportunity. It was almost amusing and typical of the hypocrisy of that crowd. How easily they forgot their moral stance when it suited them.

She sighed a little. It was too bad to be suspicious of everyone but that's how this new political climate affected people. There was fear everywhere. Nothing said aloud, just a palpitating sense of distrust, uncertainty and gloom. For some at least – because there *were* others who were delighted and happy with the new regime. Especially the farmers and peasants who had been granted subsidies and other help in an attempt to woo them over. The bribery had worked very well and they declared that business was better than ever, things had never been so good. It all depended which side of the fence you were on. Intellectuals suffered as always at the hands of extreme political regimes because they weren't so easily placated and bought off. They were independent thinkers and such dictatorial, irrational governments did not want any independent thinking to challenge them.

She called Stella who was in the kitchen cooking a meal and gave her the slip of paper. 'I'm going out now to visit this man,' she said as casually as she could. 'He may be able to help us. I don't promise, it's just a hope on my part. This is where I shall be tonight. Just in case you need me for anything.'

Stella took the piece of paper, looked at the address and nodded but then she looked up suddenly at Nina as if comprehension had dawned upon her.

'Is this Dr Galanis married?'

'No.'

'But he wants you stay the night?'

'Yes, I promised. I had to,' said Nina simply. She couldn't meet Stella's eyes and turned away.

'Nina, Nina, my dear … I think I understand …'

'It's okay, don't worry, Stella. I can take care of myself. It's fine. Nikos Galanis is an old friend of mine … I've known him since I was a kid. But I'd rather you knew where I was … well, just in case of any problems.'

She hadn't mentioned she was being followed by the police. Poor Stella was scared enough already, why alarm her any further?

Stella looked relieved and hopeful. She looked as if she was going to ask something but held her tongue and asked no more.

After leaving the Praxiteles apartment, late that afternoon, Nina walked across the street and made her way through side streets until she reached the wide thoroughfare of Vassileis Sofias. She looked around with care but saw no apparent followers. Certainly not the fellow she'd seen yesterday. Maybe they had decided not to bother, she thought hopefully. What interest was she to them, after all?

She disappeared into a shop behind Syntagma Square and pretended to be looking at some cheap clothes. After some time perusing the goods and carefully scanning those around her, she felt safe and went out and bought a bus ticket at a *periptero*, a kiosk by the bus stand. Then if anyone spotted her doing this, they might assume she intended to take a bus somewhere. Walking along Theodoras street, she entered the gates of the Royal Botanical Gardens and sauntered along between the shade of the trees. A young boy was walking along scattering seed to the pigeons that followed him in a huge chattering crowd, even flying up to his hand. She smiled to see him and wished she had her camera with her to snap the engaging picture.

She wandered around the gardens for a little while, walking towards Zappeion , and felt sure that no one was following. If they were they would assume she was having an afternoon stroll away from the heat of the day in the quiet peaceful gardens. She came back out of the gardens onto Theodoras again and flagged a passing taxi that was free and hastily jumped in.

'Psihiko,' she told the driver. Her roundabout route must surely have put off anyone interested in her movements. The taxi sped along Kiffisias Rd and took her out towards the pleasant leafy suburb where royalty still lived. Opening her powder compact, she watched out of the rear window on the pretext of powdering her nose. But she felt secure there was no car following the taxi. Stopping the driver some way from Nikos's house, she paid him and waited till he had driven away and then walked along till she reached her destination and stood for a moment staring at the house before her. The shutters were half closed although it was still light. She felt fear and a sense of disgust tremble through her and breathed deeply for a while. What was there to fear, after all? Why be disgusted? It was the oldest thing in the book, the blackmail of sex. All she had to do was open her legs and think of nothing. But first, oh first, she was determined to make sure that George was freed. That was the bargain.

Even as she approached the door, it opened and Nikos stood there. She realised that he must have watched her waiting and wondering and surely, surely he realised how she didn't want to go through with this nonsense? He wasn't going to make her keep her side of the bargain, was he?

'So, you came, Nina.' A half smile played upon his lips.

'I promised I would come.'

'And the granddaughter of Costas Cassimatis keeps her promises.'

'But does the son of Galanis keep his?'

'He does, Nina.' He smiled again and ushered her inside the hallway and into his *saloni*. It was tidy and smelt sweet and clean today, smelt of polish and herbs. A nosegay of basil hung over the doorway and there were fresh flowers on the table. Nikos had also tidied himself up and looked smart in a casual pair of cream coloured trousers and a white open necked shirt that showed the dark hairs of his chest. What was left of his once luxuriant black hair was brushed carefully over his head and he smelt of some pleasant and expensive after shave lotion. Like a bridegroom, thought Nina, her heart quailing yet again. Yet she was oddly touched as well and even a little sorry for him.

'A glass of wine?'

'Yes, why not,' She wanted to dull herself with wine, relax, lose the knowledge of who she thought she was and just be a woman. In the end that's what it was all about. Ancient rituals. The spoils of the women to the winner.

Nikos fetched a bottle from his kitchen, opened it and poured the red wine into two tall glasses.'Only the best,' he remarked, raising the glass and waving it beneath his nose, smelling its savour and looking pleased with himself. 'Only the best for you, Nina.' He sipped delicately and made a pout of appreciation. 'Try it,' he urged.

She tried to smile but couldn't and lifted the glass and took a swig of the wine without all the preamble.

'It's good, isn't it? From our family vineyards. I've been keeping this bottle for very special occasions. This is it. This is the occasion it was meant for.'

It *was* a delicious wine and despite herself as she sipped away at it, Nina felt herself softening and relaxing but not to the extent that she was forgetful of the purpose of her visit.

'I want to know what you've done, Niko,' she demanded setting her glass down on the table in front of her. She had seated herself in an armchair despite Nikos having gestured her towards the sofa. There was no way she was prepared to be that close to him yet. The coffee table was now between them and formed a barrier of sorts.

'What d'you mean?'

'Don't play games,' she snapped. 'This isn't a pleasure visit, I'm not your girlfriend, though you're trying to pretend I am. I'm here because you forced my hand and you know it.' His face fell like a child's but she didn't care. Relentlessly she went on, 'I want to know if you've kept your side of the bargain. Is George Praxiteles freed yet? Have you pulled all those strings you boasted about? Or am I here on false pretences?'

Nikos leant back against the sofa, sipped his wine and stared at her. 'I've kept my word,' he said. 'George Praxiteles has been transferred to Evangelismos. Luckily the boy got the idea and didn't try any heroics but kept his mouth shut. He does have a bad chest so his constant coughing did the trick. The doctor at Bouboulinas owed me a favour and he has plenty of influence. He spoke to Lambrou, said the boy was too ill and not much use anyway. They know the boy is connected to Eleni Vlachou through his father and she could cause a stink if he died, so Lambrou relented. He can change his mind just like that but he did relent in this case and is letting the boy free. It merely requires a phone call from me to the hospital and they'll tell his parents to collect him, take him home.'

'Then call them now.'

'At this time of the day?'

'There'll be someone on duty, won't there? You say it's all arranged.'

Nikos put down his glass. 'All right, I'll ring now. I won't go back on my word. What d'you take me for?' She gave him a fierce look and he flinched a little. She understood quite well that he wanted her to think he was noble and caring like her idol Dr Lambrakis. And that Nikos Galanis, considered himself to be a true patriot who wanted to see Greece reborn, rising again in all her glory. Once he might have fooled her but not any more.

Nikos went out into the hallway and she heard him dial a number then speak rapidly to someone. He had his mouth partly covered by his hand and after a few moments, her heart beating furiously, she sprang up and went into the hallway.

'They will free him in an hour,' said Nikos, looking up, surprised at her sudden appearance.

'I want to talk to him. To George,' she demanded. 'I want to be sure he's alive, that he's really there.'

'Hang on, hang on,' said Nikos to the person on the other end of the line. He covered the mouthpiece with his hand. 'You can't do that, Nina,' he whispered. 'Look, it's tricky enough. Trust me, for God's sake, just trust me. You can ring the Praxiteles in an hour, his parents will have taken him home by then, I promise.'

'We'll wait an hour. Then I'll ring Stella and find out if what you say is true.'

He shrugged. 'Agreed.' He spoke again into the phone and she was glad to hear his voice held some authority and assurance. Then he led her back into the room and they sat down, opposite one another again.

'You won't come and sit beside me?'

'Not yet,' she replied. 'I'll be more willing once I know George is safe home.' She leant forward and scanned his face earnestly, 'Oh, Nikos, did you see the boy? Did you actually see him?'

Nikos nodded. 'Yes, of course I did.'

'Is he really sick?'

'He's in reasonable shape, I promise.' But he turned his head away from her as he spoke and fiddled with the wine bottle. He poured out another glass for them both.

'What I wonder, is "reasonable shape"?' she asked bitterly.

'He's alive, what more do you want … a few bruises, a tooth missing – believe me that's nothing.'

'Oh, God!' She rested her head in her hands for a brief moment. Nikos watched her and lifted the glass to his lips.

'He's alive, Nina. Be glad. There are those who have disappeared, as you well know. My dear, they're all criminals, the world's well rid of them. But I agree, this one's just a wayward lad. I felt sorry for him. His parents should have kept a better eye on his activities and the sort of people he got mixed up with. Anyway, he's free now. But you want my advice? Get him away somewhere fast. The police will still be watching him.'

'Can you help me get him back to England?'

'No, there's nothing more I can do. It's up to you from now on.'

'I thought you had lots of power with this new regime?'

'I have a certain amount … how else do you think I got your young lover freed?'

'My young lover!' Nina rose to her feet and looked as if she was about to throw her glass of wine in Nikos' face. 'Are you mad, are you crazy, you bastard! How dare you accuse me of such a thing?'

He put his hands up and waved them as if in negation. 'Okay, okay, that was stupid. I'm just jealous of all this love you have for him.'

'I love him like a *son*, like a *friend*, you fool.'

'Eh, I'm a fool,' he shrugged and rubbed his chin, already darkening with new bristles. 'Come, Nina *mou*, let's not quarrel over this. I want us to be friends. See what I've done for you? I've helped you and I had to make up a good story on your behalf. *Ella, ella* … come on … don't I get a word of thanks?'

She sank back onto her chair. 'Yes, Niko, I do thank you for what you've done. At any rate, I *will* thank you when I know that the boy is safe in his own home again.'

'*Endaxi*, fine,' Nikos shrugged. 'I can wait. I've waited this long, the rest of the night is ours and you aren't going anywhere, are you?'

'No, I'm not going anywhere,' she said with a sad little smile.

Chapter 31

Athens: Max arrives at the Praxiteles apartment

Max arrived at the bus station in Athens and wearily threw his duffel bag over his shoulder, scrambled off with a dozen other passengers then looked around for a taxi. He had slept a good part of journey, exhausted by all the trauma and horror of the past few days. Images of the huge Cretan lying on the floor of the garage, his head almost beaten to a pulp, still flashed into his mind and left him feeling sick and trembling with aftershock.

Zoë's fury and strength had amazed him. Now he comprehended the story of the maddened maenads and their wild god, Dionysos. Women enraged were something terrifying and destructive. He hoped Zoë would be all right and find her way up north again. Would she return to Florina? He doubted it. He had a feeling she would try to find her way back to Turkey or Yugoslavia and disappear onto the crowded streets of some unknown city … to what fate? He didn't want to think. She was one of those women who drew violence and misery towards her. He pitied her, felt some strange bond between them, but at the same time wished to God she'd never come into his life. It was she who had almost been the architect of his death, however unwitting; she who had ruined his fragile marriage again.

He now longed to find Nina, gather her in his arms and ask her to listen while he told her the whole story. She must surely listen now that the anger had passed and her normal calm self would be in charge. Dimitri was right. Take her in your arms and fuck her, he would have said. Max smiled to himself but then a pang of sadness came over him at the memory of his dear friend. Driven from his home, split from his family by cowards and evil men. A sudden yearning to be back in sensible old England assailed Max's heart. But first he had to find Nina and make her return with him. He had promised Andrew he'd bring his wayward daughter back home.

It was some time since he had been in Athens and Zografou was a suburb he knew little about. He showed the taxi driver the address that Andrew had given him and they drove through the city as fast as they could. The driver complained bitterly about the traffic problems and told Max how people were only supposed to drive on certain days according to the number plate on their car.

'But nobody takes any notice,' the man said angrily. 'These damned people just hold us taxi drivers up. We're trying to earn a decent living while half these characters who can afford a car are just out for fun, they want to show off. They drive round and round Syntagma in these big American cars. They're doing us out of business.'

He was beginning to work up to his theme, taking his hands off the wheel every now and then to gesture and protest, honking his horn madly and cutting corners at some speed. Max had forgotten how mad Athenian taxi drivers were and was relieved to reach the quiet street where the Praxiteles family lived. He paid the taxi driver – who was still muttering to himself as he took off again at breakneck speed – hitched his bag on his back and began looking for the block of apartments he wanted. He pushed open the entrance door and entering, rang the bell.

The flat was ablaze with light and he could hear voices inside. At the sound of his insistent ring, all went quiet of a sudden. He waited some time and after a while, the door was cautiously opened and a woman poked her head around. She stared at him in amazement. He hadn't shaved for a couple of days and he knew he looked, and probably smelled, pretty bad.

Max smiled and said, '*Kyria* Praxiteles?'

The woman seemed relieved to see a foreign face and hear a foreign voice.

'Who is it?' she asked. She opened the door a little wider now.

'I'm Max Hammett,' he said, 'I believe my wife, Nina is staying with you?'

The woman grabbed his arm and almost pulled him inside. Surprised, he let himself be drawn into the flat, the door shut after him. An older man, whom Max assumed was her husband, came out of the kitchen.

'This – this is Nina's husband!' the woman cried. She sounded almost overjoyed as she announced the fact. The man came over and shook his hand, pumping it up and down exuberantly. Max was amazed at this reception. He put down his duffel bag.

'I am right, you are Aris and Stella Praxiteles?' he asked looking from husband to wife.

'Oh, forgive me,'said the woman, 'Yes, I am Stella and this is my husband, Aris. We're so glad to see you, *Kyrie* Hammett. How did you find us? You look tired. Have you come here from England?'

'I am a little tired,' he confessed, 'but no, I've come here on the bus from Thessaloniki and it seemed to take forever. And Nina? Is she still with you?' he added anxiously.

Stella looked at Aris. 'She's still with us but just today, just tonight, she has gone over to a friend whom she hoped might help us get our son back.'

Max looked at them, puzzled. Aris motioned to Max to come and sit in the *saloni*. 'Come and I'll explain the situation,' he said. Stella meanwhile looked out into the corridor and seemed to listen then shut the door of the room.

The man had a tense, weary look about him. But at the same time there was a peculiar repressed sense of joy about the couple that puzzled him.

'We are so deeply relieved, so happy, *Kyrie* Max,' Aris explained. 'Our beloved son has been returned to us, returned from hell. The police had taken him prisoner – because of his involvement with the Lambrakides, you understand. You've heard of them?'

'Nina often spoke of them,' said Max, 'she said they formed as a group after the assassination of Grigoris Lambrakis.'

'Yes, they were brought together and inspired by Theodorakis who *is* a well known communist. But George, our son, is no communist, just an idealistic boy. He thought he could do good. The police rounded him and some of his friends up and he has been tortured and psychologically damaged – he isn't well at all. But, thanks to God, he was freed today. Just now he is sleeping in his bed, exhausted, poor boy.'

'That's a terrible tale,' said Max with sympathy. 'I have friends in Thessaloniki who've had to escape the authorities as well.'

I too am a fugitive now, he thought, the image of Katsarakis falling over the cliffside vivid in his mind.

'Stella, my dear, get us some coffee and something to eat. *Kyrie* Max looks as if he could do with some food and drink.'

Max nodded gratefully. 'I don't want to put you to trouble but a coffee would be good, very good.'

'Come and sit, rest a little.'

Max sat down on the sofa and felt the relief in his bones after all those hours on the hard seats of the coach. Aris offered him a cigarette which he lit up and inhaled deeply. Aris did the same and for a few moments both men smoked and kept silent.

'So, what made you come to us, *Kyrie* Max?' said Aris at last. 'Nina seldom mentioned you. We always thought she was divorced.'

Max grimaced at this. It hurt him that his wife had never spoken of him, treated her marriage as if it was all over and now meaningless to her. 'We've been separated for some time,' he explained, 'but I'm still her husband. And her father – he lives in England – is worried about Nina. He knows she loves getting involved in situations that can sometimes spiral out of control. And he wants me to persuade her to come back to England with me.'

'But you were in Thessaloniki?'

'Yes, I've been living there a few months, a brief stay helping out some friends. Nina was with me but she wanted to come to

Athens and do some research for her newspaper.' Something in his voice made Aris look at him with a flicker of understanding.

'Nina is a wonderful woman,' said Aris, 'and she is very brave. But yes, foolhardy too. I think you are wise to take her home with you. In fact, I think she will have to leave, like it or not. The authorities searched our home and found an article she was writing for her newspaper. They are angry with her attitude and mean to deport her anyway. So you shouldn't have too much trouble persuading her.'

'But where is she now?'

'Nina left us earlier in the day and said she was going to a friend she has known for many years and that she hoped this person would help her. We have no idea who this friend is or how he managed it but it seems he has helped. She said she would stay the night there. I don't know where she is though.'

At this point, Stella entered with the coffee and laid the tray on the table. She had also brought a small plate with *tiropites* and offered these to Max who took them gratefully. He was really hungry now. He gulped down the Nescafé in between mouthfuls and meanwhile Stella said, 'I *do* know where she is, she left me the address in case anything might happen.'

Max frowned. 'In case anything might happen? That sounds worrying. What did she mean by that … who is this friend?'

'It worries me also,' said Stella. 'She went to see a man called Nikos Galanis. Here's the piece of paper she left me with his address on it.'

Max frowned as he perused the paper. 'The name sounds familiar. I think I've met this man once or twice back home in London. He's a doctor, I think. Someone she knew as a kid and then met again when he came to work in London. I gather he must be back in Greece now and she must have asked for his help.'

'Well, it worked. George is free.' Aris said triumphantly.

'That's tremendous news! It seems Nina managed to pull something off as she always does. But why stay the night?' mused Max.

'I don't know,' admitted Stella. 'Nina said she would give

me the address just in case. I had a feeling in my gut that she was a bit scared. Or that he, that this man … maybe demanded some sort of … payment in kind. He's not married, *Kyrie* Max. I asked her and she admitted he wasn't. I know Nina isn't a young girl, she hardly needs a chaperone … but …' Something in her voice alerted Max.

He stood up abruptly and said, 'I'm going to go and bring her back here.'

Aris looked startled, as if the truth was dawning on him also. He and Stella also rose and at that moment, the telephone rang and made them all jump.

Nina waited impatiently until Stella picked up the phone.

'Is he freed?' she asked eagerly. 'Is George home?'

'Thanks be to God, he is, he is!' was the joyful reply. 'We went to fetch him an hour ago from Evangelismos Hospital.'

Nina gave a deep sigh of relief. 'Thank God, indeed! How is he?'

Stella hesitated. 'He's okay, exhausted, feverish, battered … but what can you expect? He's sleeping now. Why not come home, Nina? He longs to see you.'

'I … can't. I promised to stay.'

'Nina … wait, don't hang up. Someone here wants to speak to you …'

Max almost tore the phone away from Stella. 'Nina, what the hell are you doing there? Look, come home, darling. Come home as soon as you can. What's stopping you? Are you a prisoner?'

Nina almost fainted at the sound of her husband's voice. She glanced over at the *saloni*. Nikos stood against the door, arms folded and a look of satisfaction on his face. He beckoned to her now and made a motion that she should terminate the chit- chat. She waited a few moments to compose herself and then replied, 'Everything is fine. But yes, I'm staying here tonight. It's … too far to come back, too late now. You understand?'

'I'm damned if you're staying!' shouted Max and she prayed

that Nikos couldn't hear his voice and recognise it. 'I'm coming for you. Are you alone with this Nikos?'

'Yes.'

'And I can just guess what *he* has in mind,' was the furious reply. If the situation hadn't been so grave, Nina would have found it funny. Now Max was jealous of *her*. How delightful.

'Keep him waiting,' said Max, calming down a little. 'I'm coming immediately. Keep him chatting.' He slammed the phone down and she gave a big sigh and slowly replaced the receiver in its hook.

'So, they are a little suspicious of my intentions, I gather.' Nikos looked amused. 'Too bad, eh? You're an adult, a free woman. There's nothing they can do.'

Nina smiled a little, 'No, nothing they can do.'

He came towards her and stood before her so that her back was against the wall. Moving his fingers over the skin of her throat and chest caressingly, running them over her cleavage with a peculiar sensual delight, he stared at her with a strange expression. His face was sly and furtive, almost another man's face. His narrowed eyes kept shifting off sideways as if he felt he was being watched by someone. But there was no one else there, only the inner custodians of his morals ranging in shadows along the wall; he heard them chattering in his head, knew that they were there and was afraid of them.

'Niko,' she said desperately, 'I am grateful, so grateful to you. But can't you let me go now? Let me go home to my friends?'

He glared at her. 'So, you don't find me attractive at all?' he demanded. 'Not at all, eh? No, no, Nina. You made a bargain. I kept my side of it. Now you must keep yours.'

'It's not that you're unattractive, Niko,' she said as pleasantly as she could, 'of course it's not that. You're a proper man, I know that. But I'm married. It means something to me. And I thought you were a man of principle too. You wouldn't force a woman, a married woman to be your lover. Surely not, Niko. It's not like you. You have other women in your life … why me?'

'Because I've always wanted you, Nina,' he said simply. 'God watches me, I know that. But he knows I'm a good man, a good Christian. And we both know your husband has betrayed you. He's far away, you've parted now and will soon be divorced. Max won't care, why should you?'

'But I do care,' she said, 'I do.'

'Then you're a fool.'

He took her arm now and guided her towards the bedroom. She tried to pull away but his grip was tight.

'I'd like a glass of that delicious wine, first, Niko,' she said, playing for time. She smiled at him and touched his face with her hand, playfully. 'Come, let's drink a little more. I can't make love "cold" so to speak. You need to woo me a little … yes?'

He laughed at this and said, 'A good idea. Lovemaking should never be a rushed affair.' He seemed almost triumphant at her change of attitude and they went into the *saloni* and he poured them both out a glass of wine then sat beside her on the sofa and began to unbutton her blouse. She let him do so, let his hands roam into her bra, pulling out her breasts and gazing at them with a look almost of reverence. He passed his hands over them and fondled her nipples till they grew hard.

'Ah, *now* you're beginning to desire me,' he murmured. Nina hated to tell him that this was one of the biggest and stupidest of male fantasies and that nipples always responded to touch in this way. It had nothing to do with her desire whatsoever. However, she just smiled again but drew away a little to sip at her wine, looking at him steadfastly. He kept his eyes on her body as if afraid to meet her gaze and she knew that her candid gaze unnerved him, pierced him to the marrow of his soul.

Nikos leant back to drink his wine, staring all the time at her full, round breasts and touching them now and then with the practised hand of a doctor, soft, careful rather than lustful. 'I want to savour you like a delicious meal,' he whispered. 'You're like a piece of ripe fruit, ready for the taking. I want to peel off your clothes bit by bit.'

'How romantic,' she said. She wanted to scream.

'I *am* a romantic man, Nina. Yes, I am. When you are naked before me then you will "peel" me too. Slowly, slowly. We shall make love all night. There's no hurry.'

'No, no hurry.'

They both sat in silence for a little while, sipping at their wine.

'I'll put some music on,' said Nikos.

'A wonderful idea,' she agreed. He rose and went to his little gramophone and selected a record.

'Something romantic, eh?' he asked.

'Yes, something soft and romantic,' she agreed.

He got the music going and returned to the sofa. Now he took the glass from her hand and set it down on the table. He pulled her to him and began to kiss her, this time not so gently.

'You don't seem enthusiastic,' he complained.

'Give me time, Niko.'

'I'm giving you time.' He was beginning to sound upset now. How much longer could she hold him off?

At this point there was a loud ring at the bell as if someone had their finger on it and refused to take it away. Nina's heart leapt. She prayed it was Max and not the security men.

'Oh, what the hell is this?' Nikos looked up angrily while Nina hastily buttoned up her shirt, wishing she didn't feel guilty as if caught in some naughty act she *wanted* to participate in.

'No, don't!' said Nikos, trying to stay her hand. 'We'll just ignore it.'

'You can't ignore it, Niko! Suppose it's the police?'

'Why the hell should it be the police?'

'They've been following me,' she said. 'Maybe they've traced me here.'

He rose now, fear in his eyes. 'Why the hell didn't you tell me?'

'I was sure I was safe and felt certain they didn't follow me here. But who else could it be?'

Nikos went to the door, half angry, half afraid. He opened the door and there stood Max Hammett. That was almost a worse sight than the police and Nikos stepped back in astonishment while Max shoved him aside and burst into the room. Nina was seated there looking very prim and proper, sipping her glass of wine.

'You're coming home with me!' he shouted at her and dragged her up from the sofa, spilling red wine over the floor.

'Max! How did you find me here?' she cried but felt so glad that her knees almost buckled beneath her.

'This is a bloody set up, a trick!' screamed Nikos and he threw a punch at Max who jumped aside so that the older man almost stumbled and fell.

'It's no trick, you disgusting bastard!' said Max. 'It's you who tricked my wife. I can bet anything you like, if I hadn't arrived in time, she'd be forced to get in your bed with you, if she hasn't already. I'll beat you to a pulp if that's happened.'

Nikos steadied himself against the sofa and glared at Max. 'You've got it all wrong,' he said. 'Tell him, Nina, tell him how I helped you to get your young lover freed.'

Max swirled round at that and confronted his wife. 'George is your lover?'

Nina pulled her arm away from his fierce grasp and decided it was time she took over. She'd had enough of these two crazy men.

'No, he damn well isn't my lover. Niko is just being spiteful and thwarted. What is true is that if you hadn't arrived, he *would* have got me to his bed. It was the price I was obliged to pay for his help in freeing George. Get me out of here, Max. Take me home.'

Max needed no more urging. He and Nina left and jumped into the taxi that he had left waiting outside the house. Nikos stood on the doorstep, his face full of rage and hate. It was a sight that would haunt Nina for a long time.

'I'll have Praxiteles arrested again!' he screamed. 'I'll have him torn to bits!'

Chapter 32

'Thank goodness you kept the taxi waiting,' said Nina as they sped along. She had told the taxi driver to 'put his foot on it' and get to Zografou as quickly as possible.

'We'll pay you double, just get us there fast,' she said. The driver needed no explanations. He had heard the yell of hate and vengeance uttered by a demented Nikos and had got away as fast as he could.

'What sort of bastard's that!' he said and then lapsed into silence as he negotiated the traffic.

'A complete bastard,' said Nina. She was still trembling with the shock of having got away in one piece from Nikos and finding herself clutched tight in her husband's arms again. It was a sense of utter relief to have those familiar, comforting arms about her, to look up at her husband's face and see his own relief there as he gazed down at her.

'Nina,' Max spoke to her in English now, 'you're not leaving me again. You're not to be trusted. You just get into trouble and I can't bear it. Did that man touch you? If he even touched you, I swear I'll go back and kill him.'

Nina couldn't help a smile, 'Oh, Max, now you know how it felt for me when I saw you with that girl at Agia Sofias. I know I should have let you explain … but I was so mad, I just jumped to conclusions. Now don't you do the same with me. I'm fine, truly I am. He hasn't bothered me too much. You've no idea, though, how glad I am you came along like the US cavalry.'

'I was damned lucky that I was at the Praxiteles place when you rang. Good job you left the address or none of us would have had a clue where you were.'

'You see, I'm not as foolish as you think … you *and* Dad. I bet it was Dad sent you careering down from Thessaloniki.'

'You're not foolish at all, just foolhardy, my love. But it seems you have a hard-working guardian angel. Yes, Andrew *was* concerned about you and added fuel to my own fears. He gave me the address of Aris and Stella and things were winding up anyway in Thessaloniki. But I'd have come anyway. I'd have come sooner but I was delayed.'

'Maybe it was just as well you didn't or Niko might never have had George set free. I don't know how he did it, but he did. I have to thank him for that at least.'

'And the price was your body.'

'Yes,' she admitted, 'it was. I had no choice but to agree, Max. I had to get George out of their clutches. He's a dear boy, a good boy.'

'I know, my darling,' he said and hugged her once more.

'And George, is he all right, Max?'

'I didn't see him. But I gathered he was sleeping and recovering from his prison ordeal. His parents were naturally overjoyed to have him home. But when I think what you might have sacrificed to save him …'

'Don't think of it. It didn't happen. But Max, we've got to get George away, get out of Athens as fast as we can before Niko can create more trouble … and believe me, he will. I'm sure of that. I just pray we're back in time. We have to leave at once.'

'But where the hell will we go at this time of night? Hotels will be dangerous if the police come looking for us.'

'The night can be our cover for now. Yes, I agree, no hotels, no obvious places. I don't know … I'll have to think. Maybe Aris and Stella have someone we can go to just for the night at least. Then I suggest we hire a car or something and drive up to Mistres. From there we can escape over the border into Yugoslavia.'

'Does George have a passport?'

'He should have. He was studying in England.'

'It could work. I have to get out of here fast, too, Nina. I'm in trouble as well.'

'Why? What's happened?' Nina looked fearful.

'I'll explain when we're somewhere safe. It's a long and not very nice story.'

'So I'm not the only one who gets in trouble,' said Nina but she kissed his cheek as she said so and he responded with some passion, seeking her lips and holding her to him for a long time and running his hands over her body and face with longing. The taxi driver regarded them in his mirror with an amused eye.

'My God, I've missed you, Nina,' Max sighed, 'but time for all that when we're all safe somewhere.'

They asked the driver to wait yet again. Nina decided he seemed trustworthy though these days it was hard to tell who was on who's side. However, he was a pleasant young fellow and they decided to use him for now. There really wasn't time to negotiate.

Dashing into the Praxiteles apartment as soon as Stella opened the door, Nina hugged her friend and said, 'Stella, darling, get George up and dressed. We've got to get him away. I'll tell you what happened later but for now, we've got a taxi and we're getting him out. Go on, don't stand there, get the boy up.'

George, disturbed by all the commotion,was already awake and pulling on a shirt and trousers as his mother ran into the room.

'I heard all that,' he said. 'It's never safe and I was half ready to run again. Don't worry, Mother. I'll go with Nina.'

'Her husband is here too,' said his mother. 'They'll help you get to England. Oh, my son, my dear one, take care!'

'I will, Mama, don't worry.'

'George, you'll need your passport,' said Nina. She grabbed her own things from the table in his room and stuffed a few pieces of underwear and a couple of T-shirts into a large shopping bag. 'Hurry, look for it now.'

'They took it from me when they arrested me,' said George. 'Didn't they give it to you with my clothes, Mama?'

'I don't think so,' said Stella. 'Unless it's in the pocket … but no, I turned them out and have washed the clothes. No, they didn't give it back. What can you do?'

Nina grimaced. 'We'll worry about that when we have to. Let's get out while we can. The police may be round any minute.'

They all embraced, uttering reluctant but quick farewells, George hugged his parents hard and ran out with Nina and Max.

'I have an idea where to go,' said Nina as they bundled into the taxi again. 'But I daren't ring from your parents' place in case it's being tapped. Anyway, there isn't time for explanations, we'll chance our luck. I met a friend of Vlachou a short while ago, a Maria Constantinou. We'll go to her. I doubt the security people know I met her; they weren't following me at that time.'

'You're sure she'll help?' asked Max.

'Of course she will. She's totally against this regime.'

They took the taxi as far as Omonia Square and Nina told them they should get out there.

'We'll pay this fellow off,' she said, 'then we'll get another taxi, and then walk. We need to play a bit of a game just in case. I'm getting the hang of it now.'

'It's like being in a spy film,'said Max, almost amused at his wife's craftiness. But he also knew she was deadly serious; it wasn't a game and her tactics were wise. He only had to take a look at the face of the young man she had befriended to know the boy had been severely knocked about though how much he had no idea as yet. The boy kept coughing, a nasty dry cough that sounded pretty bad.

'I don't like that cough, George,' say Nina, echoing Max's thoughts. 'But I'm glad you didn't stay in the hospital.'

'The doctor seemed kind,' said George. 'He told me to pretend I was better and then they would discharge me.'

'Hmm … he *was* kind, but not any more, George. He's angry and dangerous now . I'm afraid we've made an enemy of him. That's why we've dragged you away from home … poor boy, just as you thought all was well,' added Nina with sympathy.

'It's better if we get you out of Athens. We need to drive to Mistres tomorrow. Once there we can seek some medical help. I can ring my father and ask his advice.'

'You're so good,' said George, 'I can't thank you enough. But I don't want to draw trouble on you both. Maybe I should just set off on my own from here.'

'You'll do no such thing,' said Max firmly. 'We're both getting out of Greece and you'd be wise to come with us.'

'I feel I'm deserting all my friends.' George looked sad. 'They're still in prison. If only I could help them to escape, get out somehow.'

'Well, so do I,' said Nina, 'but we may be able to help them more from abroad where we can be free to say what we want and alert other nations. Surely people will create a fuss at what's going on over here. It's a human rights issue. What use will you be in a military prison camp? And if you're caught now, how will they treat you this time? Be sensible, George. You come with us.'

He nodded and was seized by another fit of coughing. It was a warm night but the boy was shivering and Max took off his jacket and put it around his shoulders.

The night had now drawn in and only a faint pink flush of the sunset showed in the sky amidst some scudding blue black clouds. They passed people eating and drinking in the *tavernas* and bars and walked along the main roads towards the quieter suburbs where houses were drawing shutters for the night. They took the next taxi that passed them by for a few blocks and then got out and began to walk along, mingling as best as they could with passers-by. Eventually they reached a quiet side road in the suburb of Pangrati and walked up this till they reached a smart block of modern flats.

'I'm pretty sure this is the block,' said Nina. 'Wait here and I'll go ahead and see how the land lies.'

The two men waited in the shadow of the trees in the front garden. Max yearned for a cigarette but didn't dare to light one when George kept coughing so badly. He looked at the boy with concern.

Nina rang the bell and a woman's rather shrill voice spoke over the intercom.

'*Kyria* Maria?' asked Nina.

'*Nai, pios einai*?' asked the woman. 'Who is it?'

Nina spoke rapidly and quietly in Greek. 'Can I come up, *Kyria* Maria. It's Nina Hammett, remember me? I came to see you a short while ago? It's really urgent. I and some friends need help.'

In answer the door clicked open. Nina called over the two men who followed her through the glass doors that led to the hallway of the apartments. At the top of the stairs a woman stood waiting for them and she beckoned them to come up and follow her upstairs, her finger to her lips. They came up, treading as softly as they could. With some relief, they entered a pleasant comfortable flat with cool marble floors and a fan that kept the warm night air in motion and felt refreshing. Maria shut the door behind them and regarded them all. Her air was not one of surprise but rather a calm authority that felt re-assuring.

'This is my husband, Max Hammett,' said Nina, 'and this is George Praxiteles.'

Maria took one look at them and said, 'Come and sit down, you all look exhausted. Let me give you a drink and the explanations can come later.'

'Forgive me, but have you any bread and some coffee?' asked George. 'I haven't eaten for a while.' He began coughing again and Maria said, 'Of course.' She scrutinised his face and shook her head in disbelief. 'I can see you're not well. Do you need a doctor?'

'No, no, I'll explain everything,' said Nina. 'He just needs food and a bed for the night. We all do. Is there any hope we can stay here with you and your husband just for the night? We daren't go to a hotel.'

'You can have our bed,' said Maria at once. 'My husband is out just now but he'll be back soon. The young man can sleep in our son's room.'

'We can't turn you out of your own beds!'

'I insist. We can all manage on sofas for one night. It's no trouble. You all look tired, and need a good night's sleep if there is more travel to come, which I suspect there is. Come, I want to hear your story.'

Her young son, a lad of about sixteen, entered the room and looked at them all with undisguised interest. His mother turned to him and said, 'Takis, my son, can you make us some good strong coffee and bring in the bread and some cheese. I can make some omelettes if you want that?' she turned to George who shook his head.

'Bread and cheese sounds like a feast,' he said gratefully.

'There's fruit too,' said Maria to her son, 'and cake in the tin.'

Takis scuttled off to get the food and Maria settled down to hear their story.

Chapter 33

Flight to Mistres

'The first thing is to get you out of Athens,' said Maria after she had heard George's story. Nina hadn't elaborated on her own part in it but Maria read between the lines and her intuition painted the picture with Nikos Galanis.

'I know of him,' she declared. 'They say he's a good doctor and a decent enough man but he's totally right wing, totally their man. I'm amazed he helped at all. But I see what happened, what *might* have happened, let us say. A thwarted man is a dangerous one.'

George's cough was worse now and he was bringing up yellow mucus. Maria told her son to bring some fruit juice from the fridge.

'You need to drink a lot of fluid,' she told George, 'and no smoking.'

'It's okay, I don't feel like smoking,' he said, looking glum.

It was a relief to be with someone as capable as Maria. When her husband, Andonis, returned home, he was equally sympathetic and resourceful. He thought for a while and then said, 'You can borrow our car tomorrow. It's our turn to use it in Athens anyway.'

'Take the car to Maria's cousins in Kallithea and leave it there,' he continued. 'We can go and pick it up later. From Kallithea you can hire a car to take you to Thessaloniki. You said that was your destination?'

Nina nodded. She wouldn't tell even these people about the

house in Mistres. Better to be vague. For their sake as well her own. She just had to hope Nikos would take a little time to remember her family house. She wanted desperately to get there and allow George to rest a little and improve his laboured breathing and the nasty cough.

'That's a good plan,' said Max. 'But what if we're stopped? We've both got driving licences – but it won't be our car. How will we explain that?'

'Just say you are English friends touring the country a little. Say we are your friends and we are letting you borrow our car for the day to visit Kallithea. It's a lovely place, why would you not go there?'

'Okay,' nodded Max. 'I'll drive as I'm so obviously English and tourist-looking. George can sit in the back and keep quiet. We can say he's our son or a brother or something.'

'I don't think *Kyria* Nina looks old enough to be his mother,' smiled Andonis.

Nina returned the smile. 'Thank you.'

Max smiled too. 'That's true enough. But he could pass as her young brother, perhaps.'

'He needs a bit of tidying up though,' said Maria looking at George who was almost falling asleep in his chair. 'We'll cover some of those bruises with make-up tomorrow. Go to bed now and rest, George. We'll sort something out. Takis will show you his room and give you some pyjamas.'

Takis smiled and helped George from his chair and took him away to his bedroom to attend to him.

'I'm not used to him with his hair chopped off,' said Nina looking after George with regret, 'I loved his long dark mane.'

'They cut his hair in prison, I expect,' said Andonis

'No, he said his friend did it when they hoped to escape to Piraeus. But I doubt they'd have got very far. Poor George, he's so young to have witnessed so much horror.'

'One hears all these stories,' said Andonis with a grimace. 'This boy's lucky not to have had the *falanga* or he wouldn't be walking properly now. I've heard of people crawling back to their cells on all fours.'

'I know. Thank God for that, at least. Anyway, your plan of escape is a wonderful one and we're so grateful for your help.'

Andonis nodded, 'It's the least we can do. Let's sleep on it now and you can start off early in the morning.'

Max and Nina cuddled and stroked each other when they were at last in bed but it wasn't the time for further intimacy. They were both exhausted yet at the same time keyed up with excitement and anticipation of what might lie ahead. The night was warm and stuffy with all the shutters closed in the house. It was hard to sleep and they both tossed and turned. Eventually they saw the rosy rays of the sun at dawn slipping fingers through the slats of the shutters. They both gave a deep sigh, indulged in a tender, lingering kiss, then rose to greet the day.

George was already up and looked a good deal more relaxed. His puffiness had subsided considerably and he was eating a hearty breakfast as only a resilient young man might do. Nina glanced at Max and smiled. George would recover from all this. He was young and healthy.

They sat down with him and on the insistence of their kind hostess ate as much as they could. Maria then applied some make-up to George's bruises which did improve his appearance and they all joked about it.

'How about some mascara and lipstick? You're beginning to look very pretty,' laughed Takis. George pretended to punch him on the shoulder. It was good to hear young men's laughter again despite the grave situation..

'He'll have to get his front tooth fixed,' Maria remarked, surveying her handiwork.

'We can see to that when he's safely in England,' said Max. 'He'll just have to keep his mouth shut as much as he can.'

'I've been keeping my mouth shut,' said George with some bitterness, 'and that's what I got for it.'

After they had eaten a good breakfast, Maria made them a picnic to take with them: bread, feta cheese, olives, half a cooked chicken and plenty of water.

'Here's some Luminal for George if his cough gets too

painful,' she said. 'It's all I have in the house. It's a bit stronger than aspirin.'

'I'll be all right,' George said, 'I've survived this far. But thanks for your kindness, *Kyria* Maria.'

Andonis had driven out the car from the garages at the back of the block of flats and the three travellers slipped out, put their luggage and food in the boot and set off amidst quiet farewells. There were one or two people about but on the whole the streets were empty and they soon found themselves on the road to the pleasant suburb of Kallithea. No one stopped them on the way or appeared to be following them. They eventually arrived at the house of Maria's cousins who had already been advised of their arrival and were waiting to greet them.

They offered refreshment but Max said they really had to move on as soon as they could. The cousins had already hired a car from a friend they knew and it was waiting just along the road from their house. The fugitives transferred their goods to the new car boot, made their grateful farewells and set off on the road to Thessaloniki. Only then did they breathe a sigh of relief. There was no reason why they should be stopped on the way, especially with Max as the driver. He looked so obviously foreign that anyone passing him would just assume they were all tourists in a hired car exploring the joys of Greece. He drove with care, making sure he kept to the speed limit so as not to attract any unwelcome attention.

It was late that evening before they reached Mistres. On the way they stopped briefly in the Vale of Tembe and picnicked by the river there. It felt so carefree to be sitting in the dappled shade of the plane trees, listening to sweet birdsong and feeling warm, relaxed and cheerful. It felt like normality again after all the recent madness of their lives.

'The ancient poets loved this place,' said Nina looking around, her tired face relaxing for the first time in a long while. 'Once there was a temple to Apollo here, did you know that, Max?'

'No, I didn't,' he confessed. She lay back against the trunk of a tree and let her eyes wander into the distance as if dreaming a little. Max gazed at her and thought how beautiful she looked despite the darkness round her eyes that betokened lack of sleep and a good deal of worry. It wasn't the end yet but the end seemed in sight. They simply had to hold their nerve, get George better, then plan a way of getting him out of the country with them. The loss of his passport was a worry. He appeared to have no identity of any sort with him now. But somehow they would sort it out.

They drew up at last outside the old family house in Mistres. A few villagers came over and surrounded them, asking questions and looking at George with narrowed eyes. Nina didn't feel troubled by this scrutiny. She knew these people since her childhood and knew too that they would never give any of them away. It was as safe as possible – for the moment.

The head man, Makis Cuyumjoglou, came over and Nina told him a little of their story as they all sat in the *cafeneion* with him and a couple of other men. Max downed a few tiny glasses of *raki* with relief and was now able to smoke a longed-for cigarette. They had left George tucked up in bed, dosed with Luminal and told him to have a complete rest. He already looked a great deal more relaxed and the cough sounded less hollow.

Makis heard the tale and nodded. 'Eh, what can I say? What in the world is this country coming to? Will we never be free from tyrants? But you can be sure, *Kyria* Nina, if anyone comes looking for you we'll get word to you. We have plenty of places to hide which we've used through all the troubles. Your grandfather knew them all when he was a spy in the Great War. Greeks are always fleeing something.'

'Thanks, *Kyrie* Makis,' said Nina gratefully. Again, her face let go of all the tensions that had haunted it for so long and she looked around with a sense of homecoming. Here in this village high in the Hortiach Mountains she had been born and lived her first few years. Sometimes she wished she could roll back time and be a carefree child playing out in the dusty road once more, laughing with her little friends, now all grown men and women.

Max caught her look and understood it. He squeezed her hand beneath the table. She turned and smiled at him with love. She knew he could enter into her feelings, he always had done. It was one of the reasons she had fallen in love with him. Perhaps she had first really loved him when he once said to her, 'You smile and speak cheerfully, Nina, but your eyes are always sad.'

'I think that of you, too, Max,' she had replied, 'you have this sadness underneath as well. Some people grow a carapace, a hard shell to hide the soft interior. You use camouflage. You pretend to be smiling and relaxed and can change to suit everyone. But the real you is unknown.'

At heart she and Max were one. That was what marriage was about. They would always be as one and no matter what upsetting, foolish thing either of them did from now on, they would talk it through. She would not allow herself to be so unreasonable ever again.

Later that night they went to bed and at last had time, peace and the sense of safety that allowed them to make love quietly so as not to awaken George. He was fast asleep and they could hear his gentle snores but there was no need for noisy passion. All was gentle tenderness that night and as Nina felt her husband slip into her body, she gasped a little with the sense of enormous joy that the sensation gave her. He also let forth a deep, aching sigh of relief and gladness. They were together again, they were united in love. It was like grace, like a religious experience.

Chapter 34

The fugitives spent a few days enjoying the coolness and sweetness of the mountain air after the heat and pollution of the city. George especially benefited from the sense of relief and freedom now that he was away from the horrors of Bouboulinas Street. But he still awoke in the night covered in sweat and shouting wildly and Nina would creep into his room, smooth his forehead with a wet towel and put a comforting arm about him.

'I'm sorry, *Kyria* Nina, I'm so sorry,' he said. He felt ashamed of his cowardly outbursts. That was how he deemed it. Nina assured him that it was by no means cowardly to be afraid or for a sensitive spirit to react to the terrible cruelty he had experienced.

'I could bear anything they did to me,' he told her, 'but when they dragged in Lakis, my good pal, Lakis, and beat his feet with the shoes still on. It makes it so much worse, the feet swell up in the shoes. The shoes split open and I could see his mangled feet …'

'Try not to think of it,' said Nina, shuddering, 'try not to. His feet will heal. My grandfather told me of this sort of thing happening during the Civil War. They'll heal and the boy will survive.'

'He talked,' said George sadly, 'that was the worst of it. I don't blame him, none of us would – but I know that he will always be ashamed of it.'

The villagers were so pleased to welcome them, bringing over specially prepared and delicious dishes of *makaronia, moussaka* and other delicacies from the baker's oven. They wanted to fete the visitors, especially the young Lambrakis follower who was a hero in their eyes. They were so relieved he had escaped prison and that while incarcerated there had acted like a true *palikari*, a real man who had done nothing to implicate his friends. They were determined to help in any way they could.

Everyone here knew of imprisonment and pain and torture. They or their parents had all been caught up in the varied struggles of Macedonia. First the war with Bulgaria and the Germans in 1917, then the Second World War of terrifying occupation, starvation and fear. Many had joined the *andartes* and though several villagers were communists they were also true patriots and had fought hard with everyone else to liberate their country. Then came the civil war and the decade of turmoil. Now this military regime. It was like the Nazi occupation all over again.

They remembered Grigoris Lambrakis with true love. He had opened up kitchens for the starving poor, and held free surgeries for those without the cash to afford a doctor and medicine. He was a great man who cared about ordinary people. These new rulers were trying to woo the peasants and the farmers but here in Mistres they were not fooled by such crafty moves. The Macedonians, ever-proud, slightly aloof from the rest of the mainland Greeks – an effete lot in their opinion – were men and women of honour and strength. The general opinion in the village was that these new fellows were just jumped-up peasants who had risen in the army to become Colonels, mainly because they were American pawns.

The problem of getting George over the border was now discussed. None of the villagers had ever left Mistres except to visit Thessaloniki. No one had much idea about passports. They mooted various ideas such as taking George to the coast and getting him to swim over to a waiting fishing boat which could then sail over to Brindisi. Max thought of Big Bouros who might have managed to wangle something with his old contacts but as far as he knew the poor fellow was still in hospital. Would the two lads who had worked for him have some way of smuggling George out? Max decided not to try and find them, afraid of anyone asking too many questions. Apart from anything else, Max had no great desire to show himself in Thessaloniki. For all he knew the police may well be hunting him. It was wiser to stay out of the way. He had to explain his reluctance to Nina. It was time to tell her the whole story about Zoë and the death of Katsarakis.

She listened in silence. With his gaze fixed on the floor throughout, Max recounted the story from the very beginning when Katsarakis has slashed the tractor tyres, right to the moment when he entered the garage with one intent in mind, to kill them both. At this point Nina, stopped him by putting her hand on his and he saw tears streaming down her face.

He took her in his arms and she clung to him, sobbing. 'It's my fault for driving you away – not listening to your story about Zoë. I thought the worst of you both. I didn't dream you were in such danger.'

'You can't be blamed, darling,' said Max, his own eyes filling with tears. 'I'd gained myself a bad reputation and you were angry with me. But never once did I lay a finger on that girl, nor did I want to. You do believe me?'

'Of course, I do,' she said looking up at him now and stroking his cheek tenderly.

'That's when this brute came at me,' Max went on. 'He was laughing, determined to make me into pulp and he would have done – but a garage has some hefty tools in it and I knew I had to try and reach the bench for one. It was thanks to plucky little Zoë, who despite her horrific injuries, came out like some raving banshee and stuck a paper knife she'd found in the office in her husband's side. It didn't do him any harm, all that flesh and solid muscle! But it surprised him, made him pause for a moment which gave me time to grab up a heavy wrench and floor him with it.' He paused as the full horror of that moment came back and almost choked him. Nina clutched at his hand.

'And then?' she whispered.

'And then Zoë went completely crazy. She seized the huge

wrench from my hand and hit him over and over again … my God, an angry woman! She made his head a pulp, Nina. It was horrible but she was elated, she was so glad – until the enormity of it all hit her. Then she collapsed and her strength and courage fled like air from a balloon. I don't blame her though. Frankly, she saved my life.'

'Nor do I blame her!' said Nina with feeling. 'I'd have done the same. But he was dead, obviously. What did you do with the body?'

'Our guardian angels must have been around because there's a decrepit old truck in the back of the garage. It's been there for ages, Dimitri meant to do something with it but never got round to it. I managed to coax it to life. We always keep a can of petrol around and that was just enough to get us to the coast and back. We went past Neo Monastiri and we managed to throw him over the cliff and into the sea.'

'No one saw you?'

'No, there wasn't a soul around, not even the farmer whose fields we drove into. Thankfully the ground is so dry this time of year the tyre marks didn't show up at all. We then drove away and I took Zoë to some people, some friends Dimitri has along the Monastir Rd.' Max thought it better not to elaborate on the sort of friends these were.

Nina sighed deeply. 'I hope they look after her. I wonder where she'll go when she's better and if she'll be safe now. You say this nasty man had some followers. They'll miss him, won't they – and wonder what's happened? They may know he went to see you.'

'I'm hoping he didn't tell anyone because he definitely intended to kill us and leave us there to rot. But I have no idea. However, that's why I don't want to be seen in the city, Nina. They all suppose I've returned to England.'

'Did you give the girl some money?'

'I gave her some. Hadn't got much left myself. In fact we're probably both pretty much broke.'

'We are. I'm not sure we've even got enough to pay for the train to get over the border,' said Nina, looking worried.

In the end, Nina decided to drive into Thessaloniki in the rented car. It was to be left with a driver who would take it back to the owners in Athens as arranged. While in the city, she would visit Basil and Athina and ring Andrew from their flat, reassure him of their safety and see if he had any bright ideas that might get them out of their predicament.

'Don't tell anyone I'm still here,' said Max. 'I'm not sure just where Basil stands. He's so delighted with the new regime and he has friends in the police force. Last I heard, his cousin was going out with the local bobby. I'm sure he'd never give us away and you're safe going there. But it's best he doesn't know too much. Play it by ear – say as little as you can.'

'I won't mention a thing,' said Nina, 'I'll just chat a bit and ask to use their phone. Better not to let them know, I agree, for their own sakes as much as ours.'

Nina drove the car down to the city the next morning and took it to the address Maria's cousins had given her.

'Thanks so much for going to all this trouble to help,' she said when she delivered it. The man who was to drive the car back assured her that it was no trouble and he was more than happy to help. He seemed to know something of the story and Nina wondered whether to confide a little more but decided it would be better not to get these good people embroiled in problems that were not their own.

Taking the bus to Basil and Athina's apartment, she ran up the long flight of stairs and rang their bell. Athina opened the door and stared at her in amazement.

'Nina! Oh my God, come in! Where've you been, what's happened?'

She gathered Nina to her in a big hug and they went into the large airy salon.

'*Katse*, *katse*, sit, *vre* Nina… it's so good to see you. I'll make us some coffee.'

Rather to Nina's relief, neither Basil nor the children were home yet and when the coffee, the glass of water and the spoonful of *glyko* arrived, she drank thirstily and smiled with pleasure at seeing her good friend.

'So,' said Athina, smiling back, 'what brings you to Thessalonki? I heard you were in Athens and busy with your journalist work.'

'Yes, I was,' said Nina, looking as casual as she could.

'So? Did you come back to find Max?'

Nina shook her head. 'No, it was another reason that brought me back.' She fell silent, gazing at the floor in concentration, weighing up what to say and how much she should confide. Friends were turning upon one another in these times. Was it safe to speak to Athina? Athina in her turn looked at Nina with a puzzled frown but refrained from questions.

She held out a box with cigarettes; the two women lit up and puffed away for a few moments. Nina sipped her coffee then asked, 'How are things, Athina, *mou*?'

'Eh, no complaints, business is good just now and things are quiet here. We have no problems with hooligans any more,' Athina grinned. 'We're well in with the police these days. You remember Agatha, Basil's cousin?'

'I think so. She helps him in the shop opposite the Fairground?'

'That's the one. Well, she and our local policeman, Vasilis Hadji-Stavros, are engaged. Think of that! Vasili has such good prospects. He is absolutely enamoured of this new regime, a stickler for law and order. A splendid boy, so handsome too. So you can imagine how glad we are of his help. We had some bother a little while back, just after the new government came to power. Some nasty boys hacked off our Yiannaki's lovely curls. Poor Yiannaki, he was so frightened and upset. Can you imagine that? What stupid people there are around, eh, Nina? But Basil soon found out who they were and had them dealt with. They were only youngsters so they got away with a scolding. Basil wanted to break their bones! I've never seen him so angry.'

'Well yes, he's a quiet man as a rule.'

'He is. But he said their parents were commies for sure and that these were their spawn so what could you expect?'

Nina stared at her friend and then asked quietly, 'You believed that, Athina?'

Athina turned her head away to gaze out of the window. She lowered her voice as if afraid of being heard. 'I don't know what to believe, Nina *mou*. There's been talk of tortures and bad things at the Salonika Gendarmerie. Basil says they deserve all they get.'

'Do you think that too?'

Nina looked steadily at her friend who returned her gaze for a moment, put out her cigarette, then replied, 'No, Nina. No one deserves to be tortured and treated badly no matter what their political belief. We Greeks should know better, we should set an example. But it seems we're no better than anyone else in the end.'

Nina nodded. They fell silent again, each wrapt in their own thoughts, then Nina said, 'Athina, will you help me? I wasn't sure about your feelings. I know Basil's opinions and he's entitled to what he believes. It's his nature, he is conservative and moral by nature and he believes all the twaddle this present regime is giving out about a new Greece. The phoenix isn't rising at all, it's dying. It's burning and dying. They are destroying Greece, Athina. Believe me. I'm in trouble too with the police in Athens because of some of my political writings. I need to get out of the country but I have no money left. Could you lend me some – is it possible?'

'I can lend you some of my own money,' said Athina at once. 'I have some savings that even Basil doesn't know about. Husbands don't need to know everything, eh? Of course, I can help you, dear friend. Even if you can't return it, who cares? As long as it helps you to get out safely.'

'You're a good friend, Athina. But don't let Basil know any of this.'

'I won't. But Max ... he's in England now. You know that, don't you? He left Greece a few days ago. Dimitri has closed the garage and is on the run.'

Nina nodded, 'Yes, I know that.' she replied.

'Are you still enemies, you two?' asked Athina, looking sad.

'Oh, Nina, Max is a good man. He's done nothing wrong, Basil and I are both sure of that. He became mixed up with some unfortunate girl who wanted to escape her husband. It was purely philanthropic. I know it was. He brought her here and we helped her to get away to Florina. She's safe there now as far as I know.'

So she knew nothing of Zoë's return to Thessaloniki. Nina was relieved to hear this. She wondered if the news of the missing Katsarakis was known as yet but dared not ask. 'It's all right, Athina, I've found the truth now and all is forgiven and forgotten. I was foolish and jealous.'

'Oh, I don't blame you for that, I would feel the same. But I'm so glad you've found out the truth. It made me unhappy to see you both separated like that. Max was heartbroken without you.'

Nina smiled a little. 'Was he? The poor darling. That did him good! Ah, well – all's well that ends well. I hope to be with him soon. Listen, Athina, can I use your phone? I want to ring my father in England and ask him to come and meet the train when I reach Paris. He'll make sure you get your money back somehow. He could transfer it to a bank. I will pay it back, dear friend. I wouldn't dream of using your savings.'

'Banks are useless here in Greece, you know that,' smiled Athina. 'Wait until all this is over and Greece becomes normal again. You can bring it yourself then.'

'With interest,' smiled Nina. 'Look on it as your savings growing.'

Athina smiled. 'There's the phone in the hallway. Go ahead.' She showed Nina into the hallway then went into the kitchen and discreetly shut the door behind her.

'My darling child, we've been so worried about you! Where the devil are you now?' Andrew sounded deeply relieved to hear his daughter's voice and Nina felt ashamed for not communicating before. She spoke to him in rapid English.

'Papa, it's been a difficult time,' she said. 'I'll tell you the story when we get home. I've so much to say! Just now I'm with Max ...'

'Max found you!'

'Yes, thank God. He found me and we're staying at our house in Mistres. We're all fugitives and have to get the hell out of Greece. I'm ringing from Athina Petrakos's place. She's lending me some money to get a train.'

'I can wire some money.'

'No. it's fine, better this secret way than anything official. But there's a snag. We have a young man with us who's also fleeing the country but he hasn't got a passport. What can we do about that? I don't know what to do. He did have one but the police took it from him when they arrested him.'

'How did he manage to escape?'

'It's a long story, I'll tell you when we're back.'

'I see. Is he this student you met some time ago?'

'Yes, he's the son of Aris and Stella.... Papa, he's been tortured, he's really quite ill. We're staying at Mistres till his health improves a bit.'

'What are his symptoms?'

'Bronchitis, we think. He's a little better for the rest and the villagers are feeding him up marvellously at Mistres. They think he's a hero.'

'Bless them all, they're such good friends. Yes, stay and let him rest, it's the best cure. Give him something to help him sleep and plenty to drink. There's not a lot else you can do. But the passport is a problem. I'll have to think about it. Can you get in touch with me again?'

Nina hesitated. 'It's not easy. I don't want to go anywhere too public. I don't like to come to Athina's house when her husband, Basil, is around. He's massively in favour of this government. I'm not sure I can trust him any more. People have changed, Pa. Really changed. But Athina is fine, I'm sure of it.'

Andrew paused for a while then said, 'There's a monastery in the mountains near Mistres and I'm sure they have a phone. I've used it in emergencies myself. Try to get Max over there tonight, about seven pm your time. They'll prefer a man to a woman, I'm afraid. You know what these monks are like. I'll let you know what I've figured out.'

Chapter 35

Just a little more
And we shall see the almond trees in blossom
The marbles shining in the sun
The sea, the curling waves.
Just a little more
Let us rise just a little higher.

'Just a Little More', George Seferis

Leaving Greece with laden hearts

Max returned later that evening from his visit to the monastery. Nina came rushing out to greet him and drew him indoors away from curious gazes and listening ears.

'Did Pa come up with anything?'

'Your father is a marvel,' said Max in admiration, 'he's figured it all out.'

'What! Tell us what he said!' Nina was like a child and Max grinned at her excitement.

'A coffee first and then I will.'

'Oh, foo, you're being mean!' But she went into the kitchen and made them all a drink and returned with the tray. George was seated by on the small sofa and smiled at her when she handed him his coffee. His livid bruising and puffiness was almost gone now and he looked relaxed and cheerful. The gap in his teeth was scarcely noticeable unless he laughed which he seldom did anyway.

'Andrew's phoned a friend in London, a Greek lawyer he knows whose son is a student like George. He's going to lend us his son's passport. He reckons the border police can't understand a word of English and generally check the passport in a perfunctory manner. We need to get a passport photo and fix that on this fellow's passport and that should be enough. George will be your cousin in case they notice the name difference to your maiden name. We've all come over for a holiday and are returning home.'

'But how are we to get the passport?'

'Andrew is driving to London to collect it and then he's driving over via Switzerland and Yugoslavia to Mistres. He's perfectly free to do so, no one will stop him entering. He'll come here, we'll fix up the passport and then he'll drive us all back after a few days so called holiday or business or whatever he wants to say he came for. He has a home here and is perfectly likely to come for some business, house repairs or whatever.'

Nina considered the idea. 'Yes, he's driven over before. That sounds a brilliant plan,' she said. 'It could work.'

'No reason at all why it wouldn't.'

'The only fear I have is that Niko may remember our house here and alert the police in Thessaloniki.'

'Well, let's hope not. But if the police arrive, we'll soon know about it. The villagers will let us know and hide us all somewhere.'

'That's true. They said they would.'

All three of them felt a sense of rejoicing. It seemed that freedom was at last in sight and each one of them wanted to leave Greece now.

'We can do so much more when we get to London again,' said Nina. 'I've so much to tell, Reggie is sure to give me a column of my own. That would be wonderful.'

Max smiled. 'Nina, Nina, you'll never change.'

'I won't, I can't. I'm a Greek, Max *mou* and I must say what I feel, what I've experienced here. We need to tell George's story for him. He's endured such atrocities. It almost made me laugh when Athina was fretting over a minor attack on her little boy – which was only a bit of stupidity on the part of some lads – I couldn't help but contrast it with all George and his friends have suffered. Athina herself admits Basil is still in denial about it all. How can people be so deluded?'

'It's all relative, isn't it, Nina? We can only judge life by what we experience and what we want to look at. Some people simply cannot face the evil of the world and bury their heads in the sand. They'd rather not know. It means they would then have to do something about it or see their own part in the evil, even if that part is simply being passive and unresisting. I agree, these stories need to be told by those Greeks who manage to escape the regime. It's just as important as being foolishly brave, staying here and being recaptured.' He looked at George as he said this.

'You say that, *Kyrie* Max,' replied George, 'but a part of me still feels I am a coward just running away. I think of Zo-Zo and Savvas and Alekis and Lakis ...' Tears filled the boy's eyes and he began to sob from the depths of his being.

Nina went over and put an arm around him.

'We'll fight together, George,' she promised. 'You're not a coward. Never, never. Dear boy! We'll fight and we *will* do good because some countries are beginning to listen to us. If enough people escape Greece and begin to make their statements then there will be an enquiry and that *must* help the fate of others.'

Andrew arrived as promised within three days. Nina ran out to see him and hugged him so hard he swore his bones would crack.

'I'm so glad to see you, Papa!'

'And I'm damned relieved to see you, darling. What a worry you've been to us all!'

'Oh well, Pa, that won't change, I'm afraid,' she replied with a little laugh. 'I am what I am. I can't be different.'

'So true. And we wouldn't really want you any different,' smiled her father, hugging her again.

Once indoors, he took a good look at George and pronounced him to be almost clear now of the chest problems.

'Good fresh mountain air, good food and company have restored the lad,' he declared and George nodded in agreement.

Andrew said the roads in Yugoslavia were terrible but he'd had no mishap en route. They took a photograph of George, and Andrew went down to the city the next morning to have it developed. This was then trimmed and fitted into the passport. George was the same build and height and actually similar in looks to the young student who had lent his own passport. Andrew had managed to find rubber stamps as well so that an entry date into Greece could be forged.

'There's quite a network forming back home. The Greeks are mobilising their resistance and some English have also got involved. They've got all sorts of mad ideas in the pipeline. It's all quite exciting really,' said Andrew. 'I shall certainly do my best to help them if I can. My having a legitimate reason to come over to Greece could be a valuable asset.'

'What will happen to the passport's real owner?' asked Max

'He'll pretend he's lost it and get his Embassy to issue another one once we return safely,' said Andrew.

'What about George? What will happen when we get to Dover?' asked Nina.

'He'll have to seek political asylum. We won't try the forged passport once we're past the Yugoslavian border, the Italians and Swiss aren't likely to be fooled. Anyway, there's no need, he'll be alright. Don't worry, this is a happening a lot now. Several other Greeks have escaped the country and come over to London. The thing is to get the hell out of here as fast as we can. Give it a few more days so it will look as if I've done some business here and then we'll go. I've bought some clothes and cases for you all, so it will look as if we are authentic tourists.'

They spent a wonderful few days at Mistres. The villagers prepared a feast and a young man brought out an old santouri and played some songs by Theodorakis. Everyone listened and some women cried, dabbing their faces with their headscarves. They knew the music was banned but who cared about that nonsense.

'Ach Theodoraki *mou*!' sighed Nina,'what a brave man,

what music … a true *palikari*. I pray you escape and they don't find you.'

Andrew, Nina and George got up, fingers clicking, music throbbing sweetly and began to move in a slow dance together.

'Come on, Max!' urged George and he joined them, laughing and saying, 'You'll regret this!' and after a while some villagers also joined in, hands on shoulders in a long row and with many an '*Opa*!' and clapping of hands, they all danced. Slowly people dropped away and left Max and Nina to dance together. For some reason, Max found himself totally in rhythm, something that had never happened to him before. He forgot himself, forgot his clumsy feet and English inhibitions, simply gazed into his wife's eyes with love as they circled and twined in the dance. At the end, he took her in his arms amidst the cheers of the company.

'Together forever, Nina *mou*,' he murmured.

'Ah, Max, you're becoming a true Greek,' she murmured back.

'For your sake, I'll become a Greek,' he replied with a smile.

'And I'll become an Englishwoman for your sake,' she replied.

Later that day they sat outside their house on a couple of benches and the sun was warm and delightful on their faces, the smell of delicious Greek cooking filled the air, cicadas chirruped in the grass and graceful swallows swooped and curved in their hunt for flies above the ochre rooftops. Andrew said it was raining back in dear old England.

George looked sad and gazed around him. 'I shall miss you, my beloved country,' the young man said almost to himself, 'when will I ever return here?'

Tears spilled from his eyes. His heart was breaking with pain for his country.

Nina and Max felt the same. They also felt sad to be leaving. When it came closer to the time for their departure, they took Andrew's car and drove alone down the mountains towards the sea. They got out and stood on a cliff top and looked around them at the beautiful scene spread before their eyes. The scents of pine, sage and thyme sweetened the air.

'My grandmother used to come here when she was a nurse in the war,' mused Nina. 'They used to get away now and then and have picnics or go bathing. Little stolen moments of pleasure amongst all the horrors of war.'

'Does anything really change?' Max wondered. He looked over at his wife. The wind tugged at her blouse, billowing it out behind her as she stood motionless against the skyline as though entranced. With a little bound up a small hillock, he reached her side and put his arm about her.

To the west the bay curved round the mountains and the sapphire sea shimmered before them, calm and peaceful in the setting sun. At the horizon the sky glowed deep red, mingling with a profusion of vivid flame-bright colours higher in the atmosphere. Soft little clouds like wisps of straw clung to the sky's hair while a slight evening breeze rippled the surface of the sea, breaking it into a thousand gold-tinged bars of light. The little fishing boats that floated and bobbed at their moorings on the beach below were suddenly afire with colours they had never possessed in the day. It was as though some magic brush had painted them for the pleasure of this brief moment.

The scene of peace and tranquillity melted the souls of the two onlookers on the cliff top and held them spellbound. No matter what happened, no matter who imagined themselves to be rulers of this land and these defiant peoples, Greece would always live on through the earth, the sea, the light, the colour and the beauty of its landscapes. So many people had invaded this country. Franks, Venetians, Turks, Germans – now they were all gone, swallowed up in the past and the land remained free of them all. It would be free of the present tyrants as well. Greeks remained Greeks no matter what happened to them and their lives flowed on as always.

The golden show did not distract the lovers from their awareness of one another, the warmth of their bodies, the stillness, the silence, their utter loneliness as if they were the only beings left upon this earth. Both felt their hearts beating in excitement. They clasped each other closer and their lips met in a kiss – and then again and again. They looked deeply into one another's eyes and then turned their gaze back to the scene spread before them, a scene now fading in its splendour, fading into the deeps of the night.

'We'll be back,' said Nina softly. 'In the end, things change, they always do and the phoenix really will rise again for Greece.'

Epilogue

The Junta held power in Greece until July 1974. Many people felt they were all for the good and approved of their stern ideology and the idea that Greece was to be 'reborn'. Their intolerant rule did not greatly affect the middle classes and they became popular with the rural and farming communities with whom, Papadopulos had a natural bond as he came from such a background. He pandered to this and gave the farmers financial aid and other help. On the whole the economy improved due to the encouragement of tourism during these years. Little freedoms began to creep back slowly, even allowing Western films and pop music to flourish. The fall of the regime came about because Papadopoulos began a liberalisation of the strict regime which undermined the original stern message of the Junta and showed it to be no longer valid. People began to clamour for democracy again.

Various controls against the freedom of the students led to massive anti-junta unrest. This led to an uprising of the students at the National Technical University of Athens. The students, calling themselves *The Free Beseiged* , barricaded themselves in the University. When it became obvious that they had the public on their side, the Junta began to panic. In the early hours of 17th November, 1973, an AMX 30 tank crashed through the gates and many students were killed. This led to a counter coup and eventually, together with the Cyprus/Turkish debacle, to the overthrow of the regime. By now they were both ideologically and politically discredited.

The leaders of the Junta were tried in 1975 for high treason and sentenced to death but this sentence was later changed to life imprisonment.

Yiannis Petrakos (Yiannakis) was one of the youngest students at the Athens Polytechnic who was killed duing the uprising. Basil and Athina had already felt uneasy about the new government though Basil would always remain staunchly convinced that the Colonels had done a lot of good for the country and kept it in order. There was certainly less crime during those years. However, the loss of their only son turned them against the Junta in the end. They at last saw it for what it was.

Max and Andrew made several daring visits to Greece during the seven years of power, disguised as mere English tourists but helping to smuggle in ammunition and bomb making equipment to help those revolutionaries who were trying to create as much nuisance and trouble as they could for the Colonels and their regime. They had many a close shave during these adventures. Dimitri and Petros took a part in these activities though remaining safe in their mountain retreat, issuing forth as the *andartes* had done in the old days to cause as much annoyance as they could. George Praxiteles went back to University and continued his studies and later found work in a London bank. Nina, meanwhile, wrote articles and campaigned fiercely to rouse the interest of human rights movements to condemn the Junta. She eventually rose to the position of senior reporter for Reggie's newspaper.

After the crushing of the regime, she returned with Max and George to Athens to meet up with Stella and Aris Praxiteles. The reunion was joyful in the extreme. Aris was now back working with the newspapers re-opened by Eleni Vlachou who, along with Mikis Theodorakis and other dissidents, had been forced to escape Greece for many years and who had also continued a campaign against the Junta from other lands. George decided to enter into politics, doing his best to battle against corruption and injustice.

Later, Max and Nina took a trip to Thessaloniki to visit the reunited Dimitri and Yiota. Dimitri had many amusing and wildly exagerrated tales to tell. Luckily he never realised that his workshop was the scene of so much horror and Max never told him. Max had returned the truck after leaving Zoë, taken it back and cleaned it up so that no one was the wiser. Basil never got over the death of his son and was a much embittered man but Athina was as welcoming and kindly as ever and they spent a few days with them at their flat before eventually returning to London. Max now had a thriving car repair workshop of his own in Earl's Court. Many a peaceful walk was enjoyed with Nina in the Old Brompton Cemetery and life resumed it's peaceful tenor. A couple of years later they had two children and settled down near Downlands in Gloucestershire to the delight of Andrew and Dorothy. It didn't stop Nina from her journalistic aims, her restless spirit would never quite be curbed by domesticity but Dorothy delighted in her role as a great grandmother and helped the family considerably.

Nikos Galanis never married and a couple of years after the regime ended, he suffered a massive heart attack and was found dead in his home by a neighbour.

Once her wounds had healed, Zoë Katsarakis made her way to Kavalla where she worked as a barmaid for a couple of years and then moved to Turkey. She eventually married and settled in Istanbul with her Turkish husband. She was never able to have children due to the damage Katsarakis had inflicted upon her. Max never heard from her again.

The body of Manos Katsarakis was washed up on shore some weeks after his death. The police assumed it was a gangland killing and didn't trouble themselves to investigate any further. No one, except a few loyal supporters, was particularily sorry for his demise.